THE PRISON HOUSE

John King is the author of five previous novels:
The Football Factory, *Headhunters*, *England Away*,
Human Punk and *White Trash*. He lives in London.

JOHN KING

The Prison House

JONATHAN CAPE
LONDON

Published by Jonathan Cape 2004

2 4 6 8 10 9 7 5 3 1

Copyright © John King 2004

John King has asserted his right under the Copyright, Designs
and Patents Act 1988 to be identified as the author of this work

First published in Great Britain in 2004 by
Jonathan Cape
Random House, 20 Vauxhall Bridge Road, London SW1V 2SA

Random House Australia (Pty) Limited
20 Alfred Street, Milsons Point, Sydney,
New South Wales 2061, Australia

Random House New Zealand Limited
18 Poland Road, Glenfield,
Auckland 10, New Zealand

Random House South Africa (Pty) Limited
Endulini, 5A Jubilee Road, Parktown 2193, South Africa

The Random House Group Limited Reg. No. 954009
www.randomhouse.co.uk

A CIP catalogue record for this book
is available from the British Library

ISBN 0-224-06448-7 (trade paperback)
ISBN 0-224-07367-2 (cased)

Papers used by Random House are natural,
recyclable products made from wood grown in sustainable forests;
the manufacturing processes conform to the environmental
regulations of the country of origin

Typeset by Palimpsest Book Production Limited,
Polmont, Stirlingshire
Printed and bound in Great Britain by
Mackays of Chatham PLC

F122,080
£ 25.00

THIS BOOK IS DEDICATED TO MY MOTHER

With thanks to Tomak, dammer champion

Ah, truly, shades of the prison house close about us, the new-born things, all too soon do we forget. And yet, when we were new-born we did remember other times and places. We, helpless infants in arms or creeping quadruped-like on the floor, dreamed our dreams of air-flight. Yes; and we endured the torment and torture of nightmare fears of dim and monstrous things. We new-born infants, without experience, were born with fear, with memory of fear; and *memory is experience*.

The Star Rover, Jack London

WISE MEN SAY

THE ICE-CREAM SELLER presses against the cell bars, leering, threatening, swearing I fuck you good, fuck you very good, fuck you so good you never walk again, my friend, and looking into his wired, mascara-lined eyes I find no pity, no humanity, understand he is one more bully in a playground packed with cowards. I do what I have been told and turn the other cheek. Say nothing. Refuse to hear his wicked words. But it is very hard. And jamming my eyes shut I search for sanctuary, find the judge who sentenced me earlier today waiting, his face blood-clot red and turning purple, waving a clenched fist as he delivers a thundering sermon, the fury of his tirade the heaviest reminder that I am the scum of Creation, the lowest of the low, and unfit to lick his shoes. A man can only take so much abuse and eventually I open my eyes again, the choc-ice rapist blowing a soggy kiss and rubbing his balls, thrusting hips back and forwards moaning I fuck you well. Leaning back against the wall, I slide to the floor and sit in silence, the same as the six other prisoners, every one of us with our heads bowed and bodies hunched, buried alive in police custody.

My head throbs where it needs stitching, but the guards say tomorrow tomorrow, moving nimble hands and sluggish tongues, their language foreign and me a foreigner, meaning shaped in the air. They can see the nature of the cut on my forehead, a flapping wound ripe for infection, the congealed blood and bruising, just shrug their shoulders and stroll away. When a spout of cold air bursts through the cell window it brings paranoia, killer germs arriving from the chicken farms of the East, surfing bacteria riding waves, as old as the planet.

I shiver at the thought of gangrene, touch loose skin and wince, the ice-cream seller turning fear to excitement as he licks his lips and unzips nylon trousers, flashing a limp penis. He performs his dance of outrage, craving reaction, and some men would spring forward and grab his head and smash it into the bars, crack it like a coconut, but not me. I am a peaceful man and hurting this fool would be a sin. He starts tugging at this cock, trying to work himself erect but failing, and despite the perversion what shocks me is the realisation that although he has a nose and a mouth and two vacant eyes, the choc-ice nonce has no face.

Mr Fair darts across the corner of my vision and I remember the first time I saw him over on the common, wondering why his face is also blank, but it is years later and I am on top of the climbing frame looking across foot-ball pitches to the road and houses beyond, straining to glimpse a familiar window, a barren sky dwarfing rooftops, the harshness of a frozen sun making me turn towards the dead ferns butting the playground, charcoal skeletons and evergreens bending in the same wind that chaps my face, and at school they say there are coniferous and deciduous trees and that coniferous means they never lose their leaves, and that means they never die, and even now I understand it is best not to wander over there from the playground, as Mum says, you never know, there are bad people in the world as well as good, it's better to stay out in the open, and remembering Mr Fair reminds me of fried onions and a popular chorus, and as usual he is wearing his funny hat, I can never work out if he is a dunce or a clown, and he vanishes in a puff of smoke and I am scanning the small parade of shops, see myself years before peering in a window at a teddy bear waiting for someone to guess his name and take him home and I want to win the competition more than anything, but the memory cuts out and it is the hottest day of the year and I am standing by an ice-cream van with Mum trying to decide between a lolly and a cone, and now it is winter again and I am back on the climbing frame staring at the side of the common where the land disappears, snow covering the grass and ice lining iron bars, the cold splits gloves and stings hands and maybe my skin will peel off as I swing along pretending I am a monkey who has escaped from the zoo, and releasing my grip my feet tingle hitting concrete, but I don't care, and leaving the playground behind I lurch towards the edge of the world, smiling at the sight of this primitive jungle boy trailing his arms in the snow, an easy trail for his trackers to follow.

The choc-ice queer is drooling, lost in a mantra of I fuck you hard, fuck you very hard, fuck you so hard you cry for your mother, and then I fuck her, yes, I fuck your whole family, and I jump up and try to reach him through the bars, but he is too quick, sways like a ballet dancer as he skips out of reach, and I am rattling iron promising that if we ever meet again I will fucking kill him, and he bounces up and down, pigeon chest puffed out, singing you don't kill me, no, I fuck your mother and I fuck you, until you die, that is my promise, my friend, and he is giggling and wobbling and ecstatic. Teachers insist I take the insults and never retaliate, force me to hang my head in shame, the rape man twitching when he hears voices nearby, scurrying off without a farewell glance. I mean nothing to him, it is the power that matters. It is the same with all these bullies. I lower myself back down to the floor.

An ancient man rests opposite, muscles wasted and bones trembling, and I want him to be at home in front of a warm fire with his childhood sweetheart, drinking hot tea, passing wisdom on to grandchildren, stories of hard work and noble struggle and carefree world travel, but instead he is in a holding cell with men who could kill him with a single slap, if they wanted, if they even really noticed him. He is a failure, wasting his final years. I imagine him as a young boy with a big gap-toothed smile and bigger dreams, riding his bike with his pals, playing hide-and-seek, spinning on a round-about until he is dizzy and leaping off, stumbling and toppling over in the grass and laughing at the sensation, hurrying to his mum, helping his grandmother, see myself in the past and future.

I am kneeling in front of the fireplace with Nana and she is fussing as she cleans the grate, brushing ashes into a dustpan, and she turns and points at a robin perched on the window ledge, chewing bread as he watches us work. The robin blinks and darts off, back to his nest Nana says, to feed his young and see Mrs Robin, and I return to the fireplace, lean forward and look up into the darkness of the chimney, ask if there are any dead children there, bad boys who ate too much and got stuck, and Nana laughs and shakes her head and says of course not dear, and she looks at me and tells me that I am a good boy, a special boy, and that I must not worry so much. She hopes I will never change. Tells me the secrets of living a good life and shows me the charm that will one day be mine, and I listen carefully, take her words as gospel. And I am tearing up newspaper, screwing it into tight balls and placing these in with the splintered wood and nuggets of coal, twist it into longer strips that stick out of the side of the grate. At night it is my job to light these tapers. I am only three or four and must never play with matches, except when Mum and Nana are with me, and I love the way the wood and coal smoulder before sparking and once the fire is burning my work is done and I sit back and stare into the flames, feel their warmth until it is time to go to bed. This memory is very strong. It is a happy time.

As well as the old man there is a teenager, eighteen or nineteen years old with new trainers and a ragged baseball cap, sullen wax-like features creasing fast; a man in his late twenties with a shaved head and slashed leather jacket, a bandage on his hand; two middle-aged fat men in glossy suits, meat bellies hanging over natty trousers, each with a square of cardboard propped between their oily hair and the wall. Five convicted criminals and me, the innocent man who is just passing through, a globe-trotting peace-loving romantic who doesn't belong here and doesn't deserve to be treated this way. I am sure there were six other prisoners, but when I count again there are only five. I am tired and confused and uncertain of everything that is happening, stare hard at the wall.

What is certain is that tomorrow I am going to prison.

The righteous warnings of the judge are disguised by the translator, shielding his own satisfaction, easing into my brain, stirring up a lifetime of social conditioning, the great myth of prison and incarceration and the gutter cruelty of mankind suddenly real, my skull a closed-down empty library where their simple words vibrate and re-form, tremors racing down my spine. I try to forget, thinking warped as I panic and guess the crimes of the men around me. I see the old man as a beast and a tramp, the teenager a mugger and shoplifter, the baldie a pimp and hashish grower, the two fat men hired killers and traffic violators. But this is a mad way of thinking and I raise my eyes and focus on a crack in the ceiling, force myself to see the stem of a plant, slowly count nerve endings. Even if I could speak their language I would not ask about their lives, never mind their crimes. I don't want to know. Ignorance really is bliss. What counts is how I face the next few days, and the coming years.

But I am nervous and can't settle, stand and go to the window, a small oblong with three bars and no glass. I reach for these bars and feel sherbet rust, hang my weight on them and find they are set solid, sweet powder turning to grit. The cleaner air reminds me how bad the cell smells, a squat-down toilet mixing shit and piss with a fog of dread. The atmosphere is stifling. I lift my nose higher, ready to catch the next gust of oxygen, forget about the gangrene and plague looking for a way into my forehead, thinking short-term. Outside the city is deep asleep, its street lights groaning as regiments of decent citizens sleepwalk their way through millions of secrets, a tangle of aerials and industrial cables purring beneath a crescent moon, electricity shackled but ready to break loose and snuff out our lives. All I want from mine is to run from the police station and reach the docks, lose myself among the machines and containers, climb a gangplank and stow away on a tanker bound for New Orleans or San Francisco, Bombay or Calcutta. I don't care where I go as long as it is away from this cell and the years of prison waiting for me on top of the hill.

Lifting my feet off the ground I try again to loosen the

bars, willing my weight to increase, but they are not budging, and even if it was possible to bend them and squeeze through the gap, the drop would cripple me. I imagine the judge rolling his neck and adding extra years to my sentence, launching another tirade, and I can feel his eyes on me, imagine him selling lollipops in the station, this professional choc-ice man raising his hammer and stunning the court with his eloquent threats. I turn and catch the teenager lowering his gaze. Footsteps echo outside and I return to my place by the wall, a guard appearing and counting heads, scratching his ear and yawning, moving on.

I stay awake for a long time, brain aching and forehead pounding, a storm of confusion crushing any attempt to reason things out. It is important I stay alert, concentrate and fight back, but the cell is bare, without even a line of graffiti to focus on, and my mind is weak, pulled into the courtroom. The translator returns and explains the horror waiting for me in prison, the psychopaths sharpening their knives and greasing their cocks, an orgy of mutilation and sodomy. I am about to enter hell on earth, the judge and his lackeys content, the smirks of the bureaucrats and media revelling in a warped notion of retribution. Male rape is their fantasy and my terror. I would rather die. And death has also been promised. This cell is where we wait for the terror to begin, and while night is the time when the monsters come calling, and I want it to pass, I also wish it could last for ever. I gulp down air as the walls close in and the room shrinks, chest tightening and ribs crushing lungs, jaw grinding as I struggle to breathe, blocking the court out.

A half-sleep of jolts and small electric shocks finally takes over and against my will the day is resurrected, the furious faces of the authorities screaming racist bile, pointing accusing convicting me of all sorts of crimes, and I am a hated condemned man surrounded by upright citizens sweating disgust for this novelty foreigner outsider troublemaker refugee, their contempt singeing the air, lies fired at me in words I can't understand let alone deny, the thud of fists and stamp of feet an accepted release for controlled professionals, and the eyes of the judge are about to pop out of their sockets and the prosecutor is black as he demands retribution, the court a theatre full of character actors playing set roles, the prosecutor insisting on a punishment to fit my crime, the translator adding his own malicious slant to proceedings as the ice-cream prowler sells vanilla and whistles at the bad boys being led away in handcuffs, hypocrites urging him on, keen the subhuman criminal element works as their torturers, and I crouch down and leap forward and reach for the ice-cream man and this time I grab his neck and because he is right here right now I pay them all back as I smash his head into the bars, and there is one solid crack for the judge and another for the prosecutor, one for the translator, more deep fractures for the bureaucrats and technicians, the lackeys and arse-lickers and petty officials, for the arresting police officers, back down the line, splitting the skulls of everyone who has ever done me wrong, right back into the schoolyard. On and on and on. They want me to fear the other inmates, and I do, but I hold the sacred text in my hand and swear I will never surrender and never do their dirty work. And I wake up sweating. Swallow hard. Time suddenly matters.

I want to start again, sit with my grandmother in front of the fire and feel my mother's arms around me, and watching the old man opposite I wonder if it is true that the more years that pass the stronger distant memories become. His mouth moves as he chews on empty gums, right back where he started, and he splutters and heaves a tired frame upright, stumbles to the toilet where he drops his trousers and squats down. His guts explode and splatter the stone. I press my face into my knees. The stench of his rancid failure fills the cell. I press harder, wait for the smell to fade. He cleans himself with water from the bucket, doing his best to wash away the mess, face averted as he returns to his place. I sink back into sleep, losing myself in the darkness, the faint sound of the old man's sobbing following me down.

Some men wake up in the morning and see the face of a devoted wife on the next pillow, savour soft sleepy breath and the reassuring smell of cheap talcum powder. Maybe they glimpse the half-open eyes of a loving girlfriend, expensive perfume dabbed behind delicate ears. Or perhaps they are surprised to meet the steady gaze of an exotic stranger, a passionate kiss blowing away stale alcohol. All around the world men are opening their eyes and spying women, and they are absorbing their warmth, lost in huge tides of love and respect, but for some of us, the wandering men who roam at will, the tramps and drifters and hobo drunks, well, things can turn out a little bit different. For the likes of me morning means the crack of a police truncheon on the bars of a cell, the stench of an open toilet and a haggard male face barking orders. For half a second it almost seems funny.

The cell door opens and I hold out my hands for the handcuffs, reality snapping into place as silver bracelets are secured, the policeman almost tender the way he clicks them shut. He guides me away from the cage and through a gate, along a corridor lined with sketched black-and-grey faces, artists fighting natural urges but still enlarging brows and narrowing eyes, a series of mean lips beneath piggy nostrils. Even the hair, whether short or long, is wire-like, sharpened pencils adding a jagged edge. There are no women in this gallery, but things change when suspect impressions give way to full-colour crime-scene photographs. Torsos dominate. Faces are distorted or hidden. A young girl sprawls among rusty cans and bent plastic bottles, pants protruding from her mouth, legs and eyes wide open. A man sits against the side of a car, his chest split apart, bowed head in seven shades of condensed red. The charred remains of a woman lie in a pyramid of scorched bricks, her face charcoal, teeth gleaming. I turn my head away.

We pass through a door and cross a tiled floor, the air lighter, footsteps loud beneath a higher ceiling. Five police officers sit around a school desk, each one sipping at an espresso, in between exaggerated puffs of tobacco. Slender glasses of water rest nearby. I crave a mouthful of their water and a nip of caffeine, but it is not as if I can ask for favours. They stop talking and ease back in creaking chairs, watch me closely as a sergeant signs a sheet of paper and takes charge, points at my cut head and performs a sewing motion. He says something to one of the smokers, who sighs and performs a drama of standing and stretching, the sergeant scowling and leading the way.

The outside world is cool and refreshing and I swallow as much oxygen as possible, heart muscle flexing as I will it into my bloodstream. Moisture flavours the air and the dark clouds above are about ready to burst. I notice that people have stopped to stare and am clumsy and embarrassed in front of these good folk, for the first time feeling the sergeant's grip on my arm, free hand resting on his revolver. The other officer opens the back door of an unmarked car and I slide in, peering at the watching citizens, mouths open, catching flies. The engine fires and what I guess is smug political rhetoric oozes from the radio, the driver revived and accelerating away with a flamboyant screech of rubber and static. We are soon stuck in slow-moving traffic and I have time to examine the buildings, a trail of white concrete and grey glass, people moving in and out of doors and looking through windows at the clouds, waiting for the storm, narrow roads showing off an older life behind an already exhausted modern façade.

Lightning strikes the rhetoric dead and rainwater quickly swamps the windscreen, my driver seeing a lull in the traffic and speeding up, wipers cutting a narrow path. Half of me hopes he crashes, the other wants him to slow down, and knowing I am powerless I press into the window and feel the film of the glass on my face, imagine the smell of the water, its origins and journey, lost now in iron and masonry and already searching for a route back to the ocean, its vitality a relief from the dead pong of oil and cigarette butts. We swerve, narrowly avoiding a van, the downpour harder, a stolen sea washing and then smearing the buildings, flooding gutters. But it doesn't last long, which is a shame, sunshine conjuring rainbows from puddles, greasy prisms decorating the tarmac, our ride coming to an end as we pull up in front of a smart oblong structure, the sergeant's grip firm as we enter a hospital, passing patients and visitors and medical staff who don't notice the cuffs or escort, more important things on their minds. We walk down long corridors ripe with polish and disinfectant and I could be anywhere in the world. The muscles in my legs stretch and I want to keep on going, maybe break into a casual jog, and then a sprint, run for my life, but instead we turn into a brightly lit room where a matronly nurse and younger assistant are waiting.

There are few preliminaries, no introductions or explanations. I am ordered on to a padded bench where my head can be stitched, and I am conscious of Matron watching me without emotion, as if she already knows me, or at least my type, and I realise I am one more problem, avoid eye contact, replace her with the smile of the nurse who sets about cleaning my wound, dabbing at it with cotton wool soaked in a stringent disinfectant, which stings but is worth the pain, and I enjoy her calm, know she is one of the last women I will see for a long time. The table is comfortable and the back of my head rests easy. I could drift off to sleep and stay here for years, but once my wound is clean she leaves the room.

Matron takes over, fiddles with a phial and then approaches with a syringe, raises the needle so I can appreciate its fine point. I shut my eyes. Thoughts of euthanasia fill my mind, but I push them away, remind myself that the state may be cumbersome and uncaring, but it could never be so corrupt. The needle burns and the drug quickly numbs my forehead. I feel dizzy, nausea stirring in the base of my stomach, reminding me of those crime-scene photos. Maybe it is a truth serum. The nausea settles. I want to be sick but know it is impossible. I open my eyes and catch a faint smile trickling across Matron's saggy lips, wonder again if she is a dedicated carer or a frustrated executioner, imagination playing tricks. Nausea overcomes paranoia so I don't really care when she covers my face with a white shroud, cuts a circle in the cloth where my head is split, and I can feel the pressure of the scissors but not the blade, and I see a dead man wrapped in linen and notice how Matron is ghost-like behind the material, hovering over me, concentration slipping.

Life exists in the eyes of the beholder, and I must remember that gem, at least I think that is what the wise men say, there are so many lessons and too much advice and it's easy to become confused. I am numb mentally as well as physically, Matron raising a sewing needle and threading it carefully, and she moves in close and starts digging at my wound, a devil woman weaving an evil spell, a kind lady saving my life, pulling the skin together, and there is no need for fine craftwork, no frills or decoration or wasted time. Love and hate flow along the needle as she pulls the thread extra tight, and I have surrendered, any will to fight back paralysed, love conquering hate as my thinking stops and I revel in the soft padding of the table and the warmth of the room and the young nurse has gone but I am still here and Matron knows best. When she removes the shroud I want to thank her for saving my life and apologise for doubting her, but she has already gone. Struggling to my feet, the nausea is stronger, every outer pore turned to stomach lining.

Dizzy and confused, the police help me out of the hospital, and I am skimming the ground on distant feet, tripping into the car and guzzling petrol as we patrol foggy streets packed with featureless machine men, and I am shivering and wondering if the puke will flow and whether I will be beaten with truncheons, eyes adjusting for a second, blurring, brain sharp, fading, fuzzy. I can hear a voice and wonder if it really is the sergeant saying I feel sorry for you, my friend, you do not seem like a truly wicked man, but the time will pass and even though it will be hard you will come out of prison with a knowledge few men possess, and I try to speak but can't connect, and maybe he didn't say those words at all. Perhaps he thinks I have been treated too leniently and deserve life for what I have done.

We turn into a small street packed with people, the driver forced to slow right down. I feel a little better, roll down the window and look out. We are passing through the edge of a market and the stalls shine with the brilliant colour and texture of fruit and vegetables, a stunning exhibition of aubergines peppers onions tomatoes olives cucumbers lemons bananas limes oranges and everything else ever grown in the soil, all of it stacked and arranged with loving care and attention. I feel elated. The smell is incredible. Citrus fills the car and my sickness disappears. At least for a minute, until we reach a cliff of black meat, the stench of rotting bodies destroying the citrus, a bloody tangle of limbs and torsos and hooves tumbling towards us, hundreds of skinned heads closing in, and they are so near I could reach out and stroke their eyelids shut, except the lids have been cut off, fur stripped and leaving a mess of white and bloody tissue and thick bulbous veins, goat and sheep eyes wide with shock, these defenceless creatures castrated and cut open with knives and machetes, their screams only ever heard by slaughterers elbow-deep in intestines, these animals without any rights, faces stripped of identity, and the controllers insist they feel no pain and have no individual thoughts, that their executioners are just doing a job, and as we move forward I see pigs embedded on massive hooks, guts and hearts ripped out, feel the sickness and wish I could throw up.

Back at the police station I am returned to the cell, the slashed man helping me sit down and lean against the wall, back in my place, where I belong. I am defenceless but somehow know I am safe with these prisoners, lean my head into my knees, reach into my pocket and check that my lucky charm is still there. I hold it close and say a funny sort of prayer.

When I was a child I caught a butterfly and put it in a jar, but was too young to know that with the lid screwed on it couldn't breathe. I watched it flutter its wings and heard them patter on the glass and this was going to be my pet for a few days and then I would let it go and its wings were beautiful and I spent a long time admiring the pattern and was amazed how thin they were, that something so fragile could fly so high. It was summer and everything was perfect, with the trees covered in leaves and the flowers blooming and all the time I was loving the butterfly it was slowly dying, silently gasping for breath. I went off to play and when I came back it was at the bottom of the jar and it wasn't moving and somehow I knew it was dead. We carried it to the common and buried it in with the ferns and Mum told me that because butterflies are so beautiful they only live very short lives, that they are caterpillars first and then for a single day they are a butterfly. I was sad and cried, but at the same time it seemed almost fair, though I felt even more guilty as it hadn't had its full day of life. I don't know why I think of the butterfly now, but I do.

The lawn is turning yellow and sprouting daisies and dandelions and it needs cutting and Nana says she is too tired to do it she just doesn't have the strength any more sighing I am getting old dear but only on the outside I feel the same inside as when I was a little girl it is just the body that changes and ages the spirit stays the same and that is timeless so me and Mum push the mower along and it is good to help other people out and we are still living at Nana's and it is nearly always summer in my memory or if we are indoors then it is a fairy-tale winter and the smell of freshly cut grass reminds me of mice or maybe mice remind me of the grass and the unused overgrown fields where they live in the summer and Nana sits in a deckchair and watches us laughing you missed a dandelion over there and a tuft of grass here and I am full of energy and growing and getting big and soon I will be four years old and I am going to have a party with sandwiches and games and for some reason when cut grass is raked up it is wet and there is laughter from a garden nearby and we are drinking orange squash and eating small rolls with jam and cream and the garden is full of plants and cats that sleep on the coal shed and my father's camp is built into the side of the shed it is very small for a grown-up with planks of wood nailed together and a small door off a cupboard with a letter box except when he sent me those pictures they went through the door of the real house and it is hard to know whether I have my lucky charm with me at this time as it is almost like I was born with it though I know it belonged to Nana before me and in another year I am going to start school and learn to read and write and

Mum and Nana are sitting in their deckchairs while I watch the butterflies drifting and the bees buzzing and feel the heat of the sun on my legs and they are talking but don't know I am listening saying isn't it a shame he has to go to school and part of me is scared about leaving this garden though another part wants to be a big boy and they talk about bullying and a child who killed himself because the bad children said nasty things but I won't listen to that sort of talk and at night I always have a story sometimes from Mum and sometimes from Nana and one of my favourites is Noah and his ark and how every type of animal turns up to escape the flood and this is because God is angry at the bad things men have done and I ask why only two of each animal turn up and why do the rest have to drown if it is humans who have caused all the trouble and Nana says she is not sure but maybe the animals know that it is God's will and so they don't mind going to heaven but that doesn't make any sense to me and I ask her why there is a boy and girl of every animal and she explains it is the natural way of life that men and women are a balance to each other and without one the other wouldn't exist everything has an opposite in life another half that makes it whole and I will understand when I get older can I imagine what a boring world it would be if there were only men or only women and I nod and say I suppose so though I don't like girls much as they are silly and play with dolls and another time she tells me about this magic apple in a special garden and how people messed things up and it all seems so stupid as Nana makes pies from the apples that fall into her garden from the house behind us and maybe she will make me one for my birthday and there are no snakes in this country anyway or not many I have never seen one and I never eat those apples on the ground as they are sour and some have maggots in them and they taste different cooked with lots of sugar to make them sweet and hot custard poured over the top.

Handcuffed two by two we are mixed in with men from other cells, controlled by police and prison guards as we leave the station, different uniforms pointing the same rifles, the guards unshaven and rougher. It is mental knowing they will shoot us down if we try to run, kill a man never mind what crime he has committed, whether he is a serial rapist or a pickpocket. Trying to escape is a capital offence and it is a revelation realising that the worst crime we can commit is to embarrass the authorities and their servants. A prison guard playfully swings his stick, tapping us on the shoulders as we climb into the van, more of a whack when it is my turn. The ice-cream nonce stands nearby licking a strawberry cone, leering and waving at the prisoners, and the men shout back insults, their anger obvious but impotent, and the pervert laughs and rolls his eyes and threatens more sex, more rape, catches my eye, yes, I fuck every one of you very good and very hard.

Police climb into the wagon and stand at the back, prisoners facing forward, small portholes lining the vehicle but half solid with grime, spider remains and a mummified wasp trapped in the mesh nearest me. The doors swing shut and the van shudders, vibration lingering, finally fading as we are forced to wait a good ten minutes before leaving, the air becoming more and more stuffy, men fidgeting and the tension rising, space shrinking as layers of sweat mount. And it is only when we are locked inside the van that I realise I am attached to a stranger with a tangled necklace of black bruises looping his throat and total defeat distorting his features. He doesn't look at me when I nudge him. I speak, but he doesn't hear. His hand is by mine, the steel of the handcuffs cold but nowhere near as icy as his skin. He doesn't cry or shake or do anything, just stares straight ahead.

When the van sets off it is hesitant at first, rocking us gently, this convict cargo boasting tall, short, fat, thin, old and young men hanging on to the seats in front as we rumble towards the waiting nightmare on top of the hill, going the wrong way on a clapped-out rollercoaster, stuck in our minds regretting the crimes we have committed, the fact we were caught, everyone silent except for a pixie who whispers to an invisible friend, excited one moment, secretive the next.

A prisoner with a bandaged head hears this conversation and starts to hum, tapping his fingers on the rim of his window, selecting a dead fly from the mesh web, holding it up in front of his eyes and squinting, crushing its corpse between his fingers, which he wipes on his trousers, pleased by this show of power. But he is out of tune and out of sorts as another prisoner turns and threatens him, the fly crusher broken. This wagon is a doomed ark drifting along old streets of brick and stone, our view vague, the dread we feel meaning we don't try to make it clearer.

It isn't long before we begin climbing the hill on the edge of the city, engine struggling with the gradient. Time slows and our emotions are stripped down, a change in gear making us stretch for a glimpse of the passing streets, and it is as if the realisation we won't see this world for many months and years hits us all at exactly the same second. For a moment I imagine a unity between us, but this wishful thinking doesn't last, pressure increasing the slower the van moves, the shriek of the engine a screamed order that stills us, makes us sit back and forget. The van shudders and the walls vibrate, axle struggling to cope, and as we approach the summit we are barely moving, the suffering of the engine ripping at our eardrums as we finally level out and come to a halt. The van trembles and the motor dies and even the whispering pixie is quiet, listening to the thud of boots on the ground outside.

Our container springs opens and the temperature plummets. Prisoners wince as the shouting starts. Prison guards bang on the walls of the wagon and we are on our feet and hurrying out to meet twenty stern-faced bully boys showing off clubs and guns, our police escort shunted to the side as the guards funnel us towards the prison. I raise my head and there it is, Seven Towers, the prison castle on top of the hill. A massive bank of stone shuts out the sky, merging with the rock below as if it has grown from the depths of the earth. There is a tower by the gate, inside this an open door, but there is no time to admire the architecture as we are prodded towards the entrance, and I feel myself shrinking as the sheer scale of the prison turns us into insect men, and glancing at the window over the gate I spy a white-haired figure watching us, stumble up three steps and through the door as a truncheon bounces off my arm, hinges squealing as we are pushed further into the castle, the shouting of the guards louder, a barrage of meaningless anger, and we hurry through another gate and off along a narrow walkway lined with razor wire, stopping in a small yard, the inner walls looming above us, the ramparts of the castle closing out the fast-fading light.

We are arranged in rows, the prisoner with me slow standing to attention, a guard marching over and poking him in the solar plexus with his stick. He thinks it is funny seeing the man bent forward, laughs and swaggers back to his friends. Two police officers have entered the prison and are busy removing the handcuffs, working their way along our line, the attempted suicide squeezing my hand as they approach. He hangs on until the police reach us and lets go, lifts his arm with mine. A key is jiggled nervously in the lock, the police avoiding our eyes, and when they have all the cuffs they leave fast. The guards remain, watching us closely, pointing out individuals, smoking and laughing and enjoying our fear and their role in its creation.

A squat guard stands on a crate, a low-ranking arsehole who has found a stage for his lack of talent. He starts lecturing us, puffing up his voice, and very soon he is raging, prisoners lowering their faces, the whisperer from the van shaking his head with mock sadness. We have been to court and have heard it all before, but here there is no decorum, few physical restraints. The whisperer doesn't understand this and starts talking loudly, the guard on the crate stunned. There is a second of calm before this would-be dictator explodes, another guard running over and hitting the pixie with his stick. The whisperer is surprised, stops talking and sulks, pulls funny faces at the ground, a smile emerging as he listens to his invisible friend. The dictator is rocking on his heels as he scans the rows, ignoring the facial expressions of the mad man, voice rising and dipping. After a while the effect wears off. When the tirade ends there is a pause as a clipboard is produced. Names are announced and prisoners move away, gathering in small groups before leaving through a gate. The numbers quickly thin out. Soon there are only a few of us left.

Two guards grab hold of me, angry I haven't responded. They lead me out of another gate and along a passageway, push me into a room where I stand before another boss, though this one would break the crate and has probably broken a few men over the years as well. His skin is dripping, sweat staining his jacket, yellow teeth packed with gold nuggets. He reeks of dead animals, the flesh of lambs and goats stuck between his teeth, rotting pig meat woven into his uniform. I look at his cartoon snout and pink skin and realise that this man is Porky Pig, a humble porker injected by scientists and infected with the petty, bullying mentality of the human species. I feel reassured. But he makes signs. Moves his trotters. Telling me to drop my trousers.

This is the moment every man fears, the prison revenge of a squeaky-clean dirty-minded establishment come true. I have been trained to expect this but never thought it would actually happen. Sheer terror takes over, freezes me to the floor, and I have to find a way of defending myself but my thinking is also frozen as panic churns up the nausea I felt earlier, and if the hospital was full of angels then this place is packed with demons, and it is strange that just as I am about to be raped by this pig man I notice that the room has tiny chapel windows and a long shaft of purple light is shining into the gloom illuminating a billion specks of dust and it is a beautiful sight that warms my bones and smacks of God and infinity and my own invincibility, and it tells me I can refuse or take a chance, that maybe, just maybe, this Porky Pig isn't as bad as the newspapers tell me. Refusal means a beating, and if they are going to rape me they will do it anyway, so I do as I am told, take a chance, ready for the fat pig in front of me, this mutant pork beast, and there is no way I can fight five of them with my fists and feet, even if I was a tough man, so my thumbs are going into his eye sockets and I will pluck his eyes out, if he offends me, and it is an eye for an eye and both eyes for a sexual assault. I will dig my thumbs in as far as they can go, and I know I am at the end of the line with my jeans and pants dropped and these men can do anything they want, but when my thumbs are in those sockets things will be very different and the power surges through me. I don't care if they kill me. Anything is better than being raped. I remember a song and start humming they'll never take me alive.

Porky punches me hard in the chest, over my heart, shouting his abuse, and I have had enough insults pummelled into me during my life, can handle it, just turn the other cheek, say nothing, glad I can't understand, close out his features and only see this funny pig man from the cartoons, and one two three four times he hits me, then once in the stomach so I double up, and I don't fight back, hoping he just wants to batter me, and I am strong and know I will kill him. I can take a beating. Almost expect it. And he kicks my right knee so I stumble and I feel a blow on the side of my face from an unseen attacker, and my legs are taken from under me and I curl up on the ground waiting for their kicks, but they are half-hearted and I hear my chest thumping and then laughter as my face scrapes the ground. When I look out through my fingers Porky is holding his hand up and pointing at a wedding ring, looking at his friends, and then at me saying no fucky fucky, my friend, no fucky fucky, gesturing for me to pull up my trousers and get out and understand that he is a happily married man having a little fun at the expense of a low-life outsider.

The same two guards who took me to the chapel lead me along new passageways, through gates and doors deep into the centre of the prison. My heart is beating fast, and an incredible relief wells up and turns to elation, liquid ecstasy meaning I love these men, triple glad they are not rapists. And we are passing other convicts and prison guards, two men in smart suits coming out of an office, a few inmates looking at me but most uninterested. This city is a port, a crossroads for drifters just like me, so there should be other

F122,080

foreigners here. Men I can talk with and find some sort of bond. There must be people who know my language. There have to be. Loneliness swamps me as we enter the storeroom, the man running it passing over a blanket and a plastic bowl, mug and spoon. The trustee listens to one of the guards, looks as me and laughs.

We continue on our way, arriving in a small square with solid steel gates built into the walls. Guards and trustees stand around looking bored. In the far corner there is a shed with an Arab standing outside, a plastic table with three chairs and three men drinking coffee, cigarette smoke rising against a background of whitewashed plaster and thick layers of barbed wire. The square is barren except for the shed, where a fire smoulders inside a circle of stones, two earthenware pots with tropical plants wedged against the shack, which has been painted green and trimmed red. It is a mad sight. Transported from a Middle Eastern bazaar. With a touch of the Caribbean. A mixture of handwritten scripts fills small pieces of cardboard, the word Oasis in black paint over the open window of the shed. And I laugh. Despite everything I actually laugh as I pass through the open gate before me, angering the guards. It is slammed behind me. I stop laughing and scan the yard, about to start another sort of life.

Two days ago I am sitting on a stool in a bar, sipping cold beer and chatting to a good-looking, sweet-smelling woman, the goodwill sliding down, mind blushing at the sheer joy of being alive. From the railway station it takes ten short minutes to find a hotel room, and this is cheap and central and cleaner than most of the places I have been staying. There is a shower at the end of the hall with warm water, and after scrubbing away a long overnight train journey I am out walking the streets of a new city, finally stopping at a cafe to drink chocolate and eat sweet cakes, the transparent pastry soaked in honey and topped with almonds. I sit alone while around me people are busy living their lives, hurrying to work and school and arguing with the ones they love. And I am living mine. Following the sun, moving from northern lights to southern sunsets, reaching the edge of my world and wondering which way to turn. I am doing what a wanderer does. Sleeping the afternoon away and going back out again in the evening.

The bar I end up in is warm and welcoming, with a gas fire burning in the corner and locals who are reserved but friendly. With its harbour and railway junction, the people are used to strangers. Outside the wind howls, a horizontal shower chipping at the window, hot and cold air clashing and fogging the glass. Old men play dominoes at marble tables, banging down numbers and tapping the beads they carry, which are similar to rosaries, clucking as they rock on rickety chairs, without exception their clothes black and hair white. They sip lemonade and coffee, while the younger men stick to beer. Three women sit at the bar, lost in gossip, hanging over empty glasses and a full ashtray. Two are young and thin, the older one chubby and flamboyant. None of the men seem to notice them.

Food tempts me more than romance and I am drooling at the feast laid out at the end of the counter, looking past the split skirts of the girls and the low-cut blouse of their more experienced friend to the battered fish and chopped potatoes, the aubergines and mushrooms laced with chunks of garlic and floating in olive oil, wax peppers and a mountain of flat bread, a wide selection of beans and cheese and cut meat. My mouth waters and I dilute this latest temptation with a mouthful of beer. The woman I am talking to reckons this is the sort of bar where a person can sit in a corner and slowly drink themselves to death, spend ten years drunk without ever being noticed. She is probably right. The clock behind the bar is broken and as no one ever knows the time, they never know when it is time to leave.

She tells me her name, and the sound is confused and distorted, but it sounds near enough to Marian, so I nod wisely and laugh, tell her she can call me Robin Hood if she wants, that we can run away from home and go and play in the woods, rob the rich and give to the poor, right wrongs and become heroes in the eyes of the people. She looks puzzled, trying to translate my words, seems worried, and she is looking deep into my eyes and worrying me until she finally smiles. I feel as if I have passed a test. I am proud she has found nothing to fear. But she is suddenly serious and shaking her head very slowly, I am no freedom-fighter outlaw girl, no criminal, only a victim. There is a nasty silence as I wonder what she means and try to think of something cheerful to say, and then she is smiling and explaining in detail how she works in a hotel near the port, changing the beds and washing bathrooms, sometimes helping out in the kitchen, and I nod and realise that I was right, this woman really is Maid Marian.

Unlike the heroine of the story, this Marian has short hair, although a while back it seemed longer, while her bland brown coat is really fake leopard skin. Her perfume has become more powerful and her brown eyes have darkened. She reminds me of Ramona. In fact, she is the spitting image of sweet little Ramona, pointing at a trail of postcards wedged into the edge of the mirror behind the bar, and I try to focus, vision swimming as it replaces white beaches and green rainforests with a creased view of the River Ganges and the fading smile of a Texas Ranger. Ramona nudges me and I realise she is pointing at our reflections, not the postcards, and she waves and I see myself smiling back, but I seem different, older somehow, and looking at the man opposite I fight hard and identify the romance of the drifter, a maverick scholar and gentleman of the road, experienced in the myriad ways of the world. I recognise, or imagine, admiration in Ramona's eyes, see her as a little girl sitting at a school desk, growing and moving on.

Marian is waiting for her ship to come in, and it is due at any moment. I want to point out that Robin Hood lived deep in a forest, not out in the emptiness of the high seas, but guess she won't understand. A friend at the hotel will call the bar when it docks. She nods at the phone behind the bar, to emphasise the truth of what she is saying. There will be plenty of time to walk to the quay and welcome her hero ashore. This ship's captain has promised to show her the world, and she stutters I am nervous, very nervous, thinking about the way she is translating her thoughts into English, insists she is excited, very excited. Her captain is kind and generous and wants her waiting when he returns. This is important to him. He has promised to take her to Bali, where they will be married. She had always dreamt of visiting this island paradise. It has been her ambition since she can remember. She wonders if I have ever been there, but I shake my head.

Ramona fiddles with her handbag, a shiny red plastic that manages to shine in the relaxed light of the bar. As a girl she read all about paradise in a magazine, and I nod, know exactly what she is talking about, and it suddenly feels very good to be with someone I have known for many years. She explains in great detail how the Balinese carve wooden masks and paint them to represent all sorts of gods and monsters that laugh and frown and remind her of all those stories she used to hear, her biggest dream about to come true. I watch her red lips move and want to warn her that maybe she is expecting too much, but say nothing. I just hope this seaman is decent and will treat her right. And Marian is surprisingly drunk and starting to slur her words, telling me about another place she always wanted to see.

Three years ago she went to work in Paris. She picks at the zip on her sombre handbag, grinding the metal so her fingernails bend and seem ready to snap. She sighs and leans forward and whispers how she worked in a hotel by day and danced by night and was raped in the early hours by a man who bought her a drink and thought he owned her. I don't want to hear this, but she tells me anyway, and I feel sick and guilty that I am a man. Her attacker was a migrant worker, like her, and she was drunk and couldn't explain herself to the police, as she knew little French, and her attacker melted away and her brothers sent her money to return home, although she has never told her family what happened. There are tears in her eyes, but she doesn't cry. We sip our drinks.

Emotions rise and fall. Life can seem so good and then it

kicks you in the balls and turns to mush, though the glow of my travelling life is still with me and fighting the horror and I try to keep hold of that feeling of invincibility you have when you are on your own and able to go wherever you want, whenever you feel like it, with nobody to persuade. It is the purest freedom. Running for trains and waiting for buses with a small bag and few belongings, willing to sleep anywhere and try most things at least once. At times it is lonely, but I can walk into a bar in a strange town and most of the time someone will talk to me, specially around a bus or train station, in a port or major junction, a transient place full of transient people, men and women on the prowl, heading somewhere else, taking their time and in a hurry, merging with the locals and adding an opinion, an uncertainty the police never trust, fearing the drifter, these smugglers of bad ideas and lax morals. The elation fades as I think of the drifting rapist who ruined Marian's dream, glad she isn't Ramona.

Marian smiles and suddenly everything is right in this run-down corner of the European empire, and I am finding the same place everywhere I go, a universe populated by forgotten old men playing dominoes and cards and young prostitutes playing with their health, the rootless drifters and dreamers, the out of work and overworked, the drinkers and junkies and gamblers and chancers, fallen men and women riding the railway lines, a tangle of weirdos and fruitcakes, runaways and stay-aways, the criminal element and mentally suspect, bar-room thinkers and tap-room poets, honest moralists and the amoral, religious fanatics and atheists, every one of them removed from the materialistic slog of nine-to-five conformity. I laugh to myself as I imagine myself one of these free spirits.

Marian's back aches so we move to a table where she opens her coat and turns her legs towards me. She is wearing stockings with a seam and I feel a twinge in my groin. She has good legs, takes my hand and runs it over her knee. She wants me to feel her scar. The groove is deep and I remove my hand. Three months ago she was attacked by a man on her way home from work, an alcoholic who said dirty things and tried to grab her breasts. She pushed him over and he threw a bottle, cutting her leg open. He was a tramp, a dirty man living on the streets, without a home, family or even friends. But she had her revenge. She isn't defenceless here. Her brothers found the tramp sleeping in an alleyway, with the rats, and they punished him. Marian looks into my eyes. Tells me it was justice. They made the dirty man suffer for his sins. Made him scream and beg for mercy. They showed none.

The phone rings and Marian hurries to the bar. I don't want to hear about rape or the revenge dished out to a tramp. I don't want any trouble. You hear every type of story travelling and at first I believed it all, slowly realising much of it is bullshit, especially when it comes from those who are drunk speeding tripping, on whisky sulphate acid, or stoned on life itself, but this flow of bullshit is different from the petty deceit of wage slaves, as nobody will meet again so it doesn't really matter. Fact and fiction become muddled and maybe that is the easy therapy of the drifter, tall tales and a shifting realism that makes us imaginary heroes. But I haven't worked it out, and don't really need to either, as that is the reason people break away in the first place. We don't want any trouble. Just want to be left alone.

The prison yard is empty so there is time to get my bearings, find some courage and gear up for the horror ahead. In front of me stands a two-tier block with an outdoor staircase leading to the top floor, the brickwork in weak contrast to the solid stone of the surrounding castle. The glass in barred windows catches the sun and reflects the eyes of twenty blind beggars. The yard is a mixture of tarmac repairs and older concrete, potholes spilling gravel where the lining has split, the boundary walls flaking white paint, zigzagging cracks connecting with the barbed wire above. But what really stands out is the size of the castle. It is a different scale to the newer block inside, the stone walls even bigger now, emphasising my insignificance. To the right stands a tower, a rounded monster complete with battlements and what look like slits for archers. To my left are metal sinks tucked below a corrugated roof, moss clinging to a broken gutter. Washing flutters on a line. Socks and pants and trousers and shirts and a pair of split running shoes hang by their laces, tapping together, sound smothered by the steady thump of my heart.

It takes a few minutes for my chest to stop heaving, a battle for control, and walking into the middle of the yard I keep on shrinking, the castle swelling and spreading and rocketing out into the cosmos, timeless rock drawing me in deeper as another three towers appear. Only four of the seven towers are visible, the rest hidden beyond internal walls, but with the tower next to the gate I have now seen five of the seven. Squinting, I trail the outer wall, jump at the sight of a black figure, remember the translator telling me about Seven Towers, how ancient invaders lined the walls of the castle with the heads of decapitated prisoners, and I think of the market and smell the corpses, see shaved heads, unable to tell the difference between a pig and a man, and during my lifetime political prisoners were tortured here, their pain lost in the stone. My eyes focus and the golem is actually a prison guard, rifle across his chest. I imagine him challenged by the convict below, this arrogant outsider staring him in the eye, a hawk man ready to wipe out the rodent below.

Leaving the light and entering the shadow cast by the block, ripples race across my skin, and I am expecting the worst, hesitating for a few seconds before turning cold-blooded and lethal, emotions suspended, and this is what counts, what happens next. It is going to affect the rest of my time in prison, the remainder of my life, whether I live or die, and every child learns lessons, stores experience and draws on it at a later date, and I am ready for a fight, strength channelled, adrenalin mixing with anger and creating a single-minded determination. I am an outsider with the odds stacked against me, and the others can see me any way they want, accuse me of any crime, any deviancy, and I have to make it their problem rather than mine – *that's more like it, hit them hard and hit them first, the fucking slags* – and I am coming out of the gutter strong and determined, even though it is a con, the whole lethal charade, and I have no choice but to be a part of it, play their childish games. I am past the police and their suited masters, the choc-ice rapist and that deviant pork in the chapel, the hawk on the wall, and apart from the ice-cream queer all those men are protected by uniforms, the system making them bold. There are no uniforms on this block and I can fight back, but know this will work both ways, restraints and limitations removed.

Once inside the door of the lower section, I stop so that my eyes can adjust to the gloom. The room is long and lined with twenty beds on either side, the width of another bed between them. In the centre aisle there is a long wooden table and shorter benches, a pile of logs next to a small wood burner. I look for the fire but it is hidden behind an iron flap, and most likely extinguished. At the far end a battered green door suggests showers and a toilet. The room appears empty, but once my vision settles it is clear most beds are occupied, sleeping bodies buried beneath blankets, while elsewhere prisoners sit in twos and threes, talking quietly and playing cards, the tick tock of their worry beads the only true sound. I am not sure what to do, as I was expecting chaos. A few heads turn, but without interest. A glance is enough. Yet it could be a trap. Indecision may be fatal, a sign of weakness. I can't tell which beds are free so walk over to the table and sit down, run my hands across the surface, dipping fingers into carved letters that could be slogans or psalms or cruder curses. At least it is warmer here than in the cell, a faint haze hovering below the ceiling where the smoke has settled, all around me the musty smell of men, a mix of sweat and damp, with a faint hint of urine. I wait for something to happen.

Ten minutes later someone sits down opposite and formally welcomes me to Seven Towers, what he laughingly calls a heartbreak hotel. He talks back-to-front English with foreign words thrown in, this hybrid delivered in an American twang. It is hard to understand what he is saying at first, but once I get the hang of the delivery he makes sense. The face is tired and buried beneath a black quiff, but the eyes shine bright, a rebel badge sewn into his jacket. He launches into an explanation of how on his way to the United States he was caught at the airport with a bundle of fake dollar bills. A victim of a rip-off by an unscrupulous money changer, he has been here for three months and is still waiting to plead his innocence in court. He laughs and shakes his head. Like me he is a foreigner, but an older version on the move for five years, working his way up and down Europe, a minor conviction blocking his American visa applications. With this problem finally solved and the permit in his passport, money in his pocket and a ticket in his hand, he is stopped minutes before departure. He promises to tell me his story later, as we have time, and he laughs, lip curling the same as the King himself, Mr Presley asking if I saw the Director of the prison when I arrived. His office is above the gate. I mention the white-haired man and he nods. He will also tell me about the Director later, but first I must rest.

Elvis leads me down the aisle to an empty bed, ambling like a good old boy leaving a diner with a bellyful of cheeseburger and Coca-Cola, heading to his pickup truck and living the dream. He promises to ask the guards about my bag, nods and leaves. I arrange the bed, smooth my blanket which smokes dust, pick up a pillow and bang it flat, prop it against the wall and sit down. Two men stop their chess game and stare, the blood rushing and telling me to glare back, but they smile and one says hello, another foreigner who introduces himself at Franco, the other man a local called George. Franco asks if I am waiting to appear in court or have been moved from another block, surprised then angry I have been sentenced the day after my arrest. He has been in Seven Towers for five months without a trial, and like Mr Presley is waiting for a court date. Five months for a single smoke of a weak joint, these people are fucking shit, and he trembles, lost for another insult. When I tell him how long I must serve he calms down. He doesn't ask what I have done.

There is a pause as he searches for the right words, his speech even slower than the drawl of Elvis, and although I have to concentrate hard it is a miracle finding these two so quickly. Having nobody to talk to would destroy me. And Franco wants me to know that I can present a paper to the court and fight for an appeal, and if I can impress a new judge he might reduce my term, but first I must find a lawyer. I explain that I don't have the money for a legal man. He frowns and wonders if there is nobody at home who can help me and I shake my head, and he is embarrassed and considers the possibilities, loses me in a torrent of jargon, exhaustion taking over so I suddenly wish he would be quiet. I ease my body down the bed and pull the blanket around me, Franco smiling, you must be very tired, I understand, I was the same. He turns and checkmates George. Don't be afraid to sleep, you will be safe, a man must be careful but we will watch you. And I nod and say nothing, the blanket harsh and lined with what seem to be specks of metal, yet it is comfortable and very warm, the pillow stained with the sweat and oil of hundreds of heads, and I am too tired to worry about fleas and bugs, feel a couple of nips as I stretch right out for the first time in days, the mumble of voices fading into the past.

I panic and try to sit up, feel handcuffs on my wrists and leather straps around my ankles, electric cable inserted as an intravenous drip, voltage cranked up setting off muscle spasms, my eyes burning from the bright light above the bed. My senses return. Bare bulbs rest high on the walls, one for every four beds, and these have been switched on and have woken me. I realise I am the only one sleeping, the other prisoners talking as they are herded inside by two guards. One stands across the door while the other marches down the section counting heads, making a comment every so often, some men grinning, others lowering their eyes. When he reaches the end of the ward he bangs on the green door with his stick. The tin is thin and easily dented, a prisoner hurrying out, fastening his trousers and quickly closing the door, a stench ten times stronger than the police cell squeezing out. The guard turns and walks along the second row of beds, shifting the club to his counting hand. When he reaches the main door his friend writes the number down in a note-book. They peer at the page for a while, then turn and leave. The door is locked. The room seems very crowded.

Men mingle as if they are in a bar, lighting cigarettes and talking too loudly, trying to forget there are no women present, blowing fumes that spiral away and form clouds, and these rise and fall for a while before spreading out across the ceiling, itching at the stone. The benches fill up fast. Dominoes are slammed down and packs of cards shuffled, the stove loaded with wood by a giant who dominates the nearest seat, another prisoner tuning up a mandolin-like instrument, narrow fingers twanging strings, creating a smile on his face and a look of irritation on that of his neighbour. A couple of hours of sleep hasn't touched the sort of tiredness that leaves me shivering despite the heat generated by the blanket. It hasn't been washed for years, if ever, and the material is coarse, but it already feels part of me.

The mandolin tuner stops his work and focuses on a peacock man strutting down the aisle. This dandy swaggers, an amateur bodybuilder and professional poser by the looks of him, and I can't help thinking he is a failed pimp, a disco dancer. He stops and stares, sneers and makes a smart remark, boosting his ego at my expense. And I am glad I don't under-stand. George calls out and he snarls back. The boy Franco says this prisoner is being released in the morning, and that he likes my shoes. Sentenced to five years for stamping on a youth's head and causing brain damage, he has been moved here from a farm ready for release, but following some confu-sion over his papers he has been stuck in Seven Towers for nearly a month. The others will be glad to see him go as he is a troublemaker.

Behind this stroppy character a tall man gazes into a hand mirror while carefully dusting his face with a cloth. It is Friday night and it doesn't matter where you are, what the situation, people around the world want to have fun, make the most of the weekend. They wash off the grime and dress up, leave home to drink and meet friends, to dine with family, parade along a high street or around a square, stand on corners, stroll down a promenade and look towards a romantic ocean. Some are looking for a fight. The man at the mirror leans in close and admires his reflection, doesn't care who is watching or what they think of his height and lack of weight, knows things can't get much worse. He is going to look his best, whatever happens, in love with himself because maybe nobody else is, and when this brain-damaging bully boy follows my eyes he turns and speaks, the tall man not bothering to shift his head as he fires off a sentence that makes the bully stomp away like a spoilt brat. He slams the green door shut as he disappears into the dark cave beyond, the familiar smell of fermenting piss and shit accompanying the echo.

I ignore this temper tantrum and listen instead to dominoes hitting the table, a mellow beat to match the fading cymbals, men banging their fists down in dramatic gestures, laughing as they win and lose, beads clicking. Franco says he tried to wake me when the evening meal arrived, but I was too far gone, and he is remembering the shock he felt when he first arrived, uses the word trauma, was exhausted for weeks, and his tiredness started turning to apathy, this is the battle, to keep fighting inside the mind, my friend, I was beaten by the police, on the soles of the feet, but not enough to send me to hospital. His friend was not so lucky. But it is a long time since I ate or drank anything and Franco brings me a plastic bottle and I gulp the water down. It tastes warm and sour but I don't mind. He has a small bottle of iodine and will give me some, as this is vital to fight the dysentery and other illnesses that can make life even harder, parasites eager to lodge in a convict's gut and intestines. Franco returns to George who has moved his king and is waiting for Franco to respond. I am glad, want to go back to sleep, realise they have been playing chess for hours.

The green door opens and the bully emerges. He stares at me again, but I ignore him. He approaches and I know the stance, the tightness around his mouth, and I am deciding what to do – *don't wait for him to hit you, get in first, do the cunt* – and there is no way I can know the score after a few

33

hours, whether he has a knife or if he fights with his fists. He stands rigid at the end of my bed and speaks. He is not asking how I feel, if I am too hot or too cold, if I would like a crust of his bread or a bowl of the soup he has saved. I move my feet to the floor as he rocks on his heels, chest swelling, an ice-cream seller with muscles and a heterosexual leer. He kicks the bed and is strong and squat and the chess game stops and the volume dips and the rest of the kids are chanting fight fight fight fight running to watch except we are adults and should know better and the other men are waiting to see if I will stand up for myself, some coming over to watch, the bully pointing at my shoes.

They are not exactly the latest in designer fashion, but that's not the point. It is the thought that counts. There is always a soppy idiot playing these games and there is no way I can hide, even if I wanted to. Respect is everything. That and fear. The two go together a lot of the time. I can't let him take the piss just because I am tired and can't be bothered. That would be worse than being a coward. Laziness is a sin. Every true coward on the wing will be lining up to have a dig, and I have seen the films, don't fancy ending up as another prison punchbag. It is funny though, as the weakest minds make the biggest bullies. It is playground stuff. Something you learn early. And he is looking at the Converse under my bed, which I have taken off, bends down and picks them up, turns to leave. My spine clicks into place and I want to sing.

It takes a split second to stand and grab the pumps, push him hard in the chest so he stumbles backwards and falls on to a bed. He is furious and our eyes connect and in his surprise there is fear and right away I know I can have him, if I want, but I don't need a fight and don't want to start my sentence in solitary or whatever they do to punish a man in this shithole. He is going home in the morning and doesn't need any trouble either. We both know the truth. I am on my way in and he is on his way out and doesn't want to get caught in the revolving door. He is a mean fucker with scars on his face and tattoos on his wrists, but I am desperate and on my own with nothing to lose. He stops, weighing up the options, his head dark red turning purple reminding me of the judge, and he sneers and leans forward, and I can smell soap, a choc-ice scent, think of the ice-cream seller again and punch him hard in the mouth.

He staggers and leans against the wall, but stays on his feet. He is dazed and rubs at his jaw. The men who have come to enjoy the fun back off. Some walk away. He is stunned, saw an outsider treading carefully, an easy target, misjudged the situation. This sick foreigner has to fight back. It is his choice and he knows I am the more desperate. He has to decide what is more important, his pride or the fact that in the morning he can walk out of prison and jump in a taxi, return home and see his family and friends and have a drink and maybe make love with a beautiful woman. He can enjoy good food and move freely, do anything he wants. I sit down and slot my shoes back under the bed. He does nothing. Finally turns and walks off. The dominoes snap and cards are dealt. The chess game continues.

I am no tough man. I hate arguments and violence, but know I have to survive. I glance at the bully who is at the other end of the room now, suddenly busy sorting out his belongings, preparing for his release, avoiding the glances of the men around him, and I shake my head, wonder how he can live with himself, his pride in tatters.

Pride can destroy a man. Send him to jail and make sure he never leaves. Prison promises murder, suicide, coma, death by misadventure, death from natural causes, maiming, rape, insanity and shipment to a mental hospital where state-sponsored detergents purge the brain of its secrets, turning proud men into gibbering wrecks. Pride isn't worth that. It is better to stay silent. To stand in line and nod agreement with the hypocrites, vote for the winners and turn the other cheek and pretend the blow doesn't sting and refuse to even hear the insults. Shut those eyes so tight the obscene gestures don't exist. Pride can also stop a man admitting his mistakes, guilt incubating and re-emerging as an all-consuming cancer. I lift my bottle and relish the taste of the beer, washing the weakness away. But pride also means a man can survive hard times. It makes him strong. Forces him to fight back.

Alcohol smoothes out the rough edges and I can understand every word Marian says, once she puts the phone down and returns to the table, finishing her drink and telling me her captain is coming to the bar, worried she will catch cold or be molested if she steps into the night. I am glad she is happy, my mind moving away from this crusty sea dog as I wonder if revenge connects with pride, trying to imagine the vicious punishment dished out to a confused vagrant in a lonely alley, how it must feel being paid back for someone else's crime. His sleazy grope reaps the revenge due a rapist far away and out of reach, and maybe that is what happens, an easy target paying for another man's sins. Ramona asks me if her lipstick is smudged and I tell her she looks great. My childhood sweetheart is beautiful.

Marian is waiting for a hero to carry her off into the sunset and at least he will take her to paradise, even if things don't work out, but I hope they do, and I am thousands of miles away suddenly tired and wishing Marian would leave me alone, the door opening and her captain entering. He is no singer of sea shanties, but smooth and handsome and in uniform, a big man following behind, one of his crew acting as a minder. It is obvious she sees romance in this sailor, where I immediately identify arrogance. I want to warn her to look elsewhere, think of Robin Hood deep in the forest, but she is saying goodbye and jumping up too fast as if she is afraid to be seen talking to another man, this scruffy stranger, this inebriated gentleman of the road. She skips over and they embrace, the Captain glaring over her shoulder, laying down a challenge like so much puffed-up lowlife, as if I am a nasty vagrant touching his girlfriend's breasts in a dingy corner, the sort of deviant hobo who sleeps among dustbins and scavenges with the rats. There is no need for this sort of behaviour. I have no romantic interest in Maid Marian.

I ignore his insecurity and concentrate on my beer, consider the journey ahead. Soon I will leave Europe behind and head either east or west, though I have yet to make a decision. Yes, it is a good life, moving with the seasons, focusing on the horizon and the future. Looking at the other end of the bar and seeing the food there reminds me of the hunger in my belly, but I have already eaten today and that is the only downside of this travelling life, a serious lack of cash, and I make a snap decision, stand and thank the bartender, wave to Marian and stumble outside, the wind sobering me up as I head for my hotel. There is bread and cheese there and a jar of olives, and it is late and I have had enough to drink and there is a train at nine in the morning and I want to be on it, ready to move on, already bored with this place. I try and focus on the street, but my judgement is blurred, the wind getting so far inside me I imagine garbled voices.

A hand grabs my shoulder and twists me round. The Captain stands up close shouting into my face, and I step back as I don't have a clue what he is on about, just know he is angry. I am disorientated, don't know what the problem is, certain I paid for my drinks, at least I think I did, but yes, the barman smiled when I left, so it can't be that, and Marian waved, I didn't offend her, and the Captain grabs his balls and makes a gesture and I understand. Marian is his possession and he is a man of importance. He is doing her a favour. My first impression was right, the Captain is a cunt. Behind him, his bodyguard is listening and nodding and flexing muscles. The Captain is reaching the end of his rant and I am thinking about my sleeping bag, the bread and cheese, the taste of those olives, the train journey in the morning, and I can't be bothered with all this, don't need the hassle. I want to be left alone. He finishes speaking and I try to tell him he has made a mistake. He spits in my face.

Funny thing is, I am not even angry. The wind is so cold I don't feel the phlegm and it would be easy to turn and walk away. Return to my room and sleep until morning. Nobody will ever know. Except me. And it is pride that makes me punch him in the face and break his nose, and self-defence that forces me to reach into my pocket and pull out the clasp knife I carry for protection, because the road is long and the road is winding and the road is fucking dangerous when you are an alien in a strange land. That is the other side to living free and easy, drinking around train stations and in harbours, places where you are a prime target. It is no easy ride when you are a drifter. This small knife, the one I use to cut apples and cheese, is essential and saves me as the Captain's bodyguard swings a broken bottle at my face. I duck and return, slice his hand open, raise the knife in the air but hold back from hurting him more than I need to, and he has broken the bottle earlier, ready to scar or maybe even kill me, a calculating coward who turns and runs off lost in melodrama shouting for help, and the Captain is on his knees holding his nose, moaning police police police. A voice tells me to kick him in the head, but I am not like that. I walk away and hear sirens. Start to run.

Back at the hotel I pack my bag and leave. Once outside I keep off the main roads as much as possible, wary of retribution, but when I stop at a corner I wonder if maybe I am overreacting. Somehow I know the Captain means to punish me. I find a drain and drop my knife into the sewer. The blade is two inches long and hardly a murderous weapon, merely handy for slicing fruit. I reach into my pocket and squeeze my lucky charm, make sure it is still there, stitched into the material. I stand no chance against a respected man like the Captain. Self-defence won't count for much, and as for the cause, well, I doubt anyone is interested. It will take the police time to work out where I am staying, unless Marian has told them. I am worried again, keep moving and reach the train station, which is nearly deserted. Trains pass through at all hours and I am almost safe.

Spotting a railway uniform I warily approach, ask when the next train is due, frustration growing as I try to make myself understood, relieved at his desire to help. He beams and inspects his watch, holds up ten fingers and points to a platform across the tracks. I thank him and hurry off, cross the footbridge and join a small band of waiting men and women, a young girl sleeping on a pink blanket spread on the ground. These migrant workers look at me briefly, before turning their attention to the rails. I take out the cheese and bread and eat fast, sitting on my bag. I listen to the tracks with the others, and maybe it is bad manners to eat in public as they are suddenly staring at me, over my shoulder, and I turn just as the Captain arrives with three sweating policemen, a truncheon smashing down on my head.

SEVEN TOWERS

SUNSHINE SLIDES THROUGH a gap in the clouds and flows over the prison wall, warming my face, a just reward for the first man in the yard. Morning is the best time of day, specially in this place, and as soon as the door is unbolted I am straight out, natural light dazzling after fourteen hours locked inside, crisp air diluting the murky vapours of the night shift. It is cold, despite the lingering rays, winter closing in and forcing me deeper into my jacket, hands buried, head raised towards the sky. There is no real privacy in Seven Towers, only odd moments that have to be grabbed and savoured. Pressed into the ledge running along the side of the block, feet on the ground and back against the wall, I feel good, enjoying the sunny glow of achievement. Today marks my first month in Seven Towers, and I have survived, stood up for myself and learnt fast, avoided the petty squabbles that can end with a stab wound, and despite some gastric rumbles I am healthy, kept alert and adapted to the rhythm of prison life. The biggest battle, the one raging inside every inmate's head, is ongoing.

A flock of geese pass high above the prison, wedged in tight formation as they head south, following the sun, necks stretched and beaks splitting the air. Their honking creates goose pimples, the synchronised flow of their wings making me glow inside. The sun hardens their feathers and they become a wave of gleaming B52s, relentless power driving them on, and instead of bombs they scatter seed, spreading life over death. Too quickly they disappear beyond the outer wall and I am sad but grateful for a small glimpse of freedom, focus on the clouds and force myself to admire their shape and texture, the various

43

shades of black and grey and patches of dirty white, but they drift aimlessly while the geese are determined, and that is a rare quality. Stuck in the yard or dormitory there are few new sights or sounds, the sky our window on the world. I stay positive and enjoy the silence. It won't last.

The noise level rises and falls with the mood of the men and the time of day, but it is near enough constant. There is talking, laughing, shouting and singing, and when we are asleep snoring, coughing, farting and dreamy dog-like yelps, the whisper of insomnia and schizophrenia, the creak of a bed and gnawing rats behind the green door, the same suppressed sobs from the police station. Mixed in with the sound of men living is the tick of the prison clock, a steady click of beads. Most of the prisoners have small chains wrapped around their hands, plastic beads snapping back and forward, back and forward, on and on and on, variations in speed and intensity matching shifting emotions and individual personalities. I don't need their beads, as I have my charm, and this keeps me disciplined, a reminder of better times.

The second man out is a stocky little character who helps run his family's bakery, and receives a regular supply of bread and cakes to supplement his diet, the guards limiting the amount and keeping the excess for themselves. He strolls from the block to the far wall, swivels and returns, rolling shoulder blades. Baker is well liked, makes the men laugh with his bumbling manner as much as his jokes. With the business in debt he agrees to drive a car for a friend, the payment enough to clear what they owe, but it turns out he is the getaway driver in a bank robbery, forgets to wrap the scarf around his face and is arrested within the hour. The courts offer to release him if gives up his friends, but he refuses and will serve the full three years. Baker is the boy who makes every mistake going, but doesn't seem bitter, just bemused, the bakery winning a healthy contract and prospering. I don't know what goes on inside his head, relying on Elvis and to a lesser extent Franco for my information. Without these two I would go insane. They have saved my life.

The sunbeams hover and those geese must be over the sea

now, on their way to Africa or maybe Arabia, and I look forward to the arrival of the breakfast detail, humming morning has broken like the first morning, blackbird has spoken like the first bird, sitting in assembly during another life, between prayers. I try to remember walking into the infants school for the first time, but it is a long time ago now, and while the picture is bogged down in my subconscious the feeling remains, how I was nervous but also excited, and I made myself strong, a big step for every five-year-old. It is the same for the men here, the likes of Elvis and Franco, George the chess-loving serious thinker and Baker the greedy doughnut boy and these two flash kids who act as if they are related, brothers or cousins or maybe just good friends.

Baker is joined by the chubby gangsters from the police cell, four weeks of prison food thinning kebab bellies, glossy trousers baggy and jacket shoulders oversized, hair still greased back but boxing slimmer faces. They stomp to the gate, turn, aim for the wall opposite, turn again, return to the gate, crunching the concrete and patches of gravel, working off frustration, and there is an intensity to their jerky strides that Baker lacks, walking across their path, on a collision course he will make sure he avoids. These gangster heads are bowed as they talk intensely, the loneliness of not having a connection with my culture returning, someone who speaks the same language and shares a common humour, most of all reference points that mean as much as words. I can communicate with Elvis and Franco, but it isn't the same. I am not complaining, can't imagine what would happen if they weren't here, just know it would be very bad.

Baker ambles along and I see him dusting cakes, taking his time as he removes bread from a kiln, dipping his finger in chocolate sauce, and the fact he has an extended family so near makes his imprisonment seem worse. And it is the same with Franco. He has a life waiting for him in the Italian Alps, letters arriving every week, a warm shelter to crawl back into when he is released, a place where he can hide for the rest of his days. It is easier for the likes of me and Elvis. Nobody knows our situation and few would care if they did.

The gangsters have each other, and their loved ones beyond the walls, and it turns out they are no big-time villains, just local conmen, car salesmen and licence forgers who prefer flash suits and diesel to hardcore crime. This is the nature of the C-Block boys, and it is fine by me, Baker swerving to avoid their trail, these plastic gangsters showing expert hearing, a key in the lock of the gate sending them jogging upstairs to collect their mugs. Baker licks his lips.

The gate opens and Chef enters, his too-small apron straining to hold back the blubber that comes with his vital work, two trustees struggling with a large silver pot. This is Chef's cauldron, from which he conjures potions. He is a popular sight, nose held at a slight angle to explain his genius, but he is no snob. It is an essential part of the Seven Towers package. Five-star accommodation at a bargain price, an interesting clientele with stories to tell in an exotic dialect, and the chance to go on safari whenever nature calls. And Chef is no ordinary cook, at his best when he is serving the people, two guards riding shotgun in case he is mobbed by good-food lovers. He enjoys the art of presentation, becomes angry if an overkeen prisoner approaches before he is ready to start serving. Chef is a perfectionist, watches closely as the pot is positioned, shifted to the left, a little to the right, his donkeys eager to please, withdrawing as the sacred ladle is inspected, a speck of dust removed from the handle before the great man turns to his escort and nods. A guard raises the bell in his hand and starts ringing, the lid of the pot removed and the steam exploding.

Baker almost runs to Chef he is so excited. Saliva fills my mouth as I stand behind him, sweet mist reaching out, and I am breathing deeply, absorbing as much goodness as possible. Chef laughs at a Baker wisecrack and offers a second helping. They exchange pleasantries, Baker obviously keen to get away and start on his breakfast, but remembering his manners and investing in the future. When it is my turn I am humble and extra respectful, Chef dipping his ladle into the pot and easing the hot milk towards me, making sure he doesn't spill a precious drop, finishing off with a flamboyant flick of the wrist. When I don't move he looks into me, considers the options, nods and dips his ladle back in, fills my mug to the brim. He rewards respect, needs to be appreciated and even loved, and I thank him, in his language, before slowly turning towards the ledge.

A line has formed and more men are hurrying from the block, dodging right and left as I protect my milk, clouds tightening and shutting out the sun, but it doesn't matter now. Once comfortable on the ledge, I lift the mug with two hands and let the warmth flow over my face, revel in the sugary flavour and pressing harder feel the heat sting my palms, will it along my arms and into my body, but it stays in my hands. I imagine the plastic is a silver chalice, sip at the sacrament and burn the tip of my tongue, softly blow on the surface and leave it to cool a little before trying again. It is pure nectar, the sweetest milk I have ever tasted. There is no need for bacon and eggs and sausages and mushrooms and baked beans and stewed tomatoes and a stack of buttery toast with gallons of thick tea and bottles of brown sauce and tomato ketchup when you can have a single mug of sweet milk. Chef mixes in so much sugar to deaden the taste of the bromide, kitchen workers sweetening a bitter pill. It is a fair exchange. We need sweet milk more than a hard-on.

A man has to change in prison, and after that first bowl of soup scorched tender intestines, my stomach adjusted and taste buds hardened, and while it took a few days for things to settle down I now appreciate any sort of food, love the grease that swamps every meal, a soothing film that fills the hollowness, hungry for anything that can be chewed, only leaving fish heads and the thickest beef veins. We live on soup and stew, some fish and meat, cabbage and potatoes, a watery rice that is near to porridge. Best of all are the extras, the two half-loaves of bread and three boiled eggs each week, which we can eat whenever we want. Once our appetites have shrunk the food more or less fills us, thanks mainly to the grease, but it also leaves us mentally and physically weaker. This is good for our jailers.

I focus hard on every meal, avoid conversation and concentrate on the actual eating, a complicated process I never appreciated before, make sure the three highlights of each day last as long as possible. Between sips of milk I glance at the line, see men leaning to the side and checking the pot, nervous as they puff cigarettes and fiddle with their beads, controlling agitation. They know there is enough milk to go round, but still they worry. Short and tall, fat and thin, bald and hairy, a few old men and teens, most of the C-Block crew inside the twenty to forty-five years range. We wear our outside clothes, freedom coats and jackets that wear fast, blankets wrapped around shoulders, scuffed shoes and trainers gnawing at the concrete. The line snakes over to the sinks, a bent coil of stubble and waxwork skin, bent spines and rigid posture, lowered heads and searching eyes, every single man waiting for a bowl of hot milk, and the day they are set free.

Some stories I know, others I do not, but it doesn't matter too much. These tales could be true or false. It is important to believe what I want to believe. And seeing the tax dodger standing in front of Chef I feel no threat from this tall accountant with wafer spectacles, behind him the fascist with the long greasy hair, near the end of a term served for using an axe on his cousin, and there is George the communist, Franco's friend still waiting to appear in court, charged with stealing a book on globalisation, behind him a one-legged street fighter who wears bright red trousers and only uses his crutch when he is tired. George hates homosexuals, his conservatism in sharp contrast to the fascist's attraction to the teenager from the police cell, a frightened kid who has lost his baseball cap but kept his trainers, and the one-legged brawler is no queer, keeps the communist and fascist apart, prison turning him into a peacemaker, and I swallow a mouthful of milk and stare at the kid, serving two years for stealing a loaf of bread from a bakery. Two fucking years. It makes me sick. There's no sense to any of it, but I shut down, return to my milk.

Elvis sits next to me, gulping his breakfast, the mixture soothing the biting pain in his belly. For the past week he has been suffering, knows it is no amoeba, but the prison doctor says there is nothing wrong, refuses to send him to hospital for

48

a check. He leans his head back against the wall, sighs and closes his eyes. I tell him he should demand to see the Director, complain about his treatment, but he reminds me it will do no good. There is a deadening bureaucracy that means a simple request can take months to be dealt with, as if the men running the system suffer from the same mood swings and apathy as the inmates. There is favouritism, prejudice and pettiness, where a triviality becomes a matter of major principle. It was ten days after I arrived before the doctor deigned to remove my stitches. It took a week to see him in his office, and then he had to delay a simple job for another three days. Nobody is responsible in Seven Towers. It is a form of madness. Not the screaming lunacy of an asylum, but a warped, uncertain laziness.

Prison is soul-destroying, repetitive and very boring, a waste of precious time. It is about routine, having one enforced or creating it, and on the outside this translates as monotony, but in here it is what stops a man cracking up. Even in this shitty place, where there are no workshops, dining hall or gymnasium to break the tedium, no library or classes to re-educate offenders, we build a routine around meals, the locking and unlocking of the section door, the weekly shower, games of cards, dominoes and chess, a football or volleyball match, a meeting with a lawyer or clerk for some prisoners, visits from friends and family for others. Our time is spent in the section or in the yard, depending on whether it is raining, the chaos of an argument or fight a thrill most men do their best to resist. Too much thinking ruins minds and we need things to look forward to, small events magnified and turning essential. On the outside life is ordered, so people look for change, enjoy the stimulation chaos offers, go berserk for a few hours and then can't wait for normality to return. In prison everyone is on edge, every single second of the day, whether they know it or not. Boredom sets the mind wandering, and it creates its own gossip, feeding our paranoia. There is no real relaxation and little proper sleep. Chaos is right there under the surface. All it needs is a spark.

Elvis is quiet until I finish my breakfast, loves talking about the time he is going to have when he reaches America. His visa is valid for a year and once this mess is sorted out he will leave on the first flight out, travel the highways and see the free world, his aim to one day open a garage. He looks at our empty mugs and says that America is the land of excess and this is what God intended, that Eden was rich and plentiful and all Adam and Eve had to do was obey one simple rule. He laughs and says he has no interest in religion or spiritual men who turn their backs on worldly goods, pretending that if you cannot see a thing then it does not exist. Materialism is the true path to salvation and he will eat as much as he can in those diners where a typical breakfast can be a well-done steak with eggs or a plate of waffles or anything a man desires.

He clutches his belly and is silent as he waits for the pain to ease. The milk should help, but the rest of the food makes him queasy, though hunger means he eats it, and he is craving yogurt and honey and grapes, more importantly a proper medical examination. There is nothing I can do to help, frustrated and knowing we are impotent, looking at the hawk man on the wall, back at my empty mug. He could have raised his rifle and shot those geese from the sky, but perhaps hawks only kill defenceless rodents, mangy rats and mice and injured rabbits. Once the cramps fade Elvis sits upright and starts telling me about the prison farms where men can transfer and work outside planting and picking vegetables and fruit, and he perks up visualising glorious rehabilitation centres that are new and comfortable and boast proper facilities and wholesome food, each prisoner given his own cell and a flush toilet, blocks where showers and hot water are a daily habit, the regime liberal and fair and modern. Once a man has served two months of a set term he can apply for a move to paradise. Places are limited, but it is a possibility, Seven Towers a relic of a gloomy past, these work farms a brighter future.

Raindrops tickle the yard and together we watch as grey clouds squeeze into black, the men on either side of us quickly finishing their milk and going to the sinks to rinse their mugs. Elvis disappears inside while I sit in the drizzle waiting for the sinks to clear, the rain picking up and the yard emptying, leaving me alone once more, the water thick and warm like olive oil, except it works its way into our clothes so they stink for days, and I jog to the sinks and shelter under corrugated iron, clouds pressing hard, roof rattling. The wind bellows and the rain hardens, but I am safe to enjoy the spectacle, suddenly realise Baker is out there in the middle of the yard, soaked to the skin, jacket and trousers stuck to his body, hair shining. He stands with his face tilted and mouth open, laughing his head off, and while it looks inviting I know he is going to suffer for it later.

I turn to the sinks and wash my mug, then face and hands, take the towel from around my neck and dry off, bury my head in the material and draw on old sweat, loving the salty taste, a complicated miracle, pores working their magic and expelling poison along with bowels and bladder, working to keep me alive. This towel arrived with my bag and clothes the day after me, minus my sleeping bag and music. Complaints are met with a shrug. The court already had my money and this made it to Seven Towers, giving me credit at the Oasis, the shop run by the man known as Ali Baba. The Arab keeps a book and whenever he sells a cup of coffee or glass of mint tea, an apple or banana, a packet of biscuits or a slice of his ultra-rare space cake, he subtracts the cost from a prisoner's running total. The Oasis is another glimpse of paradise, a tiny version of the farm, and survives due to the honesty of its manager, a hashish smuggler from A–Block.

The rain soon begins to ease, vision clearer, Baker shaking the water from his hair, running fingers through drenched clumps, starting to shiver. I envy him the shower but not the flu he risks, nor the threat of pneumonia. I wave the towel at him and he comes over, accepts my offer and rubs at his head, thanks me in his language and goes inside, a spring in his step and a refreshed approach to life. Baker has a positive outlook all right, stays bemused rather than sullen. I wait to see where the clouds will drift, the sun bursting back out through a gap and illuminating the block, turning the windows silver, blind eyes flickering, finally lighting up the yard. When the ledge dries out I will return, stay in the fresh air as long as possible, make the most of the rest of the morning as I look forward to the dinner bell.

The school is huge as we walk towards it for the first time and I am holding Mum's hand and she is telling me not to worry as everything is going to be all right but the building is old and looks a bit like a haunted castle and we are crossing the road and reaching the pavement on the other side where a brick wall blocks out the school and I can only see the top of the roof where grey slates shine from the rain last night and we pass along the side of the wall and reach a big iron gate where a fat woman waits she has a whistle hanging on a piece of string around her neck and a smile on her face and she is asking me my name and I am shy and trying to remember and squeezing Mum's hand so hard the sweat between our palms is turning to glue and sticking and they won't be able to separate us so she will have to either come into the playground with me or we will have to go home but she rubs my hair with her free hand and leans down and whispers not to be scared I am going to make lots of new friends and the teachers will show me how to read and write and do sums and all the things a boy needs to learn if he is going to get himself a job one day and peering into the playground through the bars I see big boys running and tripping each other up and laughing while a gang of girls take turns dancing in and out of a skipping rope singing to themselves as they hop and jump and all the time other kids are doing not much some of them on their own looking lonely one boy bouncing a tennis ball and he does this over and over again maybe pretending it is interesting and I am staring at the ball waiting for him to miss it hardly notice Mum easing her hand from mine I suddenly feel it is gone and turn in terror almost knocked over as older children push past but I stay on my feet and I want to go home see the look on Mum's face and somehow know she is more scared than me and I have to be strong and the school has tripled in size so I am small and weak the same as one of those thousands of black ants we found in the garden a few months ago over in the corner of the lawn and Mum and Nana say they are a nuisance but the red ants are worse those are the ones that bite you and we didn't kill them just let them get on with their lives though some people pour boiling water over anthills as they want to keep everything neat and tidy and don't care about insects or animals and inside these hills the ants work for each other and Mum says they are more together than humans will ever be and before I know what's happening I am on the other side of the playground asking the kid with the tennis ball how many times has he bounced it up and down and he says he isn't counting asks me if I want to have a go but I say no it is okay I was just wondering and he keeps bouncing and seems much more nervous than me he is a mummy's boy and says his name is Frank and this is his first day as well and he looks as if he has been crying maybe before he left home and crying is what girls do but I don't tell him this as I think everyone should try and get on and realise the other kids my age are scared as well and this means a little of my fear melts away as a whole new class of boys and girls are nervous some of them biting their nails and one little girl wets her pants and a boy standing on his own by the drinking fountain is looking up into the sky for some reason with his top soaked with water and this playground is smaller than it first seemed with the brick wall at the front going round the sides as well and a couple of older boys start making fun of us saying they are going to stick our heads down the toilet and flush the chain and I know one of them from our street normally he says hello and is friendly but now he is different and I wonder what has happened to him and why his face is so red and his feet are jumping around and another tennis ball flashes past and hits the girl who has wet herself and she starts screaming and the fat woman blows her whistle and shouts at the boys who did it and tells them to go down to the other end of the playground they know the rules that is the only place they can kick balls around and another teacher is with the crying girl telling her she will be fine and the bell rings and we troop into the school through two big wide-open doors and it is cooler inside and smells clean my new shoes sliding on the floor and we come to a stop and wait together in a hall and have our names read out and come forward and the teachers are nice and we are shown into a classroom and given desks and told where to sit and the ceilings are very high and the floors squeak and the lady who is going to be our teacher for our first year introduces herself as Mrs Miller and we are called by our first names but have to use Mr and Mrs for the teachers though most of them are women the headmaster is a man and after a while I feel safe and know Mum wouldn't send me to a bad place and we all come from families where we are loved and protected at least that is how it seems to me at the time and later I find out there is a boy and girl from the children's home and the little girl is sitting next to me her name is Rosie and she has the biggest and blackest eyes I have ever seen and there are new names to learn and rules to understand and later we will have a carton of milk each and a playtime and a tour of the school and then dinner in the canteen today it is going to be roast this is the favourite of the older children and in the afternoon we will have more lessons and the day will pass quickly if we are busy and I sit at my desk taking it all in and remembering Mum's good-luck kiss on my forehead maybe leaving a lipstick trace a marker for a stick to bash and how can she know if there is trouble waiting and she is older and realises bad things can happen while I don't at least not really and all I know about are the bullies and I haven't met any though I know not to go off with strange men or get in their cars and anyway the walls protect us and she must be worrying with Nana if I am going to be hurt in the playground knocked to the concrete where I can crack my head open and maybe turn into a runaway end up at the railway station boarding a train to nowhere or I might wander to the common where anything could happen and I am in two places at once now but mainly back outside passing through the gate with Mum watching and wiping away a tear we grow up so fast and she is waving and in front of me there is sheet of paper and crayons and Mrs Miller smiles and tells me to draw anything I want and she pats Rosie on the shoulder as she passes and I see Mum turning and walking off and my fear melts as I reach for a black crayon knowing that she will be waiting for me at the gate when it is time to go home.

The metal booms and I lower my fist, slowly count one two three four, push the green door open and hurry into the cave, shut it fast before the gas leaks out, blink as ammonia stings my eyes, wet mist swirling in and sticking. The last rat escapes down the drain leaving me gagging at the smell, human waste caking ancient pipes, walls sweating the rotten memories of thousands of rotting men. Electric sunlight sneaks through the haze and I try to imagine I am in a smog-bound city, ducking into an air-conditioned bar in Los Angeles or Bombay, but fail, stuck in this mucky peat bog. This is one jail experience that doesn't get any easier, twitching bowels forcing me forward. It is a rush to get in position, poison flushing out as I squat over one of two rat-infested holes serving the forty-five men on the section, belly aching from yesterday's dinner, a dirty stew laced with onions and some heavy-duty bacteria. I balance on the foot rests, avoiding ground-in shit and mucus, and can't help thinking how petty-minded the Director is turning even this basic need into a degrading punishment. It wouldn't cost much to give us decent toilets. My intestines burn and muscles heave, and I suppose a good dump is another highlight of prison life.

The Director is a wicked man. This is the truth according to Mr Elvis Presley, an honest individual who loves rock'n'roll but is sceptical of idle gossip and the group mentality, a free-thinker who refuses to bend. While in charge of a prison on one of the islands, the Director had a man crucified, this information coming from convicts who were there at the same time and have been moved to the mainland, the grim details originally supplied by a boastful guard who took part in the killing. The story has spread and is considered true. The murdered man was taken from his cell and driven to the jail dump, a remote spot on an island that is deserted apart from the prison and an army base, the Director leading a small team of ex-paramilitaries armed with nails and a hammer, the cross waiting by a freshly dug hole. A sledgehammer broke the man's shins and a crown of gorse was pinned to his head, a knife piercing his torso. The crucifixion was planned in advance and no crime of passion. It was a deviant act carried out because there was nobody to stop it happening. It is said the prisoner was nailed to the cross by the Director himself, his lackeys raising it into the full glare of the midday sun.

It was a beautiful day and the island is stunning, wide sandy beaches stretching along a smooth coastline, majestic rock formations filling the interior. The crucified man could see the ocean as he died, a sheet of pure blue water taunting him as he roasted, and while the pressure on his heart may have killed him it was more likely the sun. He must have shouted for help as his skin smoked, but only insects and reptiles and small mammals could hear. Nobody knows what he did to deserve such a punishment. He has no name and remains face-less. Some say the Director took a dislike to him, that it was a very personal killing, others believe he was guilty of a terrible blasphemy, a crime against God. This man vanished. Nobody searches for him and so he never really existed. I don't want to know that this sort of thing happens, not in my small corner, and definitely not at the hands of the person who controls my life, but somehow I understand that it is the truth. Elvis is supported by Franco and the nodding head of George, and I trust these three wise and honest men.

This isn't the place to linger though, considering life and death and the pros and cons of Roman torture. Everyone knows rats carry disease and at night we hear them scratching at the door, gnawing tin, something they don't do during the day, the idea of rabies enough to scare even the hardest men. Night is a bad time. I think of the monkey monsters, return to rats, know a plague carrier could appear at any moment, flashing razor teeth and taking a chunk out of my arse, or worse, the ultimate punishment, castration by rodent. I stand up fast, use my paper and drop it in the bin, the pipes thin and easily blocked, dirty toilet roll spilling over, and I feel the nausea, puke rising, but I am unable to vomit, reach for the jug and scoop water from the bucket, wash the mess away, hurry to the sink and rinse my hands in icy water, hold it in my palms and bring these up, scrubbing at my face. This water comes through the mountain and is colder and fresher than in the yard. I reach inside my clothes and rub some into my shoulders, force a smile and look on the funny side.

We call this place safari, a barren landscape where rats and lions and gazelles roam, a rocky high-plains wasteland forgotten by environmentalists and geologists and bounty hunters, rats dipping in and out of snake tunnels, wary of boa constrictors and electric eels. There are no tropical plants or exotic flowers on this safari, no papayas or mangoes or rambutans, no warm savannah, not even the strongest fungus surviving the toxic mist, and yet primitive man thrives, this timeless convict class chattering in barmy monkey tones waiting for the fog to lift, knowing if we dawdle too long we will meet our own ghosts. The bog bubbles and pops and sucks us in, gas creating fairy lanterns, scaring nervous minds, but the funny thing is, none of us can stay away. We all have to go on safari. Every single person on the planet has to eat, drink, sleep and excrete their poison. That's all life is, really.

I come back off safari and the section smells fine, the fruity scent of a temple decorated with apple blossom tickling singed nostrils, the exotic oils of a harem flavoured by eucalyptus, but there are no loving gods or beautiful women waiting, just this motley C-Block crew of small-time crooks and petty thieves, ganja smokers and street brawlers, bank robbers and mystery men guarding secrets. I lie on my bed, breathe the air and listen to the patter of rain in the yard, feel like a conqueror beating off the safari sickness, a dirty swamp fever that seeps into the pores and numbs the mind. I hear the hum of a songsmith, men dozing and talking, others reading books, and I follow the melody and see that it comes from Baker, the pastry boy naked except for his underpants and socks, hanging his clothes next to the heater and sitting down on the end of the bench.

Steam rises and thickens, and it is hours since he did his

rain dance and I am wondering why he doesn't put some-thing else on, why he has only started drying his clothes now. It doesn't make sense. And George is glaring and speaks and Baker is surprised and shrugs, and George is angry and Baker is mystified, and behind him the fascist man is laughing, and George is looking past Baker and targeting the neo-Nazi. Things are never how they are supposed to be, George the communist a homo-hating conservative and the neo-Nazi a rampant sodomite who looks more like a biker than a mili-taristic revolutionary. Two ideologies prepare to clash, Baker not helping things when he strips off his pants and socks and drapes them on the edge of the table, scratching his balls and wobbling naked to his bed. Nobody takes their clothes off in Seven Towers, apart from on shower day. We sleep fully clothed, never lowering our defences. Baker must have caught pneu-monia, and it is affecting his thinking.

The Red shouts and the blackshirt responds and the two party men meet on the dance floor, the aisle the venue as they exchange punches, noses sniffling blood and cheeks bruising, sleepwalkers stirring inside their blankets, the fight spilling over the table and scattering an old man's dominoes, and this competitor is indignant, takes a swipe and misses, decides it is more important to reclaim his numbers and kneels down, and the fury of the extremists makes me laugh, behind these walls their lists of dos and don'ts counting for nothing. I glance at Baker who is watching the brawl, his bemusement total, completely unaware his doughy flesh is the catalyst. He wraps his blanket tight and turns away, shut-ting the chaos out, a familiar manoeuvre, the idealists battling their way along the dormitory, clattering into beds so men stand and denounce them, and the giant claps his hands, steps forward straight into a pool of blood, and he curses and sits back down, takes off a shoe and inspects the sole, stands and hops towards the green door to clean off the mess, forget-ting to thump the tin.

The one-legged street fighter watches him go, wondering if he is taking the piss, decides it is a natural reaction, his view influenced by size, and he looks back at the fight which is slowing down, weighing up their fighting skills, frowning as punches miss and a lack of carbohydrates has its effect. The extremists reach the door and roll around on the floor, two guards appearing, angry they have been forced across the yard by the commotion, three clumps with their sticks and George and the fascist are separated, made to stand in opposing corners, a couple of naughty schoolkids learning discipline. The guards squawk orders and leave, the offenders remaining where they are, faces to the wall, tired and rubbing bruises. Baker remembers something and gets out of bed, suddenly embarrassed by his nakedness, goes into his cardboard suitcase and pulls on tracksuit bottoms and a sweatshirt.

It is the boy from Tupelo, the easygoing Mr Presley, who asks the question, Franco returning to their chess game, trying to save his king. Elvis catches my eye and narrows his gaze and calls out how did we end up in this place, my good friend, what terrible things have you done to deserve this punishment? I laugh and shrug and panic and try to work out what he means, what he knows, see myself all those months ago with an anniversary looming, a date that means too much, and I am a haunted man dodging spirits and drinking heavily, a familiar voice telling me to go on the run and get the fuck out of Dodge, hit the road and live again, two days later my ferry heading towards northern lands, and I am off to meet the midnight sun. And I think of Ramona and wonder what she is doing. Sweet Ramona with her head full of music, from the heavy vocals of Brian Hayter to the manic drumming of Mr Esso, sweet little Ramona in her Joey Was A Punk T-shirt and jet-black hair standing outside that Rancid gig shouting and putting me in my place, walking off and kneeing a snickering yuppie in the nuts as she goes. The king of rock 'n' roll smiles and frowns and nods and shakes his head in all the right and wrong places as I stutter, not sure if I am talking to myself or thinking out loud, bedbugs biting and mosquitoes circling this alien leaving the ferry and walking into a Nordic town straight out of his *National Geographic* pages, the cartoon drawings of my favourite bedtime story, fantasy worlds where good fights evil and never loses, and I am travelling light remembering the days when I was a teenage runaway with just a Harrington to keep him warm, rain soaking Converse, Christmas near and the snow falling, but fuck that for a memory, this is different, embracing dreams rather than punching nightmares, every bad thought face down and spluttering as my spirits soar strolling along deserted streets stopping in an empty bar to drink a single cold beer and eat a generous sandwich, tired after the journey but paying the barman and carrying on, arriving at the train station as a locomotive is about to leave, and my luck holds, the carriage almost empty offering a choice of seats and I am sitting by the window racing north to Lapland and the scenery is stunning a mythical mass of fjords and hills and snowy peaks and huge eternal pine forests that seem to drift on for ever and when we stop at a remote station there are woodcutters on the platform jolly blond giants with gold axes and the driver of this cannonball express could be Mr Woody Guthrie himself, but the axemen are real enough, and the sun never sets and the lights are never turned off and I am in a daze as we travel for many hours and at the end of the trip I am walking from another station enjoying the warmth of the sun following a dusty path towards the trees in the distance and the mosquitoes are nipping and a dragonfly flaps past the size of a bat but there is no darkness and no night and no vampire behaviour or monkey monsters allowed and eventually the edge of the forest is around me and the smell of pine is so powerful it could soon turn to syrup and the path bends up the hill and I am in the shade and climbing and sweating tired after my long journey calves aching the path twisting and turning and the dust puffs up underfoot and small stones nag my ankles and I stop to listen to the ferns talk remembering dark stories but there is no sound not even a blackbird or sparrow no breaking twigs and no movement and I continue on my way finally reaching a meadow where bees and butterflies work at the pollen safe in this haven of peace and tranquillity and I skirt the edge of the grass so as not to disturb anything and not leave an easy trail for my trackers and any bounty hunters who want to shoot me down, but the world is silent and it could be past midnight, I don't know what time it is, don't have a watch, and it doesn't matter anyway, at least not in this enchanted forest.

There is a tiny trail on the far side of the meadow and this leads back into the trees and it could have been made by rabbits, or a fox, and I follow it and move deeper into the pine, pushing through ferns and crushing cones, easing myself free of thorns, and I am very happy, see light up ahead and quickly reach a small clearing where billions of pine needles have formed a luxury mattress, and unrolling my sleeping bag I am wondering when a wood becomes a forest and playing at being Robin Hood and wishing Ramona was here, but she never liked being Maid Marian, said it was a kid's game, but it was only a laugh, the romance of the good outlaw hiding in a monkey-free wood and anyway, we *were* kids, and I am in the heart of this old forest just like the story book says and there is a troll who is good rather than bad and Mum says when someone is very bad I should imagine them as being very good, that is the trick to play, it is something people don't expect and can't understand, and I am drifting in and out of consciousness and there is a tramp on the common and children must stay around the swings as he is without a home or a bath and in my story there is a rabbit with wings and maybe a fox who looks at Brer Rabbit and doesn't crave the meat on his bones. There are no monsters in this wood. No witches eating brothers and sisters. No chance of the monkey monsters hiding under my bed. I think of Mum and Nana and want them to be proud of me as I have achieved one of those dreams we have when we are young but let go thinking it is a childish thing and doesn't matter when really it does, more than anything, and when I was three or four years old I promised I would go to the forest and now I am here in the Lapland of my book, sitting at the top of the world, and I fall asleep and don't dream of axe killers or troll men and when I wake I wonder if any of my ancestors are watching, and I leave the forest and walk to barren land where I watch the lights in the sky and feel the breeze and I stay here for a long time thrilled by the spectacle playing across the heavens, a million times better than the machine men create with their computers and virtual highways, a clear view that makes me think of God.

I try to remember how long I stay in the wilderness, two or three days maybe, and hunger comes and fasting is supposed to bring on hallucinations and scientists say this is the cause of Jesus' visions, this denial of material pleasure, while Elvis went the other way, revelled in the earth's bounty until he could take no more, but this is just the mechanics, courtesy of the machine men. We can create visions and voices, but have to apply rules and know what is good and bad, pick and choose and make sure these choices are correct. And the hunger chews my belly and I walk away from my sleeping bag and squat down in a gully and the fear flushes out of me, maybe life really is a circle and heaven and hell meet somewhere, a line between good and evil which is so fine it can't be seen, but I want to impress this older and wiser travelling man I respectfully refer to as Mr Presley, give him the right answer, yet don't know what question he is asking, guess my thinking is distorted, and he is focusing on the chessboard and maybe I haven't been talking, pleased I haven't mentioned the forest, spilling my guts like a soppy kid, though part of me wants to tell him about the places I have been, the beer drunk and people met, the food eaten and music heard, the things I have learnt, but instead I just keep quiet.

Franco jumps and smiles, moves his king. Elvis responds. Tears slide down Franco's face. He has been checkmated. He starts talking slowly in a hoarse tone about the mountains and forests where he roamed as a child, and how he should be at home with his family. My story is nothing special. And I have an idea and want to laugh and tell Elvis that maybe it is my genes that have brought me to this prison, but I stay silent, watch Franco stand and walk away, feel sorry for him as he bangs on the tin and loses himself on safari, hiding his weakness.

Franco sniffs his soap as we wait by the gate, tells me he is an innocent man who is incapable of hurting anyone or anything. He realises every prisoner is innocent, even those whose crimes have been admitted, but he wants me to understand that his own innocence is special. Deeper and more true. I nod and reply that every single one of us is also guilty, that we are original sinners. He laughs at what he takes as humour, but it is not a healthy sound, the heavy manners of innocence and guilt pressing in, the yard shrinking and expanding with our pulse, every one of us capable of cracking at any second. Elation quickly turns to despair, physical survival depending on mental health. And yet reality is there to be created, if a man is strong enough. I tell Franco that I understand. And I do. Every individual knows he is not the fiend he has been told he has become. A man convicted of stealing a radio has actually stolen a clock. A youth who molests women takes his mother to church three times a week. A drifter who assaults a local is defending himself. The legal experts are corrupt and incompetent, ranging from vindictive to indifferent. In our hearts we are innocent, and being locked up with so many misjudged men makes me feel better. I myself am also innocent, and my innocence is even stronger and more pure than that of Franco.

There are evil men in Seven Towers, but they are stuck on B-Block, the psycho wing. There are boys on C-Block who have made mistakes, and there are fights and a couple of stabbings, but this is low level compared to the stories coming out of B-Block. Two weeks ago a man was stabbed fifty times, every single wound penetrating his heart, one for each inmate in the room where it happened, the murder weapon a knitting needle caked in shit from their safari, the slaughter carried out by a monster known as Papa. This man is insane and wears the striped pyjamas of a concentration camp inmate, stays untouched by the guards. He wears these pyjamas night and day and is one of a number of mad men running amok. I thank God for putting me on C-Block.

The gate swings opens and ten happy convicts amble into the yard, hair damp and skin polished, eyes energised as they joke and laugh and show off revived spirits. It is shower day. Our ultimate pleasure. Right above the sweet morning milk.

Moving fast, towel over shoulder, shampoo and soap gripped, with a change of socks and pants, I join Elvis, Franco and seven others in the next team, among them the shivering Baker and the one-legged street fighter. Franco carries his bag over his shoulder, shower gear added to the book he never lets out of his sight. He has never shown me what is in its pages, and I have never asked. That is the way here. And we are excited, aching to scrub off the grime and depression that builds so many layers and thickens to leather. We move in groups of ten, different blocks washing on different days, and we are like kids going swimming, loosening limbs and scratching nits, used to the itching and fungus, the stink of our armpits and crotches something cold water never quite beats. Soon it will be payback time.

Getting off the block is a bonus, our three-man escort alert now we are in the square, two with their truncheons drawn and hanging by their legs, one with a rifle across his chest, but we know the procedure, wave to Ali who is sitting on his haunches in front of the Oasis, tending his fire. He calls a greeting and we are on our way, exercising muscles and observing new walls, feeding off different smells, the charcoal of the fire and the strange deodorant of a guard. The gate leading to the showers is controlled by an elderly officer and Leadbelly, an African prisoner often referred to as Congo. This alien lives on A-Block and some say he has been convicted of assault, others that he is being punished for having sex with the twin daughters of a magistrate, while still others believe it is because he is black. Certain men hate his colour, while others believe that he is a man of great knowledge, that the suffering of his race means he carries an inherent wisdom. Leadbelly's eyes are a misty yellow, but he is hard to age. He takes little notice of the other men, A-Block the elite wing, so there has to be more to his story.

We pass down a narrow walkway, razor wire criss-crossing above our heads, and I imagine a small bird landing on it and slicing its feet. It is vicious stuff, hard to fathom the thinking of those who invent these things. Maybe there is a celestial jail for rogue inventors, the fallen souls who imagine chemical weapons and cluster bombs and landmines. Yet it is the razor wire that worries me, the thought of a bird bleeding to death. Unlike barbed wire there is no warning, the metal thorns obvious, and then there is the home-made recipe, broken bottles wedged in concrete along the top of walls, and someone has to mix the cement and crack the bottles just to hurt a common burglar. And yet burglars are scum, breaking into houses and ruining lives, and I start thinking about the people who aren't so innocent, adding burglars to those who kill for money and torture for fun, the rapists and paedophiles and wife batterers, the rubbish who sell drugs to children and rip off the elderly and mug anyone at all, the legion of suited and booted men who do the same things legally, every bullying, selfish lowlife that exists, and I keep adding to the list, racking up the anger and surprising myself, stopping suddenly, not wanting to consider the victims, reminding myself that we are all innocent men, deep down, in our hearts.

We reach another gate which is unlocked by a famously gloomy warder, continue to a steel door, which is slightly ajar, and while prison is about innocence and guilt and crime and punishment it is also about gates and doors and bars and endless locks and keys. It is a stop-start system that drives everyone mad, including the guards, wage slaves ground down by the monotony and oppressive atmosphere. We move into a narrow staircase that spirals up inside one of the towers, and I let my hand glide over the stone, marvelling at its smoothness, steps chiselled and uneven. At the top there is a landing with secure gates to our left and right, the steel door in front chained and padlocked, hiding more stairs that continue to the top of the tower. Franco says the Sicilian elder who works on the furnace has been to the top and seen the world. A guard took pity on him, as it is a decade since he has been outside the prison walls, but this is top secret information.

To our left the corridor curves out of sight, a dusty floor littered with debris, cast iron and bent metal and broken masonry, the last flakes of a painted cross. We are prodded right, gate swinging with a chalky screech, our rifle man blocking the passage so we veer through the wooden door with a serpent carved into the frame. The temperature rises as we wait in a long, narrow room, one side packed with logs and kindling, light entering through tiny knee-high windows. Stooping to peer out, I see the roof of our block and a small part of another yard. A stick taps my shoulder and I stand upright.

The air is ripe with cut wood and smoke, furnace roaring by the door leading into the showers, and I can't help thinking of my bedtime forest, the freedom of being the only man in the world, can't stop a tinge of sadness seeing these once graceful trees split and ready for cremation, imagine oak and elm and finally pine, my selfish gene pushing this away, a stretch of imagination needed to match firewood to a mighty forest, and it is easy to crush imagination. Three timeless men sit by the furnace, feeding the fire, and I drift nearer, try and catch a glimpse of the spectacle inside, the magic of the flames. The flap of the section stove stays shut, giving off a smouldering warmth but nothing like the heat of this furnace. The fire rages, sending ripples across my skin, pleasure and terror colliding.

The old men of the furnace chug with laughter as they joke with the younger prisoners, the old Sicilian talking to Franco in their language, the younger man delivering his words fast, the Sicilian more reflective, the southerner dark, Franco light, one with black hair, the other blond, their mannerisms similar. Franco doesn't know why the Sicilian is in Seven Towers, though he has been in various jails for over twenty years. He can't ask the old man. Like me, he doesn't want to know. I wonder if anyone is waiting for these three men. They appear decent, but two decades in prison suggests atrocities. They tend the fire and seem content, as men who spend their days surrounded by warmth and happy faces should be, tucked into a safe corner of a dangerous world. The furnace men live on A-Block, privileged convicts providing a vital service and reaping the reward of our own Hilton.

I think of my grandmother, an old lady and her fireplace, see her cosy living room, coal roasting like potatoes, looking so good I could reach in and pull one out and load it with butter and baked beans, the hall cold and dark outside, full of ghosts, monkey monsters lurking in the darkest corners, under the stairs but mainly under my bed, and those bad boys never sleep. I run through the procedure again, helping Nana make the fire, cleaning out the grate with a brush, removing the ashes, arranging splintered wood, balancing coal on top, forming tapers out of old newspapers, waiting all day for the scratch of a match and the flame that consumes the headlines, creeping into the heart of the kindling where it catches and sets the coal alight. The flames grow and consume everything. And I want to smash my fist into the wall thinking of Nana dead and gone, and yet it was a good time, the best days of my life, and at least I had them, too many people don't, and I bring myself back to Seven Towers, watch old lags shovel coal, think of Nana's husband the chimney sweep, cleaning up the mess. The good times always come to an end, but then so do the bad. I won't be here for ever.

Ten men come out of the shower room drying their heads, hair sticking out at funny angles, an aura around them as they saunter, as if they are leaving a bar. We take their place, strip off as fast as we can and find pipes to hang our clothes on. No one wastes time talking, every second irreplaceable. We find a nozzle each and stand below, reach for the taps, crumbling powder on fingers, hot water bursting out. And this is the best part of every week. Scrubbing off the shit. Washing away our sins. And on the outside a visit to the prison shower block is a comedian's favourite, representing the humiliation of rape and the death of the noble working man. They even use it in TV commercials. Liberals and conservatives sing don't pick up the soap in the shower, you are naked and your arsehole is exposed and we are all supposed to be ignorant bullies who spend our time fucking each other over, literally, and I laugh remembering my first shower, shitting myself in case these people were right, their warnings honest, and within seconds the soap popped out of my hands and was caught in the whirlpool heading for the drain, finally resting in the grate, and bending down I was laughing and singing they'll never take me alive. Just because men are in prison, it doesn't mean they turn.

We are allowed five minutes and I lather quickly, attack layers of guilt, gently rub a cut on my knee, careful not to open the scab, wary of germs. I scrub every part of my body, balancing on one foot like a red-trousered street fighter and getting in between the toes, deep into armpits where wildlife is trying to start up a safari theme park, brandishing a machete and backing them off, last of all rubbing shampoo into my hair, obliterating the nits that will reappear in a few days, out of the ether. I clean thoroughly, but as fast as possible, so I can enjoy the rest of the shower. Get the job done and then concentrate hard, absorbing every degree of heat. The Seven Towers cold penetrates so deep one day ice will replace the marrow in my bones. I could stay under this nozzle for ever. It is fantastic, with my eyes shut and steam filling the room, blocking out the other men and offering privacy, organs kick-starting, blood flowing, the prison block no good for the heart and brain, the smell of soap and shampoo mixing in. Thinking mucks up the brain and stress damages the heart, and the cold numbs both, triples the damage.

As soon as the water begins to cool I reach for my towel, dry off and get dressed, hurrying so as not to lose any of the warmth. The others do the same, steam clearing and a bare room returning, partition walls separating ten dripping pipes, a tilting floor and drain taking away the final scummy dregs. We squeeze back into the log room, boisterous at first but soon so mellow Franco even forgets to chat to the Sicilian. We are forced to wait extra minutes for the next batch of dirty men, who are late, but we are relaxed and content and happy to stay near the fire. A rotten smell tells us they are approaching, and we pass back out under the serpent. My clothes pong, and however much I scrub them in the yard they are never truly clean, but the human body is worse.

We move through the gates, down the steps, float back to the square. Leadbelly sniffs as we pass, but says nothing, and the guards have been primed so I go with Elvis and Franco to sit at Ali's table, a rare privilege bought for the price of a coffee. The Oasis man welcomes us warmly and brings out his silver pot mumbling espresso espresso espresso, works his magic and examines the oil-like caffeine he pours into tiny cups, talking about the brotherhood of man and the effect gasoline has on civilisations, the nature of the mullahs and priests, the Christians and the Jews his brothers, everyone is his brother. Ali speaks to us as if we have come many miles to visit his humble tea shop, believing he is at home working in the bazaar. I reach for the cup and get ready. This is only my second visit to the Oasis, though it is possible to bribe the trustee on the gate and get him to fetch a coffee and pass it through the flap. But this is special. Off the block sitting at a table, clean and warm and lifting the espresso to my lips. Life doesn't get much better that this.

There is a small mouthful of coffee in each cup, and half of that is mud. It is the strongest brew on the planet, and Ali places three glasses of water on the table to help us wash it down. A huge caffeine earthquake rocks me, the liquid rich and strong and bitter and reaching my belly in seconds, fanning out and seeping into the stomach lining, and if the kundalini serpent exists this will stir her, and I wait for the hissing in my spine, imagine enlightenment ricocheting around my skull. I suddenly feel very calm, sit with Ali as he nods into space greeting imaginary passers-by, showing respect to his fellow traders, turning and smiling to tell me his bazaar visions are deliberate. I think of the axis of evil and know this man has made mistakes, but is not wicked. Referred to as Ali to his face, and Ali Baba on the yard, he is a decent man and keeps an honest record, providing an important service within the prison.

Franco places his bag on the table and reaches inside, presents me with his book. His mother and father sent it to him so he would never forget where he comes from. It is full of photographs and he explains how he climbs rock faces and breathes pure air, eats fresh food and drinks good wine. He has an easy life, points to snow-capped mountain peaks and frozen ice fields, turns a page and shows me sunny meadows full of flowers, a chalet on a ridge, more Swiss than Italian. He tells me his favourite food is fondue, and his mother always makes it on his birthday. He looks so sad, speaks his language for a while, sees someone else in my place. He switches back to half-English. Turns the pages. A sun-baked piazza with a fountain and statues and pavements, a little like the square we are sitting in, but I don't say anything, as Franco is very serious. His mother writes twice a week and he is lucky. He stares at me. Says one joint. One smoke and still no paper.

Franco and his friends were set up. Travelling from the islands in a camper van they pull over for the night at a campsite, wash and change and walk across the highway to a small restaurant set in the rocks, a cheap place serving sunbathers and tourists and a few locals. They are on their way home after a month on the beaches, three boys and two girls, treating themselves to a proper meal in a homely taverna. The pizza is generous and the salad crisp and the manager hands them a bottle of wine for nothing, small plates of olives and soft bread. The manager is friendly and interested in where they have been, polite to the boys and respectful with the girls. It is a perfect end to a great holiday, and they are looking forward to seeing their families again, and when they finish they leave a tip even though they can't really afford to, their money more or less run out.

Tired and full of food they cross back over the road to the campsite, continue to the beach beyond, rest on the sand to watch the sunset, one of the girls passing around a bottle of water. The manager appears with five cans of cold beer and he opens these and hands them out. The world seems good. He rolls a joint and offers it around, assures them there is no problem smoking on the beach, no problem no problem, my friends, and they talk about the fishing boats out on the sea as they smoke, discuss the taste of lobster and squid. Franco shakes his head and curses, remembering that they are content and drifting and don't hear the police until they are on top of them shouting and pointing and the manager is standing back and looking very pleased with himself.

Franco is brought to Seven Towers, one of his friends is released as he hasn't had a puff, and at least the police were honest about that, or maybe they just wanted to prove it wasn't a set-up, while on the advice of their lawyer the third male has been admitted to a psychiatric hospital where he is undergoing treatment in an attempt to accept all the blame, trying to cure an imaginary drug habit. The two girls are in a women's prison at the other end of the country.

Franco sits back and finishes the last of the water, the guards calling us back to the block. Ali claps his hands and takes out his book, fiddles with a chewed pencil and makes the necessary adjustments. Franco leans forward and tells me that he is an innocent man, and I must always remember this, and it is true, the shower cleansing our souls as well as our bodies, and he whispers that when he gets out of his place he is going to return home and recover, eat healthy food and walk in the mountains, work and earn money and become calm, make himself strong again, and then he will return to this land. It might be after one year, or two years, or even five years, but he will go to the taverna and find the manager, wait until this informer's work is over and he is leaving for home, and then I will take my knife and cut his throat, from ear to ear.

I am a good boy, a decent man, clean and free from sin, head cradled in a perfumed cushion, a greasy pillow propped on dirty clothes, my magic blanket a dusty romper suit full of childish security, protecting me from the monsters under the bed. I am so good it makes me want to weep. The hot shower means tonight's rest will be deep and undisturbed, a bowl of rice and peas filling my belly, a boiled egg for dessert, and I am so content maybe I will float in the air and join the spirits of the men who had this blanket before me, their memories embedded in the wool. Nana was psychic and could hear voices, but I don't want her gift. Nothing can hurt me, surrounded by innocence and near silence, and even though Seven Towers has high walls and many locks, there is a way of breaking out.

Imagination means a man can escape for as long as his will holds. It is a battle, but it can be done. That is where my life lies now, inside my head and out on the road, passing through scenery and scenes, tracking lost genes. It is easy to be apathetic and wallow in misery, become obsessed with numbers. Calendars are propped by beds and stuck on walls, covered in crosses, a mass of black and blue tombstones destroying days and dates. There is also a touch of red, but black is the dominant colour. It is an attack on time, which has slowed down, the opposite of travelling where the days flash past and it is easy to forget the month. I have my own small calendar, but keep it out of sight and refuse to cross off the days. It is a precaution, nothing more, and with a firm nudge the dark side of my thinking crumbles, too comfortable to resist, and I am off to new places I somehow already know. I smile as I spot Jimmy Rocker, the man everyone's talking about, a wanderer with a heart of gold, a peace-loving drifter who lives a tradition laid down by thousands of searchers in the land of opportunity, the land of the free.

Jimmy is drifting south from Memphis, part of a rock 'n' roll dream that represents the peak of Western civilisation, bent over the wheel of his pickup truck, a thousand-dollar stereo recycling two thousand radio stations, a pure wall of sound on offer, the Ramones speeding through a chorus of wanting to be sedated. When this punk classic ends, Jimmy flicks channels, settling on the pounding rhythm of Jerry Lee Lewis's killer piano. He presses the gas, safe in the knowledge that he is good wholesome folk with nothing to fear from the law, those sleepy boss men with their sweaty armpits and reflective sunglasses, shotgun bubbas who only ever bother hunting niggers, faggots, pinkos, liberals and federalist yuppies. These law-enforcement officers love simple clean-living white boys like the Rocker, just as long as he ain't no thieving trailer-rash drug-taking lowlife. But this is my trip and Jimmy is doing fine, the negatives shut out, everything sweet and delicious, while behind the bars of a rehabilitating US penal system the guys are all grinning and dancing along to 'Jailhouse Rock'. Elvis understands the nature of the dream.

Pulling into Betty May's Diner is a relief. Jimmy needs a cold root beer to ease the strain. Packed with ice, the healthy properties of the drink are sure to help revive him for the many miles ahead. He has an appointment with his old pal

Freddy Fucker, pussy hunter and playboy extraordinaire, a crazy card shark living with the infamous masturbator Bobby Two-Hand in a run-down colonial house down in New Orleans, twenty minutes from Bourbon Street. The rent is cheap and they can stroll into town to impress the many visitors. The drifting man doesn't share the Fucker's values, but likes him for his other regular qualities. More than anything, the Fucker loves his mom. Sends her a regular supply of dollars so she can enjoy her final years back in Lubbock, the sacred birth-place of Mr Buddy Holly. Jimmy knows Freddy from two years back, when they were working together at Taco Bell, over in Tulsa. The Rocker held this job for a month before drifting east, moving back and forward across God's own land, content with his lot.

This strip on the edge of town is pure traveller heaven, with expansive parking lots and all the food a man can eat for a few honest bucks. Jimmy strolls in and sits at a window booth, reaching for the menu and feeling suppressed urges. It's as if he hasn't eaten proper food for a month, stuck on a diet of soup and rice and stew and fish and every other cheap tasteless mind-numbing food he can imagine, a dull diet that makes him appreciate democratic principles. Jimmy runs his eyes down the menu. There is a great deal of choice. He is excited and doesn't know where to begin. There are omelettes packed with every kind of filling, chunky ham-burgers oozing cheese and bacon, steaks the size of plates, baked corn and huge potatoes packed with coleslaw, a wide Tex-Mex selection, tortillas and enchiladas swamped with refried beans and jalapeño peppers. Maybe he will have a pizza. Checks out the toppings. There is a buffet serving salad, with five dressings. This truly is the land of plenty, and Jimmy is plenty grateful.

Mary-Lou stands over him and Jimmy doesn't even notice her at first. When he does, he jumps. She's a real beauty, with a genuine twinkle in her eye. She is polite and shy, but he can see she is the girl for him, imagines her on a beach in California, has been told San Diego is nice at this time of year. They can find a motel near the beach and she will wear a bathing suit and he will flex his Henry Rollins muscles and tattoos. He thinks of the designs he will have done, determined Permanent Mark does the work as soon as he reaches the West Coast. He wants the best, and PM is the best around. Jimmy and Mary-Lou will live a clean life in the sun, sipping margaritas and cold beer, drinking moderately and never becoming intoxicated. But first he must order, and Jimmy selects a king-size root beer and deep-fried mushrooms with sour cream and salsa to start, a free run at the salad bar to follow, and as a main order a Tex-Mex platter, with side orders of thick-cut French fries and two portions of garlic bread. He will order his dessert later, but has his eye on the apple pie, with vanilla ice cream. Mary-Lou nods and leaves.

Jimmy follows her with his eyes, admiring the way she moves, how she wiggles her ass. She quickly returns with his root beer, understands that the Rocker is thirsty after his long journey up the hill, in the police wagon, down the highway, in his pickup truck. Jimmy neatly slips a straw through the ice and lifts the glass. He thrills at the taste and bubbles, guzzling half the contents in one hit. Mary-Lou is clearly impressed. She asks where he's come from and Jimmy tells her about Memphis, his time in Nashville, understands she is falling in love with him, attracted by his romantic lifestyle and confident yet humble attitude. She wishes she could get away from Mississippi and see something of the world. The Rocker has seen and done so much. He knows she wants to talk more, but has to work, and he can't help swelling up with pride, imagining those ruby-red lips wrapped around his salami, thinks he is going to empty his sack like Jimmy No Hands, but stops and scolds himself, remembering who and where he is, and that he just isn't that sort of guy.

Jimmy leans back into soft leather and smells the polish, watches the trucks passing on the highway outside, mountain men heading north and south with solid values and loose dreams, chasing schedules. Jimmy has no time limits. He is a drifter and can do anything he wants. Head for California right now, if he chooses. There's a table jukebox in his booth and he slips in a dime. Selects Johnny Cash's 'Folsom Prison Blues'. Enjoys the twang of Johnny's guitar as Mary-Lou brings his starter over, a huge bowlful of battered mushrooms in half a gallon of sour cream, a tub of salsa, another root beer arriving to wash it down. On the house, honey, she smiles. All the pent-up hunger Jimmy has been controlling comes to the surface as he attacks his food. Each mouthful is sweet heaven to abused taste buds. The batter is crisp and lightly flavoured, mushrooms succulent, sour cream perfection. The salsa is extremely hot. He never knew food could taste this fantastic.

Mary-Lou leaves the drifting man to eat in peace and busies herself with other tables. When the sheriff enters he stops to glance around, nodding to Jimmy with an easy smile, a friendly lawman appreciating the integrity of this noble stranger passing through his county and adding to the local economy. Sheriff Clinton sits at the counter. Drinks coffee and orders a slice of apple pie. His gun rests unused on his belt and Jimmy doubts whether it has ever been pulled in anger. Mary-Lou returns and collects the Rocker's dishes, asks if he enjoyed his starter. He says yes, thanks very much, and he can see she is consumed by love, holding it in check. And what woman wouldn't fall in love with Jimmy? He is, after all, a fine specimen of manhood at its very best. Good-looking, intelligent, toned, confident, and with a healthy, active imagination. He is admired by his peers and craved by the women he meets. He is also very modest.

Jimmy passes around the salad bar, which is nicely laid out and reminds him of a snooker table, overhead lights illuminating the feast. Macaroni salad, crispy lettuce, chunky tomatoes, crispy croutons, juicy avocados, rich black olives and a tangy Thousand Island dressing fill his plate. He is very hungry. He has been thinking about food for a while now. Running dishes through his mind. There is French bread, rye bread, walnut bread and about ten other types of bread he doesn't really recognise, being a simple man by nature. He selects one at random, a lucky dip of generous wealth. It's as if he hasn't eaten for a long time, the mushrooms making no dent in his appetite. If anything they've made him hungrier. He returns to his booth, mouth watering so much he thinks he is going to drool, starts on the macaroni salad. The pasta has been mixed with mayonnaise and tiny slices of spring onion. It is superb. My compliments to Chef, and he is glad that a fat ex-con can make a new start in life and be so readily accepted back into society. He selects another song from the jukebox, Willie Nelson warning mothers not to let their sons grow up to be cowboys. Jimmy nods along, working his way around the plate, loving every crouton crunch.

He thinks of the poor unfortunates in the world, the third-world destitute grovelling in the dust of an Indian slum, appreciates his good fortune. He has been blessed, Mary-Lou gathering his plate and heading to the kitchen. Jimmy glances at the other diners, mainly middle-aged men and women, a family, a few old-timers, two men on their own. These citizens radiate good health, big people with huge appetites, God-fearing folk who live according to the gospel and have no time for wickedness. Every man is responsible for his actions and Jimmy agrees with this sentiment. Mary-Lou brings his platter and he is so hungry he could eat a horse, has to make do with three king-size burritos stuffed tight and covered with the best refried beans he has tasted since that Taco Bell in Tulsa. Two enchiladas await his attention. There is rice as well, but no ordinary rice. It is fluffy and has a flavour he can't quite identify. He cuts into a burrito and feels the heat on his hands, dips his fork into the beans, bites deep and follows the sensation as it spreads through his whole being. It is a spiritually material, materially spiritual moment.

Jimmy Rocker eats his meal slow. It is a religious experience and takes him out of his body and into other realms. Bruce Springsteen's 'Nebraska' plays on the jukebox. He knows things will not follow that Badlands route as he feels no anger, only love. For his fellow man and woman and the riches the Lord has given the earth. He is part of the rocking dream all right. And when he has finished he sits back, thanks Mary-Lou. He is going to order some of that apple pie in a minute. Maybe have a cup of coffee. He watches Mary-Lou and imagines them in the desert with the sun beating down, this sweet waitress butt-naked bending over the front of his pickup, Jimmy a little worried she might smudge the body-work, but he is a lover as well as a drifter, and he steps forward, takes his pecker in his hand but can't get rid of the hunger rumbling around in his belly, turns his back on such wicked-ness and prepares to order.

He studies the menu again, the ache in his belly growing. Mary-Lou walks towards him and the arm of a hog-like man blocks her path. This dickwad is enormous and hassling Mary-Lou, the sheriff turning his head and seeing nothing. The hog is a bully and a creep, a possible sex offender, and Jimmy is on his feet at the same time as the man, delivers a punch that sends the jerk sprawling back into his booth, where he lies unhurt but unconscious. Mary-Lou swoons and gathers her emotions, swears she's had it in this goddamn town. She wants to leave with Jimmy. The other diners are clapping and the sheriff shakes his hand, and the owner comes out from the back and slaps Jimmy on the back, says there's no charge for the meal, son. Anything you want, it's yours. Jimmy sits down, apple pie and ice cream appearing, a mug of weak coffee to finish off the meal, Mary-Lou waiting on a stool, ready to leave, and this wandering hero eats every last scrap, standing and saying goodbye to the folks, the dickwad shaking his hand and apologising for his behaviour, no hard feelings, fella, he doesn't know what came over him. Jimmy nods and hopes he has learnt a lesson, strolls out of the diner.

Mary-Lou leans in close as the rocking man eases his truck out of the parking lot and follows her directions to a wooden house with a yellow lawn and sagging hurricane fence. She kisses him on the cheek and skips indoors, while he looks along the street, reaching into his dashboard and removing a Hershey bar. The chocolate hits home. Helps pass the time until Mary-Lou returns, out of uniform and dressed in a short summer dress, hair released from its bun so she looks even better, a real doll. An elderly couple follow with a suitcase. Her moms and pops shake his hand and say look after our girl, boy, we know you can be trusted, any idea where you're heading? Jimmy shrugs and smiles and they tell him anywhere you want to drift is fine by us. He pulls away with a reassuring wave, everyone happy and content, gets back on the road, finding the highway.

When he reaches the crossroads he stops, wants to head west, laughing softly as he thinks fuck the Fucker, no hard feelings, asswipe, but that filthy fuck machine is one no-good hombre. Mary-Lou has her shoes off and delicate feet rest on the dash, the warmth of an early Mississippi night surrounding them as they sit on this country road, moss hanging in big old trees, cotton over John Lee Hooker fields, and they are in the Delta but Jimmy can't hear Robert Johnson on his radio, just the sweet rhymes of the King. Mary-Lou leans her head on his shoulder as they look innocently towards the horizon, whispering sweet nothings in my ear, loving the purity of the road, and I guess we are Merry Pranksters without any drugs or politics, just Coca-Cola and Levi Strauss and rock 'n' roll.

I love you, Jimmy, never leave me or let me down, we are going to live for ever and see the world and settle and raise a big family and eat apple pie just like Granny used to make, you and me, honey, nobody can touch us now, the world is ours, and I breathe in the smell of this fine Southern miss, trying to decide whether to head south and skirt New Orleans, find a nice beach on the Gulf of Mexico, or head west into Texas, keep going until we reach the Pacific. Mary-Lou and the Rocker sit at the crossroads feeling fine, this woman a true angel and one of those strokes of good luck that God awards good boys like me.

It is easy to envy the free men safe in warm houses and comfortable beds, earning a wage and waiting for the weekend to arrive, two whole days of mowing the lawn and washing the car. It is easy to envy the women and children and even their runaway dogs begging for scraps and performing tricks, hurrying home when the going gets tough, welcomed back with a hug and a dinner. Everywhere I go there are decent democracy-loving people living clean money-respecting lives, secure in bricks they have turned into homes, the harsh streets the wanderers pass along seen through protective glass filters. I envy them their boredom and security and love. And maybe I even envy the Captain, with his good looks and fluent tongue, his obvious confidence and wealth, the respect of his crew and the meaning of his life. Perhaps I have misjudged the man, allowed my judgement to become clouded.

Ramona tells me how after her trip to paradise she will marry and settle down and raise a family, and her man will be sober and dull and give her the sort of security she has never had, and will never find with me. Their life will be boring, but safe. The charms on her bracelet clink in time with the beads at the top of the hill, waking dreams of a great hunter on the prowl, roaming the dockyards, out on safari in a container jungle. The phone rings and this stranger I call Marian because I can't pronounce her name is moving fast, leaning over the counter and talking to the barman. I vaguely remember Balinese masks in second-hand magazines, but don't know what they represent, if they are religious or for fun. People make masks everywhere, create puppets and invent cartoon characters, but why bother on a tropical island?

My expression stays the same as Captain Decent enters the bar and Ramona turns, looks back at the phone, surprised and then emotional, laughing as she runs into his arms. The noble sea dog lifts her off her feet and twirls her around and I wait for the jukebox to start playing 'Hello Mary-Lou' by the legendary Ricky Nelson. It is a touching scene, but the Captain makes me angry, and I try to work out why, and it could be because he is the sort of man who is always in control and never suffers sadness or drops a sweet wrapper or has a bad word for anyone, his face impassive so it is impossible to read his thoughts. He is being welcomed like a hero returning from a just war, when really he is another company man, a merchant sailor moving cargo. Yet he is a superman in the glazed eyes of this woman, and she kisses him hard, on the cheek, which seems strange, more relief than passion.

The lovers sit on stools at the bar and the sensible man is smitten with Marian, arm around her waist as he orders drinks, casually scanning the room as he waits for the barman to do his work, cheeks glowing with happiness. His gaze passes over me and doesn't pause, not for a fraction of a second, and it is as if I hardly exist, one more faceless hobo with too much drink in his blood and emotions in turmoil. He has realised there is no future in such a rootless existence. He has led a wandering life, seen the world and made the decision to move up the pecking order, a humble deckhand climbing the ranks. If so, then I envy him his determination as well as his courage. I am beginning to like this man. He is sincere and treats those under his command fairly, knows that many of his crew are independent, but also lost and lonesome. I try to remember the saying. Lonely people are rarely alone. It makes sense, but not now. I am drunk and need to leave, head for the bar.

The Captain and Marian lift their shots of uplifting spirits and gently touch glasses, drink up and stand to go, and this sweet girl turns and waves and throws me a smile that transcends time, taking me back so I become even more confused, her mask slipping, from stranger to soulmate and lover, a sailor entering and greeting the Captain, holding the door open as they leave. I pay the barman and go out into the street, feel the wind on my face, the two lovers nowhere to be seen. I lean against a wall, move to the corner and try to remember if my hotel is left or right. The wind is bitter and freezing my face. It takes me a minute or two to work out that the hotel is to the right, the warmth of the alcohol fading, a car passing and spewing fumes.

I continue, walking slowly, glance across the road and spot two people in a car. I move closer but can't tell if it is the Captain and Marian, the man holding a small box in his palm. It must be a ring. The engine is running and condensation clouds the glass. I lean in closer to see what's happening. It is obvious this mystery man is proposing marriage. They are smiling as they talk and there is a pause and they embrace and hold each other tight squeezing the life into each other and they are going to have ten children and live happy lives in a nice house and my loneliness swells up and swamps me seeing these strangers warm and united, and I lose my head and bang on the windscreen, but they don't notice, and maybe I don't exist any more, an irrelevant ghost, one more faceless refugee. I recoil and spin round, look into an alley and see a length of wood, pick it up and walk back to the car, start smashing at the windscreen. The woman screams and the man gets out. I shout at him and he climbs back into the car and sounds the horn. I realise what I am doing and want to apologise, but don't know how, this envy a poison that distorts and twists reason. I throw the wood away and hurry off into the night, before the police can arrive and cart me off to jail.

HARD LABOUR

MR PRESLEY STANDS on his head, trying to squeeze as much blood into his brain as possible. When his fleece slips down the growth in his belly hangs limp between brittle ribs, a contorted knot of flesh and worry. He has been examined and is waiting for an operation, scared now that the technicians will feed him the wrong drugs and cause brain damage or gangrene, never mind whether the lump is benign. He also believes this fear could weaken his immune system so much he won't even survive the surgery, and that by flooding his brain cells he can increase his mental strength. His face is puffy and red, skull cushioned by pillow and blanket, plates creaking under the strain. I sit on the ledge counting seconds, trying to stay even. Time passes slower each day, two months in Seven Towers more like two sleepless years. I have hardly put a dent in my sentence and resisting the numbers game has proved impossible, my calendar fixed to the wall and covered in tombstones. Time has become something to waste, and that is a crime in itself.

After sixty-three seconds Elvis begins lowering his legs, arms trembling, almost making it before his muscles fail and he comes tumbling down, catching his breath and stretching across the blanket, waiting for the dizziness to pass. Lasting over a minute boosts his confidence, and he explains that while he has no time for a backward nation such as India, where religion and class prejudice combine to keep the population firmly in their wooden shacks, he has nothing against the science of hatha yoga, the headstand a popular yogic exercise, and he is laughing and saying America and India, my friend, these are the two extremes of mankind, one scientific and free where a poor man can leave his hovel and live in the White House, while the other remains in chains, destroyed by superstition and poverty.

George is passing and stops to talk to the King, and as a communist he naturally despises both capitalism and religion, but doesn't understand English so stays calm, his temper always ready to explode. He turns and looks my way, nods before moving on, and Elvis is passing on the news that an Australian or South African, or maybe a New Zealander, is due to arrive in Seven Towers, and there is a good chance he will be put in with us. This information comes from a trustee on the gate, through a guard who has a brother working in the offices, so there might be an element of truth. I can't help feeling excited, though it is probably another false rumour. Even so, I squeeze the charm in my pocket and make a wish.

Franco sits down next to me, chewing raw fingers, nails long gone. He is deteriorating by the day, his lawyer not showing up for the third visit running. His family have sent a large sum of money to the man, for his services and also to pay an official to speed up the boy's court appearance, but since cashing the cheque the lawyer has not been seen. Franco is mentally and physically weak. He also seems to be shrinking. We are all thinner than when we arrived, but he is also shorter. Maybe he is stooping, but I don't think so. I can't work it out. Elvis also has no court date set, and while he is angry about this he has bigger problems to deal with, his health more important than freedom. Franco stares at the bright red head and flattened quiff and tells Elvis he looks like a giant tomato. And he does. We start laughing. After two months together maybe we see the same images, tomatoes on a vine, ripening in the sun, piled high on a table, sliced and added to a salad, radishes and peppers glistening with virgin olive oil, diced and melting in a rich sauce, covering a plate of linguine. Our mouths water. On the outside lonely men dream of sex, in prison we are more interested in food.

Back in C-Block boiled potatoes rest in delicate stomachs, Franco battling homesickness, reaching out to Elvis and offering a helping hand, pulling the older man to his feet. He wobbles and finds his balance, gingerly makes his way to the ledge where we sit together, three outsiders, comrade aliens, laugh again as if we can guess what the others are thinking, that we must be insane to end up in this mausoleum, standing on our heads and salivating at the thought of a hot shower, tasting imaginary tomatoes and planning rambling road journeys. But we are surviving, and when a man comes to Seven Towers he is on his knees, praying for an easy time, begging God things won't be as bad as he has been promised, that he is not going to be gang-raped or have his throat cut. He is scared and angry and paranoid. He listens to the whispers and can easily react and turn violent, start fighting non-existent enemies. The block is new territory, yet there is little to see, the other prisoners a mystery for a foreigner, who doesn't know what is being said. Only Elvis and Franco make sense to me, and they have mannerisms and hidden meanings that stay out of reach. There is no variation or stimulation, just months and years of emptiness stretching ahead, with too much time to worry about the future and regret the past. The unrelenting boredom is suffocating, an epileptic claustrophobia that has broken stronger men.

The prison guards and other inmates can use this paranoia against a new man, if they are that way inclined. A murderer will make you feel safe with a nod and a broken biscuit, while an embezzler might try a sneer and pout, playing the role of a hired gunman when all he does is cheat old people out of their savings, a small-time whore who doesn't see the long-term view. Once a man has settled in and knows the score it is easy to pick the embezzler off in the toilet, punch him in the belly so he falls in the piss but doesn't bleed, the law of the jungle restrained on safari, a fear of worse enough to make this petty criminal dirty himself. A broken nose is obvious and a flow of blood will stir the guards, while the sort of lowlife who robs grannies is the same kind who will run crying to the Director.

A recent arrival cautiously enters the yard, a teenage boy who slides in nearby and fiddles with his flute, wincing when it touches his lips, which are split. He can't be more than eighteen, accused of flashing an old lady, and he makes the mistake of telling another prisoner, punched before he has a chance to explain how he was seen urinating against a wall late at night, on his way home from a bar. This lady is a high-class snob and complains to the police, insists he is charged. Elvis reckons the kid is genuine, and as flashing is near enough a sex crime he wouldn't admit to the charge if he wasn't telling the truth. There is a pecking order, with sex cases firmly at the bottom, though we don't see them, or at least, if they are in with us, they keep quiet. Gays who flaunt themselves can also expect a beating, those who don't more or less tolerated. Flute boy starts blowing and instantly puts me on edge, Elvis calm as he discovers a Carl Perkins tune, Franco scowling. This is no mellow jazz trumpeter, more speed urchin with a penny whistle. I control myself, the smallest incident starting a chain reaction.

The volleyball match yesterday is a good example, the guards bringing the net in once a week for an hour, the games played mainly to wear out those taking part. The only ball on the yard, the one used to play football, is a basketball, so it is heavy and cumbersome and punching it hurts. The men playing mean it and there is always a row, and yesterday it is between two men from upstairs, and instead of insulting each other and swapping punches as usual, a knife is produced and one man has the other against the wall and is about to plunge the blade into his belly when Baker starts screaming. The sound is high-pitched and demented like a dying innocent plucked from the earth by hawk men, but then I recognise it as the shrill terror of a child who can't take any more. It chills our skin, especially coming from such a well-liked character. The knife is lowered and the two prisoners separate.

Baker stands in the middle of the yard, arms extended as he looks to the sky, voice moving back through the years of his life, deepening and begging God to save him, to reach down and lift him from the chaos, the rest of us silent and embarrassed. He turns and runs inside and we go over to the windows and peer in, watch as he reaches under his bed and removes his suitcase, mumbling to himself, and answering, shaking his head and laughing, and it is all good-natured stuff, but sad to see. He begins folding his clothes, and is very precise and fast packing the suitcase, clicking the latch and checking it is secure, sighing and smiling broadly. He trails around the room shaking the hands of the sleepwalkers, comes back into the yard and does the same again, formal and polite and decisive, finally turns and walks over to the gate, taps good-naturedly on the flap and talks to the trustee, the head of a guard appearing. Baker has had enough. He is going home.

There is a discussion and voices are raised. Baker's confidence turns to his more normal bemusement. For some reason he is not being allowed to leave. He has enjoyed his stay, made new friends and experienced a novel sort of life, but now the experiment is over. He has better things to do. It is nonsense. Ridiculous. The flap closes and he begins knocking on the gate, gently at first, as surely this is a misunderstanding, and then harder. He places his suitcase on the ground and starts kicking at the gate, over and over, moaning and shouting and finally screaming once more. I look up at the walls and see the guards watching, Baker headbutting the gate as he shrieks louder, some of the men going over to calm him, but he is freaking out and banging into the wall and sinking to the ground where he writhes among the hands trying to control what seems like a fit, the gate crashing open and several guards flashing their sticks, Baker instantly still and on his feet and led away. He returns three hours later as if nothing has happened, but the rest of us are shocked.

Soon I will be passing through that gate to see the Director, having served long enough to request a transfer to a work prison. As well as a full-time job and decent living conditions, every day worked on the farm means two are crossed off the calendar, so I can halve my time left to serve and also become absorbed in a task, thereby speeding up the clock. I will have a cell of my own, and with the door locked I can sleep like I never sleep in Seven Towers. The guards are said to be easy-going, dealing with moderate offenders and repenters, decent men who believe in hard work. The flute turns melodic, leads me to the life of a goat herder wandering the margins of a

sun-baked plateau, heading for a waterhole to eat my bread
and cheese and apricots under cover of a palm tree, the cross
of a chapel gleaming in the distance, a flock of sheep passing
and the shepherd waving his blessing. My goats will produce
milk and cheese and their offspring will be spared the butcher
and meat market, living contentedly in a dreamy world of
endless love and sunlight. This is the life that will be mine,
when I meet the Director. It makes sense for a man to work
for his food and lodging.

Naturally I won't be allowed to roam at first, and will have
to earn the trust of the new governor, but in the meantime
there will be fields to dig and crops to sow, outbuildings to
paint and orchards to tend. Elvis passes on descriptions from
men who have been at these farms, and there is so much food
available they actually put on weight. I see myself on the back
of a tractor bringing in the harvest, a tanned farmhand lost in
the sweat of honest toil, muscles bulging from pure graft. I
will rebuild myself and become fit. There will be no more
mental drifting, just work and sleep, work and sleep, like all
the other regular men right across the globe. Life on the farm
will suit me.

In a hundred degrees of heat, and with little cloud cover,
I move in and out of leafy shade, bees and butterflies sniffing
as my fingers glide along a vine bursting with grapes, huge
ripe bundles of energy eased into a bucket, tasting every fourth
fruit to make sure it is perfect. The boss understands and
appreciates this unselfish diligence, sugar starting off a huge
emotional high where I am free and indestructible, running
and kicking and soaring into the sky. My efforts will be
rewarded as the authorities allow me to leave the prison vineyard to work on a local farm, way beyond the boundaries of
my luxurious cell block. I will be handed over to an ancient
saint, the trust placed in me by this wise man spurring me
to greater efforts, the prize tomatoes he grows so succulent
they hurt.

The owner of the tomato farm has a beautiful relative who
manages the business side, and just happens to be a great cook,
taking pity on the misjudged convict drifter. She naturally

takes a shine to this outsider and offers asylum, feeding him big bowls of spaghetti with crusty bread coated in hummus, the wine flowing as the sun sets and I take a relaxing stroll back to my cell, gates rolled open with a smile and a joke. I am looking further ahead, across the years, into the final weeks of my sentence, and I am close to the old man and younger woman, and when he sadly dies I am devastated, asked to go and live on the farm once I am released, the saint leaving me a half-share. And I laugh. And Elvis laughs. And Franco also laughs. Every one of us thinking something different. But the truth is that a move to a farm is a strong possibility. I am looking forward to meeting the Director, refuse to believe that crucifixion gossip.

Franco snaps and shouts at the flute boy, who looks petrified, lowering his instrument and head. The one-legged street fighter yells at Franco, the foreigner who should know his place, and my friend isn't the man of two months ago. Franco shrugs his shoulders. The kid stands and walks off, shoulders slumped, and I think of the beating he received and what it must have done to his confidence, how he could understand the things the men kicking him were shouting, and it happened fast, in a corner of the yard, and he was terrified about being locked up that night, although the truth was sorted out by then. Like Baker, and the rest of us, he has nowhere to hide. But it is all right, we are all okay, and maybe Elvis and Franco will follow me to the farm, once they have been to court and convicted of a crime, and we will work together on the vines, form a new brotherhood of the grape, the old team reunited, the kid as well, and his flute will sound better there, and Baker can get a job in the bakery, and the rest of them can come as well, all these bad-boy Babel men.

The rumour comes true a few days after I first hear about the English speaker, and it turns out he is a New Yorker with a flabby face and jaundiced skin, silver crucifix tight around his neck, sunglasses hiding his eyes, and this yellow man is on the move from hospital to an island jail, dumped in Seven Towers overnight, and maybe he has seen Elvis who has been whisked away for his operation, about to ask when this fellow alien launches into a hurricane of words that knocks me back and all I can do is wallow in the luxury of hearing my language spoken properly and he needs to talk more than me, after four years in custody this is the first time he has spoken freely, to someone who really understands, and his tongue is smooth and the soothing fluency of familiar words is hypnotic and sedating and I feel no threat but start noticing how he is Homer Simpson in disguise with that big yellow head and short nail-like hair, and I am cornered, by the stairs, losing the meaning of what he is saying and forcing myself to concentrate and remember that special Homer humour, the melodious flow of his poetry turning to individual words and these words form sentences with a specific meaning and he is telling me about the many years he has spent on the road and the two prisons he has served time in, and this is no upbeat Jack Kerouac view of life not even Jean Genet or William Burroughs, you see, I am a vagabond, a fucking vagabond, came to these lands after escaping a molestation charge at home, and I never touched the kid, if I had've done I'd do more than fiddle with his dick, now that's the truth, and he laughs long and hard and it is a good job he is joking, yeah, three strikes and you're out, zero fucking tolerance, the rotten apple stretches further than New York, and his glasses hide the meaning of his life and there is something not right about his smile, maybe it is the medication, preventing brain damage and gangrene, I don't know, fight hard and make sure he remains as Homer Simpson and doesn't turn into Freddy Krueger, and he nods and says he was in Seven Towers before he went to hospital, for a week, and six months in that hospital and I didn't want to leave, but those cocksuckers say my time is up, yeah, I was over on B-Block, that's right, B-Block, that's what you've heard, well, and he stops and thinks and grins, well, what you heard is half the truth, this block is for pussies, for the little boys, now B-Block is where they put the real felons and junkies, they stick the smack freaks in with the killers and rapists, all those bad motherfuckers are mixing together in a cesspit, even Jesus Christ himself wouldn't survive in there let alone save souls, forget redemption, no, it's the system, mix junkies in with psychos and they're going to wipe each other out, those H freaks are so twisted they'll kill you for your fucking shoes, and the lifers don't give a shit, a junkie starts shouting and screaming and they'll stick a shiv in him, like this one guy in the bed next to me he's a fag and he's killed his sister and puts her in the freezer and when he can't get a ride he thaws her out and dresses her as a boy and fucks her in the ass, so you've got murder, incest and necrophilia in one hit, and the killers are murderers, no crimes of passion or drunken bar-room shooting or crack stabbing, no sir, these motherfuckers are cold, like nothing you can say or do is going to stop them fucking you up, there's no pity in there, shit, they'd eat someone like you alive, you're ripe for a gang bang, and I should know, Jesus, I was raped in jail back in the good old US of A, those niggers fucked me half to death, and the governor doesn't care because he says I'm a queer and the liberals are pleased as they hate white boys and they don't want to upset the blacks, fuck, I hate niggers everywhere, all these cocksuckers here are niggers and that's the truth, something I learnt, the prison authorities don't give a shit what happens to you, they want you infected with Aids and passing it on, try to run you down so you are so low you go and hang yourself or cut an artery, they want to decrease the prison population so they let the drugs in, bring them in when they have to, the guards sell it on B-Block, I don't know about here, you don't think so, it happens all over the world, fuck, you think these countries can run without drugs, and they say judge a society on how it treats its weakest and we are some of the weakest, just fucking each other up, ridding the outside world of the bad men, shit, you must know that by now, it's never going to change and the only thing we can do is help ourselves, and he looks up at the walls, straight at a hawk, makes the shape of a pistol with his fingers and shoots, turns back and carries on, relentless, and I sit dead still, six months I spent in that fucking psychiatric hospital and it's a hotel compared to this hole, and as long as you don't damage the furniture and act polite you're fine, that crazy farm is soaked in drugs, and I'm like a child in a sweetshop, it's a fucking whorehouse, man, uppers and downers and every colour pill God invented and guys lying about half naked and half conscious and there's no security, nothing to stop a horny faggot plucking and fucking these chickens, it's an orgy, man, a fucking orgy, Jesus Christ, half those patients are so drugged up they can hardly move, don't know who or where they are, and you've got virgin boys and senile old men, guys who were something, and half these kids don't know they've got a fist up their ass, man, it's the best sex I ever had and there's no payback, and I'm laughing and passing on that Aids the niggers gave me, keep the virus flowing, fuck up as many people as you can, play the game by their rules, and this madman lowers his voice and whispers, see, I'm working for the state, the blacks are still playing at being slaves cleaning up the jails for the Feds but I'm international, cleansing the mental wards of the world for the CIA, I'm a task force, shock and fucking awe, that's me, and he pauses, you see, the blacks hate whites because of slavery and the way they've been treated so in their racist eyes any white boy is fair game and those niggers and wetbacks specialise in ass-fucking poor whites, and as you can see, I'm not a strong man, and they ripped me apart, I had to have twenty stitches in my ass, I was torn so bad I was shitting tequila for a year, and you know what God says, and I know the Bible well, he says do unto others as they do unto you, it's the totem pole of life and you listen to a rich white and he runs down a poor white when he's talking, and a poor white runs down a black, and the nigger looks around and beats up on the animals, see, we all take it out on someone less strong than us, and Homer removes his glasses and I am looking into a child's eyes that are the most brilliant blue I have ever seen, the eyes of an angel, deep and intense and bottomless, and he pats me on the shoulder and says he is off upstairs to sleep as all this talking has worn him out, and he tells me his name is Bundy but I can call him Ted, if I want, and he laughs long and hard at this humour, wants to be seen as the meanest of the mean motherfuckers parading along the valley of death, and he looks at me properly and sees I am shaking, seems pleased, calls me a fucking pussy, spitting on the ground as he heads upstairs.

Mum is always telling me that we should count our blessings as there are so many people worse off than us think of all those poor souls starving around the world and living in poverty with no fresh water and diseases like cholera and typhoid killing babies and little children running around with no shoes on their feet and there are plenty of people nearer home as well we must never take what we have for granted and Nana agrees and says some people are greedy and unkind as they find it hard to deal with their problems or admit any sort of weakness and Rosie is a little girl at my school who doesn't have a mum or dad and sometimes she lives in a special home with other children where they sleep in a dormitory and at other times she stays with men and women called foster-parents who take children in to help them and they buy her toys and treat her nicely and the ones she has at the moment take her to church every Sunday which she enjoys as she likes singing hymns and they have a dog that is allowed to sleep in her room though not on the bed as they can get fleas and pass them on and she is my first real friend at school as she is sitting next to me that is how I get to know her and she has a smart pencil case with mouse faces on it and eyes that roll around and new sharpened pencils and a rubber that I borrow from her when we are drawing pictures and I accidentally chew it and the lady she is living with at the moment took her out specially to buy it for her first day at school and I say sorry I wasn't thinking what I was doing and she says that is okay I owe her a favour now and one day I will have to repay it and the lady she lives with won't mind as it is not Rosie's fault and she is a bit of a tomboy quite a tough girl really who I never see cry when she falls down and in the play-ground the boys end up playing with other boys and girls with girls but me and Rosie still talk to each other we don't care when someone says you shouldn't talk to a boy or girl that is stupid really and I feel lucky as although I don't have a dad I have a mum who is three times as good as any other

mum she is the best mum in the world that is what I write
on her Mother's Day card Nana told me to write that down
as it is what her son used to say and I buy Mum a chocolate
bar and hide it in the fridge so it doesn't melt and I also have
my nana living with me as well as Mum and a lot of children
don't have that so I am lucky and I buy Nana a card as well
and then realise Mum has bought her one so in the end Nana
gets two cards and is really pleased and when a bully girl says
something nasty to Rosie she pulls her hair and punches her
and makes her nose bleed and the bully is crying and I think
it is good as she should be nice to Rosie not nasty and Rosie
gets told off by the teachers but not very much as they know
what has happened and are very kind to her and sometime
during my first year at school Rosie leaves and I don't see her
for a few years but remember her face and those dark eyes so
when I meet her again I recognise her right away but that is
later and another time and another sort of life and school is great
I love the infants and learning new things Mrs Miller is a nice
teacher I especially like geography that is my favourite subject
hearing about faraway countries with pyramids and yetis and
icebergs and deserts there is so much to know about the world
and I like playing football and can run fast I win a prize at
the sports day and even though I am going to school I am
awake early to make up the fireplace with Nana who is getting
older and slowing down and becoming more frail and yet I
am stronger and taller and do more of the work and when
I tell her about Rosie and the fight she says there is always a
reason why people do things and maybe the bully is unhappy
or spoilt and thinks she is better than other people and maybe
Rosie is sad inside so she gets angry like that and we should
turn the other cheek and this is different to what Mum says
and Nana wants me to remember that everyone has a soul it
doesn't matter what terrible things they do inside they are
scared little children trying to fit in with those around them
nobody wants to be an outsider and laughed at or treated
nasty and Nana knows a lot of things as she is old and very
clever and she laughs when I tell her this but inside I am glad
Rosie fights back and it is just that she has the courage to do

what other softer kids want to do but can't as they think too much of the other person and how it feels it is their niceness that gets in the way and I am pretty soft and I don't like fights and arguments I just don't see the point and in the summer we go to the common and see lots of people we know and there is a fair and we walk around the stalls and one day I win a stuffed toy it is a funny-looking clown in some ways he is a bit like a dunce tall and thin with a pointy hat but I don't care he is mine and I am allowed to call him anything I want and Mum laughs when I say Mr Fair but it turns out to be a good name as it means two things at the same time and I put him in my room and a year or two later I don't know how it happens but one day he doesn't have a face any more and this scares me so I can't look at his head not without any eyes or nose or mouth and at night he has to go out in the hall on his own as I am scared of the dark and always sleep with my light on as there are evil monkeys who live under the bed and are waiting to get me and after a few days Mum notices Mr Fair and I tell her and she says she washed him and his face must have rubbed off it is only a cheap toy but never mind all you have to do is use a pen and you can draw another face and make it happier than before as Mr Fair always looked a bit sad to me and she is right and this is when she tells me that all have I to do when I am with someone who worries me is turn a bad person into a good person just like Mr Fair and I try this and find it works and suddenly Mickey Mouse and Donald Duck and Goofy are running around the playground but after trying this out I only play this trick when it is really needed otherwise it won't work and I will run out of imagination and this is the best trick I ever learn and there is a shop on the common and one day me and Nana are walking past and there is a huge teddy bear in the window and there is a competition to guess his name whoever gets it right wins the bear and we enter the shop and I wait for the bell on the door to stop ringing and I think very hard and guess Teddy and I really want to win this bear but there are already five children who have written Teddy on the form and I am thinking extra hard for a long time and the shopkeeper says why don't you try Rupert dear that's a nice name and so I say all right Rupert and the next week I find I have won the competition and Rupert Bear joins a beaming Mr Fair on my chest of drawers and I can't help thinking how lucky I am and it is only years later that I realise the woman cheated and told me the name and I spend a long time wondering why.

When a siren howls shortly after breakfast some men panic and run to the gate, bang on the metal and tug at the flap, Franco standing up but staying near, saying there is a fire and we are going to die, I don't want to die in this place, the furnace must have blown up, the old man has said many times it must be mended. My heart aches as I think of Baker, his childlike screams stirring my nausea, the siren snapping tired minds, churning bile. Fear warps Franco so his voice quivers and Italian takes over and maybe he is right, the furnace exploding and logs igniting and creating an inferno that barbecues ten soapy forgers in the shower, flames roaring off down the tunnel and encircling the castle. We are stuck in a death trap, and this is also the last place in the world that I want to die. Maybe they even bury you within the walls. But words are exchanged at the gate and the flap snaps shut, men walking back, talking excitedly, their panic over. Franco calms down and does his best to find out why the siren is sounding. He knows some of the language, but not enough. Men speak and mime, but he can't work them out. We are missing Elvis, in more ways than one.

Mr Presley must have had his operation by now, and should be back on the block, and I can't help worrying that a technician has fed him the wrong gas, and that he has been moved to a Homer Simpson ward where cloned yellow men are busy taking full advantage. We are eager to see Elvis again, miss him as a friend and translator. I have learnt a few words but it is hard going, and while Franco is better, he struggles, still trying to find out about the siren, the one-legged street fighter struggling to explain, hopping and making climbing motions. Elvis would grasp the meaning, even if some of the language makes no sense. He is older, with a greater experience of the world, and this adds a deeper dimension to his thinking, his morals fixed and sincere. The siren gradually slows, stutters, and finally stops.

Franco turns and excitedly explains that a prisoner has escaped. It is odd, but in the two months I have spent in this fleapit the idea has never entered my head, at least not seriously, daydreams of sliding along drains and toilet tubes like an amphibious rat man, of flying off and joining a squadron of passing geese, are just fantasy. Franco and Elvis have never spoken of it either, and I suppose we just don't see how it can be done, wouldn't know where to start, and even if we somehow got out of the castle there would be nowhere to hide. It wouldn't take long for the police to pick us up, and our sentences would be increased. But before I can go into things with Franco, Chef arrives, and we line up to collect our midday meal, a bowl of grease-marinated potatoes, and wander off to eat. And one day it will be me picking these potatoes, digging my hands into the sort of soil that smells so ripe and fine I could eat it, picking out the worms first, keeping the birds away so they have time to escape, and I go back further, breaking up the earth with a spade, planting tubers and making sure they are well watered. And Franco is still trying to talk to two other prisoners, eating absent-mindedly, a waste of a meal, and I stick with my food, finish and go to the sinks, exaggerate the cleaning. Once I have finished I walk over to the clothes line and check if my socks, pants and shirt are dry, find they are still damp, hope the weather stays clear so I don't have to take them inside.

Rain halves our options. There is the section and there is the yard. At night we have no choice, but during the day it makes sense to stay outside as much as possible. The cold can make it hard going, but there is no defence against the rain. Spending a day indoors increases the pressure, racks the boredom up another notch. I don't understand the sleepwalkers. They should be getting as much fresh air as possible, stretching their legs instead of living under blankets, wallowing in misery. Maybe they really can close down and sleep twenty hours a day, go into suspended animation like human hedge-hogs. There is little to do in the yard, but they would be moving, using their eyes. I never want to end up that way, changed beyond repair, and I worry about Franco, who always seems on the verge of tears. He calls me over. I sit down and he leans forward, food unfinished. I look at the potatoes and feel the hunger in my belly, want to ask if he is going to eat them. He is very close, looking around, talking in a whisper.

The man who has escaped, from A- or B-Block, nobody is sure, is a convicted killer, someone who has murdered his girl-friend in a merciless razor attack or practised euthanasia on his terminally ill father in a celebrated mercy killing, and he has either stabbed a guard through the heart and sliced off his eyelids before using the uniform to bluff his way out, or has got into one of the towers and abseiled down the outside wall, jumping into a car parked nearby, apparently driven by his blonde fiancée. The second option is the one I prefer, thinking of the Sicilian and the tower, knowing his chance is gone. After all his years in prison I doubt he wants to leave. On the outside time speeds past. Children grow and become adults and produce more young, while behind these walls life is sterile. The Sicilian seems content, and that must be what they mean when they say a man is institutionalised. The guilt I occasionally feel about wanting to move to a farm could be a sign of this, telling myself I will be sorry to leave my friends, when really I am scared of change. Two fucking months is all I have served. There should be no doubt. I have to look after myself.

A prisoner comes over from the gate and the other men gather around him for news, Franco one of them, caught up in the soap opera, and when he tells me what is going on, I start laughing, and Franco is saying no no no, the great escape nothing more than the guards testing the siren. For a split second he looks at me with hatred, and this stuns me, and I realise how much he wants to believe in the man breaking out. He interprets my laugh as resignation and his expression changes as he pats me on the shoulder, sits down and leans his head back against the wall, twitching suddenly, a manic jerk that reminds me of the yellow man.

Prison is ruining Franco, any last trust in the honesty of a small part of the system gone with the corruption of his lawyer. This slimeball is denying he ever received the money, and as an alien Franco has even less power than a local. There is nothing he can do from prison, the embassy showing little sympathy for his predicament, especially as it is a drugs offence. These officials have cosy lives to protect and don't need their easy ride ruined by common criminals, know that challenging a respected professional isn't going to get them invited to more cocktail parties. Franco still keeps his bag with him at all times, takes it on safari and last time wouldn't even trust it to the Sicilian when we had our showers. The cover became wet and some of the pages stiffened. Elvis wants him to get some pills from the doctor when he does his evening round, but Franco resists, says he doesn't trust their contents.

Everyone is disappointed when it is confirmed that the escape never happened, and there is a grim atmosphere for the rest of the day, but I let it wash over me, leave these moody men to fret over a non-existent event. I sit on my own, Franco inside with his photos of home, and I am wondering how long someone can stare at the same pictures before the effect wears off, and it must be a slow torture, better to shut it out of your mind, but maybe it helps his imagination, gets him hiking in the mountains again. It is a bright day and the weather holds, and I stay on the ledge listening to the beads and smelling burnt tobacco.

Two skinny, plastic gangsters traipse down the steps, and these small-time crooks with the oily locks and glossy suits have turned into upmarket tramps in giant costumes, the sheen dull and material threadbare. They need haircuts, but most men don't visit the barber. The shop is neatly enough tiled, with a leather chair and polished mirror, scissors sharpened, cut-throat razor and shaving cream at the ready, a range of perfumed powders lining the shelves, hundreds of movie cuttings covering the walls, glamorous women smiling for the cameras, hot tea on offer. The barber's shop is warm and inviting and familiar, from a distance. Franco went a week after he arrived, drank tea and had his face lathered, saw the expression on the barber's face reflecting in the mirror, razor gleaming, inches from his face. He shivers as he remembers, the three assistants standing with a single broom, giggling, the barber drooling, his features contorted and covered in a glistening layer of sweat. Franco excused himself, but not without an argument and the help of the guard outside. They say the barber cut the throats of five teenage boys before he was sent to Seven Towers, but nobody told Franco.

The crooks march in silence. It could be the letdown of the escape that never happened, though it seems ridiculous so many men are bothered. They should break out themselves instead of leaving it to someone else to raise their morale. I wonder about the automobiles they pedalled, whether they deal in classics or old bangers, quality or quantity, stolen or merely adjusted, and I am nodding off behind the wheel of a Mercedes freewheeling downhill, a child on a helter-skelter sliding towards my mother, picking up speed and racing away from Seven Towers with Ramona by my side, heading for the ocean and those container ships, deciding on New Orleans as my next destination, the Captain having his crew whistle me aboard, new wife waving from the bridge, one last transatlantic voyage before they jet off to Bali. I catch myself, know dozing means a sleepless night, and the beads clatter, the patter of feet out of time, furious shouting drawing me towards the sight of the two crooks trading punches.

Back in the police cell, a blow from either man would have knocked the other out, but no longer. I wonder if they are brothers or cousins, though they are fighting like sworn enemies, determined in their stances, keen to hurt, blows bouncing off as weak arms fail. They begin wrestling, fall to the ground and roll over and over ripping their suits, sink into a crater and begin cutting themselves on the gravel, small drops of blood specking their skin. One man pins the other down, headbutts him, grabs his skull and smashes it into the concrete, and the thud of bone is sickening, and I should try and pull him off, see two guards strolling over, and they stop and smile, and I look back, see the winner lift his brother's head for a fatal crack, and I start to stand, glad he hesitates, guards laughing. Sanity returns and he is fatter and more dignified and lowers the head to the floor, leans forward and rests his brow on the unconscious man's shoulder, stays there for quite a while, the guards uncomfortable, turning away. The winner stands and hauls a floppy loser up, with difficulty cradling this living corpse in his arms, legs straining as he carries his brother upstairs.

The beads return, find their rhythm, and the afternoon passes and we eat soup and bread and another day ends and once we are locked up for the night I play chess with Franco, gradually improving, protecting my king better as I fill in for Elvis, half worried in case I beat my friend, not knowing if he can take much more defeat. When I first play the game I find it hard to concentrate, but it is a good way of passing the time, and I realise this is why they play so often. Franco isn't as good as I first thought, and I know he is fragile, wonder if Elvis lets him win sometimes. We play five games and I lose every one. Maybe today I will beat him.

When the bolt is pulled back and the section door opens, we turn and see Elvis enter with a lopsided grin, bag over his shoulder and a spring in his step. He saunters down the aisle and the sleepwalkers wave, other men shaking his hand and nodding. The response is genuine and he looks touched, and at times like this, small flashes of a moment, I feel total unity with these C-Block men. Elvis appears fitter than when he left, on a high at odds with returning to prison, but he hugs me and Franco and asks how we are, scans the room and laughs and sniffs the air and glances over when the green door opens and closes, promises us he has missed going on safari. He just couldn't get used to the hospital's clean toilets and automatic flushing, the soft toilet roll and padded mattress, and I must see the animals, my friends, the conger eels and pythons, places his bag on his bed and disappears. Franco instantly perks up, carefully drops the chess pieces in the sock where he stores them, tucks it under his clothes with the board, our game over.

When Elvis returns he settles in and tells us about his holiday, and it is a drawn-out tale which is unusual for the rocking man, but we hang on every word, go through the details of his surgery to hear about the good food and gorgeous nurses. He insists he is glad to be back, worried his place would be taken and he would end up on B-Block. He has conquered death and kept his old bed, and while he feared a mistake, brain damage or gangrene, his biggest concern was the growth turning out to be cancer. He has been assured it is not, and a huge burden has been removed. The staff treated him like a king, and even though there was a guard to make sure he didn't try to escape, he was near to being free. He laughs and throws his head back and says he feels ten years younger, that a man can survive prison but not a malignant dose of cancer. He calls it the enemy within.

I only met Elvis two months ago and all I know about him is what he has told me, his travel stories and plans for the future, his love of rock 'n' roll and the American way of life, but it is as if I have known him for ever. If I was a child and he was my dad I would be proud of him. He has his dreams and a moral code. He will never sell out, never compromise his standards and bow down in front of a judge or director. That is the spirit of the road. First impressions last for ever, and I see myself coming on to the block for the first time as a scared foreigner, spine shaking, nausea eating at my gut, and it was Elvis who made me feel at ease, offered a helping hand.

He tells us about the nurses, the colour of their hair and shape of their lips and the way they move and treat him with respect, as a human being rather than a dangerous criminal. They ask the guard what he has done and don't feel threatened by counterfeit currency, angry he is in prison at all when he tells them his side of the story. This anger turns to outrage when they learn he is in jail without being convicted of any crime. And Elvis teases us with a long description of the hot shower he has as soon as he arrives, clothes taken away and cleaned in a washing machine. The nurses give him pyjamas and a white gown and a bed made up with starched sheets and pillowcases. He feels safe and is served food on a tray after his operation, and when he can walk he goes to a dining area where he sits at a table with metal knives and forks, the food grease-free and wholesome. There is lots of it as well, so much he is unable to clear his plate, feels bad wasting a single bite, sick the first time he eats, but afterwards all right. He reads newspapers and magazines and watches television and talks to women and has a great time. We listen with awe and want to hear more.

He is visited by a concerned doctor and the operation is explained, his mind relaxed, and afterwards a surgeon comes to see him and goes through the same routine, a distinguished man in his fifties who even asks about conditions in Seven Towers, shaking his head in disgust as he hears the details. When they take Elvis to the theatre he is calm, reasons that if he dies it is his fate, and at least he is not in prison. Yet he scorns fate and karma, believes in the triumph of will-power. It could have been the sedative, but he thinks it was something more profound. But, of course, he survives and is visited again by the surgeon and told that the lump is benign. A man's health is the most important thing in life. We have to realise this fact. And now he must concentrate on getting a court appearance.

The surgeon has promised to help him, using the operation as leverage and insisting on a trial date and a move out of Seven Towers. He believes he can have an influence, and has connections. The stitches are sore, but Elvis has tablets and cream and another visit to the hospital scheduled. He tells us life could be so much worse, and he is looking forward to a game of chess. The surgeon will help him. He has hope. We must stay strong and get through this time. He promises us the world is still there, waiting for our return, and he tells us again about the clean sheets and hot showers and good food and the sight of so many women walking around with smiles on their faces, some even carrying vases of flowers, to see women, my friends, that is fantastic, and we let him talk and talk, his new optimism and zest for the future lifting us up and keeping us there for days.

Sitting at the crossroads with Mary-Lou, engine rumbling, Jimmy Rocker decides to head south to the Gulf of Mexico rather than west into Texas. Mary-Lou has only been outside Mississippi twice in her life, and is excited by the idea of seeing the sea. Right now she looks like a young Dolly Parton, which surprises Jimmy as back in the diner she reminded him of Ramona, an old friend from way back when. But Mary-Lou is no punk. She is a country girl, in love with the honky-tonk sounds of Lefty Frizzell and Kitty Wells, Hank Williams and Ernest Tubb, and while dedicated to her family and modest in both taste and ambition, she has taken a gamble on the rocking man. This makes Jimmy feel very special, the fact he is trusted by a stranger a huge compliment, showing that his inner goodness shines through the dust of the open road. He wants to show Mary-Lou the world, and maybe they will ease their way along the coast and dip down into Mexico, a radio bulletin cutting through a Patsy Cline lullaby reporting perversion across the border, rogue Mexican cops stopping gringos and robbing the men, raping the women. Jimmy isn't taking a chance with any of that third-world shit, and swears to stay in God's own country.

Mary-Lou hugs him tight, whispers I can't wait to reach paradise, honey, take a swim in the ocean and eat some of that famous gumbo, and he can feel her breasts against him as he leans in close, thinking it's a pity her interest in the cuisine of Louisiana doesn't extend to music, the Cajun and zydeco that's made the state, and the bayou, so respected. He would put the Balfa Brothers right up there with Kitty and Hank, but respects her views. She has no interest in New Orleans either, as she's pure country and hates cities and even big towns, which is just fine with the Rocker, as he has no desire for her to meet his old Taco Bell confederate Freddy Fucker, the dirty-minded pussy pumper quite capable of charming the iron drawers off the meanest San Francisco dyke.

With their destination agreed, Jimmy pushes on into the night, staying inside the speed limit at all times, Mary-Lou brushing his penis as she reaches over for their shared can of Coke, but luckily the sugar in the can has killed any reaction. It is accidental, as Mary-Lou just isn't that kind of girl, living the cleanest of lives, the sort of civic-minded citizen who would admit to dropping a candy wrapper if questioned by law-enforcement officers. Jimmy wonders if Mary-Lou regularly attends church with her family, but doesn't pry, and doesn't really want to know.

While Jimmy would like to travel through the desert landscapes of Texas, New Mexico and Arizona, and sleep under a billion stars and ten thousand meteors in the Grand Canyon, finally reach California and tread the paths laid down by John Fante and Charles Bukowski, right now, more than anything, he wants to see Mary-Lou in a bikini. Stretched out on his freshly clean towel. Even a drifter needs to rest occasionally, and he imagines the sun on his shoulders and Mary-Lou rubbing lotion into his skin. Jimmy concentrates on his driving, heading down the highway towards Baton Rouge, the night closing in and insects bouncing off the windshield, good old boys working on their automobiles outside remote homes, engines lit up by electric lamps, warm air blowing through the window as Mary-Lou tells Jimmy about her family and childhood, the diner where they met, how she nearly married her high-school love, the kid known as Eminem, and how she called it off when he wanted to get fresh, tried to stick his dick where it just didn't belong. I shake my head. There sure are some sick people in this world.

We drive through the night and that coffee is stronger than the usual stuff you find in the States, more like crude oil, a thick sludge of mind-warping caffeine. It is hard to know what Ali would make of the Dream, if he would reject the capitalist ethic for something a little more righteous, or merely rub his hands and set up a felafel stall opposite the nearest Burger King, and I wonder how Mary-Lou would handle this Middle Eastern favourite, served with sesame paste and cracked olives, and I reckon she would love it, fucking right she would, and because she's asleep Jimmy can use the fuck word for emphasis, nothing wrong in that, between men, in a prison environment, all boys together and no women in sight, and my eyes are fixed on the white line, high beams picking out a path through the wilderness same as those old-time explorers, dazzling armadillos and bobcats that stop on the tarmac, dimming the glare so they can escape into the trees, a stag turning to look me in the eye, frozen to the spot, antlers the size of a small tree, and I am slowing right down and easing left as he runs to the right, see his face, the clearest I've seen for months, and he's no buck, this stag is in his prime and has fought many battles and carries the scars, but I keep my concentration, Jimmy driving on, every half-hour or so a vehicle approaching from the opposite direction, lights growing in size and power so he dims his brights, and the other driver does the same, the Rocker feeling the unity of the road, the brotherhood of the traveller, one car selfish and blinding him and looking into the window as it passes Jimmy is shocked to see Homer Simpson laughing at him, the evil tint of that cowardly yellow man making him shake, the back of Homer's automobile full of chained black men in prison dungarees, and in a flash Homer is gone, the sound of a flute playing on the radio, and looking in my rear-view mirror I see the kid accused of flashing the rich lady, bound and gagged in the back seat calling for help, and I try to turn around but the wheel won't budge and I press the brake and find it doesn't work, fight hard to get rid of the faces and regain control of my vehicle. In an instant, morning has broken and blackbird has spoken and a mellow Jimmy Rocker is admiring the Louisiana shoreline.

The sunrise is truly magnificent, patches of godly breath floating across purple-tinged infinity, a huge fireball roaring in from Cuba, turning the beach to golden flakes. Mary-Lou is asleep, her head on Jimmy's shoulder, cleanliness overpowering despite the sultry night the two travellers have just passed through, and he marvels at the fact that women never seem to smell, while men are rancid inside a day. Despite the beauty of the Gulf, Jimmy doesn't wake her, not yet, knowing there are plenty more sunsets to come, that they have all the time in the world. He lets the sun dance across his eyelids, dozing a little at the end of their journey, dreaming sweet dreams, Chuck Berry duck walking across the parking lot, Mary-Lou stirring and rubbing at her eyes, thinking real hard.

The Rocker removes the key from the ignition and the two romancers drop from the cab, yawn and stretch and stroll over to the beach. This place honestly is paradise on earth, the golden sand smooth and deserted, sea reflecting the heavens. They look left and right and try to decide which way to go, suddenly hungry. At the western end of the beach they identify a new restaurant built into the rocks promising pancakes and waffles, big signs showing syrup and sugar and unlimited coffee and root beer for the Rocker. Mary-Lou licks luscious lips. Jimmy points to another eatery in the opposite direction, a ramshackle hut sending out smoke signals and tropical flavours. Jimmy suggests they try this place, but Mary-Lou isn't sure, preferring pancakes to a bowl of chana. A gold-plated crab hurrying across the sand feels their shadows, stops and pretends he is dead, waiting for the two lucky drifters to make up their minds. Waffles and pancakes with sugar and syrup, or a mystery dish from the East is the choice that needs making. Sand fleas nip Mary-Lou's ankles and she squeals, Jimmy, musing at the strange appearance of an Indian cafe out here in Louisiana, reasoning that this is what the free world is all about.

When the loudspeaker calls my name I only hear distortion, Elvis telling me I am wanted at the gate. But that crackling white noise can't really be me. It must be some other misfit, a musty sleepwalker or political crank, but Elvis is no liar. The gate opens and I am let out into the square, Ali slicing cake at the Oasis, coffee brewing, my escort leading me off to see the wizard, the Director in his ivory tower. The guard opens a series of doors and we follow walkways and corridors and suddenly I am in the middle of a crowd of forty or fifty women. They are facing away from me, and I look at the back of their heads and see wiry black and grey hair hanging loose and pulled back and fastened with clips and scarves. It takes me a few seconds to realise this is the visiting area, a circular room with wire coops around the sides, visitors in the centre and prisoners along the perimeter. I am stunned. The noise is incredible. The room is dark and dusty and crowded, but a feminine bouquet beats the decay, a vibrant perfume of soap and scent and nature.

Men and women touch fingertips through the wire, the metal tight and thick, clotted with grime. The visitors are nearly all women. I identify wives, mothers, grandmothers, girlfriends and sisters, several small girls and a couple of boys. It is possible to caress the sadness, reminds me that most of the convicts have people who know and love them. The majority of the women are over fifty. Everyone has a mother. And we love our mothers, whether they are alive or just a memory. It dawns on me that all these men are children. We are older and less intuitive and have mucked things up, made a mess of our lives, but our mothers still love us. I try to guess how these women feel seeing their babies in this rabid house of correction, imprisoned like chickens, five-year-old sons interned with dangerous men, scared and lonely and depressed, their greatest fear that their boy may never come home. Some women cry but most are talking loudly and forcing themselves to laugh, making another sacrifice and lifting spirits. The hum of good news covers the tears, information doctored. Every boy is worth the world to those who love him. Most of all there is forgiveness.

After more doors and locks I am climbing marble stairs that smell of disinfectant, stone walls freshly whitewashed in a soothing cream. We reach a landing, a heavy iron gate barring the rest of the stairwell, the same sight as the tower where the shower block waits. Two steel doors block the corridor running through the walls. My guard knocks on a smaller door and this is opened once we have been inspected through a flap. We enter a large office with a row of filing cabinets along one side, desks and chairs down the other, polish replacing disinfectant. A man in a neat uniform ushers us in, talking to the guard before pointing to a seat. Another guard sits at the far door, a rifle by his side. We sit down. A man in a smart suit works at an antique desk, studying a letter. The office is plush and ordered, the tick of a clock and the rustle of paper the only noise. The silence is golden, a shock to the system, the clean decor impressive.

My escort picks his nails, then chooses a magazine from the table. It could be an upmarket doctor's waiting room rather than the outer circle of a run-down prison. It is hard to believe this office can exist so near our squalor. I feel awkward in this place, but appreciate the sterility and hush. I start wondering whether the Director has ever been on safari, ever stuck his arse over a rat-infested drain and prayed he doesn't have constipation. With a start I notice the green door which must lead to his office. It is wooden rather than tin, and the paint is immaculate, but a smile plays across my face. The guard with the rifle frowns. Nobody speaks. The tick of the clock grows louder. I realise my chair is padded, ponder the crucifixion story.

When the green door opens I jump. We enter a smaller office, with wood panelling and an ornate mirror, my face clear in the glass. It is a shock. That man can't be me. I have only seen my chin in Franco's tiny shaving mirror, but here I am in all my three-dimensional horror. The face is gaunt and skin grey, hair longer than it has been for years. I appear dirty and weak, cheekbones outlined by the light on the ceiling, a touch of yellow I hope is artificial. I fix on the image, which flickers in the glass. It can't be me. Not really. And I try to remember my name, a split second before it returns, glimpse the face of a boy. I am laughing and crying inside and have to look away. By the end of my term I will be a skeleton, a monkey monster, and fuck knows what else I will be seeing. Any regrets I have about leaving my two friends for a place on the farm vanish. Elvis and Franco are backing me, telling me to take the chance and cut my remaining time in half.

A clammy man with braid on the shoulders of his jacket stands in front of me, a huge Slug blocking out the Director's desk. He is mean and sly and probably pulls the legs off injured insects. He has thin slits for eyes and rubbery skin, but despite his size is more office clerk than elite commando, the sort who stamps orders while soldiers fight, then turns up for the interrogation of prisoners. I think of Homer and put him in the same category. Except the Slug has a uniform. And the guard with me stands nearby, making sure I don't attack the Director, while the Slug ensures I join him in a sweat session. A minute passes before he slithers sideways and I face the Director, a middle-aged man with white hair and beard, sitting at a desk fiddling with a fountain pen. His features are vague and without expression, the ultimate administrator, calm in his work. I want to look back at the mirror, see who is standing here now, a small boy facing a headmaster or a grown man meeting a judge.

The walls of the office press in and the oxygen squeezes out, lungs filling with smoke as my heart smoulders. There is no smoke without fire, that is what they say. No smoke without fire. Don't play with matches. That is more good advice. My chest heaves and skin peels as I take the place of the man on the cross, knowing the crucifixion really did happen, that it is fact rather than myth, a bent jump of faith that has me looking through the eyes of the dying man and seeing that beautiful ocean in the distance, wishing I could flap my nailed arms and soar out of the valley, dive down into the water and quench my thirst, shoot back up into the heavens and head for home with a flock of returning geese. I pull back and concentrate on open fields and fragrant orchards and a liberal work ethic, this partial freedom so near, the Director with the power to halve my sentence with one scratch of his nib.

Silence reigns in court as I wait for him to look at me and speak. I notice the framed photographs of men in various army and prison uniforms, what looks like a young Director standing in the sun next to a chapel, revolver in hand, another one on a sandy beach where he is gazing out to sea, and I run my eyes over these pictures fast, servants of the state proud of their decades of service. In a way this is my appeal hearing. Things can only get better, and I relax a little, keen to make a good impression, the Director raising his head, hands in front of his chest, the beady eyes of the Slug on me, and I imagine him staying inside while the crucified man bakes, knowing direct sunlight would kill him. I almost laugh, but stop myself. Over the Director's shoulder I see rooftops through the window, a small section of glass without bars, a few hundred slates and a yawning sky enough to make me tremble.

The Director leans forward and speaks to the Slug, keeping his eyes firmly on my face, voice relaxed, almost melodious, mouth breaking into a faint, welcoming smile. The crucifixion story is ridiculous. This is a man who loves God's children, the misbehaving scallywags put into his care for protection and rehabilitation. He understands the truth about the human soul, that we are all the sons and daughters of the Almighty. Even the Slug, who listens to the Director's message. I glance at the sky and stop trembling, know it was formed through the power of love and free will, my brain floating in gallons of rich, stimulating blood, Elvis standing on his head and returning from the dead, lifting our spirits, and I am listening to the sound of the prison god, the Director, unable to understand a word he says. It is wrong to listen to rumours and spread lies. The Director is a good man, I know that now, a patriarch who hates the sin and loves the sinner.

The Slug speaks to me in very good English, which is a surprise, and asks about my crime. He is my new translator. The Director watches me closely. The Slug also asks about my punishment, whether this is fair, and I try to explain that I am really an innocent man. I feel the sentence was harsh, although I am not criticising the system, I understand why it was handed out, and as a foreigner it is tough here, without my two friends I would go mad. I pick words carefully, know not to insult their system or threaten egos. I am not evil and a threat to nobody and will work hard if I can transfer to a work prison. The farm will benefit from my presence. The Director nods, thoughtfully, and I see the faces of holy men and women inside wooden frames, decorating the walls of the office, halos around their heads, intricate colours that glow as if they are made from stained glass, the atmosphere more relaxed now, heat coming off a radiator, and I explain how the case against me was distorted, even though I accept my punishment. I want to earn my freedom. The Director and Slug talk calmly, the boss leaning back in his chair, considering my humble application.

I am in the great outdoors again, in a field cutting hay, working in a vineyard, building walls and pitting olives, anything that needs doing I will do it, counting my days at the end of the week, on Sunday, my day of rest, and if I have to go to church then I will, ready to sing twice as loud as the other worshippers, and I am praying that I leave for the farm today, in twenty minutes or half an hour or even in a few days. I will do anything to get away from Seven Towers, and my spirits go off into orbit, the farm is the place for this Jimmy Too Good, that is where I belong, and I focus on the pen in the Director's hand, willing it to sign an order, I can taste oranges and smell lemons, look at his desk, admire the leather blotter covered with the doodlings of a thoughtful man, an official stamp with a black ink-pad, and maybe they will burn wax over the stamp to make it secure, hand me a certificate when I walk out of the front gate.

The Director lurches forward and smashes his fist down on the desk. I stagger back, steadied by the guard, even the Slug jolting. The sky vanishes and the walls collapse as he shouts and screams and stands up and turns red with rage and I am right back in court with the judge, his eyes bulging and teeth gritting. The Slug translates that I am a bad man, a guilty man with no respect for the law, no respect for the people of the land in which I am a visitor, do I think I can lie and cheat and expect favours from the very people I insult? I will not go to a farm. Things have been too easy for me and they will not be made any better. I must serve the whole of my sentence here. Every single day. He points at the door and I return to the block, don't see another soul all the way back, pass through the visiting area and don't notice the mothers and sons, shocked and belittled and feeling stupid, finally angry as the C-Block gate shuts behind me, knowing I haven't been given a fair chance.

My friends Elvis and Franco listen as I tell them about the Director's tantrum, and they are sympathetic but unsurprised. Elvis reminds me of the crucified prisoner. He explains that the system is fucked, however secular it pretends to be it is still based on the angry writings of a harsh desert society. I must see that failing to admit my guilt means I am wicked. The system insists I am denying the truth. How can the process move forward if I won't accept their judgement? Franco joins in, that is why my friend is in the hospital being treated for a drug addiction he does not have. Elvis says this is wrong, to admit to things we have not done, we must be strong and not surrender, this is the spirit that built the new world, that I am right to say what I did but can't be surprised at the reaction. Franco insists that if I want privileges I must lie and say I am wrong and they are right. It is as simple as that. I lay back and close my eyes, head pounding, nausea returning, leave Franco and Elvis to argue over tactics. I tried and failed. I am devastated, but at least I have my friends.

When the food bell rings two hours later it sets off an earthquake, hands shaking me awake, four guards talking fast, and Elvis is saying I have to gather my belongings quickly and go with them, right now, and the Director must have changed his mind and granted my request and I am going to the farm, sadness overwhelming me as I look at Elvis and Franco and realise I will miss them, touched when I see how angry Elvis is becoming. Franco is confused and asks what is happening, one of the guards pulling my bag out from under my bed and another prodding me with his stick and they are in a hurry and want to get me in the van, pulling me into the aisle and pushing me to the door out past the men heading towards Chef who is startled by the commotion and Elvis is shouting at the guards and one turns and hits him in the face and this doesn't stop the rocking drifter and he is trotting along next to me saying that the Director is wrong, a man can never be innocent in his eyes, and the Director has told the guards that I am a bad man who shows no humility and does not repent for his sins, that I have spat in the face of God Himself, and that I am being moved to B-Block.

Living a free and easy life, Jimmy Drifter moves from train station to bar, drinking with the poets and philosophers, travelling on without a care in the world as he leaves a series of beautiful women gasping in his wake. What the men in suits don't understand is that the likes of the Drifter avoid complications and break no hearts, operating with total respect for their surroundings. We take people at their word as we educate ourselves at the best university, grabbing every opportunity life offers. Eventually we reach a crossroads and end up sitting alone on an empty beach eating an apple, the fruit extra crunchy and double delicious, little meat left on the core by the time we finish. We study the seeds and lift one out, crack it between our teeth. It is bitter and we throw the rest towards the tree line where the core will rot and the seeds can seep back into the earth. One day apple trees will grow here, and we think of Jimmy Appleseed, the distant unsung cousin of the more famous Johnny.

A bus brings me out of town, a rattler packed with peasants returning from the vegetable market, laughing men and women carrying empty boxes and baskets, a few unsold apples and loaves of bread. They have had a good day and are busy spoiling the outsider, offering drinks and teasing me as I try and keep my balance, hanging on to a pole, accepting three apples and a bag of plums, finally jumping off at a deserted bend when I see the sign for the campsite. I walk down a dusty lane listening to the birds sing, heading for the coast. The campsite is easy to find. It is also deserted. This is okay by me. Summer is over, but it is still warm as I eat my bread and cheese, two of the apples and every plum, a container of olives and a stumpy little cucumber with tough skin and succulent flesh. It is a proper feast. Full, I rest my head on my bag and watch the sun sink down, find it is suddenly very cold and dark. The birds have stopped singing and there is rustling in the trees, followed by grunting. There is little moonlight and no electricity and I stumble to some nearby cabins, prise open a door and hurry inside, settle down on a bed, a snorting sound at the door, more wild pig than vicious monkey. The night is cold and I wrap up tight, glad I have spent good money on this sleeping bag.

In the morning I stroll along a deserted beach and swim in the sea, sink my head below the surface and blow air out of my lungs, rise up and breathe again, right along the bay to the rocks, then back to my clothes. I dry off and dress and walk along the coast towards the chapel. I am no sightseer, no museum hopper, but the area is said to be stunning and this information is sound. From the headland I can see for miles. I am exhilarated, by the swim and the isolation, the air and a realisation that this landscape hasn't changed for hundreds of years. The peasants on the bus could be from another century, with their traditional clothes and tougher skin, every person knowing everyone else. I walk faster, keen to reach my destination.

I pass rocks and wind my way over a granite ridge to a small bay. This is also deserted, apart from a single fishing boat gently rocking on the water. The chapel rests on the crest of a hill and stands out, shining pure white in the sun. I start up through boulders that have slid out of a crack in the coastline, quickly find a path that bends through a cornfield. It is an easy walk. Pine trees spread across the slope behind the chapel, a dirt road leading inland and disappearing round a bend. I approach the building and stop, look past the trees and into a valley where wild grass blows in the breeze, a swaying army of nodding helmets, billions of stalks moving in time to a militia band, and I can't help wondering how many billions of pods are in there waiting for an air current to lift the seeds out and carry them away on the wind. I think of Jimmy Appleseed again, switching to flowers, scattering corn. It is easy to feel humble before God, even though I am not a firm believer. The chapel ahead of me is clearly a spiritual house with an aura that has nothing to do with anger and retribution and worldly possessions. This is a place where good and evil no longer exist. It is far beyond such limitations.

Standing still for a long time, looking out over a timeless land, I am glad I broke away from the railway tracks and bus routes and congestion of city life. It is easy to end up on the traveller's conveyor belt. Without a car or bike I can only go where public transport takes me, realise I need to think differently, buy a pickup truck or settle somewhere and educate myself. I am searching, but short of money and need to work. This shortage worries me, but being out here is almost a holiday, which seems ridiculous for a drifter. Nothing matters in this place.

These peasants have few luxuries and don't seem to care. They live their lives the same as their ancestors did, and this forces me to consider my own restlessness, if there is something rotten in my genes. I think of my father and am suddenly jealous of this community and the calm its people enjoy, their

peace of mind and beautiful chapel and everything it represents and contains, every slab of stone and crucifix and hymn
and religious icon. But I control this jealousy and press on,
enter the chapel. And it is tiny, even smaller than it appears
from the outside, with six pews on either side of the aisle and
brilliant white walls. I stand in silence and smell the plaster
and incense. Feel my breath so steady it could almost have
stopped. A man's voice is a surprise, but doesn't startle me.

An elderly priest approaches and extends a hand, shakes
mine with a grip that belongs to a younger and much stronger
man. He invites me to sit under a window and drink lemonade,
explains how he once lived in London, where he studied for
three years. The lemonade is cool and fizzy and very sweet,
and I sip politely when really I want to guzzle. We chat for a
long time in a purple shadow, light flooding through stained
glass, and looking to the source I see Jesus crucified on the
cross, his halo out of proportion to the rest of the picture,
wonder if anyone knows the names of the men who created
this masterpiece. Dust particles dance in the light and make
me understand infinity and I honestly know that there is no
more right or wrong way of behaving, and it is as if this has
all happened to me before. The priest tells me that Jesus was
a travelling man who passed on the trade routes through Persia
and gained his knowledge in India and Tibet, and that only
by ridding himself of possessions and desire can a man find
salvation. He believes Jesus is more Hindu and Buddhist than
Jew, and that too many Christians have lost their spirituality.

This priest is very old. Nearly ninety he says, as if reading
my mind, and when I congratulate him on the chapel he
shrugs and says it is only a building, and while it is God's
house, God really dwells in our hearts. We drink more
lemonade, until the jug is empty, and then he takes me on a
tour, pointing out various saints framed in wood, a small icon
that is worth a lot of money, but which his congregation do
not even notice. The forgotten things are sometimes the most
precious. Its financial value means nothing to the people who
worship here, men and women who never travel far, content
in their lives. The priest smiles and places his hand on my arm,

reassures me that wealth and possessions are not important, as if he understands that I am short of money. People never lock their doors in this area as there is no theft, and no need to steal. The chapel is always open to strangers. If gangsters come from the city and rob this place he will not care. Attachment to anything, especially religious objects, is wrong. He holds his hand over his heart, emphasising that his words are important. He shuffles his rosary beads, counting but unworried, at peace with the universe.

Eventually he checks his watch and says he must leave. He has to visit a friend. She is one hundred and three years old and suffering from a cold. She is strong and independent and comes to the chapel twice a week, but now it is his turn to travel. He will walk to her house and it will take him twenty minutes. I am free to stay for as long as I want, to sleep on the floor tonight if need be. I look at the priest and know everything he says is heartfelt. This is a great man, the first I have ever met, face purple in the light, gentle lines on his forehead blood red. He wishes me a safe journey and shakes my hand again. We go outside and I watch as he walks towards the trees, following the track and fading from sight. I consider his words and feel part of his flock. With a priest such as this there is no such thing as an outsider. No man is a stranger in his eyes. He has offered me assistance. I look back at the chapel and think of the icon, the money it will bring, the food and shelter it can buy, and the fact that the locals won't even notice it is gone. The priest will be pleased.

In a few hours I will be on a bus, absorbed in the crowd, lost in another city. This is the life of Jimmy Drifter, the wandering man taking what is offered and offending nobody, and I walk back into the chapel and reach for the icon, look at the painting and see St Christopher carrying a small boy over water, shake my head as I realise the priest was blessing me in his own subtle way. It is an omen. I slip the icon into my bag and leave the chapel, head back along the coast, taking a path instead of the beach, moving briskly, the sun peeking in and out of the clouds, fifteen minutes later spotting a whirl-wind of dust in the distance and running to the crossroads and waving at the approaching bus which slows and nearly stops and I am running and jumping aboard, engine shifting down a gear and the machine lurching forward, picking up speed once more. I rest by the window and watch the fields pass, think of the chapel and the priest and all these content people, and as the bus sails away I feel my jealousy slowly fade, the peace of mind of the priest and his humble flock already rubbing off and making me a better man.

B-BLOCK

THIS IS WHERE they put the scum, men who are morally corrupt, extra retribution for the psychopaths, murderers, sadists, beasts, junkies, blasphemers and anyone else decent people scorn. The reputation of B-Block is carved into Seven Towers folklore, a slow torture wing where the knives are drawn and laced with narcotics, the terror of my arrival returning ten times over, nausea churning heavy-duty acid. Fear loosens my guts and I think I am going to dirty myself. That would be a great start, standing in the spotlight on the edge of the yard, paddling in my own muck. A new level of fact-based paranoia tells me the Director has planned this from the moment I stepped through his hallowed gates, allowing the alien to settle and make friends, find some security with Elvis and Franco, a snide bully offering comfort to a scared child and then snatching it away when he feels safe. I have walked straight into his trap, the Director sitting back and waiting for me to come begging. I am starting over, looking at the same-style wing but this time full of Homer's hardcore, another gate slamming shut behind me, bolt jammed into place, the sound echoing through the yard, shaking my confidence and turning heads.

Prisoners pack the ledge, snapping beads from palm to fist, chains tight on bare knuckles, every stroke laced with violence, bodies hunched forward, eyes darting left, right, left, right inside rigid skulls, too many faces shaded by hoods. There is no C-Block apathy here, the tension obvious, aggression fluid, metal chains and plastic beads racing a pounding heart, the scar on my forehead a beatbox neon pleading please leave me alone, please, I don't want any trouble, the eyes on the ledge stabbing into me, searching for an excuse. I am scared they will see through my disguise and identify more lowlife, the haggard skulls of splintered junkies straining as they search for revelation, a black aura lining the alien's frame, eyes flickering with recognition, muscles flexed, smoke rising from cigarettes in angry trails circling and forming spirals that hover and fade and finally melt away. My kneecaps ache and I could topple over, but instead of crumbling like a coward I kneel down and tighten a shoelace, do my best to act nonchalant and gain a few seconds, deciding what to do next.

Beyond the ledge, at the bottom of the stairwell, a pack of monkey monsters sit around a massive figure in striped pyjamas. This is the killer Papametropolis, better known as Papa. His oblong head is plastered with shaggy black hair and an uneven beard, jaw square and made of stone. He is also wearing a woolly jumper, thick socks and boots. His eyes are lowered into the book he reads and I jump seeing the knitting needle towards the back, as if used as a marker. The prisoners around him are as skinny as Papa is bulky, their heads shaved beyond stubble, a jumble of hollow simian cheeks and skeleton frames. They are watching me as one, black shadows patching eyes, monkey monsters and a gulag keeper, and I notice that their hands are empty and still. They click no beads and smoke no tobacco, merely sit in the jungle and stare. Papa turns a page and I look away fast. I know all about these monsters.

I stand and prepare to move forward, choosing the bottom tier, a man pushing me from behind as if I am in his way, or he is trying to knock me over, and I swivel and back off two steps, start to apologise and see his snarl, tell him to fuck off instead, everyone in this jail knows fuck and fuck you and some even laugh fuck you motherfucker, and he shows more teeth and moves his hips as if he is shagging a goat, grumbling fucky fucky, you and me fucky fucky, and I say you fucky fucky me fisty fisty, hold my hands up like a prize boxer. He smirks and groans and walks away leaving me on my own with the eyes of the ledge men on me, and I don't waste time, aim for the block, glancing at the inmates but avoiding eye contact, focusing on the bricks and glass as if I am honestly interested in the architecture of this fine old reform palace, fine lines dedicated to the elevation of the human spirit rather than its suppression. It is a long walk, the clank of the beads growing, a pungent smell of tobacco forcing smoke into my lungs so it is hard to breathe. I methodically place one foot in front of the other, reach past the ledge and enter the section.

The room is near enough deserted, the noise and smell of the yard shut out. A couple of sleepwalkers doss under blankets, but nothing like the numbers on C-Block. I don't hang around, find an unused bed, the nearest one, knowing it is a lucky dip whether I end up between knifemen or junkies. I bend down and sniff the mattress, make sure it didn't belong to a bed-wetter. It seems fine, regular issue, old and musty and drenched in sweat. Pulling it off the frame I give it a good shake, dead silverfish and a cockroach falling to the floor, killed by the powder that follows, and I turn the mattress over, arrange my blanket, lift the pillow and smell oil and wax, one side worse than the other. I puff it up and place it at the top of the bed, drop my bag on the floor, then, thinking, lift the bag up and slide it under the pillow, knowing this won't stop a thief, but making it a little harder. Sitting on the edge of the mattress I inspect the room, and it is laid out in the same way, with two rows of beds and the table and benches and stove and logs in the centre and the green safari door at the end. Everything is the same except for the occupants. I imagine the Director in his wood-panelled office, laughing as he signs decrees, the Slug washing away his sticky trail, smiling obediently.

The more power someone like the Director has, the greater his cruelties, and I think about the crucifixion, and maybe it is not supposed to be taken literally, the story invented by the small men to explain the actions of the big man. But his rage in the office stays with me and I understand that the Director really did nail a human being up in the sun to burn to death, and I see myself in a few years released and moving on, going to the island where the crucified man died and finding his remains in the rubbish dump, a broken skeleton in with the splintered wood of the cross, covered in mushrooms and animal carcasses and red metal. I will carefully collect and carry his bones down to the beach, wash them in the ocean and let the salty water soak in, and when they are clean I will swim out as far as I can before the currents and sharks attack, lay the forgotten prisoner to rest in deep water, where there is no chance of his remains being washed back to shore. I will say some words, though not a proper prayer, and then return to land, spread out in the sun and dry and move into the shade of a palm and recuperate, visit a chapel and drink lemonade with a man who can advise me, plan my next move to perfection.

Returning to the city I will track the Director down. It won't be hard. All I have to do is wait outside Seven Towers and follow him home to his six-bedroom villa, an acre of land-scaped gardens and chlorine-drenched swimming pool, a centre of rest and relaxation where he can play out the role of kindly family man instead of bully and murderer, watch him chomping steak with his neighbours, a collection of judges prosecutors translators politicians journalists, everyone I resent gathered in a single setting, the Slug in the background serving cocktails, out of his league. I will slip into the villa itself, hide in his wardrobe with his wife's ballgowns and mink wraps, his brats busy with their toys, tell myself I am going to do them a favour when I kill him – *cut his fucking throat* – but I can only go so far, know I am not that sort of man. I am a good boy. Control my imagination, tugged towards childhood against my will, but holding firm.

A scrawny monkey monster scuttles into the room, chattering as he lopes towards me, and I prepare to defend myself, remember they are weaker during the day, fists clenched, toes on the floor, but he keeps going, down the length of the section and off on safari. The door bounces shut and I hear him scream on the edge of a barren plateau, the soft pad of a hunter's feet on the jungle floor below, Papa strolling along the aisle. I sit back down, hypno-tised by the knitting needle in his hand, the pyjama man staring dead ahead, through bricks and time, banging on the green door to scare the wildlife before he goes inside. Tin quakes. Settles down. Screaming sets it off again and my skin crawls, but I do nothing. A minute passes before the door opens and Papa returns, needle dripping red water, and he examines me as he walks, growing in size until he is ten feet tall and the needle is a spear dipped in blood. His eyes are black and soulless and he knows all about my sort. He doesn't care about punches and damaged cars and stolen icons, beyond pride and envy and jealousy. He knows the truth. Passes and leaves the section. It is only a matter of time before he comes for me. Paranoia rules.

How the fuck did I end up in this place? Elvis asked me the question and I couldn't answer. There must be a simple reason, but I can't work it out, an injured monkey appearing, face blotched, a clot of blood on his calf where he has been stabbed. This dangerous beast limps along and I trail him with my eyes until he turns and shouts, full of hate, spitting a curse, continuing on his way, the food bell banging in my head so I grab my bowl and spoon and follow him out into the yard where he veers left to the stairs while I stand in line, the men in front of me talking among themselves, the ones behind staring past, and I search for contact, a chance to smile and nod, exchange syllables, find none. I am ignored, yet know everyone is watching, looking away the moment I turn. My spine shrivels and the intense nausea I knew two months ago is with me again, the sickly medicine of a quack anaesthetist. The line moves forward, and I know nothing, not a single word, guards swinging sticks, hands on holstered revolvers, clasping rifles, glaring at us so hard that I focus on the ground, wonder what my pals Elvis and Franco are doing, see them sitting on the ledge eating and mourning, and I am facing Chef and smiling into a chubby blank expression, and he fills my bowl with rice and beans, and when I stay where I am he adds a few more beans, thin slices of what look like carrots in with the mush, keen to serve the next man and get away.

It would be easier to eat alone, to hide inside and keep my head down, wait for events to unravel, imagine this is a chilli made with kidney beans and green peppers, heavily spiced, a cold beer to wash it down, but this is my first meal and it is not going to happen. I can't hide. Have to prove a point. Sit on the end of the ledge nearest the door and get stuck into soggy grain and soft pulses, grateful as ever for the warmth of the grease. I force myself to count every mouthful, the food line shrinking, almost finished when the monsters move. They leave Papa reading, the starving monkey he chased on safari carrying two bowls, Chef frowning at their hollow heads, dishing out one serving each, and the monsters accept their ration, this small army capable of ripping the fat man to shreds in seconds, happy eating enough to stay alive. The food detail leaves and I am inside my bowl spooning nourishment home, the only way to handle this mess, a monastic life where we eat to survive and not for pleasure. And I feel the loneliness of the police-station cell, my good luck in being put on C-Block, a flash memory of the prison chapel, the punches and humiliation of taunting guards, and now this B-Block mob completing the set. Fuck them all. Papa and the stabbed monkey and Mr Fucky Fucky, who is the same as the chapel guards, Porky Pig and his lamb-chopped teeth, and I think of the Director and the Slug, my courtroom judge and prosecutor and translator, and that horrible little I-fuck-your-mother nonce selling ice-cream cones. I finish eating and look up at the castle wall, nearly puke seeing vultures in place of the hawks walk over to the sink.

My gear is still there when I go back inside, and I make a big show of arranging my mug and bowl and spoon on the windowsill, put my calendar up, finally sit down and stare at the wall for a long time, floating with the grease in my belly, putting off the inevitable safari. It starts to rain and men filter into the room, ready for lock-up. The minutes crawl and my stomach rumbles, guts churning, and I can't put it off any longer, hurry to the green door and bang loud enough for the rats to hear, rush in and crouch down. Someone is in the other cubicle groaning and this safari is even worse than C-Block, a dirtier slice of the same jungle experience, full-on piss humidity off the equator, bouts of gastroenteritis and dysentery. Liquid fear flows and I clean up fast, wash and get out, in time to see a guard counting heads, return to my bed and nod at the men on either side. They blank me. Look away. And the time I have left may as well be life if that is how it is going to be. I scan the beds, but can't see any other foreigners, just melted skin where faces should be, the table crowded with domino and card players.

Darkness blacks out the windows and monkey monsters dim the lights in the far corner by hanging clothes over the bulbs, forming shadow puppets, Papa wedged into the angle of the two walls. The stabbed monkey lights a large yellow candle, positioned on a wooden locker, the flame jumping and settling down, adding to the shapes on the wall and ceiling. Smaller candles are spread around it, dripping wax used as glue. A faint smell of honey filters through the smouldering logs and cigarettes, candles shielded by the bodies of monsters shrouded in blankets. At the other end of the room there is an argument going on between a long-haired freak and two shaven-headed youths, the kids laughing at the older man in sandals, his verbals stronger than his frail appearance. He is moving his hands to emphasise a point, the youths unable to match his fluency, answering with a sneer. They are powerful and dismissive, more interested now in a tattooed character holding the arm of another prisoner, needle and ink removed from a silk pouch.

The tattoo man studies virgin skin, uncorks his ink and dips in what looks like a sewing needle. He takes his time, talking softly as he works, tilting his head enquiringly and making those around him nod and laugh. I squint to see lines form, realise what I am doing and lay back, lower my eyelids, keep watching, but without staring. I don't want any trouble, kidding myself I can fade into the background. I follow the needle and see an outline form, and this is given creases and developed further, two legs sprouting, a womb gorged with blood and ink feeding the embryo. The curve of the lines means they belong to a woman and I see hips form, followed by breasts, which are hidden behind a bathing costume. This man is a craftsman, drawing arms and hands, and I think even shading fingernails, but I am too far away to be sure. He finishes with a neck and head, fills in the face and makes sure it is round and happy and a perfect sweetheart for the genial Mr Fair. Hair reaches down to the woman's shoulders. He has planned ahead and left space in the shoulders for it to dangle and reach the breasts. When he is done he admires his work, looks around at the small crowd that has gathered, and they murmur their approval.

Prisoners stand in a huddle discussing the tattoo, pointing at the woman and laughing, and I start drifting along the edge of coma, struggling to keep my eyes open, knowing sleep will leave me open to attack. These men could be using the tattoo as an excuse, waiting for my breathing to settle before launching an assault, and I try to imagine the woman in the tattoo coming to life, but it is someone else's image and doesn't work, and anyway, I have Ramona. It would be best to take my mind out of the section, but I can't seem to move, hear the coughing of perverts waiting for the outsider to fade, and I am not going to give them the satisfaction. Most important of all I have to keep an eye on those monkey monsters in the corner, make sure they are not crawling along the floor and gathering under my bed. I push every good and bad thought away and concentrate on staying awake.

Lightning strikes and rocks the boys and I wake to the pop of a voyeur flashbulb glimpsing the faces of police and welfare workers vision blurred as their expressions fade and the darkness rushes back in and swamps me and the lights are out and that thunderbolt must have connected with the power supply and I can feel the electricity crackling under my skin turning it to pig gristle a royal shock to the system and it is dead black outside heavy rain clouds suffocating the moon and stars and there is some serious anger crashing around in the heavens and I hold my charm and wish for another strike but it doesn't come and the hum of the blackness makes my ears bubble there is some tossing and turning but nobody else seems to be awake how can they sleep through thunder and lightning it is impossible to see anything at all the darkness is total and there could easily be a face right in front of mine and I wouldn't know and some creatures have night vision they eat their carrots and can see without a sun or its reflection and I try to feel the breath of a stalker but smell no milky tea or banana sandwiches keep perfectly still and I am terrified of the dark always sleep with the light on at home and at times like this I can't help thinking of Mum and I want to call out to her but she won't be able to hear and I think of Nana and water fills my eyes and I don't cry none of the boys ever cry that is what a sissy does but even so we do it under the covers or into our pillows and I keep my face above the edge of my magic blanket hoping my eyes will adjust and find something to focus on but there is no glimmer and the rain is tapping on the windows and it is best to try and be calm and wait for the electricity to return or the clouds to leave and my back itches as if ants are nibbling at my spine maybe it is an earwig or a beetle but of course they don't come into these starched sheets as there is nothing here for them no food or dirty shelter and it is more than a scratch and the horror hits me and there are monkey monsters hiding under the bed and their long razor fingers are pushing at the canvas and trying to unravel loose threads and they are working their nails through the canvas cracking iron-bolt knuckles digging into the mattress and I am petrified and can't move imagining the half-skeleton heads of these semi-human monsters grinning and hungry and about to rip me to threads and eat me alive and why can't they leave me alone the sound of the jungle is inside my head and their jabbering madness is destroying me they are inside the mattress and coming round the sides of my bed clambering along the frame swinging on springs prehistoric teeth pulling at the sheets tearing the edge of my blanket and the dark is remorseless and more furry hands are reaching from above and I am surrounded by monsters and the bad boys are out of their beds this tribe of orphan monkeys stuck in a strange zoo without a climbing frame and they are about to kill me and the lightning strikes and explodes outside and I wake up and the lights come on and the dormitory is silent every sad boy fast asleep and it smashes into the earth again and dents the prison yard and I wake and sit up sweating and look around and find the section quiet full of dozing men and the monsters huddled together staring into their yellow candle.

The next few days drag and I am stuck in isolation, which seeing as there are around fifty men in the section and a hundred on the block is worse than being in solitary. The days are bad, the nights worse. I try talking to other prisoners, but nobody is interested. I am shunned, kid myself I can handle it, see zombies in the same state, burnt-out shells mumbling to themselves and never raising their eyes, one loner Dumb Dumb making no sound at all, forever fiddling with a pile of dead matches he collects from the floor and keeps in a sock. One night he produces a tube of glue and starts sticking them together. He is disturbed, but more sad than mad, and not as worrying as men who answer their own questions, nodding and shaking heads, jerking back and laughing loud when there is nothing to even smile about. And all the while the monkey monsters sit around their candle by night, on the stairs by day. They never seem to sleep. Just watch and plot their attack.

I waste time the same as Baker and those plastic gangsters and all the C-Block men I never understood, marching up and down the yard and not caring what anyone thinks, joining the flow. I spend many hours in the section with the zombies, B-Block's more serious brand of sleepwalker, eat Chef's food and wash my face and go on safari. Try to think positive. Get drawn to the Director and the farm and C-Block, and when I am exhausted Mum and Nana and the good times. At night I do my best to get back on Paradise Beach with Mary-Lou, but that Gulf sun is a low-wattage bulb now, the sultry air of the bayou tainted, the insects silent and a hunter on the move. Men wait to attack me and proper self-defence means I need a weapon, a glass knife removed from a broken window. And all the while the other inmates pretend to sleep, waiting for me to relax, more lights dimmed and grey areas forming, and there is this nagging pressure to look under my bed, like a soppy boy checking for monsters, but I fight the temptation, finally give in, find nothing but a squashed cockroach. I feel stupid, begin wondering if I looked closely enough, each night worse than the last.

When the talking stops, the voices start, and hearing men in conversation is reassuring, makes me invisible. The lights are switched on at night and never turned off and I hate to think what would happen if they were. The thought of a power cut really is a nightmare. I am a child unable to sleep, worrying about life and death, the belch of a pipe and a gust of wind slamming a door. There is more silence, which deepens, my ears burning, an insect dialect in my brain, part earwig and part caterpillar, giving way to urgent whispers. The warnings are brutal. Usually they can be blocked out. With imagination, movement, fantasy. Right now there is no escape. Arguments start, voices chipping away, snickering, turning to threats, accusations it takes great strength to ignore. Night is when we are at our weakest. And most dangerous. Tiredness wears me down, everything left dedicated to self-defence, defending the self against this other sick fucker, the enemy within with his nagging doubts and lazy cruelty. That Louisiana beach changes as alchemy reverses, gold turning to base metal, hardening to a train-station platform, worldly possessions tucked into a meagre kitbag slung over a shoulder, a one-way ticket in my pocket. Memories become twisted. Wishful thinking meets déjà vu meets fact, and I know that everything that is going to happen has already happened, and is happening at this moment. How can I see the sea so clearly and feel the sand and smell the salt if past, present and future haven't merged?

Mary-Lou is leading me by the hand towards a breakfast of pancakes and waffles and maybe I will have some freshly squeezed orange juice, and we are sitting under the shade of a Coca-Cola canopy reclining in comfortable chairs and following the pointed finger of the owner to an alligator stepping from a swamp, and I look at his boots and they are made from the skin of a dinosaur and the beast stops and yawns and shows off teeth that are no match for a hunter's rifle, technology stronger than muscle, brain over brawn, eyes rolling inside handbag fabric, tail swaying as he ducks back out of sight and loses himself in mangrove, the thud of the jungle drowning out cumbersome footsteps and cracking branches. A Hindu boy taps a coconut with a machete and drains the milk, breaks off slabs of white meat, and he is thin and shoeless and smiling and Mary-Lou is shaking her head and saying no thank you, sipping her Coke, preferring the corporate can.

Paradise vanishes in a flash of a necrophiliac's cough, the belching fart of his cancerous prison stomach. And a few days in the countryside is enough, all most people expect, the city pulling us back towards civilisation, the bustle of the opium-lost masses blocking any deeper sense of loneliness. It is hard to be lonely surrounded by people, in a crowded metropolis, but somehow I have managed it, and this is the suicide version. There is nowhere to run, no horizon or distraction, the only direction deeper inside myself, off into the tunnel, but I know I have to stay on the outside, skim the surface and ride the waves, Jimmy Rocker keeping things simple but having problems. The door is bolted and the walls shifting in and I try to get to Mary-Lou, back to the Gulf of Mexico, try to feel the space of America, its luxurious material comforts, but fail.

When you are a child there is a time when you realise life isn't how you thought. The idea of death fills your head and, because it doesn't make sense, won't go away. Time is static for a boy, until he hears about death. It is talked about and feared and obsessed over by those around him and suddenly there is a cut-off point when the good times end. A bone-crushing dread descends and stays with him for the rest of his life. Men invent religious and scientific theories and say they know the truth about life and death and, most importantly, an afterlife, but they don't. They have their beliefs and convince themselves the thing they want to believe in most is beyond doubt, and call it faith, but they are never certain. They stop listening. Tell children fairy tales where witches cast spells and ghosts walk through walls, a cartoon universe of malignant spirits and child snatchers. The life the boy took for granted is lost for ever. This fear of the night stays inside people like me.

With a physical effort I force myself back to that crossroads deep in Mississippi, and even though the Gulf has its attractions I don't want to travel the same highway again, turn right instead, head west towards Texas with Jimmy Rocker, that crazy wandering man with a cold root beer in his hand and a cheeseburger in his belly, and I am laughing, have finally pulled it off, back on the road with Hank Williams on the radio and popcorn wedged into the handbrake. Mary-Lou is next to the Rocker singing along with her hair blowing in a hot wind. She is alive and free and in love with Jimmy, and when she's by his side there is no such thing as night, only daylight where others know darkness, placing popcorn on the end of his tongue with a long purple fingernail, salt- not honey-flavoured, and Jimmy is rocking and rolling and reeling and rocking, putting his foot down as he heads for roadrunner country.

But I have no stamina. The effort is too hard and I can't do the drifting man justice, poor Jimmy accelerating away from a posse of police cars, good old boys leaning out of windows firing rifles, red-faced as they scream abuse calling him one dumb son of a bitch. He doesn't understand what he's done wrong, why these state troopers hate him so much they want to kill him for a speeding violation, so he panics, increases his speed and churns dust, heading towards the next motel, a free swimming pool and all-you-can-eat buffet, only problem being he won't be able to stop. He is in some serious shit. Approaching an intersection. Doesn't know where he's going or what he's doing. He is confused and scared and wishes he had never left home. And I fight for control of the Rocker, struggle to turn the steering wheel, but he turns right and hits a dirt road, bounces along gravel with the sheriff in hot pursuit, a clump of thirsty pines laughing as he passes. The Rocker can hear police voices over the banjo-picking on his radio, and a right-eous preacher, the Bible-bashing Billy Bob Bush is telling the world that Mr Elvis Presley is old and fat and dead and buried and they are going to string this Jimmy Rocker cocksucker up and cut his balls off and if they can't do that they are going to fry him in Warhol's own electric chair, and Jimmy looks for Mary-Lou but she has bailed out, realises she is nothing but a good-time girl who knows the drifting man is a no-good two-bit loser.

The sound of a man shouting takes over from the bashing of Bibles and engines and for a few seconds I think it is the Rocker captured and confined, look down the section and see a junkie waltzing along the middle of the room, head bobbing on stiff shoulders, a red balloon that makes me think of Elvis doing a headstand, this one covered in red paint. He reaches the door and starts banging with pink fists, forearms ripped open and blood spurting from long gashes, covering his skin and clothes, forming a puddle around his feet. The noise is incredible. Men are on their feet yelling at him while others are at the windows calling out to the guards. One man laughs. High-pitched, lunatic laughter. They are angry. That they have been woken up. That the junkie has ended up in this state. Angry with themselves for being here.

The bleeding man reels back, starts shouting at those nearest the door, turning and running to a window where he jumps up on the sill and starts kicking at the bars, his foot squeezing through and shattering glass. His foot starts to bleed, a darker red as if he has hit a bigger vein, and men are trying to calm him, those calling to the guards frantic, blood everywhere. And the junkie is young, early twenties, his red ball of a face lost in the chaos, the entrance opening and uniforms storming in swinging sticks, two guards at the entrance with their rifles lowered. The snatch squad dodge the blood and see the junkie's arms, say a few words that shut him up, and he hobbles out of the room, the door locked.

Shaking, I lie down, pull my blanket around me, wait for the talk to die out, which it does, quickly. Too quickly. As if this sort of thing often happens. And there is whispering in the distance, wind trapped in creaking lungs. I am half asleep myself, too fast, oxygen cutting off as I jolt and toss and turn, blanking out the sight of those slashed arms and artery blood-shed, back with Jimmy Rocker who is kneeling at the side of a deserted freeway with a pump-action shotgun pointing at the back of his head, Mary-Lou passing on a Greyhound, a one-way ticket to New Orleans and the loving arms of Freddy Fucker. She doesn't even look at the drifter being led to the back of a police car, Jimmy asking what he has done wrong and the sheriff turning and punching him over his heart, you goddamn son of a bitch, don't play games with a mean Mississippi porker like me, but what has the Rocker done, he is a freewheeling good-time boy, I am innocent, Sheriff, you tell that to the judge, you drifters are just rootless white trash, but I am a good boy, Sheriff, and Jimmy is ordered to shut the fuck up and tell it to the judge, this rock 'n' roller watching scorched earth pass as they cruise deeper into Texas, wooden shacks and blues men and a boarded-up petrol station on the edge of his memory.

The wandering man they call Jimmy Rocker is strapped into an electric chair. He thinks of his mother and wants her to come to his rescue, but she is far away and unaware of his plight. He thinks of his granny gently rocking. In her rocking chair. Yet she is dead. He wonders if his mother is even alive. He hears a man of God reading from a Bible, and says he doesn't believe in religion. God can help him in his hour of need, if he is out there, but Jimmy knows no supernatural power is going to save his miserable life. Jimmy is a material thinker, deals in objects he can see and touch, a dreamer, but logical and keen to consume. He has no time for theory. Miracles don't happen to men who live the life of a pickup hobo. Soft-hearted, hard-driving rovers. Honkey-tonkers. Jukebox jivers. Hot-rod cowboys. The open road is all that matters. A root beer and a burger and a big smile from Mary-Lou, his Mississippi mademoiselle. And the executioner is grinning like an ice-cream seller with a limp dick, a curtain pulled back so he is face to face with his mum and nana, these two sufferers behind glass, witnesses to his death. There is a man in the background and he wonders if it is his father, but no, he doesn't care about his old man. The executioner blesses me and says it will be over soon, son, nobody knows what you've done wrong, only you. You've let your ma down. And Jimmy goes to say something but the words won't come, a lever pulled and the electricity roaring through his body.

I jolt as the oxygen cuts out and organs smoke. I am outside my body as Jimmy Rocker shakes and shivers and begs for mercy, skin smouldering, eyes bulging. In a short while fire will spurt from his chest and his heart will melt, and the tears are flowing down my face as flames lick the feet of the Rocker, burning his Converse, features turning colour and identity collapsing in on itself as everything I love dies, the darkness descending, carrying me away.

The punch connects with the back of my head, catching me by surprise, and I am furious, for the last three days staying alert and keeping awake, dodging the sneers and insults that prove these men hate me, even turning down a trip to the showers and only going on safari when it is essential, straining bladder and bowels, knowing these corners leave me more open to attack than the dormitory, where the grasses offer some sort of protection. Sleep deprivation makes me manic, paranoid, the nausea constant, a need to vomit, but I am unable to achieve this release, prepared to maim with the glass knife in my jacket pocket, away from my lucky charm, toilet paper wrapped around one side forming a handle, fingers loose, like a gunslinger. The glass offers strength, even though I don't want to use it, violence against my nature, a sin, know another conviction would add to my sentence and start a chain reaction. But I have to protect myself, a matter of life and death. I want to return to C-Block and be with my laid-back pals Elvis and Franco, improve my chess and appreciate those mountain photos, the boredom attractive, but there is no appeal. No turning back. This is my fault and I should have appreciated what I had and kept my head down, and I must survive, staying on my feet as I turn and hit this sneak square in the face, hear a crunch as my fist connects with his nose, and he is surprised, doesn't expect the outsider to respond, but he has friends, two dirty androids trying to knock me over, other men shouting and moving back as I hit the floor pulling one man with me, feeling kicks in my back and head as we wrestle on the concrete, chimps scrapping in the dirt, and I consider the knife and decide to wait, keep it as a last resort, instead make the sacrifice and play monkey monsters sinking teeth into the man's face, bite into his cheek and feel skin pop, taste bitter milk, and he is shouting more from shock than pain and I am sucked back into the chapel and Porky Pig and billions of shooting stars in the purple haze of deep space, blasphemy spurring me on as I push my attacker away banging his head and struggling upright, a kick missing my balls and I respond with iron knuckles, cracking nuts, shaking my head and frothing rabies spitting out red mucus, a circus master swinging his stick and the animals, prisoners, moving back, checking the vultures on the wall, fight over, the three men who attacked me walking off while I stand alone with blood staining my mouth.

Leaning over the sink I wash my face, quickly get rid of the blood, know I will be all right. People give blood disease mythical powers. A coward spits and I turn and see phlegm on my jeans, stare at the nearest clowns whose pale faces remain blank, and I laugh, call them Mr Unfair, and they are wary after the monkey routine but ready to stab me in my sleep. I gob pink snot at the ground in front of them, think about howling but decide against it, don't want to act too theatrical. It is good to be mad, but not mental. There is little I can do against the odds, stuck in a new, bigger playground all those years ago rooted in another part of the nightmare as the bullies come for me, and I feel their punches and hear the chants as I fall to the ground, a rhythmic taunt that is worse than the assault, and they start kicking me and I take my punishment as I am too soft and think this is what I deserve. Eventually a teacher stops the beating and shoos the boys away, and he can see the water in my eyes but doesn't give me a hanky and anyway, I keep it bottled up, he doesn't help me off the ground, trousers ripped at the knees, blood spilling from the broken skin of a prison-yard crater.

The worst thing is there will be no let-up. There is no going-home time or cell to hide in. I don't know what to think about it now – *don't think just stop worrying and toughen yourself up and fuck every single one of these cunts, that's what you've got to do, let yourself go and stop holding back and worrying about the other person and whether they deserve it or not, you didn't dig your teeth in deep enough, you should've torn him apart, ripped his face off and chewed on the bone, torn a chunk out and chewed the flesh in front of these so-called hard men, that would scare them all right, even mass murderers fear animals, rabid rats in a drain, rat up a drainpipe, that's what they say, rat up the fucking arse, mind you, half these dirty bastards would love it, just stay alert from now on because you've upped the stakes, hold on to that knife and next time slash at their fucking throats, anyone can be heartless, it's the easiest thing in the world* – and I scoop water up and spit it back out until it is transparent and clean, stand with my jaw open so the cold air can kill off any last chance the HIV has of finding a way into a cut in my gum, a place it can incubate and breed and turn me to bone – *you've done it now, next time carve the cunt up like a joint of meat, you have got nothing at all to lose* – and there is no reason that man is diseased, he might be a sneak and dirty but none of us are clean for more than one day a week, not in this shithole, and I go back in the section to find my towel, dry off and feel good the first violence is over and I am okay, that is going to scare some of the bullies off, they want an easy target – *they'll be back, twice as strong, twice as deadly, don't worry about that, these sadists and racists and criminal class are after you, and remember who's the outsider, a thieving gypsy and wandering Jew, a no-good sponging asylum seeker who wants to rob their fortunes and fuck their sisters* – and I take toilet paper out of my pocket and wipe the snot away, walk down to the green door and bang on the tin, sink into the gloom of misty excrement – *it's a distillery, clouds of piss gas and shit fumes, watered-down spunk and infected blood* – see rats scurrying away, and they are huge – *small dogs* – and I can't work out how they manage to squeeze into the pipes – *they're still there, waiting round the bend, chomping on saliva* – and I drop the paper in a bin, the trustee responsible for emptying it slack, the role of shit shoveller one of a tiny number of jobs available, and I get out quick, walk back to my bed watching the silent man opposite – *Dumb Dumb* – the one with the matchsticks – *a matchstick man made of wood, a black gunpowder head ready to explode* – and there are a few of us, God's lonely men, that sums us up, yet we can't connect with each other – *you're beyond repair, enjoy the ride* – and I give it a try, say hello to Dumb Dumb, but he doesn't even hear me – *mug* – and I can see he is sad and lost but there is nothing I can do for him – *you've got enough troubles* – and he is sitting on his mattress absorbed in the matchsticks, and has stuck forty or so together – *what the fuck is he up to, maybe he's building a glider, thinks he can escape from Colditz, the thick soppy cunt* – forming a panel – *he is building a raft and will disappear down the drain with the rats, float out to sea and hitch a ride on a luxury yacht, reckons he'll be sitting at the captain's table, drinking his champagne and fucking his wife* – and I sit on my bed, watching the matchstick man at work.

Dumb Dumb pays no attention to his surroundings. He is methodical and focused on his task. I slide a hand into my pocket and feel the glass knife. It is thick and sharp and from the broken window behind my bed. I search out and feel the easier surface of my lucky charm – *throw it away, what good has it done you?* – reassured by its meaning. My heartbeat slows. The exhilaration of coming through my first big test eases and I lose myself in the motion of the matchstick man's hands. I try to work out the difference between the loose and glued matches, realise those in the panel have had their heads removed. Somehow I know they are symmetrical, with each match exactly the same length. As if to confirm this, Dumb Dumb holds one up to the light, smells the wood and runs his tongue along the edge, and I think of that pine forest where I slept, the dumb man measuring the match against the panel, pressing a fingernail into the wood and then biting the head off, spitting it out, scratching the end level and adding glue, attaching it to his raft, holding it tight until it is fixed. He sits admiring his work, a faint smile on his lips.

This period of calm has to be enjoyed. The three men who attacked me are not far away and I start thinking about lock-up when we will be packed in and what will happen, how they will be looking for revenge, and I won't even be able to doze and maybe the monkey monsters will join in, at least those three who attacked me don't live with Papa. It suddenly dawns on me they aren't from this section, that I have never seen them before and when they walked off they went up the stairs. It is a massive relief, and another shot of joy pumps through my veins and into my heart. This precious, compli-cated organ swells up – *you've got your knife, what else do you need, you watch those monsters, and Dumb Dumb is dangerous, don't be fooled by his passive nature, some of the worst men are calm and collected and raging inside* – and I close my eyes for a minute, but stay alert, purple light and burning matches flickering in all their multicoloured glory. Ever so gently I run a finger along the edge of my glass defender knowing the damage it

can do, remember biting that man's face in the yard and punc-
turing his skin and wonder where that idea came from, the
elation rising up and sinking down, returning with a surge of
confidence trying to persuade myself that I am the sort of
monkey who rocks and rolls and rips men apart, a mad boy
who isn't going to lay down and die.

Time passes slower than ever and after a week on the block
I still haven't had a proper night's sleep, and have yet to speak
with another prisoner. The man in the bed to my right nods
once, but when I try to talk to him he turns away. It is more
than just language. This is the scum of the prison system,
deviants who maim and rape and despise innocence, lost in
their cruelty, adding mental torture to that of the flesh. I stand
in line and collect my food, Chef at least half smiling, but he
responds to everyone except the monsters who shun his world
of grease and bromide and job satisfaction, and I sit on my
mattress or the ledge, make every single mouthful last twice
as long as on C-Block, chewing in slower motion, wash my
bowl until the plastic shines and becomes steel, but only after
the others have finished, a runt ostracised from the pack. Dumb
Dumb is a runt but secure in his matchstick haven, while other
misfits accept random punches and kicks, humbly lower their
heads and fail to respond, a childlike acceptance that makes
me seethe. I go on safari and hardly notice the stink, senses
dimming, crouching down and feeling the dampness of my
skin, no longer sure if it comes from in or outside, while at
the sink I rub icy water into every reachable pore, wetting
clothes and not caring, shivering and sinking deeper. I stare at
the ceiling and watch insects, spirally jets and bombers and
soulless drones, listen to mosquitoes firing machine guns, go
outside and hang about in the yard whether it is freezing or
just cold, knowing I will crack soon, wondering how long a
good man can survive, three times spit hitting the back of my
head, faces hard and snickering, blank eyes taunting, and at
least in solitary there would be no threat. There is a song about
not knowing what you have got until it is gone and a saying
that the grass is always greener, and I know I should have sat

tight and realised how lucky I was. There is a part of me that wants to stand up and take them all on, force these whores to either speak or kill me, to share their language or shut me up for ever, but refusing to suffer in silence would set the mob loose, and I would stand no chance, an uppity nigger daring to resist a lynch mob, and the walls narrow and the towers swell and hone in on my confusion, vulture men watching, listening, waiting for the last twitches of life to fade, and very soon the monsters will attack, the moment is near when they will stop toying and use their wire and steel and glass, paralyse my arms and legs, turn me into a vegetable – *a turnip* – and the Director will rub his hands and ship me off to the psychiatric hospital – *or a new potato* – and I will never be released, unable to walk or think clearly, a punchbag for the criminally insane, a sex slave for Homer and his homo fakers – *something more exotic, an aubergine perhaps* – and I push back against the wall, rub at the bricks – *or a tropical fruit that is smooth on the outside but rotten to the core, something like a smelly old durian* – with my back covered I look at the wall opposite, wounds in the plaster, see cracks in my armour, what is left of it – *you've always been a weakling, always have been and always will, you know what Mum says* – and my fists are useless, what sort of defence is that – *get them before they get you* – what sort of a man am I, thinking I can scoop the eyeballs from the skull of Porky Pig, as if I am enjoying a hard-boiled egg – *if you don't stand up for yourself you'll get eaten alive, you give it back ten times harder, deep down people are wicked, they spot a weakness and work their way in, open the wound and smile and wait until they are safe and then they show no pity* – but of course, I have my knife now, a thick wedge of glass that will slice a man so badly he will beg for his mother, it is my security, along with my magic blanket – *how is a blanket going to protect you from a blade, forget Papa and his perverts and all that monkey business, every one of these men is a monster, and you have to think their way, hurt them before they can hurt you, and at least you tried with the rabies act, a bit childish but a start, you're thinking clearer, but you have to get right into the groove of this prison, and it is greased and made with a sharp edge, a wound that bleeds and scars, a medal pinned to your chest* – the blanket wraps me tight but has lost its magic, there are no more flights of imagination, no escape – *fuck imagination, you've got to be harder* – and I spend my evenings peering into the section, worrying about what is going on around me, staying awake, always awake – *and the monsters are watching you, and these are no fairy-tale trolls or golems or monkeys under your fucking bed, we're talking beasts, kiddy fiddlers and sadists, subhumans who capture innocents and attach cables to their balls, pump electricity through their gene machines and collapse the wires, frizzle their testicles for money, and pleasure* – and I feel stupid, hiding under a blanket like a frightened child, it really is pathetic – *but you are right, they're waiting for you to fall fast asleep so they can hide under your bed and take a skewer and drill it up through the mattress and into your heart, skewer the mince and turn you into a kebab, masturbate into the greasy mess as you gurgle and gasp, pickled in monkey oil* – the mattress is very thin – *voyeurs will break their bonds and nibble on the leftovers, hold you down and do a Homer, turn you over and piss on your face when they've finished* – the fruits don't worry me, they live their lives and I live mine, rape a crime nobody forgives, a rapist is dirt in prison just as he is in society – *that's C-Block, this is B-Block, they're all sex cases, all bent as arseholes, just listen to Homer, that man knows the truth* – I don't see men buggering each other, of their own free will or by force – *well, maybe not, but it goes on, in the shower and barber's shop, behind the green door, when you aren't looking, and you know they want to stab you for being an illegal alien, these men are scum and you should go on the rampage, slice some of these cunts up, or pick your moment, operate at night, what have you got to lose, flash the glass, boy, flash the fucking glass* – and during the day my knife offers protection as I walk up and down the yard with the other prowlers, one foot carefully placed in front of the other, up and down, up and down with the beads, tick tock, tick tock – *why bother?* – one hand tucked in my jacket pocket, then my trousers – *holding your balls* – and what I need is some masking tape as a grip, but that is wishful thinking, unavailable, and when I sit on the ledge I admit that I am no weapons collector, no expert on the samurai sword or swashbuckler's cutlass, watching the crazies patrol the yard, up and down, back to front, tick tock, clock clicking, tick tock – *look at that long-haired cunt in the freak sandals* – the long-haired man who is always arguing with thugs twice his size passes, looks my way, eyes lingering – *what are you fucking looking at?* – and for a moment he seems about to speak – *probably going to stab you with a needle, borrow it off his pal Papa, once the big poof's finished knitting his rent boys new socks* – and I have never seen this man near Papa – *and the monkey monsters, don't forget the wild boys* – there is something about him I recognise but can't quite make out, and he continues walking, disappears inside the section – *follow him, don't let him look you in the eye, he can read minds that one, he is a sorcerer, a pagan and a warlock, you can't let people treat you like that, looking at another man is an insult, and letting him see into you is worse, come on, do something about it, stop these heathens getting too near, stand up for yourself* – and a row starts near the stairs and punches are thrown and the clicking of the beads slows, fast or slow, it is driving me mad – *the day you get some of those beads is the day you join the living dead, look at these cunts, no clue, click click and tick tock, it's driving me fucking mad, slice one of them up, that'll stop the clock, damage the minute hand and let the seconds take care of themselves, time has to end and then we can start it going again, you and me together, speed the whole thing up, escape from this slaughterhouse* – but I must fit into the rhythm, somehow, as I did on C-Block. At first I was scared, believing my conditioning, the machine that tells me men are inherently evil and that jail removes the restraints, but I settled in and survived, found a new society, and I have to do that here, learn to live without friends or language, like the other dummies, and what is that other saying, no man is an island, what the fuck does that mean, but no, it is obvious – *you would be better off in a dungeon, an underground bunker where there is nobody to offend you, just bread and as much plain water as you can drink and it will be okay to piss in the corner where it will smell but it will never be as bad as going on safari even if you have to shit in the dungeon it will be your shit and my shit but mine doesn't stink and it will be ours and ours alone that dungeon could be a timeless paradise with no ticking clock or angry voices and better than the silence we would have nothing to fear no monsters waiting for a lapse in our concentration and when we want to sleep we could sleep as deep as we want yes we could sleep soundly if we were in a dungeon sleep day and night except we'd never even know if the sun or moon is out there as with the light on all the time it would always be daytime* – and Papa is strolling down the yard as if he owns the place – *he does, in a way, the fat cunt* – and I wonder what the pyjamas mean – *he's insane, they're all insane, specially that Dumb Dumb with his stupid fucking matches, sitting there like he's in a trance* – and Papa reaches the stairwell and the monkey monsters part as if he is the Messiah, but there is nothing soft about Papa, he is a seriously hard man, well over six feet tall and with a mean streak running along every crease in his skin, a scruffy killer, king of the monkey monsters, the little skeletons with their skulls marked by scars and purple powder, the doctor trying to kill lice, silverfish infesting their jumble-sale corner of dirty clothes and blankets and burning fucking candles – *you want to keep away from the pyjama man, pick on someone with no friends, and I can't help laughing, but why not Dumb Dumb, that way you'll be a winner, nobody threatens someone when they know they'll be outnumbered, or come out second-best, that's the way of the world, forget all that shit about pride and honour and bravery, that belongs in a story book, everyone's a bully deep down, people are gutless to the core, it's the nature of war to build up superior odds* – people are basically decent, maybe even the men in here are okay, if I could get to know someone, show them that I respect their culture and that I am an innocent man – *they don't fucking speak to you, ignore you when you try to be friendly, wise up, goon, they hate your guts, why fool yourself, human beings are wicked, they kill and abuse everything around them, that is what we are* – and I am so used to the daily fights and flare-ups and the two slashed wrists this week that the punches thrown on the stairs are in the back of my mind as they happen in front of my eyes, and it continues and is getting worse, the guards by the gate walking over and taking their time, it must be prison policy, and the gate opens and I am shocked when Porky Pig enters, and he is immediately the biggest and most powerful guard on the block, and this is the first time I have seen him since I arrived and he turns his pink head and looks me full in the eyes and my nausea stirs, eases as he moves on, and once more I am grateful to the pig man, glad Porky doesn't remember – *you're a foreigner, of course he remembers* – and he instantly takes control of the yard – *he's more lowlife, not exactly a fucking detective out solving crimes, is he, just a lock-up man with trotters and a snout and meat in his gnashers* – he is even bigger than Papa – *never forgive him for what he did, the terror he made you feel, never forgive any of these cunts, we have to stick together on this, you and me, and that's your problem, you always want to forgive and forget, just don't fucking do it this time* – and Porky is massaging his stick and he must have had it custom-built as it makes the truncheons of the other guards look small, and he is swinging it now, tapping it on his leg – *back and forward, tick tock, it's only a matter of time* – back and forward, over and over and over again – *over and over again and again* – driving me insane – *driving us fucking mad* – every single tick a reminder that there are millions of seconds left to serve, and Porky looks at me again – *they're all at it, watching you day and night, inside and out in the yard, and it's because you do nothing, and with Porky, okay, I see your point, he is a big cunt all right, let it go, but the others, choose a target* – and again Porky shows no sign of recognition, and if I was being stamped to death by the whole block he wouldn't notice that either – *none of them care what happens to you* – and that makes things worse as all you have – *as an outsider* – is the protection of the machine that sent you away in the first place, and once this sloth takes over men like me are fucked – *go mental and they'll transfer you to another prison, anywhere is better than this place, there might be people you can talk to, English drug smugglers and American psychos and Australian drunks, good people, friends, or if not, at least we'll go to the dungeon, there must be one in this lump of rock, every castle has a dungeon* – and the fight blows up as more men become involved and the guards are wading in, struggling to break it up, and I watch Porky grunting, the prisoners involved haven't seen him yet, and he doesn't speed up or slow down, doesn't break his stride as his mighty stick smashes down on the head of a man – *go on, fucking kill him* – and I hear the fracture from across the yard, feel sorry but at the same time so glad it is not me, anything that diverts attention is good, and Porky Pig has other targets, trotters dancing – *I thought you were invisible, make your mind up* – and not knowing what people think is the problem, not even being able to guess from their conversation, and everyone is backing away from the guards and the man Porky has hit on the head is lying on the ground unconscious – *brain-damaged* – and Porky looks down and rubs at his rubber ears, grunts more pig language, a smile oozing out, and he just looks around tapping his stick on his leg, finally turning and walking towards the gates, stopping halfway, in the middle of the yard, another warder taking out a pack of cigarettes and offering him one, providing his lighter and clicking the flint, and they stand together smoking as if they are not scared of anything or anyone, two magnificent pigs in control of the market – *don't ever forget anything that happens you must remember to move on you have to fight these demons and Porky is part of the problem a fucking pig making you stand in front of him with your trousers down punched and kicked and humiliated how can you close these things out never forgive and never forget and never use such a magnificent word as magnificent in jest go on take that knife out of your pocket and walk up to him and wipe that smirk off his ugly mug and chop at his nose to spite his face and it's true you will be beaten and abused and they'll add extra years but you will be sent away to the dungeon, a bright white void where we will sleep, just to be able to sleep and dream normal dreams is all that matters, even the best international spies can't survive sleep deprivation, and the lights will burn for ever, trust me, this is no catacomb I am talking about, just a brand new dungeon of peace and tranquillity and liberal consciousness, and we have to get out of here, we have to do something.*

The boffin who invented heaven and hell was on drugs, his imagery confused. Hell can't really be packed with saunas and spa pools, the eternal punishment block a lunar landscape dotted with burning coal and scorched craters, wrongdoers so lost in torment that when a devil woman parades in fishnets and six-inch stilettos they are too ashamed to even peep.

Sweating from every pore they would rather pray for forgiveness, wishing for a transfer to heaven, that winter wonderland of frozen celibacy. They must be pretty sick if they want to leave the warmth of hell and spend eternity in a refrigeration unit, a stark complex where saintly men sit in rigid silence, studying for business degrees. The great inventor has obviously spent no time inside Seven Towers, where the cold blunts our senses and filters so deep it freezes the soul.

If I am going to die in Seven Towers then this is the place I want to go, right here in the shower, and after almost two weeks the experience is extra special, knife under my clothes, within reach. There are plenty of men waiting for another chance to catch me off guard. They track my moves every second of the day and night. The loneliness is crushing. Only Dumb Dumb offers distraction, and I watch him from a distance, wary of being sucked into his psychotic world, this sad fool searching for spent matches, rifling through the dustbin by the door, slowly working on the wood, staring at it for hours while the other inmates play cards and dominoes and argue. Dumb Dumb's work ethic makes me feel decisive, and I think of my glass and wonder if I will ever have the courage to slit my wrists. I could do it here, in the shower, just slump down in the mist and watch the blood bubble and finally seep out of my veins, joining the whirlpool and mingling with the soap and dirt, peacefully drifting into a better sphere. I will haunt this shower for ever, scrubbing at the grime and cleansing myself, but there is no such thing as a glorious rock 'n' roll suicide, no romance or release or sense in the act.

I return to last night and know the notion of suicide and its reality are two different things. They say a man who kills himself is clear in his mind when he does the deed, that he feels no doubt or confusion. And I see men moving to the far end of the dormitory, hours after lock-up, hear crying, prisoners shouting through the windows, stand and walk over to find out what is happening, stand at the back of the crowd with the lonely boys, peering over shoulders. At first I see an albino face, mystical in its purity, and I try to work out why I never noticed this saint before, but although the eyes are wide and open I realise they are glazed and unseeing, and that something is very wrong. Looking at the bed where the albino rests it seems he has a different blanket to the rest of us, a novel texture and colour, and then I see the mess on the floor below and it is clear the blanket is soaked in blood. Papa pulls the cover back and the man is naked, white hairless skin turned to marble, wrists open and hands clasped across his heart. Papa leans down and lifts the drained corpse and carries it in his arms, reminding me of the gangsters on C-Block, reaches the door which is open and the first guard pukes into a corner, and we are hovering in silence, a column of mourners, and the head lolls back and hangs loose as if the man is twitching and alive, but we know he is dead, Papa allowed outside by the second guard, the sick one following them with his hand over his mouth.

Acid pours out of me and I rub at it with my soap, imagine sweet apple and a bottle of satsuma body lotion, far away in a five-star hotel with central heating and a king-size bed and television set, the steam of my prison offering privacy and cover for an attack, soap smelling of detergent and sweat, and I am angry at the marble man for committing suicide, wasting his life and clouding the time I have under the hot water. This shower is the height of civilisation, and yet it is a very dangerous place for me now, but I stay still when the temperature rises, the hotter the water the better, loving the sensation, waiting for a knife to come through the fog, and it doesn't matter, at least it would be an ending. If the water was scalding I doubt I would move, just let it melt me down like soap, follow my blood and spiral away into the drains and run off through the tubes and into the sewer, eating shit all the way, into the sea with the rats, using Dumb Dumb's raft to float to a cargo ship, shape shifting, grasping a glass wand, blood across my palm.

The pipes choke and hiss and whisper words I half under-stand, through the nozzle rattling rusty brackets hanging loose on the wall, and I apply another layer of soap, work up a lather, doing my best to ignore the spirits moving among us, and it is the best resting place for the prison dead, their whispering mingles with the clatter of water hitting concrete. Soon I will understand what is being said. It is a strange moment, conversing with pipes, and so many words sound like so many other words and after a while the brain misfires and picks up sound alone, building its own sentences. A man must be kept weak and muddled or he will be harder to control, and it is the same with the heroin in the block, just as Homer Simpson told me, Porky Pig coming in with the doctor in the evening, when he does his rounds, an ice chest of official pills, the pork man conducting his business in the corner by the stairs, out of sight of the vultures above. The heroin makes a difference, quietens the junkies down and eases things for the rest of us.

The temperature drops and I rinse away the last suds, hand on the tap ready to turn it off when the cold arrives. The heat is more than skin-deep, a proper tonic, the highlight of my life – *what a life, you've made your bed and you have to lie in it, maybe die in that sagging mattress and spunk-stained blanket and crusty pillow, a proper little fleapit, and because this shower gives you a few minutes of calm every week you think you're in heaven, you fucking mug, is this the best you hope for, two weeks without a shower and what sort of smelly cunt have you turned into with that scruffy scalp and armpits breeding bugs and nits in your hair and mould between your legs, you fucking stink worse than the rest of these subhumans, these dirty rapists and child molesters and wife batterers, you fucking useless cunt, you're as guilty as the rest of them, dragging me in here like this, I hate you, wish you were dead, go on, cut your wrists like the marble man and put us both out of our misery, you won't survive much longer, I fucking hate you, every man in here fucking hates your guts, every woman in the world* – and the tap is bent so I move a little to the side, pick my moment, quickly turn it off and hide inside my towel, angry when I realise there is still soap on my back, can't believe it, and there's no way I will wash it off with cold water, brush it away with the towel instead.

Once dressed we file into the furnace room and wait for the next group of prisoners. The funny little man with the long hair stands next to me. He speaks. To me. This is a shock. He tells me his name is Jesus. I laugh. No, that is what the other prisoners call me, and I remove my smile as after two weeks of being ignored the last thing I want to do is upset this man, he can operate under any name he likes, and call me whatever makes him happy. He says that they call him Jesus as he has long hair and is a carpenter by trade, a spiritual man who wears sandals. I wonder what to say, if my tongue will work. He glances at the others who are scowling at him, I guess for talking to me, explains how he spent two years in India and was caught at the border with hippie hair and a bad temper. That is the reason he is in jail. His appearance and the fascism of the authorities. Can I believe this? I nod. They have put me in B-Block because I do not show the Director any respect. I will tell you about the Director. There is something he did on the islands that it will be hard for a stranger to believe, and I know the story but don't tell him, glad to hear it again. But first he must ask me something.

I am attentive and polite as I listen, the meaning of what he says lost at first, and I concentrate hard, struggle to understand, and Jesus is asking me a very serious question, peering into my eyes in a strange examination, asks if I am all right, do I know what he is saying, and this pulls me back and I hear clearly, realise he is asking if it is true that I raped a woman and then killed her. The blow hits me in the solar plexus and I lean back against the wall, can hardly breathe, stuttering as I shake my head, unable to speak, finally answering no, in a whisper, voice crumbling, no, of course it isn't true, I haven't done this, who said so, do I look like a rapist, and it is a dumb response, as if there is a rapist model, but the shock must register in my face as well as my voice as Jesus is looking at me as if he is a holy man who can separate fact from fiction, the sort of spiritual teacher who forgives and knows that we are all brothers and the sons of our mothers. Jesus nods and says I did not think you were a rape man, and part of me believes he is a fool, but mostly I want to thank him.

Jesus explains that the men on the block hate rapists. He talks to the other prisoners and they look at me and ask questions. I in turn watch the Sicilian take wood to the furnace, notice how carefully he lowers the logs to the ground, and how neatly he arranges them in rows. Maybe he has forgotten his own terrible crime, and I wish I knew what it is he has done to end up in Seven Towers for such a long time. Maybe he is the real rapist and time has absolved him, and if this abomination doesn't exist in the minds of his comrades then maybe it never really happened, but then I consider the victim and know that for her it will never be forgotten. But the old man is no rapist, I just don't want him to be, and when I look at Jesus and beyond him to my jury I see that their expressions have changed, understand the hatred is no longer present, the monsters nodding, and one of them even laughs. Jesus says that the man with the big smile is known as the Butcher, and he wanted to stab me in the shower but Jesus managed to put a doubt in his mind, had the attack delayed until tonight, when he would have hunted me behind the green door, so it is good they know the truth. The Butcher slaps me on the back and grins. He is a friendly man. And I can't help thinking they are idiots to believe me, just as they were fools to trust the rape story in the first place, the guards opening the door and waving us forward.

It must be the Director feeding this story into the system, and I have to remember that inside Seven Towers there is no real truth, that there are rumours and suspicions and it is a case of convincing those around us of our basic decency, but it is a sadistic trick to play, and for a few seconds I hate the Director, wish I could kill him, but this passes and I force myself to pity him instead. I hate no man. And yet an exchange of punches, a broken window, the theft of an image, these are crimes that can be forgiven, but not rape. What sort of man does that to a woman, or another man, or to a child? A rapist would hide his crime, invent an offence that shows he is a good man, and perhaps he would erase the memory of his crime from his mind, unable to admit to himself that he is a beast, the dregs of humanity, and maybe I really am guilty, the decency left inside me closing out the horror of what I have done. I could be conning myself, but how would I know? The fact that other men heard this story and looked at me and believed it tells me something I don't want to hear, lays a suspicion and a doubt, and don't spiritual men say everyone is capable of every good and bad deed, that we are all saints and all sinners, that any one of us could have driven the train to Auschwitz.

The guards escort us back to the block and I hear only Jesus, push away my suspicions and enjoy the easier atmosphere. It is more broken sentences and odd words, but this is my prison patois. It is slow going yet I am very happy, see a reason for my treatment and hope Jesus will spread the news. We reach the yard and he is looking at one of the guards high on the castle wall, raises a hand up as if he is holding a rifle, wiggles his trigger finger, and for a moment I think of Homer, but know that Simpson is another extreme, a victim and a perpetrator, Jesus holding his hair out and taunting the vulture. He turns to me and says he will never visit the barber's shop, and that when he is set free he will spend a week at home before returning to India with his sister. He tells me about her in a hushed voice, a spiritual woman who can levitate through meditation. He has seen it happen. He looks at me intently and says that she is not a woman that a man would want to have sex with, although she is beautiful, and again he asks me if I understand and I say that I do. And that is the truth.

Listening to Jesus I watch the truth pass around the yard, notice that it is one of the men I fought with who passes the information through the flap in the gate, and my eyes drift towards the nearest corner and with a start I notice a tree. It is black and harsh against white plaster, its bark lined with deep ridges, a rock-like appearance to its trunk, branches and twigs. The barbed wire spooling along the wall behind it has turned to ivy and sent out feelers, grabbed the trunk and dug in its suckers. I focus on the tree as Jesus talks to me, learn of his determination to return to India and search for enlightenment, a form of blasphemy in the eyes of the Director, and I nod and appear interested, at the same time identifying old sap around the tree's wounds, wire breathing as it dispatches more feelers, the tree already dead. I can't imagine it being planted deliberately so it must have sprouted from a seed dropped by a migrating bird. It is hard to know how it could survive on this barren rock, but it did, growing and living and finally dying, and then turning to stone.

What sort of man do these fools think I am, these hypocrites who commit acts of violence and theft and see themselves as superior, do they really think my lust is sexual, or a craving for power, no, I am merely living the life of the rootless drifter taking what he wants without a second thought, and concerned mothers everywhere warn their children about monsters such as I, it has been the same through history, it is my lust for life that pushes me beyond the strict morality of conservative society, and I see Iggy Pop covered in white powder and remember the yellow skin of Homer Simpson and I am humming Iggy's words as I move from my room into the cold streets of the metropolis glad I am no idealistic Robin Hood no noble man of the forest, pleased I was never a child, and I remember Mary-Lou riding with a stranger, sitting at a bar minding my own business sipping a cold beer, guzzling a cold soda, these temptresses provoking fornication and urging this man to degrade himself and risk Aids and death by HIV, cruci-fied in order to satisfy a natural urge that big capital has manip-ulated and force-fed out of all proportion to its true value which is after all one of procreation and the spreading of selfish genes, this good boy pitied as his immune system fails and he rots in front of his loved ones, how are these people going to feel seeing innocence corrupted in such a sordid way, and the good boy is a bad boy or he wouldn't be on B-Block with the lowlife, but nobody knew what he was like back then, with his smiling face and trickster nature, oh yes, this rape man is one mean motherfucker, right around the world this Jimmy Too Bad waits with his dark secrets and light veneer, and this B-boy is on the rampage across the soiled fields of Europe, a freethinker who has moved away from the moral-ising of false moralists, phoney preachers preaching false doctrines that have nothing to do with his lonely life, and this lack of restraint must be my natural search for freedom, and to be accused of rape brings the reality home, the meanness of the system and the depravity men see in me, and I am a faceless stranger who comes rampaging out of the night, power surging along the back of my legs and moving into the pit of my stomach, another ball of energy coming down my spine from what is left of my brain, an explosion in my groin as I step forward to conquer and take what I want, the notorious drifter of legend moving on, a merciless outsider who wreaks havoc on stable communities, a jobless ex-con with no attachment to time or place, a man so in love with life he feels no remorse, the notion of consequences a limit on his freedom and the magic of the moment, and this rape man is a libertarian, a seeker, and I wait in a dark alleyway and smell the rotting vegetables, old sauces and nappies, cardboard that has turned soggy with the rain, hear the rats talking as they sniff through the remains of civilisation, gnawing at the face of a battered tramp so badly hurt he doesn't feel a thing, and none of this matters to a man like me, all I see is my prey as she walks along the pavement and it could be anyone in the wrong place at the wrong time, it is the bad luck of the draw, this is not personal, just the lust of a man following the sun and living a life of uncaring hedonism, the sound of crying inside my head something I scorn, and this is what I have become, just what they say I should be, and reaching out my hand I am grabbing life and smothering the mouth so the screams will never be heard, and the woman struggles but I am too strong and hold the cloth over her nose so she breathes in chloroform, pull her back into the alley and God is on my side as the fog comes flowing in off the sea and through the docks and I am the forgotten brother of Jack the Ripper roaming the streets of Whitechapel feeding on the poor, protected by superior forces, and it is lust that keeps the world spinning, and I am a ripper but also serving the needs of humanity, expanding the boundaries of the city's gene pool, and this temptress stops struggling and I am pulling her into the dark and there is this emptiness in me as I fight the accusation, the judge shouting that women are sacred, they are the mothers of the human race, and the Director is raging and the Slug is slithering, where is my pride now, and I am confused and spinning out of control as I am labelled a B-Block monster find myself in a room in a hotel, curtains shut and my victim gagged and tied to the bed, and I strip and mount her, begin to move with a power I never knew was in me, and I am swearing and angry and somehow this doll is awake and crying silent tears and I place a hand over eyes and nose so she has no face and I can see the face of Jesus the English-speaking saint looking for some sort of explanation from his cross on the wall above the bed and I know that Jesus forgives men their sins, and I put my hand around the slender throat and begin to squeeze and tombstones are rattling on a calendar and I press harder as I finish and feel bones break, look down at the head and see she has stopped breathing, skin as blue as the eyes, and I lay in my dirty bed and untie frail wrists and ankles and hold her in my arms, glad that I have done nothing wrong, that I am a good man, a good boy who does the right thing, and I am lonely and my friend will never leave me, never die, not really, and now I know she will love me for ever.

SILENT NIGHT

MY LIFE CHANGES once I find Jesus, shifts again as the winter darkens and Christmas approaches. The block is still a madhouse, but the hatred directed my way fades, and while there is still only one person I can talk with, this is a massive relief. It also means I can sleep. Prisoners fight each other and turn over beds and break windows and damage themselves, beads clanging, chords rapping, but the paranoia eases and Jesus promises to watch over me on that first night. My sleep is deep and life-saving and for a week I am a zombie, lost in an emotionless void. Then the rain comes. The downpour starts in the morning and last for days. Torrents fade to drizzle and build up the strength for another push, clean air entering the section. We are forced to stay indoors, only venturing out to collect our food. The sun dies and the lights are left burning twenty-four hours a day. I count my blessings.

Jesus is a spiritual man with a political edge, a belief in duality meaning he tries to see both sides of any argument. An active anarchist before heading East, he arrives in India and sets about smoking bushels of mind-bending ganja, six months later staggering from the hedonism of Goa towards the chaos of Bombay. It takes another three months for his brain to recover and by this time he is shacked up in Old Delhi. One Monday he wakes revitalised and crosses to the newer side of the city on a subconscious mission, discovers a treasure trove of religious wisdom in the old pamphlets and forgotten colonial memoirs of a second-hand bookshop. He spends a day flicking, examining these texts, and buys so much reading material he has to hire a rickshaw to carry it back to his room. He soon develops a deep interest in Hindu and Buddhist thought, and begins living the life.

He tells me the story of the Buddha, an Indian prince who was so upset by the suffering of mankind that he dedicated his life to finding a cure, leaving his old material existence behind and going on the road, never sleeping in the same place twice, dressed in rags, begging for food, realising that attachment was the real cause of unhappiness. Learning from the Buddha, Jesus moves around India and stays at ashrams where he learns to meditate and practise yoga, attends festivals where millions gather, their ranks brimming with the wildest wanderers on the planet. Jesus says the alleviation of suffering is the only real freedom and he is fighting his own attachments, knowing that the material world doesn't last and is therefore an illusion. He talks about the Buddha for a long time, and it makes sense, as is I already know a lot of what I am being told.

He also tells me about some of the other prisoners. The knifeman known as the Butcher is, apparently, a gentle giant. He has a meat stall in the market but has never killed so much as an ant, not until the day he returns from work and discovers his wife on all fours with his cousin behind her. He is drunk and carrying his work tools and stabs each of them to death before removing his cousin's genitals and placing them in the mouth of his wife. After two days drinking whisky, he dismembers the bodies in the bath and begins selling the meat on his stall. He is complimented on these choice cuts and business booms. His sister-in-law, who has long been attracted to him, and knows about the affair, consoles the Butcher, believing her sister has run off with the cousin. They are soon having sex in the same bath where the bodies were mutilated, specks of dried blood pebble-dashing the soap bubbles. The Butcher avoids detection for nearly a year, but is a soft man, and over a glass of beer breaks down and confesses. If he was tough he would have got away with the murders. His sister-in-law goes straight to the police.

Papa is a mystery. There are different versions of his truth. One sees him as a safe-cracker moving along the coast breaking into mansions and luxury yachts, stealing diamonds and jewellery and million-dollar paintings, hurrying across the nearest border when the job is done. Here he goes on a spending spree, blowing what remains in a casino. But years of success means he becomes careless, robbing the villa of a billionaire and not bothering to move on before trying to buy a Porsche for cash. The salesman alerts the police. Before entering Seven Towers he has never committed an act of violence, but the high life has spoilt him and he can't cope with being interned. He has a breakdown and the hospital overreacts, dishes out electric-shock treatment, paid friends of the billionaire increasing the voltage. Since then he has been a vicious thug where once he was a high-class thief capable of charming glamorous women. Another version says Papa is a psychopath, that the electric-shock treatment was to revive him after he had been badly beaten by police officers out to avenge a comrade who Papa attacked with a hatchet. Jesus says there are other versions, but what is certain is that he is now a dangerous man who has killed other prisoners and we should do nothing to upset him. Keep out of Papa's way and we should be safe. Although insane, he is not a bully. Jesus has no idea why he wears the pyjamas.

Most of the junkies are inside for relatively minor offences, stealing to feed their habits, snatching handbags and breaking into cars for the sort of sums the safe-cracking Papa spends on a casino beer. A couple of men have been accused of living off the immoral earnings of crack-addicted girlfriends, one strangling a drug dealer over a minor weight discrepancy, another losing the thread on acid and wiping out a colony of bats with a blowtorch. This man was beaten senseless when the story was revealed. Most of the B-Block boys seem to like animals, and that goes for C-Block as well. It is obvious in the way we watch birds in the sky, point when they settle on a tower, smile at the prison cat picking its way along a wall, dipping paws in and out of the barbed wire, and even insects attract attention. Only the rats are hated.

The junkies are obvious, questioning eyes cramped in shrivelled skulls, skeletal bodies in scarecrow clothing. We are all undernourished, and it is not possible to stay clean, everyone tormented in some way, but there is a darker sadness about these drug freaks, another sort of mental turmoil. It is hard to feel sorry for these freaks when they are breaking windows and screaming their heads off, picking fights at two and three in the morning, banging on the door at sunrise, opening their forearms with glass, but it is clear they belong in hospital. Sticking these chemical brothers in with lunar crazies such as the Butcher and Papa, men like Flip Flop, a strangler of rich ladies who survives due to the lack of a sexual motive and his thick biceps, and Pretty Boy, a macho queer who slaughtered a paedophile who raped his seven-year-old nephew, then drank the pervert's blood from a plastic goblet, is madness in itself. This small-mindedness is typical of the Director and his arse-licking lackeys, the judges and their cock-sucking cronies.

According to Jesus, the junkies are either weak-willed and easily led, or deep thinkers who understand life and its complex nature, the inevitable result of this knowledge inner turmoil. Usually they are a blend. Life for the smack and crackheads is tough, whether from experience or a genetic flaw, and Jesus is soon ranting about drugs and the curse they place on social cohesion, this poison supplied by selfish capitalists taking advantage of human frailty. Yet the organised criminals are on A-Block, enjoying easy lives on the luxury wing, the rest of the prison crammed with men who act on impulse and can't control their behaviour, emotional crooks without contacts or serious money. As an anarchist who has fought state capitalism and globalisation, and a spiritual seeker who believes enlightenment can only be achieved through strength of will, Jesus denounces drug use as a physical answer to a spiritual quest.

The rain lashes down, quickly forming puddles in the yard. Lightning smashes into the rock and lights up the dullness of late afternoon, a fluorescent glow that X-rays every prisoner. I see the fried heads of men stripped clean by the biggest electric shock of all, fifty monkey monsters jumping for joy and not sure whether to laugh or cry. The voltage singes nerves and makes me want to check under my bed, but the flash is lost in a split second and I fight the urge, laugh out loud as Jesus's sermon takes on another dimension. He could be as mad as the rest of them, a zealot preaching his own version of an ancient wisdom, a hippie drifter who reaches the cross-roads and hitches in the wrong direction, sucked into another version of the same old dream. The voltage fades and he is a good man once more, one of the best and most original I have ever met.

Jesus doesn't seem to notice when the lightning strikes and I think of Jimmy Rocker reaping a righteous reward deep in the heart of Texas, paying for his greed and lust for life. The Rocker is a pinhead, stuffing his face on fast food and carbonated soda, the beat of his heart tuned to a bubblegum jukebox, Levi jeans and expensive tyres symbolic of his demise, his worship of material gods. Behind the secular veneer lurks some hard-core fundamentalism. Things are not as they seem, and I laugh again, thinking that Jimmy Rocker really is a dumb fuck if he thinks he can do whatever he wants. Jesus stops talking and stares, leaning his head to one side, trying to read my mind. I pull myself together, listen to the rumble of pagan fury and wonder about my pine forest, Thor firing off rockets, find it reassuring that we are sheltered, the room almost cosy, and Jesus is talking again and I am juggling words, hearing about the monsoon in India, flash floods and tropical rain that brings out millions of hibernating snakes.

You see, my friend, in India the people are very poor but they have belief. He says this is hard for us to understand, yet true. While the West is a slave to consumption, producing so much food it creates obese depressives and clogged arteries, the ordinary Hindu makes do with essentials such as rice, dhal, bread and vegetables. They are too decent to eat animals, while we needlessly kill hundreds of millions. I nod and wait for him to continue, think how Elvis loves hamburgers and T-bone steaks but could never kill a cow, and I recall him saying this, the very words, in a rare moment of seriousness, Elvis a gentle man who just wants to have fun, and this makes him funny and easygoing and generous. He is much less intense than Jesus, lacks his edge, although this wandering baba is more intelligent, and you see, my friend, the multinationals will rule the world and yet we can free ourselves if only we can renounce greed and live our lives according to spiritual principles.

My friend scans the room before moving forward, telling me that prison can be heaven or hell, the choice is ours. I should think about this. Inside Seven Towers we live in basic conditions, and I smile, he is right, Jesus frowning, you must listen, please. And we exist on basic food that leaves us thin and light-headed. And there are few temptations. Again, this is true, I have worked it out for myself, so, my friend, prison can be a monastery for the right man, if he is strong enough. Such a man has to be willing to shut out the noise and not fear possible harm, know that everything he sees is an illusion, and that it will pass. I nod, half knowing what he means, but unconvinced. It is a path to consider, my good friend.

Seven Towers is no monastery. An insane asylum perhaps, but there again the original holy men were often accused of madness and blasphemy. Wasn't Jesus himself crucified for his faith healing and socialism? And the next day he is back telling me about the swamis he met in India and how the spiritual quest is built into the Eastern tradition, confusing stories of dreadlocked young ganja kings wandering naked through bazaars smothered in the ashes of burnt elephant shit, fed samosas and chapattis and bowls of dhal by respectful shopkeepers, worrying tales of retired civil servants donning loincloths and hitting the road with their oldest friends, leaving wives and children for a few months of dharmsala freestyling. Jesus talks for a long time, enjoys an audience and the chance to practise English, and I am captive all right, he could talk to me about anything and I would listen, another storm raging, pushing me into his vision, a two-week fast undertaken in a hillside town perched high above the Ganges, where he claims he saw nature spirits, clouds of consciousness that make me smile in my cynical way, imagining a misty safari. Even so, my skin tingles the same as it does thinking of the great American road, the sheer freedom of sitting behind the wheel of a Dodge pickup with a full tank of gas, open-minded enough to listen and understand that anything is possible.

There is a pause and maybe he feels he has said too much, left himself open to scorn. This is a problem, goes back to that crucial stage between childhood and that point when we realise

166

we must keep our feelings hidden. To break the silence I ask Jesus about the men who sit with Papa. I don't describe them as monkeys or monsters or monkey monsters or any other childish expression, as that would be exposing my own weakness, and he sighs and explains that like Papa they are a mystery, their identities and crimes unknown. They huddle in a mass and enjoy Papa's protection, keep to themselves and don't speak to outsiders, and he asks if I can tell them apart and I admit that I cannot. He nods and says this is because they share each other's clothes, keep changing their appearance, visiting the barber's shop together every week, without fail, strength in numbers, keeping their hair cut to the bone, hoods pulled up for winter, shading their faces. I think of monks, good and evil so near each other, and he asks why I am laughing and I tell him, and he shakes his head and says that they are bad men.

Porky controls the flow of smack on to the block, but Jesus believes the Director is the man in command, a classic hypocrite. He points to various prisoners on junk and explains the situation. The nature of men and the nature of their crimes can't be separated, but the added tension on B-Block is also connected to drugs. Heroin is available to those with money, and this leads to problems. Many men have next to nothing, hardly enough for a cup of coffee, let alone smack. They don't want the doctor's substitute. They crave heroin and this causes trouble between the haves and have-nots. Rich junkies and poor junkies go to war. Then there are fights with the other men, criminals who despise drug addicts as weaklings. Add convicts suffering from withdrawal, a constant stream of smack fiends flipping out and trying to hurt themselves, the fragile mental state of the psychos, the loneliness of everyone, and the anger and violence is constant. Jesus says it is a wonder things are not worse. But life has been quieter these last few days, and he agrees. We are experiencing the Christmas spirit.

Prison is full of mood swings, from fuck-off funny to fucked-up sad, small events as spectacles, huge happenings unseen. This pendulum keeps swinging in a positive direction as more days pass and men slap each other on the back and shake hands, sharing jokes and bread, the volume sinking to a normal level, beads clicking in time. Christmas is nearing and our thoughts are turning, the religious finding solace in the date itself, while the rest of us should be depressed but are in fact quite happy. Jesus claps his hands and says that someone understands the potential for trouble at this time of year, and the heroin is flowing in a seasonal glut, taking the junkies out of the equation. Even the poor men are feasting in the build-up to the hardest few days in the prison calendar. This is the Director's work, as he wants his regime running smoothly. A riot would look very bad on his record if it came at Christmas, especially after the trouble last year.

In the outside world people are preparing for a festival of eating and drinking and family values, an exchange of presents and holidays from work, the best of human nature apparent, a time for children to sit around a pine tree and see huge forests decorated with fairy lights and tinsel and glass balls and a nativity scene where Baby Jesus smiles in his humble cradle surrounded by frolicking lambs and wise men bearing gifts as they sip cocoa and hot milk and nibble chocolate. People are happy and strangers greet each other in the street, stumble home drunk and disorderly and bearing gifts. And the days are passing and Christmas seems more and more special with Jesus's wise words playing in my head and I am thinking about the Virgin Birth and considering miracles and all sorts of mad stuff I know from childhood but never really thought about before. I realise that I am godless. Without a faith or higher knowledge. It is children who seriously believe in Christmas, and looking around the room I return to that notion of the prisoners as small boys trapped in men's bodies, missing their mums, and maybe it is the season of goodwill affecting me but it has become as clear and as honest an insight I have ever had in my life.

Two days before Christmas five new men arrive. They are brisk and efficient and dressed in neat suits they have worn to court. Prisoners gather around them excitedly and there is a great deal of hand-shaking and noisy talk, some laughter but mostly a seriousness that shows these men are special. Suddenly the B-Block boys are holding themselves differently, and I notice that even Papa and the monkey monsters come over to listen. Jesus is at the front of the crowd so I will have to wait to find out what is happening. Dumb Dumb sits cross-legged on his bed gluing matches together, glancing over, returning to his work, and seems happy enough, the good mood having a knock-on effect as prisoners drop matches on his blanket where more recently he has been walking around collecting them, knowing the Butcher will hand over his treasure with a smile while Pretty Boy frowns, the only ones who refuse outright the monkey boys, Papa shaking his head, and I have the funny feeling that they are somehow disappointed. Dumb Dumb is another one I should ask Jesus about, but keep forgetting, deep down probably preferring to avoid complications, the matchstick man happy to enjoy his work and count down to the big day.

Peering out from under the covers I try to guess what time it is but it is hard as I don't have a watch to look at and it is mainly grown-ups who carry time around with them on their wrists and are always checking to see if they should be doing something else and it must be morning by now but outside it is still dark and I wonder what Father Christmas has brought me and I want to look in my stocking but I have to wait for Mum and Nana to come and wake me and I shut my eyes and am very warm and comfortable in these sheets and blankets and I have my baby security blanket wrapped around my legs it gets smaller as I become bigger but it is extra soft and I don't often think about my father but as I wait for Mum and Nana and morning to come he is in my head and maybe it is because today is such a special day when the Baby Jesus was born in a stable and slept in a manger and I wonder what Dad looks like and what he is doing at this moment and maybe he slept in this room when he was my age I will have to ask and he must be a good man or Mum would never have loved him and I am sure she loved him once upon a time and she says she will tell me about him when I am older there is no mystery and nothing bad to worry about everything is fine as long as the three of us stick together and maybe he will send me a card or he could be dead even but I must be young enough not to feel sad at this thought and Father Christmas will be pleased by our chimney as it is very clean we had a fire last night so that will make the grate a bit dirty but it is only ashes and Mum says he will bring my presents upstairs and put them at the bottom of the bed and she says I am always worrying about something Father Christmas knows all about chimneys as he has been squeezing down them for years and anyway he likes the smell of ashes and pine and a glass of whisky and a couple of mince pies.

Christmas Day dawns and the church bell rings, shaken by a festive guard wishing he was at home with his family. We stand in line, strangely mellow, knowing we are in this together and suspending the friction, for once in tune with each other. Every single one of us is missing out, but the season of good-will exists, and there is laughter mixed in with the murmur of voices, the sugary smell of breakfast stronger than ever. They have doubled the bromide to stop an orgy of sodomy and murder, in his warped fundamentalist way the Director linking sperm and violence, hoping to avoid a repeat of last year when three prisoners were stabbed and one died. The killer is in an insane asylum, but the Director is cautious. When I reach Chef he repeats a seasonal greeting and I return it in his language, which makes the great man smile even more, watch as he fills my mug. I sit down next to Jesus, who is chatting with the Butcher and another man. I wedge the milk between my knees and reach inside my jacket for the bread I have been saving, dunk it in and watch as it expands and turns soggy, a great Christmas treat.

Mum and Nana are sitting at the bottom of my bed and I am bouncing around on the mattress as Nana tells me she has been downstairs already and made up the fire and lit it so the front room will be nice and warm for us and I don't mind that she has done it without me as today is different from any other day and as I am bouncing an apple rolls out of my stocking and falls on the floor and I lean over to pick it up and looking under the bed I see a dark shape and know it must be a monster and I am scared and then happy as I realise it is the Yogi Bear toy I asked Father Christmas for and he wants to know if I have been a good boy and I look at Mum and she smiles and nods and says yes he is a very good boy indeed and I thought maybe I really will get Yogi Bear as a present and seeing him down there I realise it is an extra surprise and I am wondering how Father Christmas crept up the stairs with nobody hearing and sometimes I put Mr Fair down there to protect me but he doesn't do much good he is too small and Yogi will help me if I need him he is bigger and I grab the apple and pull myself back into bed and start taking apples and tangerines and chocolate and a police car from my stocking and there is a rubber ball and water pistol as well and I say thank you Father Christmas wherever you are and he could be back home in his winter wonderland by now surrounded by huge forests covered in snow and there is a pause and I am trying to work out how Yogi is going to surprise me if he will come alive when Mum drops the ball and accidentally knocks it under the bed saying sorry dear can you pick it up and of course I must realise that her and Nana are really Father Christmas.

The Butcher wraps a massive arm around Jesus's frail shoulders and squeezes tight, embarrassing the birthday boy who mumbles a few apologetic words, the dismemberment man roaring the sort of laughter that coils out of his stomach and starts Dumb Dumb fiddling with his spoon, creating a whirlpool in his mug. He has left his matchsticks inside, which is unusual, as he usually keeps them with him the same way Franco clings to his book of photographs. He was busy last night, cutting matches to exact lengths and creating panels, working later than usual, using his teeth and removing splinters from his gums, flicking them on to the floor, almost frantic, suffering just like the rest of us. Jesus turns away from the Butcher and shakes his head and smiles and asks me how I ended up here. It is the same question Elvis posed and I panic and start telling him about my desire to see the world, to keep a childhood promise and sleep in an enchanted forest, and he shakes his head sadly, no, no, my friend, that is not what I meant.

The Christmas tree sparkles above a pile of presents and the nativity scene where plastic shepherds wait in a mountain of cotton wool surrounded by lambs and goats and I have put a lion and two tigers in there and a mother pig and her piglets on the roof of the stable and Mary is twice the size of the lion but it doesn't matter and her son is tucked up in a brown blanket only his featureless face showing and the Three Wise Men are sitting on their camels but one has been knocked over by a star that has fallen from the branches and it is a real pine tree filling the room with a smell I will always remember and I wish I could stay like this for ever wide-eyed and glowing and it really is magic with the fire burning and the flames dancing in time with the lights the warmth of the coal merging with the warmth of our family Mum hugging me and Nana kissing my head and we are pleased just to be together Nana putting a plate of sausage rolls on the table as we sit around the tree me and Mum on the floor by the presents and Nana in her chair and we start handing out gifts and Nana's record is playing a choir singing hymns and I am excited to have these presents to open but mainly it is Mum and Nana who make me happy and maybe this is also when I realise Christmas is about people.

Following breakfast the morning passes as we wait for dinner. My holy friend confides that the Butcher will miss his feast more than most, as he usually celebrates with a mountain of fowl and beast. Jesus runs his eyes over the wire lining the inner walls, then scans the ramparts and towers, finally comes back into the yard. He draws breath and explains that Christ sacrificed himself, while men now sacrifice lambs. Self-sacrifice, that is the difference, my friend, the inner battle. I glimpse the Butcher at work on his wife and her lover, see the blood and gore of his crime, lean steak cooking in a pan. I turn to Dumb Dumb, and watch him closely, absorbed in his mysterious task, the new arrivals also interested, and Jesus tells me they are officials from the farmers' union, which is taking on the government over a new law curtailing their power, and that they have been sent to Seven Towers by a vindictive judge. But they are unbowed, and their dignity and

172

dedication is obvious, every single prisoner showing respect. These men are here because of their principles, and that is worth a great deal. Dumb Dumb uncorks his glue.

We are sitting at the table eating our Christmas dinner and my plate is full of roast potatoes and Brussels sprouts and parsnips and Yorkshire pudding with stuffing and slices of turkey covered in thick gravy and it is great especially the roast potatoes and I am cutting into them and soaking the fluff and Mum and Nana are talking about the cranberry sauce and Mum is telling me to slow down the food isn't going anywhere I notice the ribs of the turkey and the carving knife laid over the stuffing and Mum and Nana raise glasses of sherry and I have a fizzy drink and it is a good time and memory and I ask Mum why we eat turkeys and she says it is tradition and I ask her how many turkeys die at Christmas and she says millions and seems uncomfortable and I feel sad for a few seconds but don't want to spoil things and keep eating and have seconds and eat that as well and think I am going to blow up and then along comes the Christmas cake and Nana's apple pie with the custard I love and when we are finished we sit in front of the fire tired and relaxed and Mum reminds me how we should always remember how lucky we are to have so much food and love.

Christmas dinner is served late. We are hungry and for the first time the calm is threatened, the reason clear when six guards enter the yard flanking a string-bean priest in black robes, matching beard cushioning a wooden cross. The escort is on its best behaviour, erect and reverent. One guard carries a bowl, the priest a staff and a large twig. The men on the ledge stand to attention and I do the same, careful to respect their traditions and avoid offence. The priest walks slowly, nodding at individuals, dipping the twig into the bowl and sprinkling water on the ground. He blesses us and moves into the section. We follow, crowd inside the door and watch as he moves along the beds sprinkling holy water, zombies jumping up and standing with their heads bowed, and when he reaches the green door he opens it and starts to enter, recoils, his face pale with shock, and for a moment I think he is going to be sick, but he recovers and flicks a few drops into the mist, pulls the door closed and turns away, blessing the second row of beds. We stand aside as he heads for the upper level, wait in the yard until he returns. At the gate he looks at the gathering and makes a sign in the air before leaving. There is a further moment of silence and then the beads start clicking.

We eat chocolate and play games and watch television after dinner and all the time the fire is burning and I keep glancing over at the flames and Nana is saying that one day if she wins a lot of money she is going to have central heating put in but Mum says the fire is cosy and and romantic and Yogi Bear is dozing next to Nana and soon the light is fading and I go to the window and look out and feel the wetness on the glass we hoped it was going to snow but it hasn't and it doesn't really matter it is raining and Nana says we should go to church as it would be nice to see the candles and hear the hymns even though we are not really church people and the wind rattles the glass and it seems a shame to go out into the cold and Nana thinks it would be the right thing to do but Mum says no we don't want to catch a chill and they are smiling and talking about something I don't understand and I know Nana believes in heaven and I have seen men and women come to see her and sit with her in this room right here and I would rather stay in the warm and play draughts with Nana until she falls asleep in her chair reaching over and choosing another chocolate finding a Turkish Delight one of my favourites.

When Chef finally arrives the light is fading and the hunger is biting, those men walking down the line after being served doing so with wide grins. The Director appears on the block and stands with two guards on either side, rifles pointing at the ground in front of us, more a show of his fear than our strength. This is the first time I have seen him since he sent me to B-Block and I keep my eyes averted, but notice how he holds a patronising smile that reminds us that he is the king of this castle, playing at being Father Christmas, his presence our gift. I stand behind Jesus, close to the dumb matchstick boy. We don't speak. And when I reach Chef he is happy and loading my bowl with rice, roast potatoes and a generous chunk of chicken breast. There is no meat shortage today and it looks well cooked, with little grease. I walk over to the ledge, change my mind and go inside, sit on my bed in idle luxury and enjoy one of the best meals of my life.

I don't want the day to end but I have been awake since early in the morning and after eating cold turkey sandwiches with crisps and peanuts and then cracking walnuts and almonds with Nana I fall asleep in front of the fire still hearing the sound of the television where people are clapping their hands and cheering and laughing a lot and Mum helps me up off the floor and leads me to the couch and she goes upstairs for a blanket and I hold on to Yogi Bear and rest his head on a cushion next to mine until they are ready for bed and I listen to their talk and somewhere Nana is telling Mum about the voices she hears when people come to sit with her and this gives her a faith that makes her stronger as she is getting old and this is a hard thing to accept as time is shorter and every day is more valuable and you want to live for ever but she believes in life after death more than most people and what makes life really worthwhile is seeing babies born and growing into children and bringing their energy into the world and they have an appreciation of the small things which as we become older we lose and as well as that excitement honesty is their greatest gift and I turn over and feel happy and the words sink in and I will never forget this day.

After lock-up there is a special service for foreigners and while I have no real religion I go anyway. It is held in the room where Porky and his pig men marked my first minutes with the threat of rape, but the place is transformed, a gold crucifix set up on a table in front of maybe twenty plastic chairs, an aisle in the centre. What I take to be a priest in jacket and trousers waits with a Bible in his hands. Candles burn and create shadow puppets from the handful of gathered prisoners, and I think of the monkey monsters but know this is not their place. Suddenly I notice Franco on the other side of the aisle, try to catch his eye, look for Elvis but can't see him. I try to move across to Franco, but a guard stops me.

Franco turns and looks me in the face and I smile, but he doesn't see me, his eyes bloodshot and vacant. My friend doesn't even recognise me. I feel terrible, listen to the priest, his sermon making no sense, yet I know he is a decent man, and the flames on the candle dance and an outside light illuminates the stained glass, and the candles slowly melt and fill the chapel with the smell of honeyed wax, and I recall dust particles and shooting stars and meteor madness, smile at the wonder of the universe. And suddenly we are singing a common tune, using our own languages, and there are tears in my eyes and this incredible happiness merges with the sadness and creates an emotion I have never experienced, but which makes me feel immortal. Wiping the weakness away, I move my eyes between the purple light and the candle, knowing this is another day I will never forget.

The time between Christmas Day and New Year's Eve passes in a lazy amble, and it is no different inside Seven Towers, the junkies knocked out on heroin and the rest of us comatose on memories. Everyone is on holiday, except Dumb Dumb, who one fine morning after breakfast stretches his arms and legs and snaps into gear and starts spreading his panels out on the bed in front of him where he sits cross-legged like a silent sage from the travels of Jesus, eyes moving fast as he tries to figure out the jigsaw, his determination obvious. I notice other men watching and realise I am not the only one interested in his work. The dumb man has a new momentum, mind sharp as he concentrates, shifting the panels into formation and preparing the sacred glue, leaving nothing to chance. I can't help glancing over to see if Papa has noticed, find his head raised and eyes narrowed. The atmosphere is electric, maybe twenty prisoners watching the master in action. And this Dumb Dumb turns out to be an architect and a carpenter, lining edges with solvent and slotting the pieces into place, holding the wood tight and moving fast to achieve maximum bondage. There is a faint hum when he reaches under his pillow and pulls out three elastic bands, a sigh of approval as he tightens these around the shape he is creating, allowing the glue to fasten. Inside half an hour his secret is revealed, as he has quite clearly built the lower floor of a house.

Hundreds of matches have been used, each one serving its purpose before being expertly cut to length. Dumb Dumb props the structure on his pillow and examines it from the other end of his bed, eyes never straying from his creation, oblivious to everything around him. This allows prisoners to wander in close, finally the farmers arriving from the table, where they have been watching intently. One of the union men speaks to the master builder, but he does not answer, just smiles and nods his head, and the mere fact Dumb Dumb reacts at all sends small shock waves through the crowd of well-wishers. It is a great moment, men grinning as they reach into their pockets and return to their beds, searching for matches, urging him to complete the job. And all the time Papa studies the drama from a distance, selfishly withholding his materials.

During this period Porky Pig is coming on to the block twice a day, the junkies more pale and fragile than ever, the pig man even entering the section to look at the first stage of Dumb Dumb's house, staring hard and appearing perplexed, keeping his distance. I talk to Jesus about India, try to find out more about karma and its rules, how much it can affect our lives, and also his plans for when he is released. He says he must wait until the new year before he thinks about his future, as he believes it would be bad luck, the passing of the old and the arrival of a new year a hard time in this environment. He believes the Director has been clever keeping the junkies and criminals well fed. Jesus was expecting trouble, but it has been avoided. We enjoy our easy living while we can, the match-stick house an obvious symbol of this new optimism.

On the day before New Year's Eve we are lining up for our dinner when a shudder passes down the queue. I step side-ways and look to the front, see Chef standing over his pot, anger swelling an already chubby face. It is a horrible sight. This genial character is seething and I don't have a clue why, turn to Jesus who shrugs his shoulders, every man hurrying back down the line looking into their bowls and shaking with an infectious fury, refusing questions. We edge forward and voices are raised, Chef turning to the guards and shouting abuse, the officers embarrassed, holding their palms open to show they are not to blame. I wait behind Jesus as he is served and see his shoulders shrivel. He takes his meal and hurries off. I am dismayed when Chef snatches my bowl and empties his ladle, pushes my food back and waves me away. There is no extra today and as I walk away I look at the grey liquid and the meat inside, take a few seconds to register, recoil at the sight of a small tongue floating in a greyish liquid. I don't know what sort of animal the tongue is from, but it is whole, a marble mosaic of red, brown and blue patches, what looks to be green mould lining the edges, stringy veins dangling from a pinker base. My skull screws in on itself, mouth dry and throat parched, vocal chords frozen.

A couple of men eat the tongues, the rest do not. There is a dustbin by the sinks and today it sees unwanted food. Outrage sweeps the block and the men swamp the yard. Food is what keeps us alive, and while it is bland and greasy it is also some-thing to look forward to, a reason to keep going, and this muck is an insult too far. We are raging and the Butcher, Flip Flop and Pretty Boy lead an attack on two of the guards. Punches are thrown and knives pulled and the keepers backed into a corner. A warning shot is fired by a guard on the wall, but the men don't back away, the vultures too scared to fire at the crowd in case they hit their own men, hawks coming round the wall but also holding off. I am in the yard and feel sorry for the guards as they are kicked and forced to pull their revolvers, the order to serve rotten tongues can't be their doing, the men from the union calming the situation before anyone is killed, the guards shaken and pinned into a corner. These union officials have had boxes of oranges sent up to the prison for us, but the Director has blocked their delivery, so it is surprising they act as peacemakers, though Jesus reminds me that they are good men dedicated to negotiation rather than violence.

Two shaken guards are finally allowed to leave the yard, return half an hour later with twenty of their brothers for early lock-up. An uneasy calm settles as Porky Pig brings the smack in, half the mob following him to his corner while the rest of the men, the harder element, sneer at their meekness. Porky does his business and the core of thirty or so left allow themselves to be shut inside with the rest of us. The night is tense but there is no fighting, the farmers keeping the men together while others go to the house and watch Dumb Dumb chopping off heads and lining his matches with glue. There is little I can say or do and later when I am lying on my bed the anger settles and I think logically about the tongues. It doesn't make any sense. The Director is vindictive but I would have never thought so stupid, as this is a kick in the teeth that is only ever going to stir up trouble. Then the sight of them returns and I am angry again, the easiest thing is to escape and I am trying to get back on the road and move forward, but can't pull it off, tumble backwards into the past.

I am walking down the street with my mum and we have bought a load of *National Geographic*s at a jumble sale and Christmas is coming around again and it is trying hard to snow and we are carrying them home under our coats and when we get indoors Mum will make me tomato soup and toast and the memory is clear as I hear the swish of tyres on the main road and the wind is pushing harder forcing sleet into our faces and we have our heads down pushing into it and I must be strong and look after Mum worried the magazines are going to get wet and be ruined and the paper is glossy and geography is my favourite subject at school and the photos are brilliant it is a big world inside those pages and outside our lives and I am older and maybe a bit cleverer and we turn the corner and our house is in sight and we are almost safe and we reach the front door and Mum is searching in her bag for the key and I look at the curtains and see Nana's face near the glass except it looks more like Mum and I am not sure for a few seconds and wave and am careful not to drop the magazines and my fingers are numb from the cold and Mum struggles to open the lock and I am shivering and the door is open now and a gust of warmth hits us and we are hurrying inside stamping our feet dripping water laughing and joking and closing out the cold night air.

Mum takes my wet coat and hangs it up, finds a towel and rubs my hair so it stands on end, laughs and says I look like a drowned rat. I dry my face, smell the washing powder she uses, a pine scent that follows me through life. Mum wants me to have a hot bath and I don't argue, starts running the water, the cold will get into my bones and never leave, and I am wondering where my nana is, fighting the panic, have to see if she is in hospital or the living room, battle to get the timing right and control the memory, force a decision out of a mixed-up jailed mind, feel the relief when I see her sitting in her rocking chair. But she is older. It is only a few years since we were making up the fireplace together and Yogi Bear sits quietly next to Mr Fair and Rupert in the corner by her chair and I play more with toy soldiers and tanks these days. Nana is frail and sometimes unsteady on her feet. She knits jumpers and sews socks and has that smile that never changes, right now her needle working its way through a ripped trouser knee, pulling the material tight. She has been in hospital, but is better again, and I wave from the door and tell her I will come in soon, I have to have a bath first, and I remember Mum telling me we can't be wet around Nana as she will catch a chill and that would be dangerous for her.

Sitting in the bath I play with my clockwork submarine and can hear the television singing and the clink of glasses as Mum pours Nana a glass of sherry and this new house we are living in now is smaller but warm in every room and we have been here a couple of years ever since we had to move out of Nana's house when the people who owned it wanted it back and I like this house but miss the fireplace and how me and Nana used to make it up in the morning that is the best time of day and it was our special job and I'd like to have a fire like that again but only with Nana really the radiators are nice and they are in every room and there is a boiler that gives us hot water all the time and this bath is great and with my eyes closed I go on all sorts of adventures and see myself flying planes and driving trains and maybe I will be a policeman when I am old enough and stop all the badness in the world but there is plenty of time to decide and I am in my pyjamas and dressing gown and go into the living room and kiss Nana and her eyes are sort of misty these days for some reason and I spoon tomato soup into my mouth when Mum brings it in on a plate with toast and crisps and Mum and Nana are having another glass of sherry and we will be putting the Christmas tree up tomorrow and I can't wait.

When I have finished my soup I sit on the floor next to the radiator and study the pictures in the magazine, marvel at those mountain forests and weird lights in the sky, twisted and distorted colours swirling like a drop of milk in my tomato soup. One day I will go to that place. Nana laughs and says to promise her, and I do. When I am grown up. And she asks if we had a nice time and I am telling her there was sleet and then Mum asks her if she wants a cup of cocoa and she says yes please dear and Mum is by the window and squeals and tells us it has started to snow. Nana wants to see and comes to the window and Mum turns off the light and goes to put the kettle on and I look through the curtains at the falling snow, feel a hand resting on my shoulder, and we stand there for a long time, me and my nana. And here in Seven Towers my eyes are full of tears and I crush them before they have a chance to destroy me. It is hard going back to these happy times, knowing they can never return. I do my best to think of something else.

Street lights show off the snow and it is falling very slowly, drifting and going wherever it is carried by the wind, fluffy beautiful snow made by God in heaven. And Nana is telling me about my father and says I am a lot like him, he was a good boy, a good man, and one day she will see him again, whether here or in the next life. He is off having adventures and maybe he will come back soon, we never know, and she peers into the night looking for a figure she recognises and tells me I should always believe in God, whatever happens in my life God will watch over me, He knows what is happening and has a reason for everything, and when she goes to live with God one day she will watch over me. She will always protect me wherever I am and no matter what happens. I sort of understand what dying means now and become scared, and

I panic and hug her and she asks if I remember how we used to make the fire up together in the morning and I am happy again as I answer of course, it wasn't that long ago, and I wish we could have a fireplace here, it would be much better, and she laughs and says the radiators are progress, clean and efficient, an open hearth a thing of the past, but much more interesting. She pulls me close and says I have to be a good boy because sometimes boys without fathers can go off the rails, get into trouble at school, and when they are older with the police, it often happens and she doesn't want me to be a bad boy. For my own sake. I have to listen to my mum. She is my father and mother and everything to me. Nana asks me if I understand and I nod and say yes, I think so.

I want to jump up and batter someone who won't feel the pain, a punchbag who deserves his punishment, know this is rubbish thinking and bullying in disguise, that it would be better to smash windows like a junkie, but that only lets the cold in and is harming myself. I have to control these emotions, the soul-sapping memories that have so much time to seep back into an idle mind, and yet prison makes us sentimental, stirs a soppy romance we could never admit to on the outside. I close my eyes and breathe deeply, right down into an empty stomach, do my best to believe Nana is watching over me as she promised, and she would never tell a lie, or even a small fib, reach for my charm and understand that she is very near.

Paradise is long and white and set in a curved bay, the sand hot under my feet as I turn away from Mary-Lou and leave pop and fizz and physical pleasure behind for a more spiritual life, heading East at the crossroads, towards the pungent smell of okra bubbling in a balti dish, shredded sugar cane cooled and ready to serve, pulling me on, and gold flakes turn to billions of priceless grains of sand, the sea calm as it reflects a million galaxies. Baba Jim strolls easy, a wandering man who needs only a loincloth and food bowl to see him through the battles ahead, and when he spies a tiny white chapel he wonders what strand of Christianity it preaches, watches as the cross melts and the tower stretches into the shining needle of a Thai pagoda, looks closer and sees it broaden and sink and become the multicoloured chaos that is a Hindu temple, animal gods mingling with superhumans carved in sandstone, a smell of sandalwood replacing okra and garlic. India is the only place for Baba Jim as he swings from one extreme to the other, following the example of his mentor Mr Jesus Christ, riding the pendulum the same as the Buddha, following his abandoned search for the American dream with a very personal Indian summer. He has come to this exotic land as a passive observer, determined to listen and learn, and he could have followed the overland route through Iraq and Iran, as the carpenter is said to have done, and Christmas should be about forgiveness and generosity of spirit and freedom of thought and expression, everything Jesus tells me is correct, and the steel returns to my blanket, this freedom sledge that defies gravity and the limits of Western science, and I want to walk in the Himalayas and catch a glimpse of those sadhus and swamis I have heard so much about, drifters following the Ganges to its source. Any land where a man can wander naked while covered in the ashes of burnt elephant dung, at the same time puffing on a chillum loaded with the rawest ganja, and be fed and watered and treated as a noble saint, well, this is the place for Baba Jim. My magic blanket skirts the Oasis lands of Ali Baba, soaring across the Arabian Sea as I ignore the Judaic family and its endless rowing, fly deeper into the Christmas celebrations, following Jesus's advice and turning my back on the Rocker who is doomed to a cleaner, more modern crucifixion. The dream of this material democracy is righteous and shows little mercy for the weak and unwilling, and Baba Jim wants no more labels or brands or designer burgers, the kind of rover who is happy enough riding the railways with a motley crew of betel-chewing, sanskrit-quoting hoboes, heads topped with the mightiest dreadlocks known to Rastafari. Jim is a ragged rover recalling tales of hippie exodus through old Kabul and Baghdad, but Baba is arriving from another direction, circling India and coming in overland from Nepal, following the sun down from the mountain top where he has lived with tigers and yetis and Yogi Bear himself, big hairy monsters who lurk in the rock and crave human flesh, faithless monkey monsters and Kali-worshipping thugs, cruel assassins of innocent travellers. Baba has spent many months in a monastery, where an enquiring mind is pushed to breaking point and can either collapse or achieve realisation, and he has been breathing high-altitude air, fighting back the sickness, living like a pauper prince in a Nepalese lodge where Chef serves basic rations of noodles and momo. This is a great journey he is beginning and Baba Jim is heading into Benares jammed inside a packed bus, the men on the roof grabbing the best ride, the giardia he has picked up in Kathmandu making him squirm, roaring into the city with a sense of relief at finally being set free, running to the nearest station hole and releasing the poison. Once he has settled near the ghats he eats gut-cleansing curd and fills up on plain rice, kills the amoeba in his intestine with chemical solutions. Revived and adjusting to the chaos of India, Baba finds his stride, Benares a metropolis of good food for a man fresh out of the Seven Towers monastery, and he is soon working his way along a long row of food halls, the northern curries of the Moguls with their bread and chunkier dishes contesting a friendly rivalry with the southern dosas and sambar. Baba Jim crouches over his banana leaf and asks for refills of rice and four flavours of vegetable, poppadoms and chutneys, enjoying cauliflower and lentils and tomato and the okra he smelt in another life, a sweet lassi to wash it down, masala tea and sweet cakes from the counter. But Baba is only eating to feed his soul. This must be remembered. It is essential he keep his body healthy and for this purpose alone he is forced to try each cafe, sometimes following a northern with a southern, purely in order to maintain a balance. It is food for the soul and he takes little pleasure from the experience, using will-power and mental deceit to dull his senses. He sits in small cafes plastered with postcards of Hindu gods, and in one such establishment he meets a humble baba living on the banks of the Ganges who he buys a bowl of chana and a samosa or two on the side, and this baba tells Jim that he reminds him of Ganesh, that Jim is half-man and half-beast, and Baba thinks about this for a while and wonders if it is a compliment or an insult, finally decides he can be half-boy and half-elephant if the man opposite so wishes, although he has much more in common with another animal. Jim is floating on a dogma-free cloud of liberating purity, celebrating the birth of a man who preached tolerance and forgiveness, that decent people should hate the sin and love the sinner, and I find myself in a monkey temple with all these hairy human faces around me, and they are snarling and spitting and talking gibberish, a rabid bunch of crooks who rob visitors of their bananas and nuts. Baba Jim stays beyond their reach, and most are congregated on the steps leading to a shrine to Hanuman, and he sees the face of this monkey god and winces, though he knows Hanuman is not evil. A swami in a crisp white gown and red paint on his forehead explains that these monkeys guard the temple, and although they are ferocious he should not be scared, as we are all the creatures of God. Baba wonders whether to tell this holy man about the monkey monsters, but keeps his mouth shut, maintains his dignity and listens as the swami tells him about a temple in Rajasthan which is home to thousands of rats. You see, my friend, the people worship these rats as they house the spirits of holy men who have chosen to reincarnate as lowly rodents in order to use up their bad karma faster and achieve enlightenment sooner. It seems that these souls are keen to escape the cycle of birth, death and rebirth, and I remember being told everything happens for a reason, and that could be happening right now, Baba Jim burning negative karma every single day of his life, and he has been punished in the past and will be punished in the future and maybe he is being punished at this moment for something he did a long time ago and I am thinking about this, thinking very hard, trying to remember, but there is a blockage and it all blows away and I am back on my carefree journey with no fears or worries, and it makes so much sense, heading for India and living the roving life of a baba, unbothered by possessions or material desires. Benares is a centre of learning and a sacred city, its ghats drawing millions of pilgrims who climb down their steps to bathe in the Ganges, and Baba Jim sits on a ledge watching the spectacle, and while he is struck by the poverty and has heard about the horrors of the caste system, he can't avoid the romanticised view of an outsider, and realises that, strangely, Jimmy Rocker's journey lingers, the garish imagery of the Hindu pantheon reflected in the neon strips of America, Hanuman meeting up with Porky Pig via Ganesh and Mickey Mouse, music blaring deep into the night, rockabilly and ragas clashing, innocence guarded by some hard-core religious doctrine. He knows there are contradictions galore, wants an easy life, tries to sleep but the heat of the city is too much, a whirlpool of mashed-up sensations keeping his mind racing, and he craves the open road, not ready for Benares and its mazes of the mind, catching an early train south to Madras and continuing to Kovalam, the desert in the heart of India baking in a hundred and twenty degrees of heat, and he sees elephantiasis and leprosy and this idea of karma is not much different to heaven and hell but exists in the here and now, and yet it can only work if there is no judgement involved and few Westerners are capable of this. I see Baba sitting on Kovalam beach chewing on a mango, a half-empty bottle of Cobra on the blanket he has spread over the sand. He shouldn't be drinking but doesn't want to become narrow-minded, the sort of materialistic spiritualist who scuffs the path to awareness, tries to block out the things that come naturally. This path isn't about denial, but about accepting reality, and he is approached by a beautiful woman who reminds him of someone he knows well, but is singing about a sweet virgin Mary, the love of Bob Dylan's life, and the mango is sugar-sweet and the Cobra laced with bromide and the lust of the sexual man is blunted and a pure childlike innocence reigns. Sarah wants to lead the baba man back to their hut, but he points out that sex is for procreation and the act is not to be taken lightly as children are the result of this sacred union and Sarah begins doubting herself as a woman and a human being, feels the drifting baba man doesn't love her any more. Jim realises she is immersed in the world of illusion, and of course he is man enough to understand that as a wandering aesthete, a dedicated fakir, he has to adjust, must not become attached to his own views, and so Baba allows himself to be led into the trees, to their hut, towards a ceremonial coupling. They pass a temple and hear music, and it is a Christian temple with Hindu imagery and he sees Christ next to Ganesh and an old photograph of an ancient priest in a brand new plastic pink frame, and they are singing a hymn he remembers from school, and the old man in the frame is Father Christmas and he thinks of the journeys he makes with his mother to see the fat man who is laughing ho ho ho asking the boy what he wants and he says a Yogi Bear toy like the one on the counter and Baba Jim is all grown up and with his lady, removing a gecko from the timber as lizards frighten Sarah and he is in tune with the natural world so the gecko sits in the palm of his hand and he can see through its skin to a weave of tiny veins and big glass eyes peer at him with admiration and he feels so brilliant he wants to sing and dance and float in the air on his blanket and soar over nearby Trivandrum and shoot off to circle Ceylon hunting for his princess and the ecstasy he feels is incredible, he knows the whole mental game is a balancing act, needs to stay on a high, the rusty pendulum of joy and sorrow, good and evil, stuck in its rhythm, and he has to resist the temptation, stay true to his sacred mission, explain things to Sarah who of course understands, and Baba refuses to become a fantasy figure, a cartoon fool the kids laugh at in the playground, called names he doesn't understand as he is naive and innocent, and they are turning nasty, going on and on, and when they ask if it is true he is a murderer a dark karma cloud descends and he can't answer.

The last day of the year in marked by anger on B-Block, despite the grovelling of the Director. Our morning milk is sweetness itself and there is rice and fish for dinner, an extra half-loaf of bread each, but the tongues are not forgiven. The Director has misjudged the situation and is worried, the hard core spreading the message that we are about to riot. A major New Year's disturbance is the last thing the Director needs. Chef has let it be known that it was the Director and Porky Pig who insisted the tongues were served whole and on their own, rather than returned to the supplier or disguised. Their pettiness has backfired. And the tongues have another, symbolic meaning, the B-Block scum dropping every available match on Dumb Dumb's bed as they show their solidarity with the silent builder. Only Papa resists, the monkey monsters hard to judge, although they appear to be sulking.

The farmers stand in the yard trying to ease a volatile situation, while Porky arrives early, heavily guarded and unable to resist a leering smile that is more man than pig, his protectors forming a semicircle, rifles trained on the crowd. The nutters from each tier, about thirty men in total, stand together, flanked by the rest of us. A core of violent men serving long sentences and another thirty or so easily led barmies is a frightening sight in such a confined space and Porky, for all his swagger, is scared. Some prisoners want to take their chances with the bullets and hack him to death, suddenly angry at his blatant drug trafficking, but there are the junkies to consider, the chaos that will erupt if they are left without their fixes. Porky is spat on from the top of the stairs, dodges a couple of rocks, dishes his dirt and gets out. He must report his welcome to the Director as an hour later the loudspeaker crackles and the prisoners stop to listen as the governor of the prison apologises for the tongues, blaming an administrative mix-up. Everyone knows this is a lie, but it is also a climbdown. It makes us feel as if we have some power and softens the mood. The Director and his prize pig have been humiliated. I find myself grinning as Jesus translates, yet annoyed I am so easily pleased.

I spend too much of the afternoon reliving that service in the chapel where I saw Franco. I tried to get over to him at the end, but the guards kept me back. I wave and again Franco stares blankly. It could be that he isn't expecting to see me, but he appears broken. I don't even know if he has been sentenced yet, B-Block quarantined from the rest of the prison after an incident earlier in the year, involving a knife, a grudge, the throat of a gangster off A-Block, the hand of a B-Block boy, and two coffees at the Oasis. The lack of a work regime or educational facilities means there is little movement inside the prison, so getting news from outside the block is difficult.

Even when it comes to showers and visits, we are kept apart. Jesus can bribe some information from one of the gate men, but there are no trustees on the block. I don't like asking favours as he has enough trouble looking after himself, but I ask anyway, wondering where Elvis is, hoping he has been released, though this would mean tough times for Franco, stuck on his own. Elvis could be free and cruising into Texas with Mary-Lou at this very moment.

Some of the men start preparing for the big night early, for some strange reason going through the green door and crowding around the sink instead of using the one in the yard, scrubbing and preening, changing dirty shirts to ones that just smell, combing hair and brushing teeth, and we are off to a rocking party where we will drink beer and schnapps and meet women and listen to music, while the family men aim for a restaurant serving squid and lobster and champagne, musicians busy on traditional tunes and a compere counting down to midnight. We walk up and down the yard releasing endorphins, beads tapping, trotting on the spot and talking to ourselves and wishing we were on a street corner choosing a bar or a cafe. Even the monkey monsters walk along the side of the yard, Papa alone at the section door. And when Chef arrives with the evening soup it is a genuine stew, and a good one as well. It is thick, with more beef and potato and less grease, and served with another half-loaf of bread. Chef is back laughing and joking with the boys and when I reach the front I realise he is drunk. The Butcher informs Jesus who tells me that Chef has added a bottle of wine to the stew, or rather half a bottle, as the rest has gone down his throat. We eat the stew and it is quality food, our second good meal of the week, reason that this must come from the top, the Director making a major effort.

When I have finished eating I go over to the outside sinks as normal, find the drain blocked and the nearest trough full. It must be why the others have been going inside, why I am the only one here. I look into the sink and jump back, the tongues floating in the water. In the dull light they could be rotting crabs, legs snapped and trailing, the stink of decaying flesh making me gag. I tread back and bump into Jesus who says someone has collected the tongues from the rubbish bin and picked and rinsed off the dirt and laid them to rest in this grave. A methodical, painstaking operation, I ask who is responsible and he turns and nods at Papa, the pyjama killer busy scolding a monster. I can't work it out. Jesus tries to guess which animal they come from, suggests lambs, piglets, baby goats. A tear rolls down his cheek as he thinks of the sufferers, insists he would rather die than stand by and see these creatures butchered.

We move away and sit down on the ledge and he explains that nobody really wants the tongues, the slaughterhouse selling them at a cheap price. We guess that they can be cut up and mixed with offal, shredded and lost in meat loaf, stuck on spits, put into dog food, while in some countries they are a delicacy, but here, undisguised, they are a grotesque reminder of man's cruelty. This is disgusting, my friend, the tongue is the communicator, and removing it is castration. Jesus is a vegetarian and looks as if he is about to start crying, so I leave him alone, go off on safari, wash my bowl and worry about the mist sticking to the plastic, seasoning the surface with piss, get straight back out and return to the yard.

Walking towards the gate my calves tingle, pushing weak veins and buried thrombosis, doing my best to erase the tongues from my mind. We all end up doing this in the end, marching up and down, killing time and trying to wear down reality. I reach the wall by the tree and turn, go to the opposite end of the yard, back and forward clicking heels, do this many times before stopping and stretching my arms and finally placing a hand on the trunk of the tree. I enjoy the texture of the bark, which is rough and smooth and a little warm, although this must be a trick, Jesus leaning against the flap in the gate talking, waving me over. He has asked about the hashish-smoking Italian and it seems Franco has been sentenced to nine months and is lonely as his friend, the dollar man, who has also been sentenced, has moved to a work farm on the orders of a judge, who has been influenced by a surgeon from the hospital. Nine months is a lot less than I have left to serve and Franco should be grateful. With the time he has done he should be out soon. If that was me I would be doing cartwheels and I wonder why he seemed so defeated in the chapel. It must be his nature. But I am pleased for Elvis, who now has a job digging the earth, and will halve his time and soon be on that highway heading west, his soul free and intact. This is good news and perks me up.

The sun fades and the lights are switched on in the yard. There is little rush to get us into the section, a new softer approach being employed. A flock of tiny birds dips into the castle and sways between A- and B-Block, sees the dead tree and settles in its branches. After finding a crack in the rock and a patch of soil to sink its roots into, this tree grew to be four times the size of a human being before it finally gave up. Maybe that is what happens with long-term prisoners, strong men who keep going for years before they finally snap and surrender, end their lives as institutionalised wrecks. I want to grab Franco around the throat and shake some optimism into him, explain how lucky he is, but he is a weakling caught in the wrong place at the wrong time, a holidaymaker with a stupid book of photos, who doesn't appreciate how lucky he is having a family and a home. He is a fool feeling so sorry for himself, but thinking this way is unfair, though we all do it sometime or other. There is nothing wrong in being weak, or maybe the right word is sensitive.

Jesus points at the prison cat creeping along the wall, dipping in and out of the wire, sneaking up behind the birds. The prowler lowers himself and moves on his belly, claws itching and mouth twitching, sleek and handsome, so mesmerising we don't see him as a ruthless killer, within pouncing distance when clapping hands warn the birds. Turning towards the source I see Papa smiling as the birds rise into the sky, darting one way and then the other in a twisting tornado of spitting wings, separating into two long strands as they skirt the nearest tower, coming together on the far side and speeding away into the dusk. The cat pauses, stands and stretches its legs, arches a stiff back, pretending it doesn't care, doing its best to saunter as it walks off.

Once we are locked up for the night the party begins. The Butcher has got hold of one of Ali's famous hashish cakes, and this is placed in the middle of the table and carefully cut so there is one thin slice for every prisoner who wants a piece. The psychopaths Flip Flop and Pretty Boy flank the Butcher as he makes preliminary marks on the crust with a sliver of glass, ensuring each slice is exactly the same size. It is a surprise when he reaches into the front of his trousers, to the top of his thigh, and brings out a long silver knife. He wipes the blade on the sleeve of his shirt and the more nervous prisoners among us step back. I hope he doesn't have the rest of his work tools with him, and that flour and egg won't be too much of a disappointment after liver and kidney. It is a decent enough cake, with a nutty flavour and a hint of carrot, icing around the rim. Ali must be living a good life on A-Block, and the hashish is bound to hit me hard, and it does, quickly as well.

Sitting on the edge of my bed I am grinning for ages, watching old men grimace and examine cards and dominoes, younger versions drumming beads as if they are jazz men, the teenage flasher singing a song and dancing on the spot as other men clap out a beat and roar with laughter, and it is like my first night but without the bully who wanted my shoes, and what the fuck did he want them for anyway, to prove himself, that was it, but they are falling apart and I need a new pair but there are no shops in this abandoned mall, and there are the same sounds and a woozy understanding of what is going on, and I am thinking that this is the end of a year that started so well, try to remember where I was, but it is gone, memory lost, is that all this travelling life amounts to, and through the celebrations Dumb Dumb builds his house, measuring and comparing matchsticks in his zombie way, except I know he is no fool, deep down he is intelligent, maybe a genius, thinking all the time, absorbed in an inner world which is out of bounds to trespassers, and I start wondering who is going to live in the house, he is going to need a wife and children and maybe a dog and a cat, and how many kids is he going to have and are they going to end up the same as their father, a dumb fuck who looks and doesn't see, listens and doesn't hear, and he is going to need furniture for his family to sit on and sleep in and eat at, and maybe that will be the next stage, once his house is finished he will start building furniture, elaborate chairs and beds and tables, and I wonder if he will paint this furniture, and maybe he will build some matchstick men, and I wonder how he will give them faces.

The ganja wears off and the night settles in, zombies buried alive as zombies prefer, the Butcher beaming at everyone, Jesus enjoying a friendly row with his two favourite thugs, Papa reading his book as the monkey monsters gaze into their candle, Flip Flop sitting opposite Pretty Boy at the table, playing cards, other men busy with dominoes, and despite the happy scene there is an underlying tension, all due to a simple number on a calendar. Even the Director is scared of us rioting. Any other time and he would have the guards battering us with their clubs and the hoses hooked up. He would love it as well, but tonight, and at Christmas, things are different. And it is obvious the smackheads have had an extra special hit from Porky, lying on their beds as normal, one or two twitching, something I have never noticed before, and maybe they are savouring greater experiences than ever, I don't know how it works, I am a drinker not a drug man, and there are a lot of men like me, put next to heroin for the first time in our lives and this fact only makes sense if Homer Simpson is right, that the authorities want the criminal element hooked and overdosing and never reoffending. It seems enough men enter prison for a simple crime and come out drug addicts, while others leave in a coffin.

It is approaching midnight when one of the junkies stands and walks into the aisle, starts staggering and bumping into beds, stirring prisoners doing their best to blank out the occasion. At first nobody realises there is a problem as we are used to the H-men freaking out and smashing windows and mutilating their arms with glass and wire, occasionally severing a vein in their wrist, like the marble man in the bed, slashing at their necks and armpits, searching for major blood flow. The jerks and screams become familiar, lose their shock power, and we are grateful for the calm tonight, sedated junk freaks stuck in their pleasure palaces, but looking at this frosty character even I can see something is different. Pretty Boy leans over another junkie who is lying very still, on top of his blanket, and the pretty man is calling other prisoners over and they are trying to shake the freak awake, but he isn't moving, and it slowly dawns on me that they are dealing with a corpse.

I don't know his name, he is just another convict I can't talk to, but I think of his mother and father and brothers and sisters sitting in that restaurant with the squid and lobster and champagne, toasting the memory of a child and not forgetting their grown-up son, never turning their backs, and Papametropolis is holding the stumbling freak around the waist, trying to control his jerking arms, and Jesus is jumping up and down and shouting in his language and the thugs are at the window calling for help, and all over the section men are shaking other men awake and Pretty Boy is sitting on the edge of the dead boy's bed holding a cold hand and staring at the floor, dribbling horse foam, the zombies coming alive and rubbing red eyeballs, blinking as they realise they are no longer at that party with the beautiful women, and the monkey monsters move in formation, spreading out and reaching junkies and slapping their faces and there is this huge tangle of arms and legs and moving contorted heads as the H-men are pulled upright and beaten back to life and some seem okay while others have turned to marble, and the farmers are hanging back not knowing what to do, I doubt anyone knows really, Papa taking control and issuing orders to the Butcher who moves to the door carrying his knife in his hand and the noise is spewing from gasping mouths, tongues lashing, three marble men carried off on safari and the door is left open and the smell of shit and piss and sickness floods the room and I can hear the taps running full pelt and know they are using water to revive these sad boys on the verge of overdosing before the year is finished talk about fresh starts and hope for the future and there are guards in the yard and faces looking in through the bars and finally the door opens and the Butcher is holding his carving knife behind his back as the guards enter and prisoners are explaining the situation and I half expect to see Porky Pig trot in knowing the Butcher wants this porker all to himself but of course he is at home beyond payback and Jesus is saying the smack is too strong my friend the smack is too strong and his face is contorted with rage telling me don't these idiots know they are executing themselves and Porky and the Director must be laughing at our stupidity and there is nobody here who is going to be able to accuse them of a crime and even if they do where is the evidence and these injuries are self-inflicted just as much as when a man harms himself with a piece of glass and the guards are trying to help and it is funny as I realise that apart from Porky and one or two vindictive fools I never think about the men in uniform don't even think of them as human more like rusty out-of-date machine men and they don't go in for big-time bullying like they do in the movies instead wander through the passages doing a job and not caring one way or the other until men maim themselves and start dying in front of their eyes and then they become human and the Butcher is twitching the knife in his hand and there is a father in his work clothes with his back turned towards the murderer and mutilator a sweet man who just happens to have cut his wife and her lover into pieces and fed their meat and organs to the general public taking the best bits for himself and the thought makes me laugh out loud and as I am watching him his smiling lips turn down and his face changes and it is the most evil expression I have ever seen as if he is gloating as once again he has the power of life and death, at last, and his arm is moving and I look away and the guard passes me he has moved at the right moment and Jesus is calling asking for my help and I am on one side of a marble man and the Butcher is on the other and we are helping him out into the yard where spotlights pick us out as if we are performing on a stage and we stumble to the gate where we are stopped by rifles and the Butcher is staring up into the lights and one of the guards points us back towards the section and I return with the Butcher's heavy arm around my shoulders and his voice babbling in my ear and I don't even wonder about the knife and it feels good this trust between bad men and it really doesn't matter what he has done in his life and what he wants to do in the future just as long as he doesn't hurt me, the door finally slamming with at least one man dead and four on their way to hospital.

It takes a long time for things to quieten down and longer for me to stop shivering. The passing of another year has been lost in the chaos. The surviving junkies don't know how lucky they have been yet. And I think of popping corks and men and women linking arms and kissing and hugging in their funny hats covered in streamers and balloons tied to their wrists with music pumping out and the ground covered in spilt beer staining our clothes and nobody caring and this prison life existence is shit, the callous way the minions in charge needlessly make us suffer. Jesus stands over me and there are tears in his eyes, and everyone is shocked but particularly this sensitive friend, and the farmers are suggesting a hunger strike to protest against the tongues and the heroin but aren't thinking straight, the convicts have other plans, and I laugh in a sick way that surprises me, the pendulum swinging from a famine to a feast and right back again, and I am just hopelessly arching my shoulders and spouting happy New Year, Jesus, happy New Year, my friend.

The shop opposite the park is a food heaven disguised as a delicatessen, immaculate displays showing off a huge selection of fresh fruit and vegetables, newly baked bread and exotic cheeses, barrels of olives and pickles and hummus and stuffed vine leaves, an elongated counter packed with meat and fish, a wide range of nuts and pulses, cultured yogurt and sweet cakes, wine and beer and milk, thick slabs of chocolate, figs and dates. The choice rises through floor-to-ceiling shelves, a hungry man's dream come true. The establishment does excellent business, the proprietor keeping his work surfaces and refrigerators spotless, and although he employs a cleaner he can't help mopping the floors himself, morning and night, every hour polishing the marble counter he has spent a small fortune importing, an antique treasure shining beneath gleaming chandeliers. Of course, he stocks essentials as well as luxuries, but his prices are high, and he has little time for idlers.

I stand outside the shop looking through manicured glass, watch the people come and go, smelling fresh bread when the door swings open, and I return to the park and listen to my stomach rumbling, finally pluck up the courage to return and go inside, searching for a simple meal of bread and cheese. I move through the aisles, sneaking glances at the shopkeeper, seeing a skinny man who eats all day yet never puts on weight, his miserable expression in contrast to an inner metabolism that burns energy faster than a space probe. He is hen-pecked by his wife, a snob who disrespects him, their children following her example, and I squirm seeing him belittled in front of his customers, wish he was a proud man who could break this cycle and pass his new-found self-respect back to his customers, serve a wandering man bread and cheese with a smile rather than a frown, ask how the drifter is feeling and maybe add a few of those sun-dried tomatoes for free, insist he sample a couple of apricots and a handful of pumpkin seeds.

The shop owner compensates for his wife in the quality and range of his goods, the cleanliness of his premises, closing his ears to a family that licks its lips as he keeps them in idleness yet offers nothing in return, hands extended as their arrogance shields an inner knowledge that they are more scrounging than the drifter who smells of train carriages. Scum rises to the top. But this man has no balls and doesn't like the way I dress and tells me to hurry up, in a not too roundabout way, and because I am hungry I lower my head and pay for bread, cheese and a small pot of olives and though this food is overpriced it tastes fantastic when I sit in the park, on a bench with the birds. The idea of this snob making me look foolish in front of myself rankles, but I feel no anger, actually feel sorry for him. But he can't get away with his behaviour, and I am not interested in his takings, what I really crave is the contents of his shop. Especially that cheese display, the loaves stacked in wicker baskets and smelling of wheat and rye and walnuts and sunflower oil. There is a wide range of chocolate on offer. Oranges and melons and a fridge full of ice cream. I decide to visit the delicatessen tonight, find a room and sleep, return again with a truly empty belly.

I wake at ten, excited and suddenly starving, know this is going to be a great adventure. I stroll back to the park and scan the front of the shop, see that the delicatessen is in darkness. With the street empty I nip down an alley and work my way round to the back, stand on an old fridge and crack a small pane of glass, open the window and lift myself inside. Once in the shop I stop to let my eyes become used to the layout, light filtering in from the street and touching the metal supports and shelves. There is no rush, the upstairs a travel agent's, which means the owner lives off the premises. I have time to choose whatever I want. And it is one of those dreams small boys have and the main dream of men in prison or away fighting a war or stuck on a mountain or travelling through a desert or out on safari. Best of all, this is a just raid, repaying unnecessary rudeness.

It is hard to remember the last time I tasted chocolate, and I reach out and take a box, unwrap the cellophane and open the treasure chest, select a strawberry cream and pop it in my mouth, let the chocolate melt and the fruit ooze through, a rich taste that pisses all over rice and peas. Christmas has come early, and I choose a truffle and hazelnut whirl, eating as I walk, heading for the wine rack and taking a bottle at random, look around for an opener which I find on the counter, pull out the cork and take a glass from a box, pour myself a drink. I toast life and start building myself a meal on a convenient china plate. I unwrap and cut slices of cheese, pile up the olives and slice loaves, which are still soft, one piece from each for variation. The most succulent tomatoes in the world are on sale here and I take three, chop up a red onion, open a bag of salted peanuts, and I am moving back to the food I grew up on, the tastes of childhood, taking a packet of crisps and a can of Coke from the fridge, some ginger biscuits, and my plate is already loaded so I sit in a chair at the back of the shop and eat fast, stuffing it down, forgetting my manners. It tastes great and I remember to concentrate, refuse to waste a mouthful. I finish my glass of wine and survey the food at my fingertips, reaching to the ceiling.

I am full but decide to wait a while, let my hunger return.

This is a once-in-a-lifetime opportunity and I have to do it justice. It is the same with those all-you-can-eat meals, and it doesn't matter if it's an American smorgasbord or Indian thali, it is the nature of the ordinary man to eat as much as he can. This is for free, but the owner won't even notice, and while I feel sorry for the way his wife and brats talk to him I also think fuck him, just because he is gutless doesn't mean he should take it out on me. In a way he is lucky he was rude to this man and not a nutty boy. Others would pull him over the till and splash his blood on that precious marble. All I am doing is eating a little of his produce, levelling a tax. This right-eous approach makes me glow inside, and the taste of the olives lingers and after half an hour I go back for more, add big spoons of macaroni salad, move to the potato salad, take half a quiche and handfuls of nuts mixed with raisins, mouth watering as I hurry back to my seat where I go through the same routine, reaching for the wine and pouring another glass, see a freezer full of cold beer and bring back five bottles, crack one and feel the goodness, mix macaroni and potato, the time passing as I rest and eat, rest and eat some more, filling myself to bursting point, and there is a small part of me that says I should leave, but a bigger part telling me to keep on going.

There is so much food on offer it would be a sin to walk away. I have never eaten like this before and may never do so again. And I start wondering if I should make this a regular thing, pick a shop like this every day and raid it, nobody would ever bother to track me down, and I like the idea, that while others rob banks and leave a trail of destruction across states and nations, I slice cheese and bread and hurt no man, merely fill my belly and move on. I finish the beer and know I should get going, that if I am caught they will think I am trying to steal the takings, and I decide to build a double-decker sand-wich before I leave, in a minute, feel heavy and close my eyes, so full of food I laughingly doubt I could even stand up, living like a king and spending nothing, a real glutton. I wake up squinting into the beam of a torch, an angry shopkeeper and policeman staring straight back.

CONTROL

THE NEW YEAR smashes through the windows and it must be some forgotten ganja crumbs making it shine so bright. But nobody here is starting fresh. There is only one resolution. As soon as the door is unlocked B-Block is going to erupt. The hard men have been plotting deep into the night, the rest of us angry enough to back them. The junkies get on our nerves with their moaning and vandalism, but they are part of the section, and in their way victims. Felons with nothing to lose, the likes of the Butcher, Flip Flop and Pretty Boy are excited at the coming riot, Papa and his monsters agitated, even the peace-loving Jesus and the diplomatic union officials ready to make up the numbers. The Director and Porky Pig are about to be punished for the tongues, as much as the heroin, their innocence and symbolism making it a perversely darker crime. It is a rotten world and part of me wishes there was no new year, no more days or nights or rambling hopes and fears, just a disembodied state where I can float along deaf and dumb and left alone. The other part wants a riot. One man has died and four are missing, having their stomachs pumped if they are alive, veins drained if not. And we don't know what has happened upstairs yet.

Locked inside we are weak, with little to damage except our beds and the windows, while setting fire to the place would be suicidal. Out in the yard things are different, even if we are hemmed in and easy targets for the riflemen on the wall, hawks replacing vultures as the dead boys stir. We can drive the uniforms on the ground out and control the block, make demands and even take hostages. The hard core want these hostages, while the softer men would rather take charge and issue demands. In the end there can only be one winner, but at least we will be transferred to other prisons, and for the first time I wonder if this is a good thing, that maybe there are worse jails than Seven Towers. If we took hostages we could appeal to the state and see the Director and Porky tried for murder, returned to us for punishment. But the machine will never admit a crime. Even if they are convicted, the Director will end up on A-Block, smoking cigars and drinking tea, eating Ali's space cake as he waits for his inevitable, successful appeal. Our powerlessness means that if the psychos take hostages, it will end in a bloodbath.

The choice isn't mine, the reality of what is about to happen stark and real and too dark to dwell on. I force the Director and Porky Pig into court, a jury of twelve monkeys good and true considering their case, Papa the presiding judge, pyjamas washed and ironed and his head topped with a white wig, knitting needle tapping for silence. Things turn personal and revenge gets the better of me as the judge, prosecutor and translator arrive in handcuffs. Five bad men stand trial and I am the new prosecutor, using fluent English, which is understood, to attack the characters of the defendants. A minimum tariff of ten years, without parole, and definitely no work transfer, is the sentence I demand. I insist any release or privilege, be it a bar of soap or cup of coffee from my old friend Ali Baba, depends on a full admission of hypocrisy. No man is innocent, and their confessions will be broadcast all day, every day. Papa agrees to my demands. The glare entering the courtroom grows in intensity, as if confirming the fairness of the hearing.

Dumb Dumb tumbles out of bed and goes over to a window, the years falling from his face as he jumps and excitedly points outside, Jesus trailing him down memory lane and following the dumb kid's gaze, turning to the room and imploring the men to have faith, his words filled with an urgency that stirs everyone, boys jumping out of bed and hurrying to the glass to see what is happening, and I watch their expressions and see the anger drain away, and I am on my feet and part of the crowd pushing for a view, the light blinding in its brilliance, my heart hopping and turning a somersault as I realise that during the night it has snowed.

Everyone is smiling, hands resting on shoulders, mouths moving, and I am as excited as the rest of these overgrown boys, looking from one end of the yard to the other, noticing how the snow has settled, and it is deep and crisp and even, except where a breeze has formed a tiny ridge, but what I notice most is how still the world seems, an incredible calmness overcoming us. Leaning against the glass I see frozen crystals where wayward flakes have crashed and turned to ice, forming silver starfish, and emotion cripples me as I stand with Nana watching the snow fall and there is no wind or sleet just a gentle tumble of so many individual flakes and they dull the noise of the traffic so cars move silently dominated by the snow lorries turning into sleighs drawn by Rudolph the red-nosed reindeer, and I am looking up at this woman who has lived more than seventy years and she is a girl once again forgetting the cancer I know nothing about, her face shining with a quality none of us ever really loses, and I understand this is a special moment and I hug her waist and she ruffles my hair and we stand together at the window knowing age means nothing, watching the snow drifting for a very long time, loving the way it settles and finds peace.

The door opens and we are standing at the edge of the yard, oblivious to the cold, lost in awe seeing barbs of wire as soft buds, razor blunted and balancing thin lines of chalk, blocks capping internal and external walls, drifts sagging gutters, the dead black tree dusted white and luminous. The yard itself is smooth with the craters filled and gravel coated and we are scared to walk over it as our footprints would ruin the effect, reminding me of a sunny meadow. The light is stunning, as if under the snow the mountain is glowing. There are tiny stars on the window ledges, birds watching us as the sun rises, and there are the paw marks of the cat, but no blood or feathers, sparrows and robins one step ahead. We hesitate, boys chatting and teasing, junkies forgotten, and this is what we wish for at this magical time of year, and if I was religious I would guess it was a message to trust in natural justice, heaven and hell and long-term karma. When Chef arrives we line up by the wall, leaving the bulk of the snow untouched. The milk tastes sweeter than ever, more snow falling and covering our yard-side tracks, so it seems as if we are weightless.

The swing of prison emotions is as extreme as ever, the horror of the tongues and hot-shot marble men confronted by the beauty of our snow-white castle. And the following day two of the junkies return, one staying in hospital, another dead. Two men have been taken from the upper floor, and both also return. It is made clear that these deaths are self-inflicted, although Porky Pig is not seen again. The Director makes an announcement that tells us drugs are illegal on the outside and illegal inside Seven Towers. The doctor pushes his substitute and the most chronic addicts are transferred to another jail, with a proper hospital wing, something this dilap-idated place lacks. The snow remains soft, constantly topped up with new falls. When a snowball fight breaks out it churns up the whole yard, boys pouring out of the sections to join in, though there is no chance of this game ending in the usual brawl. We are tired and wet and laughing by the end, devas-tated when we realise what we have destroyed. Straight away it starts snowing and we are reprieved, the carpet repaired in minutes, deepening as we stand back and watch.

The snow lasts for a week before turning to ice. This hardens and the yard is transformed into an ice rink. Huge icicles form along the edge of the roof, stalactite glass amazing a new arrival, the giant Leadbelly who for some unknown reason has lost his gate-keeping privilege and been shunted on to B-Block. The African is captivated. He stands and looks at the spectacle and repeats magnificent magnificent. He treads warily on the ice, giggling and smiling, face opening up, and this must seem like a miracle for someone who really is used to lions and gorillas and the full jungle experience, and his response makes the prisoners smile, although the Congo boy is shocked by the B-Block safari. Sometimes the sun catches these huge shards just right and they turn blue and purple and twinkle as if electricity is popping inside, a brilliant shade of turquoise that makes me think of icebergs and polar bears and the underwater crystals divers capture on specialised cameras, a series of prisms shaped into spears that will skewer a man if one falls.

The monkey monsters prefer the ice rink to the snow, bundling out in a ball of skinny arms and flailing legs, hoods hiding hollow heads, scarves over the lower part of their faces, chapped noses protruding, running until they fall and skid along on their padded bums. They laugh like the maniacs they are, Papa silent as he stands watching, mouth relaxed and eyes fixed. It is a timeless landscape, the ice holding for another week, freezing but beautiful the way it emerges from the snow and becomes part of the wire, the grooves of the dead tree packed but the bark refusing to crack, steel ivy sucking on the trunk and branches dripping solid-water thorns, and all the while the towers preserve chunks of snow beyond the reach of the sun. All we need are some skates and we could perform a prison ballet, Seven Towers on Ice, spotlight beaming from our Disneyland pillars. And this is also a good time, despite the heroin, the tongues of innocents, and maybe we start believing they could be accidents, the big freeze affecting the way we think, dulling our desire for mayhem. The moment passes. Peace settles over B-Block and I return to marking crosses on my calendar with a strange new vigour.

The authorities always get it wrong. With the snow calming everyone down the Director should keep things sweet, punish Porky and remove any lingering anger, improve the food and capitalise on the doubt he has created. Instead, when the ice finally melts, he orders a crackdown. The door bursts open at six in the morning and the goon squad charges in, swinging clubs and barking orders. They target Flip Flop, Pretty Boy and three other men in their beds, batter them unconscious before dragging their bodies off the block. A tear-gas canister is set off by the green door and still half asleep we are forced outside, spluttering and trying to get our coats and shoes on, disorientated by the attack. The goons are talking fast and Jesus is scared, says the Director has ordered a control to beat all other controls. Our guards have been replaced by former soldiers and civilian heavies, a private team of bullies organised and handed a logo by a security firm. The prison guards we are used to dealing with have been given extended leave or moved to other blocks. Porky has been promoted, transferred to an island with the role of deputy governor. It seems the Director is determined to add more discipline to the Seven Towers regime.

We stand in the yard with the goons facing us, staring at our faces and making comments, none of which I understand, the sarcasm clear in their sneers and phoney laughter. We have been caught out. These men are fit and cocky and act as if they are on speed, testosterone meeting steroids and urging them to crack skulls and splinter limbs. These bully boys are very different to the normal brew, officers who are older and apathetic, half sent here from the police force as a punishment, the rest long-serving jailers passed over for promotion and transfer. They do their time and look forward to retirement, dreams and ambition forgotten, and while they lose their tempers and can be petty and small-minded at times, most are all right. This lot are another breed. Posing in crisp uniforms and polished boots they imagine they are an elite, believe the propaganda, really think they are special with their toy guns and rubber truncheons and tear gas. They are in their twenties and loving the chance to push us around, any conscience soothed by the plain fact we are in prison and therefore deserve anything they fancy giving us. I notice they haven't opened the upper tier, splitting B-Block in half, a glimmer of fear in their caution. Above us, faces push against the bars, the commotion an early bell for our brothers, the gas drifting from our section a warning.

The Director struts on to the block flanked by more goons, and the bad boys in the sky shout and bang their mugs on the bars, opening the frames wide for full effect. An apple flies out and hits a bully in the face. His nose swells up in seconds. The clatter of mugs is disorganised at first, frantic and angry and fixed on volume, but it quickly dips down and links together, transforming itself into a rhythmic protest, a locomotive rolling out of the stockyards and picking up speed, building an irresistible momentum, crushing everything in its path. The Director's entourage stops and a box is produced. The Director stands on his pedestal and tries to gloat, the rhythm of the train firm and proud, drowning out his voice. He squints at the faces by the windows, and one of the junkies from our section starts thumping his hands together in a slow handclap, and in seconds we are all clapping together and falling in with the rhythm. The glass trembles and my skin tingles. We are united. The goons don't know what to do. One steps forward and swings his truncheon at the nearest convict, a panty sniffer known as Alan. He crumples to the ground.

We surge forward and a shot is fired into the air, and this echoes around the inside of the castle, the goons protecting the Director, levelling their rifles, the bully boys raising truncheons and pulling revolvers. We shout and swear and make gestures but no one is willing to be the first gunned down. We have no power and should have taken our chance on New Year's morning, instead of being seduced by the snow. We are scum and this is our punishment, made to look foolish by hired muscle freaks, two goons sprinting up the steps to the top tier. There is a pause and then shouting and finally gas spewing from the windows along with the puke of those trapped inside. I recall our happiness at seeing the snow and match it with their panic, the locomotive coming off the rails in a tangle of bent iron and smoking lungs, falling quiet as the Director delivers his lecture, face red with excitement, power surging, arsehole trembling. Barrels hold us back, the sound of coughing lost under the smell of vomit. When the Director has finished we are made to stand in silence for what seems like half an hour, heads bowed as if we are truants, before being locked back in the section.

The smell of the tear gas lingers and we busy ourselves opening every window, the wind picking up and blowing in, men walking around picking up scattered clothes and over-turned beds. A monster pushes another monkey up against the wall, spitting noise in his face as he starts to strangle him, bone fingers pressing deep into the windpipe, Papa pulling the attacker off and forcing the two to hug, which they do, faces hidden. Jesus tells me life will be very hard now. The drug cycle is about to be broken. There will be no more smack on B–Block and no easy rides for the remaining addicts. It will be up to the rest of us to control them. The Director believes he has been too generous, allowing lax guards to undermine his tolerance. We will be taught a lesson we won't forget, and those of us plotting to riot will be singled out and punished by the courts. He says there are informers among us, that he knows everything we say and do, day and night, and maybe even knows what we are thinking. After all, we are stupid men. Amazingly stupid. Jesus says some of the inmates are so messed up they probably imagine the Director sitting inside brains, controlling every move, when really he is covering his back.

While some clothes have been torn and scattered, it is a token effort, the goons more interested in the men than their possessions, and I become scared, relieved when Dumb Dumb pulls his house out from under his bed, sits and runs a hand over the walls, and as the section calms the boys come over to inspect the building, drop matches by his glue, point out small details to each other and imagine how it will look once it is finished, and they breathe easier and time stands still for a while, the calm eventually broken by the sound of the breakfast bell.

The door is still locked. Chef waits by the gate with two of the old guards carrying his pot and four goons smirking at their struggle, the bell rung a second time by one of the goons, men shouting that the door is bolted, and Chef is confused and speaks to the goon with the bell who shouts and shakes it in front of his face. That cauldron is full of hot milk, the sweetest potion in the world, and Chef tries to lift it and come to us but is kicked and forced to stay where he is, humiliated, and we watch Chef as he stands alone over his fast-cooling milk, finally ordered out of the yard.

We are kept inside for the rest of the day, missing dinner, finally let out in the late afternoon. Chef avoids our eyes as he serves us, Papa standing in line for the first time, placing a hand on the chubby man's shoulder, glaring at the goons who look at each other and do nothing. We sit on the ledge and eat our fish, and I finish fast so I don't have to look at the heads. Jesus hands me a set of beads. His sister brought them during a visit but he doesn't need them. I hold the present in my hand and feel the links of the chain, the smooth plastic. I wrap it around my hand and let the tiny tassels hang on my palm, begin moving, making sure they don't slip over my fingers. It is harder than it looks. My mind focuses on the beads, a change from Dumb Dumb's matches, and I forget my surroundings and listen to the other beads and again it reminds me of a train, moving through a town watching out for children and dogs. I feel the hunger in my belly and concentrate on the beads, the throb easing, remember the lucky charm in my pocket and feel a pang of guilt, reach in and absorb the vibration, which seems to be weakening.

For three days running the doors open at six and the goons are on us, free with their truncheons as the whole block is forced to stand in silence in the middle of the yard, a spotlight trained on us from above, manned by hawks and eagles, a sign that we are still alive. With Flip Flop and Pretty Boy gone, only the Butcher and Papa seem capable of leading us, and they do nothing. Jesus believes they are waiting for the right moment, hints at a secret plan to control the prison, but it is not going to happen. If we weren't so segregated, part of a larger complex and properly linked, we could probably run amok, but the odds are stacked against any rebellion. The professionals, men capable of cold calculation, devious characters who can plot and plan and stay unattached are living easy lives on A-Block, playing the game, uninterested in prison politics. We do not have these men. The Director knows only passion stirs the B-Block boys, however warped, and so he has let the temperature cool with the gift of snow before coming back in hard. Our morale is low and there is some fighting, mostly at night. Skin is bruised and a junkie stabbed, the goons uninterested in searching us or our belongings. And in days these new-model bullies are bringing in fresh smack, expensive gear that only satisfies the well-off few.

Junkies crowd the doctor in the evening, and he is dishing out all sorts of pills I know nothing about, a selection of uppers and downers and sidewinders, chemical time capsules that set some men ranting so hard their teeth rattle while others turn into edgy brothers of the zombies. Flip Flop and Pretty Boy eventually hobble back in, bodies sore and teeth broken. Jesus says they were beaten in the chapel and that the Director supervised what he calls an interrogation, asking about plans to burn down the prison, especially interested in the union men, whether they are talking politics and planning a hunger strike. Their ordeal has affected them and they talk to the farmers about a passive revolt. The notion of a hunger strike passes through the section again and is taken up by the monkey monsters who huddle closer together and seem to like the idea, most prisoners refusing, as apart from the weekly shower, food is our only pleasure, and it would also make us so weak we would be incapable of doing anything. The talk lifts spirits, at least for a day, but soon fizzles out.

We settle into this crackdown routine, this super control that is far beyond the occasional inspections that normally occur every month or so, a lazy sifting of belongings by haphazard guards, the term control a perfect translation. The days are as boring as ever, the nights more hellish as every junkie struggles to cope. Men flip out and try to wreck the place, but there is little left to break. They are beaten by other men, or removed by the goons and fed a sedative, returning with cut mouths and bloody noses. When one man slashes his forearms they are stitched up within the hour and he is dumped back in. Dumb Dumb retreats further into his building work, his mission respected, Papa the only one still not acknowledging the house taking shape. I even notice the monkey monsters admiring it from a distance. For my part, I have Jesus and the beads and my lucky charm, and I remember that there are always people worse off, keep adjusting, sinking down and building up, a weird confidence emerging.

When the loudspeaker calls Jesus to the gate he leaves the block with a look of excitement, and I assume his sister has come to see him, wonder what she is like, sure our visits had been suspended. I think nothing of it, reason he has gone to see his lawyer, who has had some luck with the courts in seeking an appeal date. Jesus isn't away long and when he returns there is a huge smile devouring his face, but when he sees me he frowns and hurries inside. I follow him in and he is packing his bag, ask what is happening, and turning his head away he tells me he is leaving Seven Towers, that he is being trans-ferred to a farm where he can work off half his sentence. He says I am very sorry, but you will survive, my friend, you are stronger than you know, yes, you will be all right, and there is a pause and he shakes my hand and tells me to be careful and protect myself as two goons stomp into the section and tell him to hurry. Shocked, I follow Jesus into the yard and watch this good man walk away, boys slapping his back and offering congratulations, and I am pleased for him, feel no jealousy at all. I am alone again. My world collapses.

Baba Jim stands at the edge of a bustling desert outpost and watches the buses rumble out towards the oasis town of Pushkar on the far side of the hill and he is swallowing dust and waiting for one of these ramshackle contraptions to stop surrounded by a hundred Rajputs loaded down with clothes and blankets and cooking pots and thousands of people are streaming towards Pushkar where every year they gather to race and sell camels and enjoy the fun of the fair and Baba Jim is a smiling Mr Fair in his plastic flip-flops and three-day stubble his fixed smile plastered with Thar sand and he is working his way back from Jaiselmer on the way searching out the Karani Mata rat temple which is full of reincarnated holy men and he buys sweets at the gate and feeds these spiritual rodents and thinks how lucky they are to live in India where they enjoy a life of luxury and there are nets above the yard to keep the birds out all those hawk men waiting to swoop down and kill the vermin below and the vultures are only interested in dead meat and Baba has heard about the Pharsi towers where the dead are left for the vultures to claim as to pollute the earth with burial or the air with cremation is wrong and Baba Jim remembers the Jains with their mouth nets protecting the smallest of insects and this is a long way from life on safari where it is survival of the fittest and Baba shakes his head in sheer wonderment as the temperature rises and he is back on the road and it must be over a hundred degrees and he is careful with his bag making sure the oil that has stained the material doesn't ruin the lightweight cotton of his trousers and around Baba Jim mothers smile and their beautiful daughters lower their eyes and while the baba man is only human a red-blooded hetero-sexual male who fully appreciates their fine lines and delicate bone structure and the sort of dark eyes that would drive a weaker more physical man insane with desire he is beyond such physical attraction as he moves through a romantic land-scape with noble motives appreciating Rajasthan's arid beauty the searing heat and sandy vistas the only food he craves and when a bus finally stops he climbs up to the roof and sits on the luggage rack with another fifty men and boys while the women cram inside and more passengers hang to the back and sides and the movement of the bus creates a breeze and Baba relaxes and allows the air to wash his face and dust and sand shaves his chin and reminds him of fresh snowflakes in winter and a beach in summer and he marvels how despite all these different times and places everything is always more or less the same and he is musing as spiritual men do on the opposites of hot and cold and good and evil and he feels nothing but correctness as the bus struggles to scale the hill with its engine rumbling and he wonders if the crankshaft will break or the big end explode and thieves run from a tired prison wagon and the bus is crawling as the passengers urge it on and rock rises on either side closing out the sun so Baba shivers and relishes the shade and they reach the summit and the Rajputs around him are calling him Babaji Babaji and he knows this is a term of endearment and feels at one with the world as the driver coasts down the other side of the hill picking up speed and moving faster and he doesn't seem inter-ested in the brake pedal the wind gushing around Babaji and now they are on flat land and soon approaching Pushkar and he sees men with ancient rifles over their shoulders and swords in their belts and coloured turbans on their heads and he also sees a flat field covered in snow with two runaways sitting on the edge of the world and that is the thing with imagination it can work for or against a man and there is a point where you have to control the dream and stay lucid and this baba man knows it is a hop skip and short jump from happiness to sorrow and when the bus pulls into the bus station Baba loses himself in the flood of humanity and he is alone and yet not alone and finds a hotel where he can sleep on the roof for half the price of a dormitory bed and he quickly unpacks and smoothes out his sleeping bag on the mattress and finds a tap and fills his water bottle and adds iodine drops and lets it settle and goes off to explore Pushkar and Baba Jim is moving with the crowd through narrow streets where stalls sell every type of Indian food but he is not hungry the nature of his quest and the heat suppressing hunger although the okra looks good and that pile of pakoras needs denting but he stays focused and presses on and spends many hours wandering and spots a baba riding an elephant and he follows watching intently as Elephant Baba works the food stalls and cafes and every samosa man hands the elephant an offering which he accepts lazily passing it to his mouth with his trunk and this elephant man is more of a swami with long hair combed back and greased he has the face of a Hell's Angel with a full beard and knowing smile and Baba Jim understands that sitting astride an elephant gives an ordinary mortal special standing in the community and he studies the skin and ears and the huge bone at the top of the creature's back and understands why elephants are considered wise and he remembers Ganesh and how that chana sage in Benares pointed out the similarity with Baba Jim and he follows Elephant Baba for a long time before finally breaking away a troupe of eunuchs hassling a stall owner giant transvestites making their own laws and Jim reaches a square and sees the tree he has been told about and he thinks it is a banyan but he is not a knowledgeable man so is not sure and it is surrounded by a concrete platform and the smell of hashish nearly knocks him out and the branches hang low and so do the swinging balls of the naked babas gathered below and this baba is an outsider among babas and sits nearby drinking cane juice watching events unfold at Baba Central and there must be well over a hundred of these mad fuckers and they are a wild bunch of Hindu ragamuffins stark bollock naked or with Tarzan loincloths and he sees the dust on their skin and the fuming chillums and it is just as he imagined and these men are stoned and babbling and chanting and Jim knows Elephant Baba is on a different level to these hashish gurus walking barefoot these are the frontier babas who don't care about rules and regulations and his gaze shifts and settles on Sarah who has appeared from nowhere and is sitting opposite and they talk as fellow-travellers always do and she has a luscious smile and is a human being the same as anyone else and can't be ignored because of her sex and the temptation she presents as that would be unfair he has to forget his urges and appreciate the inner beauty of all sentient beings and it makes sense that later in the day they rent a room as this works out cheaper than two roof spaces and as Sarah says the desert is hot during the day but very cold at night and this is a land of extremes and so they share the room and Baba is happy with the arrangement sees himself as a Gandhi-like figure and when he looks at Sarah she sometimes reminds him of Ramona and in the evening these two platonic friends roam the fairy-light streets of Pushkar and Baba eats a great meal and for some reason it feels as if he hasn't had food this good for months and they sit in a long hall served by wide-eyed boys who can't be more than ten years old and these kids know the score but their innocence is what makes them shine as they work so hard and stay so upbeat it makes Baba ashamed of his self-pity and he reminds himself that he is eating to replenish the body and protect the soul and stock up on energy dealing with a sweet lassi and a plate of that okra he saw earlier and the sort of puris that would make a messiah sink into the pit of gluttony and Baba needs nourishment and orders more puris and a bowl of tarka dhal and some samosas to keep the elephant company and Ramona smiles and seems to admire this drifter and how he has stayed true to his youthful rebellion even if this new life is a bit too hippie for her and Sarah clearly loves his freewheeling style and contagious humour and when they head back to their room stars light the way and Baba is tired after his long journey and stands under a cold

shower watching cockroaches scurry along the wall and he
snuggles into his sleeping bag for the sake of modesty and
begins to fall sleep his eyes heavy and view misty but he can
see Sarah come out of the shower and she is naked and drying
herself and he can't help but admire her body the pouting
breasts and slender waist and somehow he knows she has the
sweetest fanny in the whole of Rajasthan and there is a flicker
of interest as his balls tighten but he remembers the sweetness
of the lassi and rolls over and turns his back on Sarah and
Mary-Lou and Ramona and in the morning they walk through
the streets and drink tea and eat a breakfast of idli and sambar
and wander to the edge of town where men are buying and
selling camels who leer and belch safari odours and Baba and
his friend walk out to a hill that rises steeply into the sky and
they follow steps hewn from rock and he is sweating and has
to stop twice before reaching the building at the top and it
is either a temple or a tiny castle and they are high in the
clouds and Pushkar is toy-like in the distance and they are all
alone and Baba is looking out from a turret and sees a hawk
glide past at exactly the same level as his eyes and the air is
still and the world silent and he actually hears it change direction with a gentle lowering of a wing a faint hiss that sums
up the wonder of the universe and he places his hands on the
wall and the stone is cool and he peers over the side and
marvels at the trees and bushes growing from near vertical
surfaces clinging to outcrops and in the biggest tree he sees
vultures resting in the branches watching the land below and
Sarah leans over to see and recoils at the drop accidentally
brushing his groin and he concentrates on the hawk as it scans
the hillside searching for rodents gliding so effortlessly Babaji
forgets its murderous ways and imagines himself jumping into
the sky and kicking his legs and soaring to great heights and
diving in and out of clouds knowing he can go anywhere he
wants he doesn't have to follow roads and tracks and stop for
fences but stays in the tower and looks back towards Pushkar
and soon they have been in Pushkar for a week living an easy
life and everything is perfect but Baba has to get back to
Benares as this is where he will find true freedom as he was

ignorant when he passed through before and realises there must be an end to his aimless drifting through open spaces and Sarah wants to accompany the celibate man and he can see up her skirt and she isn't wearing any fucking panties talking about the Kama Sutra and tantric sex and his balls are down by his knees and he realises that he is a dusty baba under a craggy tree but draws on his inner strength and focuses on the true nature of his journey resisting these carnal cravings and drawing inspiration from Jesus Christ and all the other men trying to break free from their mortal chains and escape this prison of the flesh.

The room rocks along the same as it did before Jesus saved me, and with the door bolted and lamps dimmed, candles sizzling over in monster corner, my solitary confinement resumes, sober men yelling and junkies sulking – *like silly little girls pouting over a boy packing them in, that heroin they've fallen in love with isn't worth the agony, where's their self-respect, no, fuck them, let the selfish cunts wipe themselves out and take their dirty genes into the incinerator, it would save the helpers a lot of the trouble of mending their broken hearts, money that could go on worthy causes, they should be embarrassed letting the system break them so easily, their names aren't fit to fill a plaque, never mind a headstone –* and the old blanket is fluttering, ready for action, a strong mind that will guide it towards salvation and this control is cruel and merciless with the Director punishing the outsider, driving me towards other realms, and this the second time he has stuck me in isolation, and he is a professional, good at using the rules to hurt people – *it's nothing personal, he hardly knows you exist, you want to forget those preachers Presley and Christ, you're better off without them, a couple of idealistic cunts who need to get back into the world, drink a few beers, smoke some skunk and snort a little coke, fuck one of those travelling girls –* maybe the Director has a wall chart, takes advice from a psychologist on how to break men without using sticks and stones and leaving broken bones – *fuck off, do you really think he cares, he doesn't have the wit, for a start, and when he's in a restaurant sucking oysters out of their shells and sipping a fine wine and rubbing the leg of the next* man up the ladder, *doing whatever it takes to boost his career, do you honestly believe he remembers any of us, it's the same with that prison cat, if that feline was smart enough to catch a bird he would torment it and once its frail heart gives out and it dies of fright he'll move on without a second's thought, it's what they do, part of their nature* – and the card men hardly speak, doing their best to ride out the control with the domino boys, and my teeth are chattering – *probably got pneumonia* – thank God I have this blanket – *don't thank him, he's the one responsible* – and I am killing time – *chopping it up* – burying it deep – *deeper deeper* – doing my best to concentrate and not think – *thinking has already damaged your health* – too much thinking is bad for the brain – *fool* – and Jesus was great, a free spirit who has seen the wider world – *right* – and done it properly, not flitting from city to city – *bar to bar* – station to station – *drink to drink* – hostel to hostel – *woman to woman* – he knows what freedom means – *no responsibilities* – and he has found some sort of meaning to his life – *life has no meaning, it is empty, take what you can and move on, don't get tied down by people or places, it all ends the same way, fuck them and leave them, that is the nature of the drifter, really, you know that, think of the old man, he walks off into the sunset without a backward glance, doesn't give a fuck* – and I am cutting matches with my teeth – *you want to leave that alone* – helping the dumb man build his house – *of course* – and I lift a matchstick up and study it – *too long, too short* – inspecting splinters as if they are fur, a variety of length and width, and it is delicate work that requires skill and concentration – *forget the house* – and there is a lump in my throat as I imagine the dummy as a child standing in a playground with children around him screaming abuse and laughing in his face – *Dumb Dumb! Dumb Dumb! that's what they sing* – and I know it is not true what they say, that he has no soul – *he's made mistakes, walk away or face up to the facts, that's all you can do in life* – these dumb boys might be quiet but they are thinking all the time non-stop and considering every option, they are weak and sensitive and using another sort of defence, raging deep inside, and I wish everything could be all right with this sad useless cunt – *don't swear, it doesn't suit you, mind your language, it gets you nowhere, you soppy fucker* – poor Dumb Dumb, and I will give him the matchsticks tomorrow, maybe he won't want them, and I think about this for a while and finally put them in my sock remembering that I have friends far away, out in the open – *come on, what's happened to Baba Jim, has he fucked that tart yet, it's only a matter of time before he gives her the large one out in the desert, he must be gagging for it by now, how long can a man say no when he's got a naked woman wandering around sticking her tits in his face?* – and the thing about my good friends Jesus and Elvis is they both have strong ideals, know what they want out of life and follow their chosen paths, good men who will never sell themselves short, men of integrity – *they're human like the rest of us, and even if they have done and planned so much you have to choose your own way, find your own answers* – it doesn't matter – *no, it doesn't, nothing matters* – and I take my beads out and I am getting better, study the other prisoners and find they all have a technique, the beads an extension of their feelings as they flick them back and forward, stop to caress the plastic and metal – *now you're well and truly fucked, you're going to end up one more timeless clown sitting on the ledge covered in stubble smelling like a rubbish dump and whenever there's a disturbance or protest you'll be caught up in it and for every six months you serve you'll be handed another year in return, think of that, you should've kept your mouth shut and stayed where you were, over on C-Block with that other weak cunt Franco* – how was I to know? – *you'll be here for decades and one day the Sicilian will be dead and they'll say let's send that dumb foreigner up to take his place and okay you might get to live on A-Block as a special privilege, but you'll be another institutionalised moron, and you'll probably be happy, that's the saddest thing, your brain will be warm custard and you won't remember who you are and where you come from, you hardly know now, sitting there with someone else's beads and your charm untouched, you're always hiding from the truth* – fuck off – *you fuck off, and then you'll be up in the furnace room and think that's living, talk about great expectations, you're a fucking wanker* – it wouldn't be bad, I would be warm and building fires with Nana and smell pine all day long and think, everyone would be happy when they see me, I would be a popular boy with no enemies and

I could look out of the window into the yard and I wonder
– *what?* – I could probably have a shower every single day of
the year and spend maybe ten or fifteen minutes under the
hot water, and it would feel so good, so very fine – *maybe the
guards will take pity on the pathetic tongueless lifer and rent you a
whore, or you could buy one, use those toothless jaws to blow the
new Director, rent your senile arse out to the barber and any passing
Homer trade, and the goons will send you a girl and leave you in
the shower and she will soap you down and slip her fingers under
your skin and massage the bones, stick her hands behind your ribcage
and feel your heart beating, and you'll trust her as she's a woman
and won't let you down, sharp talons so near to snipping veins, and
she'll work hard to massage your heart back to life and scrape the
cancerous lumps off your spine and she'll have the body of a high-
grade pole dancer and will sink to her knees and wash every inch of
your body with her tongue lathering up the soap and begging for some
of that vintage bromide-mutated semen filling your rancid scrotum and
she will give anything for a dose but you'll be so old and knackered
you won't even be able to get it up* – and I could wash my clothes
in hot water and clean them properly, hook up a clothes line,
I think there is one there – *yes, the Sicilian hangs his underpants
by the door* – and they would dry fast in that warm environment, and yes, I would be content, and I might be old but
Nana will be old as well, or maybe I'll regress and become a
boy again and Mum will look after me and make tomato soup
and toast and we could look at those glossy photographs of
the big wide world together, it would be like going camping
with my dad, except I never did that, you're right, I never did
anything with that lousy drifter – *I reckon you're going senile
already, do you want to spend the rest of your life moaning, fuck me,
the furnace room might be soft living, but it is full of losers* – I just
want an easy life, to serve my time and learn how to handle
these beads – *you're an outsider, you can't become one of these men
by mastering a handful of beads given to you by a low-life hippie,
don't forget where you came from* – every single one of us is an
outsider and Jesus isn't a hippie, you sound like the Director
– *fuck off, you really are the loneliest cunt on this wobbling blue-
eyed globe, you and you alone* – you are wrong – *nobody wants*

you, where's the visitors and the book of home and the letters, you are bottom of the fucking pole, a vagrant hitching rides on boxcars and getting beaten with an iron bar by company goons, forget Jimmy Rocker and his pickup, you're Jimbo Hobo, what woman is going to look at a filthy tramp, even the worst cat-house cast-offs wouldn't come here to shower with you, and as for this other fool you're always talking about, Leper Jim sounds a bit better than Baba Jim, eating scraps from a monsoon gutter and disappearing up his own arsehole with all this sanctimonious spiritual shit when the people around him are starving to death, he doesn't even know what to do with that Sarah slag, and I bet she's a pig, appears in porn films with Porky, no, you're in the foundations of the totem, buried under fucking ground – and in one version of the totem B-Block is top of the pole, and this has to be the right approach, B-Block boys the cream of the prison brethren – we are the big boys all right, remember how scared you were when you came in here first time, fucking shitting yourself, and now you're one of them, an outsider, mind, but nobody hassles you – if being passive is a quality then C-Block deserves respect, while the professionals live on A-Block – the pussies and the cynics, two emotionless extremes without true class or passion, one controlled by fear, the other money – and there is the block without a name – for the sex cases – it might not even exist – then they are in here with us right now, in disguise – no, there is a place within the walls – it must exist – and the hawks can perch on any wall, take their pick of rodents – they are watching you all day long thinking I wish one of these gutless cons would give it a go, I do my target practice and want some real action, climb a wall and cut the wire, attack a guard with a knife, your shard of glass, and keep that ready as Jesus has forsaken you, just give those hawk assassins an excuse, and they are thinking I need to ease the frustration I feel as it is cold and boring stuck on the wall, year after year, the wind howling and banshees pickling brain cells, wishing I was somewhere else, but a man has to make a living and one of these days I am going to go home and handcuff the wife to the bed, and fuck her like I want to fuck up those queers in the yard, do them with a bullet in the gut, and when I've finished I'll blow the back of her head off, leave her on the bed and turn her into a marble girl, tell the police one of those released prisoners has done this to me, a decent citizen, and they will swoop around the city pulling in men who escaped my reach the first time around, send them back to the yard to await further investigation, offer me another chance to do my job – and we will all be free one day, most of us, and I see Franco and his friends retrieving their van from the pound and leaving the city, passing the same taverna where they were arrested, slowing down and spotting the manager talking with other innocents – *they shouldn't be smoking hashish in a backward country, these people are savages* – and Franco honks the horn and they heed his warning and escape – *it is always a romantic happy ending with you, but life just is not like that, my friend* – Franco heading home to his family who are waiting with the best tomato sauce ever invented, garlic bread and mozzarella balls in a tomato salad – *food glorious food, it's all you ever think about* – and there will be ice cream and cappuccino – *that Franco is gutless if he drives away* – sitting on a comfortable couch with his family – *while that greasy cunt gets away with grassing* – that is the best way, move on and leave your problems behind – *unresolved* – it is for the best – *these things have to be dealt with, they always come back to haunt you* – red wine and a fruity cake and more coffee, gallons and gallons of strong coffee – *Franco can pull up around the back of the taverna and wait until the grass closes for the night, do as he said, cut the man's throat from ear to ear, that's what you have to do, fuck that judge up, break into his house when they let you out of here and kill him, find the Director and make him suffer* – I don't hate anyone, but I almost hate the Director – *take him to a rubbish dump and nail him to a cross* – when I am released I am walking out of this prison and drifting down the hill, jumping on a bus and losing myself in the crowd, and they won't know I am fresh out of jail, won't suspect a thing – *they'll smell you* – it will be the day of my shower – *they'll smell your clothes* – these will be scrubbed before I leave, by the Sicilian elder – *you won't get the sweat out of them, not ever* – maybe Ali will order me something new – *they'll be wafting Seven Towers gloom, it's in you now, this depression, it has changed how you think and look and the feel of your skin and the pattern of your life, infected your mind and corrupted the blood that flows through your veins* – the girls will smile – *wondering what has this man done, is he a cruel man, an evil man?* – they will know I am an innocent man – *a fornicator, a sodomite, a sadistic sexual predator?* – that I have done nothing wrong, not really, deep inside where it matters – *hey there, girls, on your way home from work, a dab of perfume behind petite ears and a twinkle in virgin eyes, fancy some prison-style love, haven't you read the newspapers, listened to your politicians, we're all shit-stabbing rapists, perverted monsters* – and I will get into that bar by the docks and stroll to the counter and smile at the barman, let my gaze wander over his merchandise, order the coldest beer in the fridge, the little beauty right at the back caked in ice, and he will crack it open and I will decline the offered glass, drink it straight from the bottle, pick up where I left off – *I can taste it now, guzzling the lager down, ordering a glass of ouzo and another beer to chase it into my belly, and I am going to get pissed, drink till I drop, like I always do, let myself go and take my chances* – it is better to stay off the drink, one beer and a plate of decent food and I will tip him and leave and find a bakery, buy some cakes, a chocolate éclair and a doughnut, recognise the man serving and swap prison memories – *what time is it?* – and I won't miss the train this time – *make sure you don't, let's get there early, you're talking sense now* – and I am standing on a street corner with Mum and the jam is squirting over my face, sugar on my lips – *they were good times, while they lasted, but everything comes to an end and it doesn't matter if it's a cold beer losing its fizz and going warm or the éclair and doughnut, they get eaten, vanish fast, at least the way you eat them, me, I take it slow, and that's the way things work, everything fades and dies and I try and tell you this about your time in prison and sometimes you believe me and other times you don't and what a fucking shambles you've made of your life, and Nana used to love those éclairs, remember, she was a lovely lady, I remember when she died, and I don't have to tell you what happened, after she went away to hospital and never came home again, and that wasn't the end of it was it, no, Mum didn't deserve what happened to her, did she, and I miss Nana, but you have to live in the present, I understand that, and maybe I even miss Dad, sometimes, the no-good tramp, but more than anything else I miss my mum.*

★

The people who run this place they call home won't leave the light on at night telling me kindly that I am a big boy and shouldn't be scared of the dark and anyway it would keep the other boys awake and there are six or seven of us in the dormitory and at night I can't get to sleep as I am worrying about the monsters under the bed and I am scared I will wet the sheets again when it happened before they told me not to worry as it was an accident and the doctor called Tony says I must try not to feel guilty about anything but I know that if I wet the bed the others will make fun of me and we have to stick together in this place and most of the time we do and I am nine I suppose or maybe a bit older it is hard to remember and some light comes through the curtains from the lamp-posts outside things can always be worse that is what I must always remember there could be a power cut and then I wouldn't know what is going on around me and at night I always sleep with my charm in my hand the metal ring on the middle finger and I squeeze it tight and never let it go and know that it is going to help me in my life and make me strong and the people running this place are nice but it is not the same as being with Mum and Nana and every week I sit with Tony and he tries to get me to tell him things but I never do even though I like him what is there to say I don't know what he is talking about some of the time and there is a garden with areas where we can and can't walk and flower beds full of all sorts of flowers in the summer and black earth and frost in the winter and I am outside looking at a spider's web that has caught raindrops instead of flies and someone taps me on the shoulder and when I turn round this girl is standing in front of me and I see her black eyes and know right away it is the little girl Ramona who I sat next to when I first went to school and she asks me why I am here and I tell her my story and I have never told anyone before and I didn't even know I knew myself and she says it is better to forget these things and she is on her way to a nice people's house in a couple of days and promises to write and she does send me a letter right away and I write back and this goes on for a long time I suppose we are pen pals and it is great in the garden until one day a kid has to go and say something that I don't want to think about and I try and make this boy go away and I turn him into Porky Pig and this makes things easier as he is no longer a bad boy but a big friendly pig with rubber lips and pink skin and a friendly smile and I feel sorry for pigs because they are treated badly and made fun of and what have they ever done to hurt anyone that is what I would like to know but this kid keeps going on at me on and on and on until my head hurts and nice Porky vanishes and I just see a mean kid and I punch him in the face and his nose bleeds and they say it is broken and when he is crying I feel sorry for him and his nose turns to a snout and his porky face is hurt and I want to say sorry but something stops me why should I anyway and I have to go and see the man who runs the place and he tells me I must not resort to violence I must ignore these things and he has no face that I can make out and so I call him Mr Unfair in my head because it seems wrong I have to listen to people saying bad things about me and I reach into my pocket and squeeze my lucky charm and think of Mum and Nana and know *I* am a good boy and he is all right really maybe *I* am being unfair calling him Mr Unfair he says he understands things are tough for me right now but they are also tough for Porky though he calls him by another name I don't notice and maybe it is Frank but it can't be as the weakling in school was called Frank and there could be two Franks but it is too hard thinking like this and Mr Fair is telling me we must all work together and it makes sense I promise I will try much harder in the future and am glad he is helping me but I want something more maybe my mum to hug me and later on I start another school and some boys and girls know about me and say things and I keep my mouth shut I just want to be left alone and a few days later bigger boys gang up on me push me into the wall and I see three ducks Huey Dewey and Louie and the reason is I love watching cartoons as they make me laugh make everything seem more real somehow and seeing these rubber ducks means I laugh as they are trying so hard to be tough but are just ducklings why do they bother and laughing makes them mad as they want me to be scared but they are nothing compared to the monkey monsters and they start hitting me in the tummy and then in the face and finally push me on the ground and I am still laughing as it seems so stupid and then one even kicks me in the face and I lose my temper and jump up and see only a boy with an ugly look and I grab him around the neck and bang his head into the bricks and I pull him back and pretend I am a monkey monster and bite his face that will scare them you see a monkey monster is a monster monkey who is half-man and half-monkey and he is evil and looks a bit like a skeleton and the headmaster says that I have behaved the same as a mongrel a wild dog and I want to tell him I was pretending to be a bad monkey but know he won't understand and he tells me to get my hand out of my pocket and I let go of the charm and he hits my hand six times with his cane but I don't cry I turn him into Father Christmas and even smile at this friendly old man from Lapland thinking how one day I will sleep in one of his forests and me smiling only makes him more annoyed and he says I am a bad boy and I frown as I thought I was a good boy I will have to ask Tony and he seems angry when I tell him what the headmaster said and writes something in his book and Tony says I must not fight in the future and should tell a teacher if I have any problems and he asks me what Mum would think and Tony doesn't mind if I put my hand in my pocket and he is okay and I see what he is saying I know I have to make Mum and Nana proud and I am doing my best I really always do my best and later on I am in the playground again and there are more boys and girls around me and they are saying horrible things and I just look blank and imagine they are Mickey and Minnie Mouse and their twins and cousins and pretend I don't understand a word they say, but of course I do.

The water tank feeding the showers breaks down, or at least this is what the goons tell us, the Butcher wrapping his arm around my shoulders and squeezing tight, saying no water, my friend, no good water – *he's killed two people, maybe more, and carries a dirty great carving knife down his trousers* – the Butcher is a sweet man, wouldn't hurt a fly – *this control is half-hearted* – it is bad enough – *a murder and dismemberment specialist strolls around with a deadly weapon and they call this a crackdown, they should be body searching you every day, stripping the men naked and hosing them down in the yard* – the Butcher wouldn't use his blade on one of his own – *yeah, right* – only the goons – *take a good look at the goon squad* – they aren't so cocky now – *they were ready for a battle when they arrived, but time has passed and the atmosphere of the prison has quickly soaked into their skin, they're feeling the strain of boring days and nights, watching their backs, not as brave as they thought they were, and soon they will leave and the real guards will return* – it is a shame they don't stay and learn what it is like to be here long-term – *but it's nice to see them skulking off* – we didn't need a riot, Seven Towers broke them down, it is only the Director and his administrators on the outer boundary who seem immune.

We go without a shower for two long weeks. The bugs stop nipping and start biting, gnawing and breaking skin, causing scabs and infection. The section needs fumigating. The stench is sickening, safari conditions spreading. Men are itching and scratching hard and the tension increases, pushing us to breaking point. The goons are weak, their boots dull where once they shone, nervous and keeping their distance, our ghostly vapour making their noses twitch. When the goons start itching some of the old guards are brought in to kill the bugs. We pull the beds into the yard and they fumigate the room, use spray guns on us, take the blankets away to be boiled. They supply us with buckets, mops and disinfectant to clean the section floor, and we work hard, arguing for a turn on the mop, frothing disinfectant, and we really polish the room and burst through the green door and get stuck into so many layers of excrement, the first time the cave has ever been cleaned. We keep working even when the job is done, shining windows and mopping walls and scrubbing the floor for a second and third time, everyone demanding a turn. Lice and silverfish are wiped out, cockroaches crushed, and it shows how much we want to work, to have something to do, the mood pulling back from the brink, and in the evening the dormitory is heavy with chemicals, but it might as well be incense, the physical exertion making us feel so good, new old blankets a treat. We sleep well, still itching, waiting for the shower that will make everything right.

The following day we are told the water tank has been replaced, but now the furnace is broken. Nobody believes this – *it's part of the punishment plan, the Director sits up at night planning new manoeuvres, ways of making us suffer, yet it is not personal, not really* – but we don't care, scrambling to get off the block and over to the showers – *you'll miss out if you don't hurry, cold water is better than no water* – and I wait my turn, patiently, playing with the beads – *I'm warning you, don't sit back fiddling* – and I am more dextrous, almost a master – *come on, our turn* – and I follow the others through passages and locks and up the steps into the tower, past the serpent and the Sicilian and his gang of scoundrels, the smell of wood stronger than ever, senses turning it to pine, and the Sicilian is scowling at the goons, waiting for his life to return to normal, and I undress fast, stand under a pipe scratching at my armpits and picking off bugs, the water rumbling and hitting hard – *fucking hell, it's freezing* – spine shrinking and penis contracting, body temperature free-falling, and clutching the soap I focus on the parasites – *horrible little cunts, now your time is up, bug boys, this is napalm warfare, just smell that soap drenched in insecticide and defoliant, wipe these fuckers off the face of the earth, and they are small and deadly and screaming, listen to their shrill buggy voices begging for mercy, and will they change, will they fuck, there is no such thing as rehabilitation just harsh, merciless justice* – and the parasites really are screaming, they lie and cheat and take the piss and expect me to forgive and forget, but it doesn't work like that, not today, and I am scraping at the filth, from head to toe, rinsing off, starting again – *I want to watch their bodies fall away and hear their last gasps and see termite corpses trapped in the whirlpool heading for the drain that leads into the depths of the mountain where the rat men wait for these weak goons feeding on your blood, and they can't take the pressure, molluscs hanging on for their lives, peel them off and laugh as the manky cunts drift into the sewers where they belong, low-life mercenaries, let's pray one of them* commits a crime and gets sent to Seven Towers, there'll be no A-Block luxury for these boys, just some old-fashioned B-Block retribution – and there is a moment when I know they are no more, but I keep on scrubbing, cold water turning my body to marble just like an overdosing junkie, there is no warmth and no mist and the men around me have passed through the pain barrier as well, cleanliness the aim of this visit, a final flurry as the pressure slackens, rinsing away the suds and drying fast, the Butcher with his towel around his waist taking a long yellow piss into the departing whirlpool, laughing his head off, and we are all laughing, glad we are rid of those parasitical bug boys.

We leave the shower and go back into the furnace room, pause at the barred gates outside, waiting for another batch of scarecrows. I look along the tunnel and wonder if it really does circle the prison. I think of the seventh tower, which I have never seen, guess it must be the same as all the others, but would like to glimpse it one day, just to make sure. The next group reaches us and the smell is incredible, and I am angry we are forced so low down the food chain, but these prisoners perk up, lifted by our appearance. Goons lead us down, disappointed we are not broken by the cold, and the boys are grinning and joking and our escort shrinks, these muscle men with flabby brains. And I start laughing again so the others look at me with apprehension, even the Butcher seems worried, but it is just that everything is so petty, ridiculous that life has sunk to this level, and I can honestly say I don't give a fuck, blame nobody but myself.

Back in the square I try it on, talk my language and point to the Oasis, say I want to buy some glue for Dumb Dumb. The goons are confused, distracted by an argument elsewhere, and nod me over. I stroll to the cafe and Ali shakes my hand and pulls out a chair. I snuggle in close to the fire, pocket the glue. He grins and for some reason insists the Muslim and the Christian are brothers, it is the Jew we must fear, the wandering Jew, and he seems near to tears, moved by this notion of unity against a common enemy – *mad fucking cunt* – and it seems that Franco has been moved to A-Block and is teaching Ali more English. The Arab explains that Franco is to be released next week. I feel great happiness and tell the café owner to say hello from me, that I hope he makes it home safely and doesn't stop at the taverna. Ali Baba is confused, says no beer here, my friend, and then goes into his shed and brings out a plate of biscuits, sets them down on the table. He stoops by his fire and pours coffee, places the cup and a glass of water on either side of the biscuits. I drink and eat and watch Ali adjust my account.

I run my hand over the surface of a yucca, one of the plants he has had brought in to decorate the Oasis. The leaves are perfectly smooth with deadly razor edges. While it is warmer here than on the block, it is still cold, so Ali has wrapped poly-thene around the bottom of his plants. He sits with me, warming his hands, asks how I am and I say okay and he says this control is no good. He stares for a moment and continues, promising that the Director is a bad man, and that all the directors around the world are also bad men. He looks into the flames and I follow his gaze, become absorbed, think of my grandmother's house, how we had to leave it behind and move on, to another house, and how later she died in the hospital and left me and Mum alone.

Ali motions towards a pile of wood and I go over, take kindling and feed the flames, glowing coal and crackling wood, stories around a campfire. Ali sighs and says we have to keep warm, in a few months it will be spring and then summer and it is very hot in this prison during the summer. I have heard the heat is stifling and brings its own problems, the infestation we have just been through a regular occurrence. Ali talks about cockroaches and a plague of rats and the anger of Allah. He has seen the seasons in Seven Towers and I will do the same. He asks if I want more coffee and I realise I haven't finished what I have, raise the cup to my lips and find it is still hot, absorb the caffeine and love the effect. This is better than an ordinary espresso, an Ali Baba special, and I guzzle the glass of water, and when most of the coffee has gone I sip at the muddy dregs, taking in every last drop, called back to B-Block by the goons.

Late in the afternoon I am on the ledge eating bread and

stew, goons by the gate self-consciously swinging their truncheons, trying and failing to maintain a cocky stance. The loneliness is still inside me, but I am stronger, picking up some of the B-Block language, more resilient, maybe resigned. I think back over the months and remember how both Elvis and Jesus asked the question – *how did you end up here?* – and I assumed they were asking about my journey – *you pretended* – but they meant something else – *why did you leave home?* – and I shrug my shoulders – *why did you?* – what made me lose myself in foreign lands – *sleeping in dormitories, talking to strangers* – sleeping in corridors and luggage racks – *drinking in the darkest corners of Europe* – on my own – *as if you have a death wish, need to be lonely* – what am I doing in a foreign prison when I could be at home – *you have to work it out, my friend, I know the answer, it is not hard, all you need is the courage to face the truth* – and I am wondering if the drifting theory is right, the search for adventure and freedom the ultimate life, moving beyond the shackles of boredom and routine and responsibility, finishing the food and washing my bowl, oblivious to the cold water – *you're a different man* – and for the first time in my life I feel hard.

This same night, as I lie in a fresh blanket, which is as magical as the last one, staring at Dumb Dumb building his house, listening to the messages being tapped out by the beads, an old friend enters the section. He doesn't recognise me, but I know him. The sound of cards and dominoes stops and the babble of voices dips as he stands inside the door, which is swinging shut behind him, the thud announcing his presence. It seems that many men recognise this new boy, which makes sense as most of us convicted in this city follow the same route, taken from the courts to the holding cells of the central police station, from where we are processed and made to wait for the next wagon heading up the hill. It is the way the system works. The face is blurred, but the features don't matter. It is the way he moves, the tilt of his head and tread of his feet. The monkeys begin to snarl. No, I am definitely not the only prisoner who remembers the ice-cream seller.

★

Baba Jim, known as Babaji to his friends and admirers, out of respect for his pure childlike nature, the Christlike purity of his unselfish giving, the miraculous ability to heal with a touch of his hands, to make his worldly self invisible to the human eye, lifts the tea to his lips and gently sips a scorching brew. Created by the chai-shop guru known as Sri Ali, the mighty Babaji is not averse to crossing religious boundaries. He will drink tea with Hindus, Muslims and Sikhs just as long as it is cooked and sweetened with vast amounts of processed sugar. Baba has learnt the power of levitation from a yogi deep in the heart of Rajasthan, a cantankerous old goat who plays games with his disciples, juggling duality so the younger aspirants question his awareness and more experienced seekers nod in recognition. After criss-crossing the subcontinent Baba is back in the holy city of Benares and has established himself in a small, fifth-floor room near the ghats, realises that he has come full circle, that the best drifter searches within, wanders the maze of his mind for the correct answers. Here he sits on a wobbling balcony and studies the ancient books, the steady chanting of the devout in the temples below, a constant throb of eager pilgrims filling the alleyways, the tapping of japa beads reminding him of his good fortune at being a free man. Baba's knowledge of Sanskrit is self-taught and offers a huge alphabet and level of meaning beyond the narrow constraints of his native English. While language is considered the core of civilisation, what dull scientists believe elevates human beings above the rest of the animal kingdom, Baba sees it as a distraction, a social grace that gives voice to an inner confusion, weak men absorbed in trivial pursuits, tossing ideas around and creating endless layers of debate that go absolutely nowhere. Those Raj men had the right idea, believing in a stiff upper lip at all times, understanding that too much thinking is bad for the soul. During his lonesome travels, the baba boy has come to appreciate the joy of being beyond the languages around him. While conversation is at times unavoidable, he strives for inner perfection with a solitary, inner existence. The sound of men arguing in the room above is annoying and breaks the calm he has established, and this could easily turn to irritation and finally anger, but he knows he must crush this low thinking, surf the waves of disappointment. Baba Jim leaves his room and loses himself in the ancient labyrinth of the city's back-streets, stone corridors packed with men, women, children and cows. Baba loves drifting through these mental tunnels, every path eventually leading to the same place, and he is subconsciously remembering every nook and cranny, the tiniest shops buried in the darkest corners, small pockets of sunshine illuminating stone platforms where goats sunbathe, cool corners where dead men sit and smoke and drink tea. The stone is crooked and rises above his head, but Baba knows he can leave at any moment, the gate always open, the heat and pollution shut out. There is safety in numbers and even though he is an outsider nobody cares. He hears no insults, knows none are delivered. When he emerges from the alleyways he waits on the side of a larger road where traffic spews spent gasoline and young studs in mechanised rickshaws zip past wobbling heads, older men pumping pedals and slowing down when they see the white boy, touting for business, which Baba politely declines as he sets off across the highway. He ducks into a dosa house, body covered in sweat from no more than a minute's exposure to the midday sun. Propellers shake on the ceiling and the vinyl tables have been wiped down, water evaporating fast. Baba hurries to the far corner, a picture of a goddess he can't identify on the wall behind his platonic pal, the maid known as Sarah. The blonde bombshell is receiving some unwanted attention from four Bollywood-styled wankers who believe any woman travelling alone is asking for their four inches of limp dick, but the baba man would never insult these movie-affected virgins for fear of destroying fragile egos. Instead he confronts them in his own special way, placing a hand on their leader's head and allowing the power of love and forgiveness to flow through his fingers and enter the young man's soul. The sex pest is stunned and immediately apologetic, and realising the foolishness of his arrogance berates his friends, who are swayed by Baba Jim's presence, and repent. These harassing plums take turns apologising to Sarah before leaving, and Baba notices an expression of deepest respect playing across her stunning features. The boys tending tables bring him a dosa and a sweet lassi, Baba staying away from the bang variety which has confused the thinking of many a wanderer. Baba is remaining true to his ideals, following a path that sees him renouncing worldly goods and the notions of both competition and violence. He is an easygoing drifter, a wandering baba, a rover who has no room for anger. He turns the other cheek at every opportunity, determined to leave no resentment in his wake. He leans forward and feels the vinyl on his palms, eats slowly, sweat drying as the fan spins above his head, listening attentively as Sarah tells him about her home, how at times she misses her former life but is happy to be near Baba, even if their relationship can never be consummated. She admits she has erotic thoughts about his lean body, turned on by his elevated spirituality, his avoidance of physical contact, and she begins to tell him about her dream in the early hours of this very morning when she masturbated with his image in her mind, and Baba holds up a hand to stop her, orders another sweet lassi, demanding additional sugar, the sorry woman hanging her head and begging forgiveness, which is granted. Life in Benares continues and a platonic relationship is maintained, Baba appreciating the feminine qualities she adds to his life, never so cocksure as to assume he is anywhere near leaving the cycle of birth, death and rebirth, and if he is honest he would admit to a strong attraction to Sarah, enjoying the conversation which he is trying to cut out of his life, and he knows not to push himself too hard, keen to avoid the harsh, backfiring discipline of the zealot, the newly converted who believes he knows it all. As an outsider Baba Jim can take what he wants and ignore the negative aspects, well aware that being an outsider has its benefits, that there is no ultimate right and wrong, just the middle path, and as time passes he begins to deal with internal issues, for some strange reason finding himself drawn to the ghats lining the Ganges, and in particular the biggest burning ghat. Baba has of course visited the sacred river before and knows a cremation must be respected. He has never stopped, passing by and glancing nervously at the pyres. He mainly visits the bathing ghats, beneath the shelter of crooked temples that threaten to tumble into the river but never do, the Ganges rolling past, like so many before him Baba marvelling at its special power to absorb pollution and revitalise itself, the scientists bewildered by its magical properties. Eventually the wandering baba boy begins passing the cremation ghat every day, drawn from the beauty of life to the mystery of death, and he ambles and then lingers and finally sits nearby and watches the untouchable men build their pyres. He remembers other fires and can identify with the log carriers, knows wood is scarce and that many people are too poor to afford it, but do their best for the ones they love. It is especially auspicious to be cremated at this ghat, remaining ashes and bone tipped into Mother Ganges. Souls are immersed in cosmic consciousness and Baba spends more and more time here, seeing less of Sarah who begins to fret and one night explodes and says he must forget the dead and remember the living, and Ramona flashes in front of Jim's eyes and he sees her in the street, shouting the same words, and he wants her to understand that there is no difference, not for the likes of him, and eventually Sarah calms down and life continues. Baba listens to her concerns and tries to keep away, and for a couple of weeks he is his old self, passers-by smiling at this good man, eating dosas and drinking sweet lassis, watching the river roll, and then ever so gently his mood changes and he is strolling past the cremation ghat, and one fine day he sits nearby for hours and falls into a trance fixed on the pyre as it is built up, Jim captivated by the way the wood is stacked and interwoven and he moves further forward and hears the ringing of a bell and the sound of chanting and singing and there is a crowd of people approaching and he is lost in the spectacle and he forgets about Sarah and Ramona and his previous life as he is a different person that other fool is dead and he hears the voices and thinks he can understand a little of the meaning and something is wrong and he feels hands touching him and realises he is being wrapped in a shroud that covers his face and his forehead is pounding and he can see monkeys and a vague face that could be a witch or a saint and he tries to struggle but is weak and he really wants to live he doesn't want to die but is on the way to his funeral this is his karma and he thinks of the rat men those rodent babas in a special temple and knows he shouldn't be attached to his body and must die easy it isn't death in the negative sense and he is laid out in the middle of the pyre and more logs are stacked around his head and he can hear the click of beads and tick of the clock counting down and a swami with a long white beard is carrying a burning torch and he leans down and smiles at Baba Jim, lights the wood, which ignites quickly so Baba can smell the smoke and the piss and shit in his pants and he knows he is off on the biggest safari of all, and he is telling himself not to be afraid, to be brave, there is always someone worse off, and the first flames touch his ankles and send electricity racing through his meridians, and he is willing his soul free as the fire closes in knowing his face will melt and he will disappear into the firmament his miserable life forgotten and he is fighting hard to truly believe this ceremony is a cleansing process, and for the best, struggling to accept the inevitable, knows he should feel no emotion as he moves from one realm to the next, understands nobody is angry with him, and that he has done nothing wrong.

The one emotion every man has is anger, at least that is the way it seems to me, and maybe there really are people who never feel it, but I have never met them. They could be there in the Bible belt living clean American lives of plenty, or in the *Bhagavad Gita* ashrams of India living clean lives of abstinence, holy men cross-legged in the Himalayas and drifters tramping across the Sierra Nevada, but there is no one like that on my hilltop. A man who never knows anger is an ideal, and there is anger everywhere around me, it is clear to see, whether below the surface or out in the open, simmering and seething rage, a terrible wrath craving vengeance. It only needs a spark, and when the ice-cream seller walks on to B-Block he is entering a true nightmare. This is no mind game, no mental torment he can try to resist, losing himself in the insane ramblings of other ostracised boys. This anger is hard and merciless and a million times more vicious than mere resentment.

Pure unfettered anger boils and spills over, a dream sequence he has created, mentally torturing a good percentage of the B-Block men. How many I can't guess, but too many of us know the choc-ice queer. He already has two black eyes, but it is never going to be enough, his cruelty coming at the worst possible moment for those who have been scorned and belittled and much worse sentenced to years in jail. Stuck in a police cell we are at a low point in our lives, with time to think and worry and regret our sins, terrified inside and trying to still our bowels, getting to grips with the nausea of incarceration. And I remember the ice-cream rapist standing at the bars with his pouting face pushed into the steel, laughing at me, rubbing grit in fresh wounds and rubbing his balls, undoing his flies and exposing himself, promising to fuck my mother, and I feel the scar on my forehead throb, the hatred I feel bitter and twisted and a focus for all the other anger I have inside me, a lifetime of anger aimed at one pathetic man, the ice-cream rapist's biggest mistake thinking he is somehow better than us, that he could never end up behind the same walls as the men he taunts. It is a common fault, I do it all the time, think I am better than other men, incapable of rape or murder or other heinous crimes, and I am an innocent man, a guilty man, guilty as fuck, a hard bastard right up there with the worst offenders, no better and no worse. The choc-ice rapist thought he was immune. The Director plays the same game, yet he does have protection, our rulers don't fuck each other over, know not to set precedents. The rapist is a morsel, a tasty offering, the scum of the earth, the Director and Porky Pig and judge and translator rolled into one, on the front line and stupid enough to believe a strawberry lolly and vanilla cornet can buy him the same immunity. He must have done something pretty bad to end up on B-Block, without segregation or special treatment. I want to know what crime he has committed, understand he is weak like any other playground bully, and he looks sad, and his face is coming into focus, but I still can't make him out properly, I can't see inside him to the child, and an hour passes and I can hear the drums, a thump of booming beads that makes my scar ache in a strangely

pleasurable way and they bang harder and faster and I jump
when I hear the noise, a terrible shrieking worse than any
monster, and it is coming from behind the green door, some
men walking to the opposite end of the section, others on
their feet running towards the toilet, and I am with the mob
as we push into the mist and don't smell the piss, a glowing
fog rolling into the valley from the Congo hills of Africa, and
the rapist has been pushed deep into the tomb and men are
shouting at him, prodding his chest, and I don't know the
meaning of the words coming from my mouth but I am delivering righteous noises from way back in time and there is a
roar that erupts so suddenly I understand the nature of everything that has happened, and we are accusing him of fucking
our mothers and fucking small boys and fucking beautiful
women to death and setting fire to them so they burn alive
with the memory of their last seconds on earth and we are
accusing him of everything that is more rotten than us, every
unspeakable crime that makes him the lowest form of life, and
he truly is the rapist from the police station, he has raped a
retarded youth in the cells, after giving him a choc ice, and
demanding payment, in kind, an empty cell and a frightened
boy, and he has made the mistake of being a bully at the wrong
time, standing at the bars in that no man's land between judgement and punishment and threatening I fuck you good fuck
you very good fuck your mother so hard she will never walk
again, my friends, and you are my friends, all of you boys are
my friends, my very good friends, and my friends fuck you
all very hard very good, and he is laughing, he is crying, he
doesn't have any friends in Seven Towers as a punch connects
with his nose which splits and he is kicked hard in the balls,
and a funny man starts rubbing his groin offering to fuck the
ice-cream rapist, I fuck him good, fuck him hard, unzipping
his trousers, and while we are lost in our anger we are no
calculating perverts, and the queer is kicked and punched and
runs from the room, more scum to be dealt with later, and
we return to the rapist, and he is sobbing and holding out a
hand and showing off a wedding ring begging for mercy he
is sorry so sorry my friends forgive me take mercy on my

family my wife and mother please forgive me I am a weak man and I am not a homo it was only to scare you I was joking and he laughs, and this makes things worse, more perverted, and there are blows coming in and the ice-cream seller pisses his pants and shits himself, staining beige trousers – *I want none of this, I am staying on my bed, with my lucky charm, have you really forgotten?* – and I am near the front of the mob no better or worse than anyone else in the world and we are one powerful body seething with righteous anger knowing the choc-ice rapist is scum who laughs when he helps destroy innocence, abusing small boys locked up in the cell waiting to be reformed and set on the right path and we remember that we are the innocent men and feel good, the Director in his office stroking the documents that sent the ice-cream seller to the B-Block boys and the Director is rejoicing in the old ways, the myriad joys of crucifixion, but it means nothing to us as anger is power and we are unstoppable and descending on the nonce who is on his knees praying and God just isn't listening as we kick him in the head and he falls to the floor where he is stamped on and crawls towards the cubicles maybe he thinks he is a rat man and can escape down the hole swim through the sewers and reach the open sea find a ship that will take him away to a new life a convict colony in Australia where he can take his anger out on the Aboriginals, anyone who can't fight back and isn't protected, and if he doesn't make it and drowns he will live in the rat temple, and he pulls a bin down and dirty paper covers his shoulders and the back of his head, more kicks connected with his groin and stomach, men trying to crowd into the small space of the cubicle, his head on the stone ridge where we crouch and release our poison, a boot pressing the broken nose into the hole, the rapist choking, blood clogging his nostrils, and I can hear his heart beating, straining to cope, and then the glass comes out, long shards of broken ice that gleam in the fog as the bulb's full-moon lunar pull breaks in, and the pervert is going to be cut to ribbons, he seems to know, without seeing the drawn knives, pulled to his feet and held by the arms, all we need is a cross, and the glass slashes back and forwards and up and down and his skin splits easily and the eyes are all we can see through the blood, they are the eyes of the scared children he has abused and the eyes of the piglets screaming for their mother's sweet milk that is turned into ice cream and the choc-ice man is bellowing and begging for his mother, he wants his mum, and the piglets and all the other innocents in the market are screaming as the knives are raised, tongues ripped from their mouths, but they have done nothing wrong, the nonce pulled back over the hole, face pushed to one side, his jugular opened with a steel blade, and the ice-cream rapist is twitching and struggling but is held firm by the man in the striped pyjamas who seems to be whispering a hymn or psalm or maybe a nursery rhyme, and the blood is gushing, skin turning marble white so I think of the prisoner who slit his wrists so quietly and with so much humility beneath his magic blanket, and the rats must have smelt the gore by now and be on their way, and finally this no-good rapist is dead and our anger is spent and the walls of the cave contract, the Director considering the details of a convict's death certificate, the B-Block boys standing around the corpse for a few minutes before returning to the section and settling down for the night.

THE PRISON HOUSE

TWO MONTHS AFTER the death of the ice-cream rapist, deemed suicide by the Director, the loudspeaker spits more distortion and my dream comes true. I have learnt words and survive on a jumble of guesswork, scar shimmying as I decipher meaning, basic contact rather than conversation, a million times better than nothing. I am a hobo living on scraps, who knows he has an inner strength that will see him through the night, if he can just stay concentrated long enough. The battle never ends, voices prodding in directions I don't want to go. And although still an outsider, I am also a part of B-Block. The Congo man has settled in the next bed and we make signs, but he learns no new meaning, remains rooted in the red earth of Africa. Dumb Dumb is busy with his matchsticks. Papa and the monkey monsters sit on the stairs by day and stare into their candle by night. I have still never see them sleep, but know they must. The Butcher wanders the yard searching for his wife, and his smile has faded. The handle of his knife is clearly visible above his belt. Flip Flop and Pretty Boy have moved their beds and are neighbours and I occasionally hear rhythmic creaking in the early hours, feel no curiosity and stay buried beneath my blanket, yet notice they rarely collect their milk. More junkies have been released or transferred, while those left have a fresh supplier from among the old guards, who have returned in place of the goon squad. The man serving the smack reminds me of Mickey Mouse, his cheerful smile a welcome sight, and while the clamour has subsided, chaos reigns. The boys do what they always do. Play dominoes and cards. Punch and kick and prepare to stab. Focus on their beads and count the minutes.

Work is what keeps me sane. I have my own work, which

is my duty. It is also my penance. I don't care what anyone thinks. I do what I have to do and they can do what they want. We are conditioned to judge others, but it is best not to. The B-Block boys are grit-munching scum and we are also diamonds, rough cut but still managing to sparkle. And it is a mutant monkey who taps me on the shoulder and jabbers jungle dialect, moving wicked fingers that stretch towards the loudspeaker, and I hear my name clearly, realise they are calling for Mr Ramone. That's me, Jay Jay Ramone, lover of sweet Ramona, a drifting prison punk who has managed to keep his nose clean. And this monster pulls back his hood and his eyes are clear and intense, a huge rubber mouth grinning and splitting the lower half of his skull, and I reckon this is the boy who was stabbed with the knitting needle the day I arrived on B-Block, but am not certain. His joy worries me, and yet strangely I feel no fear. He turns and lumbers back to the steps where his friends wait, Papa nowhere to be seen, his book closed and propped against the wall. I reach the gate, nervous at being called, realise I have been summoned to see the Director. I have done nothing wrong.

Two guards are waiting, and glancing across the square I see Ali staring into space, waiting for a big spender to open his wallet. I am led away, off through the visiting area where mothers lean on dirty mesh trying to absorb their sons, feel the love and regret of the chicken run, the touch of brittle fingers on chewed stumps, shocked when I see Papa towering over a tiny peasant woman in a shaggy shawl, tears streaming down his face. But I am not allowed to dwell, the guards shooing me on, along a passage, moving forward, thinking about Papa, trying to work him out, climbing the steps to the Director's office. There is a short wait in his outer sanctum, and then I am inside and standing in front of his desk, the Slug to my right, slow-moving and in the same place as my last visit.

The Director stares at a sheet of paper, clock ticking down ready for an explosion, and I convince myself that I am absorbed so far into the system I am beyond the Director's reach. What else can he do? This jumped-up headmaster pauses, lifts his head and speaks, an insignificant fool but a great dictator. Kitted out in a fancy-dress uniform, he signs decrees to starve the boys of their smack and feed us on slaughterhouse tongues, sends ice-cream men to their death, covers us with lice and fills our beds with silverfish and forces us into cold showers, rubs our noses in shit every day of our lives, crucifies mystery men on paradise islands. Maybe he is going to put me in with the sex cases, the child molesters and serial rapists and snuff men. The Slug nods and turns, watery skin smooth and sleek and smelling of a pungent safari aftershave. It is hard to grasp what he is saying, as it's a long time since I heard my language. It takes a while to understand.

It seems the Director has received a sum of money and is moving me to a work farm, where I will have a job and be able to reduce my sentence. Every day I work will count for two days served. The Slug pauses. He is smiling. The Director is beaming. My heart races. It doesn't make any sense. It must be a trick, a lie to raise my spirits before dashing them again. I am alone, yet they claim someone is bribing my way out of Seven Towers. The Slug reads my mind, explains that the Director is trying to create a system where the prisoners play a bigger role and at the same time put something back in. Why should the taxpayer pay for my crime? We must remember the victims, honourable citizens who never break the rules. I am a bad man who has refused to admit his guilt, and yet the Director, with typical generosity, realises that as a foreigner I have immoral, less decent ways. It must be hard to be so alone, with only my arrogance for company. As an alien, and a drain on his nation's resources, the Director is willing to overlook my lack of remorse, for the sake of all those hard-working, law-abiding people on the outside. His smile fades. I must pay for my stay in prison, in financial as well as custodial terms. The Director signs a form and passes it to the Slug, who hands it to a guard. An order is given. Father Christmas dismisses me with a bored flick of his wrist.

My mind is full of questions as I return to the block. Am I really being moved? Has someone seriously sent money to the prison? Is the Director lying? And if so, why? But despite my scepticism I can't help thinking of the farm and how the weather will improve soon and I will be sowing and reaping, wallowing in fresh produce and honest toil. I pass through the chicken run and Papa is still behind the wire, facing his mother, and I notice the Butcher talking with a woman who reminds me of the photo of his wife stuck to the wall by his bed, but all I can think about is leaving Seven Towers behind and working in the open air, circulation kick-starting as I take a fork and turn the earth, break down clumps and move worms. I will mark out drills and carefully scatter seed so as not to waste a single plant, nurse their potential, and once these seeds are covered I will water the soil with painstaking care so as not to expose them to the birds. There is light at the end of this tunnel and I come out of the concrete and into the square, wave at Ali Baba who frowns and doesn't seem to recognise me, but raises a hand anyway. Business is business, and he reasons he must have sold me a blanket in the distant past.

I enter the yard and my escort follows, prisoners I hardly know grinning and slapping me on the back, questioning the guards, and it is true, I really am being moved. The sick feeling that has become a part of me lifts. I feel taller and stronger, but strangely my emotions are stretched. I should be unconditionally ecstatic, but a small part is actually sad. It seems wrong leaving the other boys, some not yet sentenced, others with years already served, a shock that everyone is so pleased. Prisoners return from their visits, and normally they are miserable at this time, but see the crowd and come over, hear the news and offer congratulations, their affection genuine. Only Papa scowls and hurries into the section without a word. The Butcher drapes an arm around my shoulders and says potato, my friend, many potatoes. Yes, digging potatoes is the best job in the world, and I stand still in the middle of the yard surrounded by men who are chatting and laughing and mimicking the picking of grapes and eating of apples. I am stunned, rooted to the spot, and don't know what to do next.

A guard points towards the section and I move on, back into the musty room I know very well but will never see again, pull my bag from under the pillow and undo the zip, needlessly straighten wrinkled clothes, feeling as if I should do something, but I have few belongings and pull the zip again, leave my bag sitting at the bottom of the bed, walk around the room shaking hands, carrying on a noble tradition. Zombies offer dry and damp skin, but every clasp is firm, the common bond of institution boys. Emotion clatters around inside me as I return for my bag, shake the hand of the Congo man, and he grins and says magnificent magnificent, crushing my fingers, and I kneel down and reach under the bed for my house, see only empty space, realise it has been stolen. Terror grips me and I stand, turn on the nearest prisoners. I have to find my house. I start shouting, but they are just as surprised. Some are looking under beds and moving blankets while I sit down shaking, trying to think, paralysed, remembering all those matchsticks and hours of planning, the cutting and aligning and gluing, lost in the work, doing what has to be done, making amends, however token, and now a thief has taken it, but I will find the house, I am going nowhere until I do. A monkey monster appears and trots down the section, looks behind the green door, turns and shouts, fog bellowing out like never before, and I am being urged over, hurry down the aisle and crash into the jungle, eyes smarting from the smoke pouring from my burning home.

Flames crash out of the downstairs windows, the bricks below scorched and buckling, front door exploding and firing spears at the firemen trying to break in with axes, and I look at the upstairs window where Mum is banging on the glass, face pressed forward and nose squashed, and the fire is lashing the front of our house, sleazy serpent tongues hissing and igniting the windowsill so she jumps back, fists pounding glass that wobbles but won't break, and she is fading as the smoke closes around her and pain distorts her face and I am trying to run and save her but firemen are holding me back and I am kicking and punching but they won't let go saying there is nothing I can do and they are doing their best to rescue her and I am shouting and she is screaming but nobody can hear and the room is white with smoke and she is coughing and panicking as the flames rise up inside the house as well as outside and she is headbutting the glass which splits but doesn't break, blood flowing over her face, and Mum is the best person in the world and she is on fire, engulfed and lost and melting, her face collapsing and turning to bone, and I want to die as well, try to get to her, struggling and going mad, slapped by a fireman who wants to save my life, the roof crashing down and burying my mother in a house that is now a tomb, nothing left but taunting flames dancing high into the night.

Papa stands by the sinks with a sad expression. Monkey monsters shout and point to the house. He sighs and tries to reason with them, but they are rabid and start throwing punches, and this is the first time Papa has been confronted, and he accepts their rebellion while backing them off with his knitting needle, careful not to hurt anyone, on the defensive. He leaves the toilet, a patient teacher dealing with irrational children. The Butcher slips his knife out and follows Papa through the beds and out into the yard. A jug of water is thrown on the burning building and it hisses and pops, and I understand the monster in the pyjamas has destroyed my house and killed my mother and I try to break away from the firm grip of the firemen who have turned into prison guards, mouth frothing and feet kicking out, the B-Block boys trying to calm me down, a truncheon connecting and knocking me out.

I am carried from the house and placed in an ambulance and the police are talking to neighbours as the flames rage and they are saying poor boy and how did the fire start and what will happen to him now he is all alone and has no one left his grandmother is dead and his father could be anywhere and he has no brothers or sisters, and I am holding my charm tight and floating with Mum feeling the pain, jump in time, lost in the minds of Baba Jim on his funeral pyre and Jimmy Rocker in his electric chair, and I think of Dad who left us, and Mum never deserved that, she did nothing wrong. She did not deserve to die. She was innocent. A victim. We forget the victims. Men like me. It must have been the boy in the pyjamas who killed that poor woman, and that is what they say in the playground, and the clatter of the schoolyard is breaking me in half and the bullies surround me and chant Dumb Dumb, Dumb Dumb, why can't you speak, Jimmy boy, has the cat got your tongue or has it been cut out for telling lies, why don't you talk and tell us what you think, is it because you are a mental kid and a bad boy and is it true you killed your own mother?

Big boys don't cry and good boys don't make a fuss and I am sitting with helpers in an office somewhere and they are kind and bring a bar of chocolate and a plastic cupful of orange squash it tastes as if it comes from a machine but I don't complain just eat the chocolate and drink the squash with my gaze fixed on the carpet there is a long hair in the material and I am wondering why the vacuum cleaner hasn't picked it up as it is early in the morning and Mum cleaned offices and she would have made sure the job was done right and the eyes of these helpers peer over glasses and their lips form questions and I stare harder at the floor aware of the melted faces around me all this black and blue flesh and those monkey monsters escaped the fire while Mr Fair and Rupert and Yogi Bear all died as well as Mum and they whisper in the dark below my new bed and gnash their teeth and two policemen come and ask more questions and they say they feel sorry for me and one goes out and brings back a sandwich and a can of fizzy drink and I keep quiet but know it is wrong that they feel pity for such a wicked boy.

I am in another room sometime later with more helpers and they write on pieces of paper and put these in cardboard folders and I say nothing much just look out of the window and think of Mum and they talk about confusion and denial and shock and it doesn't mean anything to me and I imagine that I am leaving my body and floating along the ceiling and I see myself in a big building somewhere I can't remember really there are other boys in the room and they call it a home say it is a special place to be for lucky boys and I am not allowed to leave although the people running it are very nice but I miss my mum and my nana as well and run away and am found at a bus station by the police who bring me back.

I think about Mum every second of every day. I see her burning to death and when I get older I learn to close it out. It makes me feel so bad I pretend it never happened. And I am in the chapel and the light is dazzling my eyes, and for a moment I feel the same as when I saw the snow, standing next to Nana looking out of the window, street lights playing tricks, turning it yellow and orange and purple, and the Slug is making slurping noises, his shoes near my face so I can smell the polish, his clipped translation informing me that the prison van is ready to leave for the farm and if I don't go with the guards right now my transfer to paradise will be cancelled.

Passing out of the prison gate the universe comes roaring forward in all its brutal brilliance, punching into me so hard I gasp. It doesn't matter that there are bracelets on my wrists and guards on either side, this is a massive taste of freedom, fresh air rinsing smelly prison clothes, its coolness chapping pallid skin, and looking ahead I see a landslide of slate flowing down the hill, dipping into the sea and leaving the sky to dominate Seven Towers, emphasising the claustrophobia of life behind its walls. It is impossible not to glance back, and I make a wish for my friends on B-Block, resist a strong urge to know if the Director is watching. Eased into the wagon, one hand-cuff is unlocked and fastened to a rod running along the back of the seat in front. With my free hand I find the charm in my pocket, feel the vibration and am relieved, ignore the beads, hold on tight and hope for an easy ride. My luck has changed. Doing the right thing has paid off. I am on the move.

Two other prisoners are added to the van before it leaves, and the first man is tall and graceful, nods politely, says something I try to work out, but he has no time to explain and turns away, closes butterfly eyes, lids fluttering, no offence caused. The second man is younger with a blank white eye and a vicious scar crossing his cheek. He ignores us, which is fair enough, as we agree what is important, shifting close to the nearest windows, ready to record every sight. The farm will be easier than Seven Towers, a modern complex with better facilities, but it is still a prison. We pull away cautiously, and the pang I felt in the yard returns, and I think instead of the matches burning, remember Mum screaming and fight back, see the Butcher fondling his knife and wonder what he did to Papa, try harder and concentrate on this ride, the best distraction possible.

We are soon gliding downhill leaving Seven Towers in the past, and I am pressed against the mesh registering a jigsaw of houses heaped into each other, shaded pencil impressions in the fading light, another type of plaster and brickwork and the more familiar whitewash, ornamental wire over glass, faint light in dark nooks, fragile balconies emerging from stone flats, food smells promising homely meals and conversation. We linger at a corner as the driver waits for a car to turn, horn squeezed as a reminder, invisible band playing a waltz as an elderly couple emerge from a cobbled street carrying groceries, boys surging past on bikes, following a smoother asphalt path, our van lurching forward, faces lost as the driver accelerates along an open stretch of flat road, mortar blurring and changing colour, slowing, shape and colour coming back into focus. Torn posters advertise films and a politician with a black moustache, promoting death and destruction and peace and love. We speed up again and I glance at the others, recognise their concentration, pencil turning to crayon as we move deeper into the city, a kaleidoscope of imagery that has to be absorbed fast.

I inspect the wire over my window, find the regular dust and crumbling insect remains, and travelling uphill we briefly tried to grab the world outside but were too cramped and anxious, unaware of what was valuable, everything so familiar it was impossible to appreciate. Relief and excitement control disorientation, and I am shackled and clutching at this brief excursion but knowing things are getting better. I am very lucky. There are many prisoners much worse off, the world crammed with the poor and starving, the disabled and deranged, crime victims who really deserve sympathy. We stop and start, a reminder of Seven Towers, the motion of the van bringing me back as we stop opposite a corner cafe where free men sit at tables sipping coffee and small glasses of spirit, and they are talking with free women who raise small cakes to their mouths, and I watch these females closely and appreciate the delicate way they move their hands to express a point, surprised when Ali Baba brings out glasses of water, sure I saw him back at the Oasis. I wish we could stay longer, but hurry on, through bigger and newer buildings, offices and warehouses, joining a wider road with hundreds of machines, a dual carriageway that flattens out and takes us from the town, into the descending night.

The rhythm is steady and the darkness soon thickens, a heavy black that is pricked by yellow road lights, spooks passing in cars and trucks, an army of glow-worms announcing a village, a neon junction of new tarmac and dirt-track lanes, white-haired men on a concrete platform, toying with beads as they make their beer last, others at uneven tables shuffling dominoes, old boys stuck in miniature chairs, and I picture the fields beyond, the olive groves and wilder woods and not too far away the sea with its fishing boats and container ships, and when the darkness closes in again and the road lights vanish thousands of stars appear and maybe the tail of a comet and I realise it has been a long time since I saw a night sky, can't remember the last time I even looked. And the growing joy of being transferred weakens my resolve so I start wondering if I maybe misjudged the Director, gullible believing in crucifixion and heroin hotshots. He has reached out and offered a helping hand, the idea of a cash payment the mask of a modest man. He has saved me from the psychopath known as Papa, the cruelty of a metropolitan man who destroyed my house of redemption. Papa is the evil one, refusing to give me his matches, hoarding them with his monsters. But I still the weakness that constantly reassesses and reinvents truth, concentrate on the present.

The journey takes a good two hours and after a period of darkness, with the stars shut off by dense cloud, I see light in the distance, a ball of electricity that spreads and turns into a glowing orb, a UFO lighting up the void, and even before we slow down and turn along a freshly coated road I know this is the farm. Neat white lines channel the tarmac, a gleaming perimeter fence up ahead, linking steel watchtowers topped with glass control rooms, the farm wide and low-lying, a clean patch of progress in the wilderness, more space station than ship, and beyond the brilliance of the lights are the fields where we will work during the day, the farm offering shelter and protection. We stop at the gate and I can smell tar, eager to get inside, see papers exchanged, the guards smart and clean-shaven, computers flickering in their office, the gate razor wire and steel, everything open and efficient compared to Seven Towers. The barrier silently lifts, our van gliding over bitumen that could be a parade ground or runway, shades of blue beyond the overwhelming whiteness. I already understand that the farm is about space and modern thinking, transparent boundaries and receptive minds, fresh food and hope for the future.

There is no macho posturing from the guards, a different breed to both the goons and the Seven Towers regulars, the door opening as soon as we stop, handcuffs removed by a sprightly professional who relays instructions and waves us out. The glare of a spotlight is welcome, documents traded and signed on a clipboard, chilly night air warmed by electricity. There is no lecture or delay as we are led to a gate and off down a deserted corridor that smells of bleach, the mood informal and relaxed. I wait for a twist, but there is none. It is a sparse environment that feels ordered and decent, every-where incredibly bright, a clean start. More papers are exam-ined at a glass door, and I watch the guards, trained professionals with none of the anger of the goons or unpredictability of our own rejects. There will be no chapel welcome here, and instead of a bawling dictator on a box and a Porky Pig drug dealer, I am separated from the others and guided along another walkway and through a secure door, finally entering a cell block that practically dazzles.

To the right is a shower room and two guards wait with a towel, plastic basket and orange boiler suit, a bar of soap and spray gun. They motion for me to strip and I oblige, wrap the towel around my waist and drop my dirty clothes in the basket. One points to my bag and as I unzip it he puts on rubber gloves, kneels and searches the contents, removing more clothes. My knife is back in Seven Towers so I have nothing to fear. I suddenly remember my lucky charm, heart popping as I point to the basket, and they move aside so I can rummage in material that already smells different, reaching into the pocket of my jeans and loosening the safety pin. The charm rests in my hand and the guards gather round to inspect it, one frowning and another remaining impassive, the third smiling and saying very good, my friend, very good.

I stand on tiles inside the shower room and remove my towel, lift arms and bend forward, go through the manoeuvres that show I am free of drugs or weapons, and once this is done I am sprayed with a chemical solution, something to kill the germs, and these men are unaggressive, pointing me towards a nozzle where the cold water shocks and revitalises, turning warm so I can wash with the soap, charm held firm, the vibration merging with my heartbeat, and the soap is rich and strong and I realise that theirs are the first eyes to look at my good-luck charm since Mum gave it to me, but it doesn't matter, I can't survive without it, hear a guard speak and rinse off, dry myself and dress in the boiler suit, a pair of plastic sandals appearing and handed over, and I slip these on, feel clean and revitalised like never before.

Leaving the shower I notice a camera for the first time, security discreet but tight, and walking further into the block there is a control room where more guards sit watching television, one screen focusing on the empty showers. I am led to a cell and motioned inside. No bolt is dramatically slammed into place, but I know when the door eases shut that I am locked in. And the cell is very clean, with a washbasin and sit-down toilet, the bed welded to the floor, a new pillow and crisp case, two blankets folded and positioned dead centre. Amazingly, there is a radiator. This really is a luxury suite, windows barred to keep the badness out and goodness in, and I can see what seem to be large storage sheds to my right, darkness beyond the silver lines of the fence straight ahead, to the left a barrack-style building. In the morning I will have a good view. Best of all, I am alone. I stand over the toilet and watch the water turn yellow before pulling the handle which sets it flushing with the genius of the modern age. Turning the tap, I clean my hands in warm water. The silence is amazing, solitude even better. I take my clothes off and stand naked next to the radiator.

I inspect the cell for signs of life, a spider's web or trapped moth, but there is nothing. A switch lets me control the light, which is a relief, the bulb covered by a modest shade, while the door is solid with a flap. I have privacy and protection, so happy I remember those two abandoned drifters, Jimmy Rocker convulsing in his electric chair, phone ringing and the voltage cutting off, Mr Lewis coming over to tell him he has been reprieved, confiding you sure ain't no killer, boy. Jimmy thanks Jerry Lee, knows he is going to be okay. He has faced death and will live again. His truck is waiting with a full tank of gas and an ice chest brimming with cold beer, Mary-Lou warming the passenger seat, the open road calling. And I see Baba Jim on his funeral pyre, Ganesh pushing through the crowd and a mighty trunk pulling the good boy clear. Jim is carried to an ashram where he quickly recovers, mind clear and focused as he returns to the maze. Both these wanderers emerge miraculously unscathed, eager to continue their quests, never knowing the nature of the accusations levelled against them but happy their innocence has been proven. I put the boiler suit back on and stretch out on the bed, close my eyes and breathe easy, beyond the reach of the monsters and at peace with the world.

The police call me a runaway but I am merely returning to familiar surroundings and have done nothing wrong just want to be on my own for a while and walking from the bus stop I can't help admiring the Christmas trees in windows some artificial and others so real I can smell the pine and sometimes their lights are shining even though it is daytime and the elderly and the young are at home waiting and hopefully nobody is alone the pavement has been salted and is gritty the rocky surface of a moon meaning I stomp along next to a road that has turned to sludge passing the shop where years ago a small boy won Rupert Bear in a competition and I stop and look in the window but the woman who ran it isn't there and it is a different sort of shop selling fancy food where before it was normal tins and toys the things people need and the common is ahead of me across the road and it is white and crisp and it is also empty with it being so cold out and I cross over and walk along the edge sticking to the path which has turned to ice sliding a few times and once I almost fall throwing my hands sideways as if I am a skater and when it is time I cut over to the playground noticing how the ferns have sunk back into the earth and the trees seem bigger and they are without leaves and remind me of burnt skeletons and I prefer pine both the smell and the fact they are always the same and seem as if they can live for ever and I used to be warned about the ferns told to keep away just in case and I never knew what just in case meant but I am fifteen now and have a better idea that there are bad people in the world and as I pass I spin the roundabout and push a swing hear the jangle of wood on metal reach the climbing frame and haul myself to the top where the wind is colder on my face and I am king of the castle looking across the snow and the clouds are shredded purple and red and lined with orange and the years have passed and I have lived with foster-parents but it never works out and I go to another home and one day I see a familiar face and Ramona still has the deepest blackest eyes and she recognises me and we sit outside and swap stories and this is a while ago now and today is the anniversary of the fire and I always remember the date and swing down and hit the ground and walk over to the ferns and find the rotting tree where Mum and me hid Dad's old sledge many years ago so as not to upset Nana and I pull it into the open and shake off the dirt and rotting leaves and set off away from the ferns and over the common trudging through virgin snow turning and seeing my footprints and feeling sorry they are messing up the smooth surface but know all good things come to an end and there are two flowing grooves from the sledge and the wood is rough and splintered and the strips of tin lining the runners are rusty around the nails and it is heavy and well made and has lasted a long time but glides easily over the snow and I reach the edge of the common and stand looking down the slope and it is a long way down to the bottom and if the sledge doesn't slow down I will overshoot and end up crushed in the road beyond and I look back over the common and see Ramona in the distance and she is wrapped up in her leather jacket with the bright red handbag she always carries and she is running and panting so I can see the mist in front of her face and as she gets nearer she is laughing and shouting wait for me, Mr Ramone, wait for me.

Following the best night's sleep of my life, the heavy clang of the wake-up bell sounds more like a delicate wind chime. There is a faint click as the door unlocks and I yawn and stretch and wonder if breakfast will arrive on a tray. White emulsion captures the sunlight coming through the window and I roll out of bed and stand at the window looking towards the horizon where the sky meets a forest, flat green fields in between. The buildings to my right are prefabricated hangars for packing and storing fruit and vegetables, the land beyond the barracks to the left rougher scrub, a bulldozer waiting to make it level. The see-through boundary means I am part of the world again. I feel great, sitting now on my own private toilet and reminiscing over life on safari, the stink of nostalgia and the threat of rodent castration. Strangely, I do not linger, not even here. I strip down to my pants and wash, stretch and touch clean toes, move my head in small circles, feel the tightness, dry off and dress, stroll out into the walkway and follow the smell of cooking, joining a flow of sauntering prisoners.

Nearing the gate my calm is shattered, but in the best possible way. At first I worry it is another happy vision, the hallucinating glory of a trickster who has lost control of his miraculous powers of mental persuasion, as instead of a forced Porky Pig or Homer Simpson I spot two old friends. As I approach these drifters it is clear their identities are rock solid. Mr Elvis Presley and Mr Jesus Christ turn when I call out, and seem more shocked than I am, but quickly recover, know anything is possible is this bizarre prison system, and we shake hands warmly, momentarily speechless, an old school reunion down on the farm. The roving rocker and the wandering baba have found each other, and despite their different routes I guess the journey is the same, all roads leading to salvation, an honourable life where we can sow and reap and atone for our sins. Guards smile and urge us on and we talk our way down another corridor of steel bars, a flurry of excited words that take time to untangle, entering the dining hall in a contented silence.

Prisoners stand behind a long table and serve us from trays, and I am given bread and eggs, thick slices of what seems to be mutton, hot tea from an urn. My friends guide me through the process, wiggling their heads, telling me there is no work today as it is Sunday, the three of us beaming like fools, glad to be reunited. I follow them to a corner table where we can eat and talk, and I am hungry but unused to solids this early in the day, easily filled by the quality of the food. Elvis and Jesus wait for me to settle, realise I am excited and trying to come to terms with the change, let me breathe before Elvis asks about Seven Towers and how I survived B-Block, and I tell him Franco is free and probably at home as we speak, getting stuck into those ripe tomatoes, but it all seems a long time ago now, and Jesus wants to know about the boys back in the section, and I tell him what has been happening, the dignity of this complex making everything in Seven Towers seem even more confused and insane.

We clear away our plates and don't have to wash them as there are prisoners allocated this job. Their aprons remain spotless and they move fast, my friends explaining how the farm operates as a smooth-running machine, the incentive of two days served for every one worked the best possible motivation. Everyone has an aim, the guards rarely needing to assert themselves. If the rules are broken, the offender is returned to a normal jail. Zero tolerance is enforced and the system works. There are no junkies and no psychotics, and neither has seen an argument since they arrived. There are no drugs, disagreements controlled. Elvis and Jesus agree that this is a paradise, but point out that no prison is perfect. They look at me and I smile, nod back, yawning from too much good rest, know it will take time to settle into the routine.

I follow them back to the block and they explain there are hot showers every night and a laundry where I can wash my clothes so they will actually end up clean. The clothes I arrived in will be returned to me, once they have been boiled and treated for infestation, although many men prefer the boiler suits, but it is a personal choice as this is an easygoing regime. There are no mad men here, just conscientious reform-minded citizens eager to start their lives over, begging for a second chance. I return to my cell and brush my teeth, lie on the bed for a while, realising how comfortable the mattress is, too tired last night, letting the food settle, enjoying the silence, an unnatural quiet that will soon become normal once more.

There is a room where the men congregate, and my friends come along later and knock on the door, show me the layout, chairs and tables on a carpet floor, a television set and table tennis, wide windows and no bars, a yard reached through normal doors, enclosed by a mesh fence topped with neat razor wire, its silver glint truly beautiful. A guard sits in the corner of the room, the yard overlooked by a control tower. I stand in the yard, which is more of a concrete garden, a bed of plants next to the block, even tarmac under my feet, and looking off into the distance the sky dominates and gives such a fantastic feeling of space it makes me wobble. Rain begins to spit and I stroll back inside, look at the control tower with its machine gun and spotlight, blank glass and steel roof.

Sitting with my friends we talk and talk and it has been a while since I have been able to do this and we discuss the places we have been and the places we will go when we are released and at first I am tongue-tied like a boy who has been lonely and has a pal at last and wants to impress him but doesn't want to come over wrong, as if he is desperate, and then I ramble on and as we talk I get the impression that something has changed with Jesus, as he doesn't talk so freely, before it was ideas and ideals and now it is just places and people and maybe it is the same with Elvis, as he has always talked about places and people and now he speaks about theories, both of them with a new edge I don't grasp. It must be me. It will take time to settle in, but I will be fine. It is the same with the food. When we go for dinner it fills me up fast and I feel sick, the meat rich and plentiful and my stomach used to soup and stew, bread and rice, scraps of beef and fish, some root vegetables and a couple of boiled eggs a week. I look at my friends and wonder.

In the afternoon I sleep and dream, toss and turn in a warm bed, and in Seven Towers most dreams were conscious inventions, any sleep light as I was too alert to let myself relax, always hanging back waiting for the monsters to pounce, listening for teeth grinding under the bed, but now when I dream I feel as if I am awake, and there is a tapping on my door and Elvis and Jesus are peeking in telling me to come on and follow them, they have a surprise for me as today is a day of rest and God created the world in six days and on the seventh He did no work, and didn't I ever wonder where the seventh tower was? It is true, I never saw that seventh tower, and they smile and talk about those six deadly sins committed by six deadly sinners and when God peopled the earth He told His men to go forth and multiply and scatter their seed and I am a farmer now and soon I will be sowing and the men from the union didn't stay in prison long and they sent us crates of oranges and I try to smell the sugary scent of the milk but all I sniff is soapsuds, and I am gliding along the hall and the lights are shining but I know they will never be as bright as that New Year's morning, the memory makes me smile, that was a special time, I will never forget that sight and I will never forget Seven Towers, and accompanying my friendly guides I pass through a succession of open gates, a guard nodding as we turn into a small corridor lined with cabinets and buried inside are files with the details of every single prisoner from right around the globe and these papers detail their crimes and punishments and the thoughts they have before and after their judgement day and the causes of those thoughts. Life is a chain reaction. Elvis and Jesus emphasise this point in their lectures – *I hate these freaks with their endless opinions* – and I am amazed at their saintliness – *they both think they're the clean-living sons of God* – men who have reached a crossroads and chosen the right path. We approach a green door. I stop and tell them I am not going on safari with the rats and those alligators that pull you down into the drains and drown you and then leave the corpse under a log to marinate, but they laugh and say do not worry, friend, this is a different shade of green and we are safe, we will not be crucified in this place, we can do whatever we want, and these are honourable men and I follow them inside and see a woman sitting on the side of a bed and at first I don't understand then see she is naked under a fur coat and they explain that in this more modern prison a man can work hard and employ women, and this girl satisfies a natural urge and I should know that the bromide they put in the milk will make us sterile if we drink too much. I look at Elvis and Jesus and I think of Jimmy Rocker and Baba Jim and those characters try to live decent lives, really do their best, and I won't pretend this prostitute is not attractive, she is, and it is so long since I have been with a woman I am aroused and tempted and she is dressed as a cartoon hooker with long silky legs and full breasts, and I think of Baba Jim the Kama Sutra hobo in an Indian brothel where they use Nepalese runaways and poor girls kidnapped and sold to fat low-life pimps with Bollywood hairdos, and I think of Jimmy Rocker in a Mississippi cat house balling slave girls ruined by crack cocaine and shipped in by skinny low-life pimps, and I think of myself and the sex every man needs to survive – *she's a good-looking girl, rubber man, and she's working for a living so it isn't exploitation, everyone has to work hard and take the job they are given, that's what life is about, and everything those two cut-throats say is right, are you going to waste your chance because of some dumb principle what makes you special every man has to eat to survive and so what if this is the Director's way of rubbing your nose in the shit and nailing your decency to a cross and this is a fine time to find some courage you've got to take what you can get and look after number one and fuck everyone else what has anyone ever done for you, come on, do yourself a favour, let's fuck her* – and she pulls back her coat and I see Mary-Lou and Sarah – *fuck them both* – but most of all I see Ramona – *no, not Ramona* – and I see the mothers in the chicken run when they are younger with their babies hungry doing what they must to survive and I want no fucking part of it – *all right, don't swear, I don't like you cursing* – and I hate Elvis and Jesus for bringing me here – *I always said they were wankers, but you never listen, stuck on your romantic notions, the wonders of the open road* – and they are walking over to the woman and inspecting her body and Elvis reasons that she is a good-time girl and Jesus insists she is a harlot and deserves everything she receives, and it is an honest transaction, we are men, after all, and they seem hurt by my reaction, soon the bromide will wear off and I realise that things are different to Seven Towers, and they are laughing and unzipping their trousers and I turn away and smash a fire alarm that brings the guards running, return to my cell and shut the door, burying myself under the covers.

When I wake up it is dark and my friends are peeking around the door and telling me it is time to eat and I drive that stupid dream away, glad to be talking and in such good company. We sit in the canteen, but I can't stuff any more down, my stomach has shrunk and the quantity and quality of the food is too much. They concentrate on their meals and there is an uncomfortable silence when I ask them about the work, knowing I shouldn't interrupt during a meal, and they say that it is hard, it will be difficult at first, but I will adjust. They hope I will be strong enough, and I nod and say I don't mind sweating, secretly hope I can keep up with the rest of the men as my old diet has left me weak and I don't want to fail. My friends have put on weight and are fit. I return to the cell block, go to the shower room, the water hot and constant and I can stay for as long as I want between six and seven every evening, any time on Sunday. There are plenty of cubicles and a guard at the door, surveillance camera an added protector. I scrub at that bad dream and stand under the water for ages, feel the warmth seeping in, at peace again as I promise I will shower every day and drive the cold out of my organs, never forget how I felt in Seven Towers. I finally dry myself and dress, return to my cell and sit on the bed, take my lucky charm out and stare at it for a long time, wait until the doors are locked before settling down for the night.

Waiting for the morning chimes I see slender strips of metal dangling from the branches of an apple tree, on the edge of an orchard brewing cider, remember the dead tree in the B-Block yard, turned to stone. Perhaps being forgotten is worse than being ignored. I think about how I was a bad boy and grew into an evil man and it must be in my genes, wonder if this defect will be passed on. Mum and Nana must be ashamed, except love often knows no shame, and my father sent me a postcard from America when I was a child, and a while later he sent one from India. I never heard from him again. He could be in America as I think this, driving down a highway with a cold beer in his hand and Dolly Parton on his arm, or sitting cross-legged in an Indian ashram, ten days into a fast, lost in holy visions. Perhaps he is dead.

Today is a rebirth and soon I will start proving myself in olive groves and vineyards, work off the terrible crimes I have committed in foreign fields, become a trusted worker who never gets drunk and abusive, and cherishes life, takes even the smallest of responsibilities seriously, the sort of honest grafter who would rather die than let his comrades down or abandon his family. I have come through the hard times and the Director is a righteous man who has offered me a chance to atone for my sins, and the burning matchsticks make me feel sick when I think of them, Papametropolis in his gulag pyjamas, but this is nothing compared to the memory of a house made from bricks and mortar and exploding glass, and I get away from towns and back into the fields, heading towards a pine forest in a child's book, off across a flat common towards the swings and slides and climbing frame.

I hear ticking and listen to oil circulating in the radiator, and I could grow plants here, get hold of some sunflower seeds or peppers, a jade tree or cactus, create an Oasis in the cell. And I think of the cold, dirty world of Seven Towers, the constant noise and fear, the madness of Ali Baba and the Butcher and Baker, the Sicilian elder and young Italian, Flip

Flop and Pretty Boy, Porky Pig dealing smack, the plastic gangsters and marble men, Homer Simpson passing through, the monkey monsters and safari rats, amazed at how much I became a part of it, the farm perfect but without passion, and yet passion is bad, boredom good. I repeat this mantra. Seven Towers and this nameless work prison are two different worlds, the past and the future and both part of the present. I think of our house burning and my mother dying and it won't go away, all those years of burying it and hiding my crime counting for nothing. But work will shut it out. Hard, slogging, repetitive, soul-inspiring work.

When the chimes finally tinkle they have swung the other way, sirens announcing a bombing raid, and I wash and accept heavy boots, overalls and thick gloves from a guard, take them with a head full of naive dreams, always a boy, tugged back to the house. Papa has resurrected memories that are better ignored, and I hate him for it, in a split second of realisation suspect he is the one with the answers, that it is not Elvis or Jesus but the psycho in the pyjamas, and maybe his monkey boys aren't proper monsters, and I remember the man who told me I was being called to the gate, and I have got something wrong here, the thought nagging and growing as I put on my work clothes and the barriers collapse and I am sitting on the bed with my head in my hands reliving that moment a week or so after Nana died and she has gone away to heaven and every night I lie awake I just can't sleep because she has vanished and I miss her and when people die they rot away and turn to dust and Mum is crying a lot and now there is just the two of us and I ask Mum and she says Nana has been buried in a cemetery and one day we will go and see her, when I am older, and I have to be strong, and at night I think about her lying under the ground and it must be freezing down there in the earth and I hope her coffin is made of strong wood and I see her face decaying and turning to a skull so she looks like a monkey and the monsters under the bed are whispering and I wonder if Nana will become one of them and she could speak to dead people men and women came to visit and she passed on words from the other side she had a strong belief in life after death and I know for certain she will never turn into a monster but I feel sorry for her as she must be freezing and stuck in the dark without any light or warmth and I think about the fire we used to make in the fireplace of the old house where we lived before and even though it was cold that front room was warm and cosy and these are my childhood memories and part of my personal history the best days of my life and the house didn't belong to her so one day we have to move to this house and it is different more modern and warmer but without fireplaces and I miss building the fire with Nana in the morning we used to clean out the ashes with a dustpan and brush and using coal and kindling and newspapers make a great fire and in the evening I would get to light it and my two strongest memories of being with Nana are making the fire up in that old house and watching the snow fall outside the new house and when she left the first house the men who owned it came and ripped down the little tree house in the back garden it wasn't really a tree house high in a tree it was nailed together next to a coal shed and I watched it burn but when you are young these things pass easier they don't seem to mean as much as when you are older, no, it didn't matter, not really, and I keep thinking about our old fireplace and how Nana loved it so much and maybe she is watching and on this terrible night I can't sleep and I go into the living room and take newspapers and put them in a plastic bowl that sometimes holds apples and I find my mum's matches and the thing about adults is they always tell children not to play with matches and that is right for babies but I have lit fires and know what I am doing and I watch the paper burn and I sink into the flames and see Nana's face in the patterns and it is warm and I put more paper in to keep it going and I sit on her chair and drift off to sleep.

Breakfast is being served but I am not hungry.

Firemen carry me outside and I am coughing and choking and feel sick but can't vomit and I am looking for Mum and there are fire engines and police and the house is in flames and Mum is dying in front of me. I am a murderer. I have killed my own mother.

I follow Elvis and Jesus and stand with a group of twenty men at the end of the cell block, two guards arriving to take us to work. The men seem subdued and the novelty wears off, eventually, we become used to change and take things for granted, but I won't let that happen, promise to remember how lucky I am, appreciate every crumb that falls my way, the New Year's resolution I didn't make in Seven Towers. Work closes out every bad thought, concentrating the mind on a task so it doesn't split and riddle itself with doubt – *you'll never get rid of me, we belong together, you useless gutless wanker* – and I am keen to start, skin clean and teeth scrubbed, ready to knuckle down, shut everything out and work until I collapse with exhaustion. This is going to be a fine time. Every day counts as two and freedom is worth any price. I am a lucky boy, standing at the gate, back at the crossroads and heading in the right direction. I am invincible.

The gate opens and we are in a huge yard, more car park than prison, to our left the forest, the flat fields before it dissected by the road I think I arrived on, cutting through the arable land where I may soon be working, up ahead the hangars where they store the produce and maybe machinery, and I imagine myself driving a tractor, or a harvester cutting and bundling hay, though that will be in the future, once the seasons have worked their magic and I have won approval. The men turn right, and glide over more pristine tarmac, through a gate and into another yard. I hear humming ahead and realise we are taking a bus to the fields, and it makes sense that we will work further out, and I feel the freedom in the air, walk along a path lined with storm fences and see goats and sheep and cows in a field, my spirits rising even higher as I watch them munch on grass, and I can taste the milk and cheese and feel the wool, hear a truck and imagine the grunting of pigs in its engine, and the wind rustles in the trees and sound really must carry as the pine forest is behind me and I can hear voices in the wind and can't make out the words and it is funny how the wind can sound like men chattering and men can sound like animals panicking and we are approaching one of the giant sheds and the noise rises and freezes my skin.

Pigs are being unloaded from a truck and I smell something more rotten than a safari in the jungle, Noah licking his lips and finding civilisation. Machinery hums and the volume grows with every footstep. I hear grunting and groaning and the screaming of junkies. We turn a corner and enter the storage shed and the ceiling is glowing with the farm's own blinding white light, a generator pumping hard. In a corner, lined along a shelf, are hundreds of skinned heads. Jawbones protrude and there are no tongues. For a moment the heads appear human, but I know they belong to sheep and goats, think of the meat on my plate and the plentiful supply of mutton, remember goats with horns and beards that make them look like friendly men, and there are ramps and fences and stone slabs and metal hooks and bolt guns that are being loaded and knives lined up on counters and there are electric prods and iron bars and drains and troughs and a bull staring at me with huge brown eyes and a gun pressed to his forehead and he is powerful and proud and honest and feasts on grass and is too gentle to beat the slaughterers and I think of lions and leopards and wonder why men only eat creatures who shy away from a fight, why gentleness is translated as weakness, and there is an explosion and the bolt fires into the bull's head and shatters the bone and his eyes are rolling into me and men are dragging him away and his hooves are kicking and veins rattling and his bowels flow and the machine men with me are moving to their positions and Elvis and Jesus are telling me to follow them and the bull is hauled up using hooks and a thick chain and this is attached to a conveyor belt which moves him forward so he is struggling over a drain where another man takes a machete and slices his chest open and shit and piss are spurting out with the blood and bubbles are flowing from his gums this noble creature demeaned and disorientated and dying made insignificant by machines and the manipulating minds of humans who would run from him in a fair fight and the smell is sickening and cowardice flows with the blood across a tiled floor clogging the drain with congealed meat and another bull is prodded and beaten forward with sticks and he can see what is happening and his terror makes the air vibrate and my friends are pushing me on with anger in faces which are twisted and warped and I look at the skinned heads and gag and they say this is normal, you will be all right, it is a shock at first, and they lead me into another section and are telling me this is where I will work and soon it will be easy, I will get used to my job just as they have, and they are watching my face and I can hear lambs bleating somewhere and when I look past the holding pens I see a pen holding piglets, noses twitching with excitement they are so young, and they miss their mums but haven't realised they will never see her again, that calling someone a pig is an insult, and that humans crave their flesh, and a man lifts a baby pig up and takes him to a bucket, holds his body over a cauldron and slits the throat with a knife, muttering as blood splatters the metal, legs kicking as it tries to escape, swearing and cursing it for trying to live, and the piglet hammers frail limbs as it screams and screams and cries out for its mother.

Stunned, I grab an iron bar and head towards the killer, Elvis and Jesus pulling at me, shouting and asking what good will I do by refusing to work – *they know what you think, what I think* – that I will be sent back to Seven Towers and left to serve out my time with the rubbish of society – *hypocrites* – and I look at their faces and see two pathetic men – *gutless fucking scum* – and they say they hate the work and feel the same as me, but it means we will be released and if we don't kill the animals someone else will, and here they stand, my two decent friends, with their empty ideals and fake dreams, talking and talking and never saying a thing. They look at me and are ashamed. I push them off and run forward, smash the bar into the face of the piglet killer – *at last, I hit the cunt twice more, his head splitting as he sinks to the ground, and the robots swarm in on me and the piglets cry and try to run but there is nowhere to hide and I am swinging the bar at the machine men and they are trying to grab it and flashing knives they are too scared to use in case they lose their jobs, and I catch someone else on the head and he goes down, and they jump me and the bar is gone and I am clawing and biting like a monster monkey and that really gets them going and the guards are running in and pulling me up and I am bustled towards the door and manage to break loose run back and kick the piglet killer in his bloody face his victim twitching in the gore of its death and the guards are hitting me with their truncheons and I hardly feel a thing pushing past them and staggering outside into the clean air of a dirty world and there are more blows on my skull and back and there is no point looking for the good in people as most of them are cowards and their words meaningless and I stop in the middle of the yard and sink to my knees, lean forward over their perfect tarmac and release the nausea, let the whole lot come up in a flow of sickness, ridding myself of their injustice and my guilt and the sheer rottenness of life.*

Prison is a voyage of discovery, a journey into the depths of the night, the longest night of the human soul, and maybe it is a wicked thing to say, but it has been a blessing in the heaviest disguise. Seven Towers cleans me out. Teaches me nothing but forces me to learn for myself. When I am set free I will do so with my head held high. This is my education. My revelation. Because the road may be long and the road may be rough but who gives a fuck, this is about more than time and space. My innocence is beyond their hypocritical courts and squalid punishment, their grubby bribes and choices, their pathetic attempts to make me lick their shoes and thank them for the privilege. I turn down their freedom and, still shaking from my glimpse of a hell ten million times worse than incarceration in a run-down jail, I am alone in the wagon and on my way back to Seven Towers.

Dazed and in shock I pass through misty fields, see birds flying from telegraph pole to tree before rustling feathers and soaring off into the sky. I am sad for the innocents in the slaughterhouse, sorry for their executioners, machine men who have sold their souls and destroyed any last grains of purity. I ride with the motion of the van, fields and forests passing as Elvis and Jesus work on the necks of piglets and lambs. And I despise them as much as the Director, probably more. The farm is a factory and no place for this weakling. They can keep their daily showers and rich food and solitary confinement. Give me the chance to go on safari and five minutes

271

of hot water a week, a musty blanket and crowded dormitory, surrounded by men of passion who have killed and mutilated in the heat of the moment, mad fucking monkeys who never sleep and that psychopath in the pyjamas, the man who burnt my house down and made me confront a fire that happened years before. And I am muttering to myself as if I have gone insane, and maybe I have.

The countryside flows in a wash of green and yellow, merging rock with vegetation, head throbbing. Buildings grow by the roadside. People pass. Cars honk. And we are moving into the outskirts of the city and I watch but feel no pang of regret, notice the women and think of Seven Towers and how it is full of men. It is a solid male world. The effeminate and the non-believers and the homosexuals are all male, and until a man enters jail he doesn't understand what women mean, that without them only half of life exists. There is a time, whether it is in court, a holding cell, on arrival or the long months and years inside, when every man cries for his mother. Even old men sitting in a police station sob in the dark and wish they were small and could start again. Most men don't even know they are crying. We don't want to go to school and learn this new way of behaving, don't want to stand up and fight for our lives in the playground and the prison yard.

The van chugs through the streets and stone blots out the sun. I smell carbon monoxide and hear the roar of engines, the hum of a slaughterhouse generator. There is a great deal of traffic and it is a while before we start climbing the hill. The next time I leave Seven Towers I will be a free man, and I think of this as we slow down and the engine whines, and it is a long way off, double the time the farm offered, but I don't care. And when the van finally stops the driver walks back along the side and opens the door and two guards shake their heads as they usher me towards the gate. I don't look up at the Director's window. This time I am not making a point, just uninterested. I place a hand on the wall and feel the energy in the stone, imagine the chatter of jungle voices, and now I am inside Seven Towers and walking in alleyways and small yards, passing through the visiting area, which is deserted. I stand in the square and wave at Ali who is talking into empty space, concluding a deal. He seems relaxed. Alone and busy and returning the greeting.

The gate opens and shuts and I am back on B-Block. The faces are crystal clear and I feel my hand being shaken and the Butcher slings an arm around me. He is grinning and I realise the monkey monsters are with him, hoods pulled back and eyes shining as if they are spacemen. Pretty Boy waves and Flip Flop smiles and I walk inside and find that my bed is waiting. My bowl and mug and spoon are on top of my magic blanket. I bend down and smell it, recognise the odour. A monkey man slides past and grabs the end of the bed, pulls it along to where the monsters sleep. I follow him and sit down, look around and hear the rattle of the green door as someone goes inside, imagine rats scurrying for safety. Papa enters the section and stares without expression, refuses to look me in the eye. I should be scared as he is carrying his knitting needle, but for some reason I am not. He rummages around under his bed and takes out a plastic bag, comes over and pours hundreds of matchsticks on to my bed, turns and walks off.

Teetering on the edge of the world the drop seems more like a cliff face than a slope and I am wedged behind Ramona on the sledge and there is fear in me as she turns and smiles and seems embarrassed that we are so close together and every time I see her beautiful black eyes I feel awkward they are so intense and dark they are almost purple and she calls me Mr Ramone again and I suppose Robin Hood and Maid Marian is for children and she says we are a couple of surfing birds about to catch a wave to some sort of paradise and the wind hits the cusp of the hill and makes our eyes water so we lower our heads and the squall of a seagull means we glance back at the road on the other side of the common where a car with a flashing light has stopped and two policemen and a social worker are messing up the snow leaving tracks and I look around but see no seagulls see no birds at all and these mechanical scarecrows are shouting and waving and the slope seems steeper than ever the snow hard from this angle more like concrete and there are cars and buses roaring down below and not much space to stop we could easily keep going and skid under their wheels and be crushed to death and Ramona tells me heigh-ho let's go if we die at least we will go together and who fucking cares anyway and we ease the sledge forward and the front sags and tries to find its balance and my arms are tight against her holding on to the guide ropes and we rock the sledge and find our courage and it slips over the edge and straightens and we are moving and picking up speed and laughing at first and shouting and finally hunched together and concentrating on staying upright and it is so many years since I have felt a hug or been near someone and it must be the same for Ramona and we feel the icy wind on our faces and I am holding on to Ramona with all my might as we wobble and the ropes keep us upright and her hands are tight on my forearms and we are going faster and faster and everything is misshapen and fuzzy we are lost in the whiteness of the hill and the rush of wind and adrenalin become the same and I feel very warm rocketing into the hemisphere not caring about anything just me and Ramona two teenagers sizzling along cracking the universe open we don't need to breathe or even hold our breath the blue of the sky is the white of infinity smashing the speed barrier the sound barrier any sort of barrier and I feel so alive I hope we never reach the bottom of the hill but of course we do and I half hope we will keep going into the road and be killed by a bus but the snow is deep and we stop quickly the runners sinking down with room to spare the road empty and our excitement turns to joy as we stay close and I can smell Ramona and she turns her face and kisses me on the cheek and leans her head against my shoulder and I cradle her not knowing what to do not wanting to do anything watching the police car pull up and we are warm and it would be good to stay like this for ever and one of the policemen is talking about under-age sex when we have never even kissed until now and drugs that we don't take and they call us delinquents as we are juveniles and runaways which is true and he sees us as sinners though I don't understand why as we have done nothing wrong we just have this bond they can never grasp and I look at the policeman and see Goofy acting foolish and smile but keep it inside and all the time Ramona has her face buried in my jacket and she is whispering in my ear if you are ever in trouble I will know and I will come and help you it doesn't matter if it is ten or twenty years from now and one day we will get married and have a son and we can call him Joey or Dee Dee or Jimmy Junior or anything you want and we will be the Ramones and live like a proper happy family and I know she is telling the truth that this dream is going to happen and sweet little Ramona asks if I am all right and I have never felt better and we made it down the hill and wasn't it brilliant and she nods and says she will never forget it and she is led away to another car that has pulled up with a second social worker and she waves and blows me a kiss and goes back to the place she is living and the other helper takes me in the police car to my home in the dormitory and he offers me a piece of chewing gum which I accept tasting peppermint and watching the streets pass and seeing people huddle against the wind and the police are all right now the one who was talking rubbish sees we are only a couple of kids and I think of Ramona and her black eyes and whatever happens in our lives in the meantime I know now that one day we are going to live happily ever after.

Marching up and down the prison yard, pumping blood into soft muscles, doing my best to speed up the clock, it is a month after returning to Seven Towers that I notice something strange about the tree. My heart beats faster as I hurry over and discover a tiny bud. It is a brilliant bright green and looks as though it is made of plastic. I want to touch it but don't, worried it will break. Emotion fills my eyes, but I control myself, run a palm over the trunk and feel the cracks, the harshness of the armour that ensures its survival. The tree was dead and now it is alive. And within days it is covered in hundreds of sprouting buds and these develop fast, determined to flourish, and the days grow longer and the light is brighter and the sun warmer, and soon the tree is covered in blossoms and insects emerge from hibernation and the bugs start nipping and I am standing in the yard when a butterfly lands on a branch in among the promise of new apples, and I walk over and wish I could reach out and touch its patterned wings, feel the multicoloured fuzz, watch it live its single day of life. It seems early in the year for butterflies but what do I know, and it senses a current and its wings flicker and it is a long flight out of the prison and I worry it is too small and frail to escape but it rides the waves and glides out of the block and towards a tower this tiny dot turning and disappearing over the outer wall.

I sit on the ledge with the other men and feel proud that I am no better or worse than any of the prisoners in Seven Towers, that I have the same strengths and weaknesses, one of the boys and no longer a dumb outsider, and like so many others in jail I grew up without a father to guide me and my mother said he was a drifter, his wanderlust meaning he was selfish and ran from responsibility, just left her to it, and Nana must have missed her son but never said a bad word about him, and perhaps I would like to meet him, find out what he thinks, if he regrets the direction he took, but most of all I would like to punch him on the nose. But I am a good boy, an okay man, not perfect, I have made many mistakes. One day I will find Ramona, at home with my son not yet conceived, and I was always tormented, never satisfied with what I had, and one day she had enough and turned her back but I was too proud to admit it was my fault, she said I was like the dad I never knew, and I packed my bags and got on a train and slept in a forest as I promised I would do and wandered around Europe, a romantic life I glimpsed in my travel magazines.

I see the mothers in the visiting area, middle-aged and old, with grey specks and white hair, shawls wrapped tight, sadness filling frail hearts as they fight back the tears for the sake of their wayward sons. They are always there. And we want to go home, and home is where we were as children, when we were innocent. I am not alone. We miss our mums, every single one of us.

It is true that I am a proud man, but I have never envied

other people, never coveted their possessions, greed something for those who lack pride, and while pride has caused me trouble it has never driven me to uncontrolled lust, and I have been angry since the fire but it has never made me kill another man, but more than pride my sin is sloth. I have been too lazy to face up to a crime that was never a crime, a childish accident that had tragic consequences and which I let ruin my life. The fire was the mistake of a sad boy who missed his nana and wondered about his father, who wanted things to never change, to live in a house that was warm with love and the protection of women, for his grandmother to never leave. An accident brought the world crashing down on his head, and it doesn't matter where you are, prison is about retribution, and while there are men here who are truly wicked, most are okay, confused maybe, and violent certainly, some very deadly sinners in fact, but they are God's children, good boys straying from the path, and I am proud and lazy, and these three monkeys I sit with are envious and covetous and greedy, while the ice-cream rapist died for his lust and Papa carries the sort of anger that sends a man to prison in the first place. But if there is a God then I am all of these men, and all these men are me. On the outside it seems ridiculous, but in Seven Towers it is the truth.

The mist has cleared and the faces around me are sharp and the language easier to understand and nobody is ever going to call me Dumb Dumb again. These are my mucked-up, fucked-up friends, and maybe one day I will see that seventh tower but I guess I already know what it looks like, and when the guards come into the yard for lock-up they swing their childish sticks and I walk back into the section knowing the time will pass and once my two years have been served I can return home and find Ramona, strong and full of a new knowledge, understand there are no more boundaries. All I have to do is stay alive.

Secure for another night, I smell the salty magic of my blanket and hear the reassuring snap of dominoes and cards, the tick of beads I no longer use, the murmur of voices, and measuring matchsticks I wallow in contentment, sitting with monkey men who aren't really monsters, glancing into the big yellow candle and seeing a familiar face waiting for the bell. And on that day when I venture back out into the world I will thank my lucky charm, and I reach into my pocket and squeeze it tight, take out Nana's old keyring and smile at my three wise monkeys, their faces carved in wood, and this is how I try to live my life, saying and hearing and seeing no evil, fulfilling a promise and doing the right thing, and I can't help feeling pleased as I look back into the candle and see this good boy – *this cheeky monkey* – walk out of the school gates and straight into the arms of his mother.